Blurb

His alter ego is a rebel and a bully.
Wait until he meets hers.

I don't deserve to have good things come my way.
I tend to turn them bad.

But when my bandmate tells me McKenna Beckley's in town,
well ... I'm tracking down that good thing.

Only, she's not the Mack I remember.

The sweet, shy, bookish schoolgirl that I screwed over has
disappeared, and in her place is a gorgeous, curvaceous and
jaded woman who's gotten herself into some bad, bad things.

Me? I haven't transformed one bit. I'll always be the jerk she
remembers.

Second chances? Nah. More like a second chance at ruin.

Problem is, it might just be my own.

KETLEY ALLISON
DARK & SPICY ROMANCE

Part One

SENIOR YEAR

CHAPTER 1

Mason

I SAG against the seat on the city bus, clutching the torn, creased pages of my notebook with the goal of not having sheets of loose paper shooting across the dirty, down-trodden floor and losing weeks worth of music.

My right eye throbs, bulbous and swollen. I rub it, thinking I'm already down at least twenty pages of work when my dad stormed into my room, looking for a bong and instead finding his son's "fuckin' fartsy fairy notes" under his mattress and tearing them up right in front of my face.

Said face then crashed into the bedroom, fists flailing, teeth snarling, but Dad crushed my teenaged bones with one solid, meaty punch.

When I came to, I was on my stained bedroom floor, Dad was long gone, but he left me the thoughtful gift of one fully functioning eyeball.

The bus rattles through the streets as I stare vacantly out the window, my thumb fanning the dog-eared pages of my notebook. I've messed with them enough that the creases are soft and the paper is almost back to the pulp it was made out of.

The driver yanks the bus to the righthand curb, picking up additional passengers. I usually don't pay attention, since we're now in an area often termed "affluent," a neighborhood I don't want and will never be a part of. I'm talking perfectly manicured gardens maintained by guys from my side of town, cleaned penthouse apartments done by workhorses who are my neighbors, and nannies and pet-sitters who are more familiar with proper care than their nip-tucked, Botoxed, and spin-classed bosses' asses.

Yet, none of us stay beyond our allocated hours to enjoy the fruits of our labor.

Chewing the side of my cheek, I watch the small cluster of over-privileged fucks board the dented, greased-up, motor-coughing clunker because they can't stand a little drizzle of rain with their six-dollar lattes in the mornings.

A small, curly, reddish-brown head peeks through the huddled mass. My jaw pauses.

She's the third to climb up the vehicle's stairs, swiping her MetroCard with practiced ease, because for some reason, she takes this eyesore every goddamned day. I'm fairly certain it's because she wants to be environmentally conscious, to the extent you can be when your father is a finance genius and your mother a top attorney at a white-shoe firm.

It's kinda like shopping for and buying organic foods, using green cleaning products, and purchasing only certified cruelty-free cosmetics and soaps. Oh, and the six-dollar latte in her hand made with compostable material.

You know, those Earth-saving things that cost a shit-ton of money.

I accidentally lock eyes with her as she's coming down the aisle, one shoulder laden down with a heavy bag full of a laptop and textbooks. Her eyes are moss-green and tipped up at the edges, cat-like and watchful before her eyelids shutter and she looks away.

Can't be caught staring at the dirty boy from across the tracks, now can we?

Sadly, for the both of us, the only seat available is next to mine. Everyone who boarded before her managed to avoid the beat-up hooligan whose ripped, hand-me-down clothes smell like weed even though he never smokes or ingests it. I leave that stupid shit up to my father and younger brother, but unfortunately, that smell is fucking porous and has sunk into every inch of our floorboards and fabrics.

She freezes with her hand clenched around the top rail for balance. I can tell she's debating, her cultured manners wondering if it'd be rude to pass by so obviously and stand the rest of the way. As if I'd be insulted.

I decide to make it easy for her. "Move it along, Tubs."

She winces. I crack my jaw and resume staring out the window. The girl's not fat. She's got curves in all the right places, including those gorgeous tits that have blossomed recently. But, every girl is insecure about their weight, at least the ones I hear moaning about their muffin tops at their lockers, so I know the jeer will hit its mark and she'll avoid me like the rest of them always do.

My half-closed, swollen eyelid saves me from appearing startled when I feel the seat shift with weight on my left, and she settles herself beside me.

"My name is McKenna," she says tightly while staring straight ahead, her arms folded over her bag while balancing her coffee. "But you know that. Mason."

My top lip lifts into an automatic sneer. "I don't do names. Or small talk. If you're gonna sit there, do me a favor and shut up like a good Catholic girl, yeah?"

I expect another wince, but instead get a clash of green against my blue. "Do you always talk to people like this?"

"No, because people are usually smart enough not to start a conversation with me." I point to my fractured eye socket. "Since they usually end up with this."

"Then I guess whoever you spoke to last got to you first." She angles her head. "Did you get a swing in, or were you knocked out cold?" She stares down at my knuckles. "Too bad. The evidence shows you didn't even get a scrape in."

My throat swells. My cheeks go hot. She can't know she's talking about my dad and that he was the one who threw the punch—he always makes the hits—but I'm furious with her, anyway.

"Get up."

She raises a brow. "Excuse me?"

"Get the fuck out of that seat before I throw you on the floor."

Finally, the wariness I've been waiting for settles behind her expression. "Relax, Mason. I was only—"

"You don't know me." I get right in her face. "And you don't get to sit your Princess ass down and pretend to spar with the poor boy to make yourself feel better for doing a good deed. Are you gonna offer me your homework, next?"

She squeaks when I grab for her tote bag, unbuckling the straps and shaking out the contents, including a MacBook Air that makes a satisfying sound as it hits the floor between us.

"My laptop!" McKenna cries.

I stop her from reaching for it by grabbing a spiral-bound notebook that's toppled onto her thighs and briefly fan through. When I see her words and notice that it's actual prose, I hesitate, realizing she writes down her thoughts in a lot of the same ways I do, but that beast of mine reels the niceties in—the one that hates and loathes and can't stand happiness—and I tear out the pages and rip them in half in front of her.

"Thanks for the offer, but I don't need your school notes," I say. "Not sure if you've noticed, but I'm not made for education."

Her lower lip shakes, but her gaze doesn't back down. In fact, she stares steadily at me, defiant sparks going off in those cat eyes, and my cheek tics angrily at the sight.

Then, because I can't help myself, I grab her coffee from her hands, lift up the lid, and splash it all over her while stepping over her legs and swinging around to the middle exit so I can get off at the next stop.

Gasps abound, including some dude in the back yelling, "You turd fucker! C'mere and try doing that to me, little man!"

That's me. Mason "Turd Fucker" Payne.

"You!" the driver screams, his glare lasering through the rearview mirror. "I've had about enough of your disrespect! Get off my bus!"

We're not near any stops, but the driver brakes hard and yanks open the doors. "I said, *get out*, you delinquent motherfucker!"

Fuck, I love New York.

On the last step off the bus, I say to the back of McKenna's trembling ringlets, "Nice talking to you, Big Mac. Send me a wink the next time you see me in English class, yeah?"

And then I'm gone.

CHAPTER 2

Mckenna

I TAKE my seat at the front of the classroom, pen poised, back-up pencils sharpened, and wait for Miss Lucas and the rest of the class to enter.

I'm always the first to step into the classrooms, mostly because I enjoy the peace and quiet of sitting in an empty room with the white noise sounds of slamming lockers and laughing, chatting students riding through the air behind the safety of a closed classroom door.

I use that time to pull out my secret novel and sneak in a few chapters before I have to focus on teachers and schoolwork.

The library is my other favorite place, and this morning I checked out the newest historical romance novel I've been dying to get my hands on. It's fairly new, with only a few others checking it out before me, so the spine lightly cracks and the paper is crisp when I flip the book open and smell that gorgeous, pulpy, dried ink smell. I squirm deeper into my plastic scoop chair attached to a right-handed desk (I'm left handed, but there are no lefty desks in this school), and start the first chapter.

Thump.

My chin jerks up.

I shove my reading glasses higher on my nose and glance

around. I'm alone in the room, and the sound didn't come from the hallway, either. I'm sure of it.

Thump-bang.

A high-pitched giggle follows.

I carefully close my book, my attention drawn to the broom closet to the left of the teacher's desk.

Thump-thump-thump.

A female moan bookends the noises, after a few scraping sounds, like fabric brushing up against wood.

Suppressing an eye-roll, I cross my legs and get back to reading. Whoever's in there will tumble out at some point, but I'm not about to leave the room and give them privacy they don't deserve. This is *my* time, too, and I'm not about to spend it being shoved and bumped by elbows and hips—some more deliberate than others—at my locker.

Never mind that my cheeks are going hot.

Or the fact I'm envisioning all the dirty things that could be going on in that closet, helped along by my voracious reading of all things historical romance, what with skirts being lifted and dapper heads with tousled hair sneaking under, their hands caressing ankles, then calves, and kissing thighs, until finally—

"Oh—*shit.*"

The voice draws my attention back up, and I really wish it hadn't, because I'm staring at my English teacher, Miss Lucas, with an unbuttoned blouse, wrinkled skirt, and a missing shoe.

"McKenna!" she exclaims while frantically closing her shirt over a lace bra, only she's finding the wrong button holes. "What are you doing in here?"

I state the obvious. "Waiting for class to start."

"I—right—well." Miss Lucas looks around, probably searching for any type of authority, but finding none. "Could you please wait out in the hall until the bell rings?"

"I could," I say, "but I'd rather not."

Miss Lucas smooths down her brassy blonde hair. "It's not a request, McKenna."

I'm not used to defying authority, but in this instance, I'm desperate. "Miss Lucas, please, if I could just stay here. I'll, um, close my eyes if you need me to…"

Miss Lucas's eyes go wide, like she can't believe I'm honestly asking to stay when I've just caught her in the act. I can't blame her. Most students would've scurried out long before. But I've never been like most people.

She glances behind her at the closet door left slightly ajar and still containing whoever is in there with her.

I chew my bottom lip as Miss Lucas debates her fork-in-the-road moment. She can't threaten to send me to detention, since what I've witnessed will trump any disciplinary action she tries to take to the principal. She also can't quite believe that I'm still sitting in the front row, paperback open, waiting to get back to my chapters.

"McKenna." Miss Lucas sighs. "I realize we're in a predicament and you don't owe me anything, but if you could *please*—"

"She ain't gonna move," a male voice says from the closet. "Big Mack's too afraid of the big bad she-wolves in the hallway."

Every part of me stiffens. My shoulders. My fingers against the pages. My freaking kneecaps. I'm too familiar with that voice and all he brings with it. So conditioned am I that tears automatically spring forth, but I blink them back, allowing the boiling water to burn the back of my eyeballs rather than give him any satisfaction.

Mason Payne ambles out of the closet without one fuck to give. His chestnut hair is a mess, but in that sexy way where it falls across his brow and he has to use a heavy hand to smooth it back. His eyes, so blue the sky wishes it could clear enough clouds for that color. And those dimples, those indents flashing in ways the heroes of my novels would die to unleash on their heroines.

It's not fair, for someone so beautiful to wield the power of such cruelty.

Miss Lucas stutters, her hands moving as if she's going to try and shove him back in—which I truly wish she would, and please find a deadbolt—but she falters, raking her fingers through her hair instead.

"Fuck," she whispers. "Goddamnit, Mason, couldn't you have stayed in there five more minutes?"

Mason's sly gaze is on me as he zips his jeans and drawls out, "Nope."

"McKenna, I—" Miss Lucas pauses to lick her lips. To think.

Part of me should feel sorry for her, since she must know what it's like to be under Mason's thumb. Maybe I should even commiserate with her, since we both know the only person coming out unscathed in this scenario is Mason Payne himself. He will be the hero of this story, the guy who bangs the hottest, youngest teacher in school, while she most likely loses her job or worse, gets jail time, and I spend the rest of senior year further in the social trash pit than I've ever been, subject to Mason's whims, boredom, and posse of mean girls that follow him around like his personal pitbulls.

I want to ask her, *Is he worth it? Is sex in a closet with Mason Payne between classes really worth losing your life as you know it?*

But I don't dare. I'd rather not draw more attention to myself than I already have.

"Besides, Big Mack won't say anything, will she?"

Flinching, my peripheral vision catches Mason coming up to my desk, his long, dextrous fingers curving over the edges of the wood. This is the most random time to remember he's in a band with a few of his friends and that he's the bassist, hence the thought of his limber hands and how he uses them. Except, I'm picturing them inside my English teacher instead of coaxing guitar strings.

My flinch turns into a wince.

"Aw, don't get shy on us," Mason says as he bends close. Whenever I'm in his scope, my cheeks tingle. I feel those metallic eyes of his seeing through my white shirt and picking apart every inch of me. It's an uncomfortable feeling, a foreign one, coupled with a *zing* I'm having trouble identifying.

I keep my head down, unwilling to show him the rouge on my cheeks.

"Mason," Miss Lucas snaps. "Class will start any second. Take your seat."

Mason looks over his shoulder and smirks, that dimple of his a mere arm's length away. "When you took a seat on my face I wasn't nearly as rude, Miss Lucas."

Miss Lucas hisses in a breath, her entire face splotching. I swallow, wondering why the hell I decided to stay in this classroom and witness this R-rated exchange instead of running off school campus.

Oh, yeah. Because of Mason's minions, who I'm convinced wait in the halls for me.

I jolt when fingers trail down my shoulder and play with my shirt collar.

Mason's hot breath coats my cheeks. "Say one word of this, Big Mack, and you'll regret it."

Unable to resist, I meet his eyes, and I'm confronted with what I fear the most: emptiness. There's nothing behind them. No savageness, anger, rage, or worry. Mason's a shark in territorial waters, and he claims the ocean as his own.

"I—I wasn't going to," I stutter.

Mason tilts my chin up. His lips are close, so close that the skin under his eyes clues me in that he's grinning. "Because you're a good girl, right? A classy, stuck-up, rich snot who has no sense of survival." He cocks his head. "Like right now, a scared, mousey girl, unable to stick up for herself because she's so afraid of the big. Bad." *Snap.*

I flinch as he bites the air between us, nearly catching my lips in his teeth.

Mason chuckles.

"Wolf," he finishes.

"Mason, really," Miss Lucas says. Now that her outfit is straightened, hair is smoothed, and second heel is found, she strolls over to us. "Threats aren't the way to keep secrets around here."

"It is with her. Big Mack cows easily." Mason laughs at his own joke.

Miss Lucas grabs Mason's arm to pull him out of my comfort zone and points to the seat beside me. "Last I checked, I'm still the teacher and you're my student. Sit. Then I'll tell you how this will go down."

Mason licks his top lip, sliding his gaze to mine as his lean, muscular body folds into the neighboring chair. "See how I like my women, Big Mack? Strong, hot, and rough."

Miss Lucas ignores his comment. I thin my lips and keep staring at my desk.

"McKenna, are you still looking to pad your extracurriculars for your college applications?" she asks.

The question is so out of place that I glance up and answer. "Yes."

Miss Lucas nods. "Good, since I have the perfect solution. Take on another student to tutor in English."

I glance between Mason and Miss Lucas, noticing Mason's deepening frown. "I, um ... what?"

"Look, kid," Miss Lucas says, "All of our asses are on the line, here. If we all get something out of this, no one will want to speak up."

"I might." Mason raises his hand. "Since you've been touching me inappropriately, Miss Lucas."

"*You* are going to end up back in my classroom next year, Mason, if your GPA doesn't rise. McKenna can do that for you."

"Can't you do it for me?" Mason asks with a buttery smile. "Cheat my grades a little? Then I'll eat you out just the way—"

If anyone wants to get out of this school and never, ever come back, it's me, in this moment. Forever. I'm desperate to bolt out of this chair, but smart enough to know that these two will chase me down relentlessly until they're sure their secret is safe. Well, Miss Lucas would. I doubt Mason cares how this scenario will play out.

I'm not so sure about Mason and his motives, but what I *am* sure about is, "I can't tutor him, Miss Lucas."

"Yes. You can," Miss Lucas says. "Because doctoring his grades in any other way would cast too much suspicion. If you do, and Mason's grades become passable and believable, I'll also become one of your personal references in your application. My father is a Yale alumni, which I know is your top choice. I'll even get him to write something out for you." Miss Lucas leans her palms on my desk. "If you do this for me and pretend you saw *nothing*, anything you need will happen for you. Do you understand?"

Mason scoffs beside me, his arms crossed. He's glaring so hard, the side of my head might as well crack like a raw egg.

What's worse, I have the astonishing urge to explain myself to him.

"I'm *not* accepting any handouts," I say, though it's unclear who I'm addressing. "I don't want or need favorable treatment. I won't say anything, okay? I won't. If you'll leave me alone, I'll leave you guys alone. Okay?"

"Is that a threat, rich bitch?" Mason asks.

I jolt. "What? No!"

"'Cause I ain't ever leaving you alone. Not until the first day of summer, and even then, I may not want to give you up so easily."

I seethe through my teeth. "I'm *not* tutoring him, Miss Lucas!"

"You are," she says, then turns away from the both of us. "Because *I* need the assurance, too. That's the last I'm going to hear of it."

Who has the power in this scenario? Shouldn't it be me? I could go to the principal right now and—

"Don't even think about it," Mason mutters beside me. "I will make your life such absolute hell if you narc."

With my bottom lip trembling, I retort, "Maybe I don't care anymore and I'm tired of being pushed around—"

Mason gets up and swipes my paperback off my desk. He fans through once, musing, "Hmm," before he opens the book to a random page and shoves it down his pants.

"Uh. *Uh*, oh, yeah," he says while grinding against the pages, his gaze drilling into mine.

With one side of his mouth tilting up, he pulls the book from his pants and flings it at me. It hits me square in the chest, and I instinctively fumble to catch it.

"Since you'll never get good dick in real life," he says as he stands, "I figure I might as well have you smell it on those fake-ass men of yours."

Mason strides to the back of the classroom and flops into his regular seat right as the rest of the class funnels in.

I bite down hard. Swallow against the hot swell in my throat. Fight through any threat of tears.

Mason will not see me fall.

With trembling hands, I stick the book I was so looking forward to reading back in my bag, resolving to return it to the library as soon as this horrible class is over.

I hate Mason Payne.

Hate him more than anything.

CHAPTER 3

Mckenna

HE DOESN'T SHOW.

Not that I should be surprised. Mason and I both don't want this.

I close my binder containing notes on *Catcher in the Rye*, sit back in my chair in the empty classroom, and stare at the ceiling, because I'm well aware of my fate.

We may not want this, but Miss Lucas does, and she has the capacity to make the last few months of my senior year more insufferable than it already is.

I clean up my small area of study materials, throw my backpack over my shoulder and head out into the hall. It's after school hours and I'm content with the smattering of students lingering by their lockers, none of them threatening. All the predators have gone back to their natural habitats.

Which means, I'm pretty sure I know where Mason is. He's practicing with his band somewhere. What I've heard, by being present when nobody notices me, is that they gather in his garage, usually with a small gaggle of girls they bring with them to watch. Mason and his three friends: Rex Sloane, Wyn Chance, and Easton Mack, none of whom are as nasty as Mason. Maybe because they have no idea I exist.

"My goodness! Look who's loitering the halls after hours! Do your parents know you're past curfew, little dove?"

The female voice sends an instant irk down my back, the kind that stiffens your spine and your upper lip all at the same time. I don't bother to turn around as I walk, but I pick up the pace.

"It's four in the afternoon," I say, staring straight ahead. "I don't have to be home for my bottle until four-thirty."

"*Oh*, she has spunk today." A hand lands on my shoulder and jerks me to a stop. "Hold up, Big Mack. Where are you off to in such a hurry?"

I'm forced to make contact with gold-brown eyes and honey-gold hair. April Landers stares down at me, clad and shiny in her cheerleader's uniform. Her two other minions, Courtney and Melissa, blonde and ebony-haired respectively, flank her in matching school colors.

April's full, sparkling and wet-glossed lips stretch wide. Her manicured nails dig harder into my shoulder.

"Do we have to do this right now, April?" I ask. "School hours are over. I should be off your shit-list during recreational time."

It's such a cliche, I know, to be bullied by cheerleaders, but high school is nothing *but* cliches until you manage to escape it.

"You've been avoiding me," she says.

"Probably because little kitty cat's afraid," Melissa pipes in, her squinty hazel eyes growing smaller with glee.

Considering the last time I saw them, they stole my underpants and pulled down my gym shorts, and it was the day I wore a skirt to school, they honestly couldn't blame me.

I clutch the strap of my backpack tighter, muttering to the floor, "I just want to go home."

"So sad." April clucks her tongue. "But according to a text I just received, you're coming with us."

My brows furrow. "What? No, I'm—"

"You are." April's hand moves from my shoulder to my bicep and she pulls me into a stride. "Mason requires your presence at his home in forty-five minutes."

"Since when d—" I clamp my mouth shut, swallowing the rest of the words. I have my answer, anyway. April *always* runs Mason's errands and jumps his bones when he calls. She's his rescue lapdog, and what's worse, she's proud of it. Pride dances across her features whenever he pays attention to her, whether it be to toss a french fry at her in "jest" in the cafeteria, or a quick make-out session as he passes by her seat in class before taking his own.

I'd almost feel sorry for her if I didn't constantly fantasize over setting her hair on fire.

"Well," I say, despite being jostled and surrounded by her friends like Mason's personal Secret Service agents, "tell him he was supposed to have shown up at the English classroom, and since he didn't, I'm going home."

"No can do, Burger Girl," April says. "You're getting in the car with us and I'm taking you to him." She looks down at me with a sneer. "Though God knows what he wants with you."

I don't think I want to know, either. "He doesn't live anywhere close to where I do. How will I get home?"

Courtney—the blonde—snorts behind me.

"That's for you to figure out," April says. "Hitch a ride with his druggie brother or something."

I decide against running, since these girls, with all their cheer training and spin and smoothie classes on Saturdays are well ahead of me fitness-wise, and I also stop struggling. Resisting their hold means my brain is focused on the physical, when I need it to flip to mental strategy.

These girls are prettier than me, but I'm smarter than them. I have to hold on to that. I have to survive.

We make it to April's scarlet red Volvo SUV, a personal gift from her father, and she stuffs me into the backseat with Court-ney. April and Melissa take the front.

April cranks up the music as she starts the engine, Top 40 hits flowing into the car and crashing against my ears. I'm half-surprised it's not Mason's band I'm hearing pound through the speakers.

"I thought you were Mason's biggest fan," I say before thinking.

April and I lock eyes in the rearview mirror. She says, "Excuse me?"

I point to the stereo. "I figured you'd be listening to his music."

"That garbage?" She scrunches her face, and unfortunately, remains pretty doing it. "I'd rather not ruin my leather interior with those sound waves. I do my part, cheer him on, be the bestest girlfriend, but everyone knows they're not going anywhere. Especially Mason. He's bound to be working cars just like his father, maybe even boosting them."

I can't help but ask, "So ... why do you like him, then?"

April giggles. "What can I say, girls? I have a weakness for bad boys."

"And slumming it," Courtney adds.

Melissa and April answer with a chorus of laughter.

A part of me almost feels sorry for Mason and the people he's chosen to surround himself with, but then I remember who we're talking about and I stare out the window, my upper lip curling in disgust.

Let him have her. He deserves it.

"We should get some fast food," April says, out of the blue. "Huh, ladies? Afternoon workouts *starve* me."

Both Courtney and Melissa state their approval. April's sly gaze meets mine again in the mirror.

"What do you say, Big Mack? Want a burger?"

I bite my cheek rather than voice a retort. The silence doesn't deter April.

"Burgers it is!" she says, then pulls into the nearest drive-through.

April gives her order through a spout of giggles and also adds a bunch of milkshakes. When we pull up to the window to pay, my bag is swiped from my lap.

"It's on you," Courtney says as she digs through the front pocket for my wallet. "Or didn't you get the memo?"

I reach for my backpack to snatch it back, but April's words stop me.

"Could I have some extra ketchup and honey packets? Like, a ton more? I mean a *ton*. And add some mayo ones, too."

She stretches her hand back to accept the debit card Courtney folds into her palm. My hesitation prevents me from intervening in time, and before I know it, I've footed the tab for these bitches.

April tosses the food to Melissa, as well as a brown paper bag containing only condiments and guns the engine back into the street.

In a matter of minutes, pristine buildings containing marble and brass turn into downtrodden brick and sagging porches. Window frames hang at the corners, the glass panes broken, with stapled cardboard over holes becoming more common than the windows themselves.

The smell of fried food seeps into our enclosed space, and because I can't control it, my stomach rumbles.

Courtney smiles. "God, when did you last eat? Twenty minutes ago? Ready for another round?"

In answer, I swipe back my bag, clutching it like I would a teddy bear as I try to figure out what these girls are planning.

April makes a sound of displeasure as she makes a right turn, yet does it, anyway. "I think this is it … Ugh, he lives in a dump. No wonder he tries to keep it from me."

Her words put my suspicions on high alert.

If April doesn't know where Mason lives, it means she's never there. She's not one of the girls that watches him play—clearly, since she can't stand his music—yet, she's taking me to see him. Allegedly at his request.

Even though Mason can't stand me.

I note the exchange of glances between April, Melissa and Courtney. And the lack of conversation. Katy Perry has filled the silence, but her peppy song sends foreboding ghost-fingers against the back of my neck.

What are they planning on doing with me?

I envision all the worst things, like them holding me down and stripping my clothes off, then dumping me naked on Mason's driveway.

My mind *dings* with a revelation.

The condiments. All the ketchup, honey, and mayo … are meant for me. For my body.

I can't believe I allowed myself to get into this car, to let them have control over me in such a small space.

But I know this car. My stepmom has this car. If I could get to the passenger-side door…

April stops at an intersection, the red light nearly as harsh as the color of her car, and I unbuckle and leap between the two front seats, practically falling onto Melissa.

Melissa squeals. "Hey! What are you—ugh, freak!"

This model vehicle automatically engages child locks in the back seat. I have to press the unlock button on either the passenger's or driver's door before I can get out the back, and that's exactly what I do.

Melissa flails, too surprised to grab me, but April hooks my arm as I slide back through the seats, and Courtney wraps her arms around my waist.

"Let go of me!" I cry.

"Stop, you psycho!" April says, her hands like claws as she

reaches over the console. Her face screws up like like she's coming through the depths of Hell.

Courtney holds firm as I grapple for the lever on the rear door.

These girls may be strong and limber, but in a tight space, I'm stocky and and have way more girth to throw around. I push back with my legs, making Courtney lose her equilibrium, and since April can only use her arms and cars are honking at her to drive, I have seconds before I lose the meager amount of control I have and am forced to stay in the car with them.

Realization smooths April's expression and she whips around to the steering wheel, her foot pressing on the gas.

Right as the car starts moving, a blast of cool air hits my face as I get the door open and scramble out. I run without looking back and am nearly hit by an oncoming car in the next lane, but I wave an apology and scramble to the sidewalk, my backpack hanging at my side.

Hands on my thighs, I bow over and take deep breaths, the adrenaline feeling like I've been shot.

I peek through my falling hair, but no one is coming out of the car after me.

"Have it your way, Big Mack!" April screams through the open car door before Courtney closes it. "Good luck making it out of this cesspool alive!"

An unwrapped burger hits me square in the chest through the rolled down passenger window, followed by an un-lidded milkshake that I dodge just in time.

Tires screech as April makes a U-turn and drives away. In the opposite direction.

I blow out a breath, lifting my bag's strap to my shoulder and ignoring the sharp mustard smell now coming off my blouse, and move in a slow circle, gaining my bearings.

Being right doesn't mean I've saved myself from further misery.

I've landed in front of a corner bodega, the awning blinking and buzzing with dying lightbulbs behind the plexiglass. Words are missing, but it looks like Hal's Ubs and Wiches isn't doing very well. There's a man smoking a ... crackpipe? ... near the entrance. He sits on the ground, one leg stretched out, and eyes me underneath his beat-up ball cap.

Now that the light has changed, traffic is thin, and I hear far-off screams and loud, foreign bangs more often than motors. It's mid-March and I'm losing sunlight fast.

Suddenly frantic, I hold my bag in front of me—thank God I decided to use it as a weapon against April's face then drag it out of the car with me—and search for my phone.

I have to call a car. Search for a cab. Get the hell out of here.

My skirt feels too short. My bare legs feel exposed. When a man passes by, thin with holes in his shirt, and not the fashionable kind, he sends an appreciative look to my chest. Gulping, I clutch my bag higher up.

I scroll through my apps in my phone but don't see any cars available. Glancing at the bodega and trying not to panic, I think, maybe it'll be safer to wait inside, ask the owner to call me a cab—

"I wouldn't go in there, Shorty," the man with the crackpipe says. His voice is whispy and raw, but I understand every word. "Hal sex trafficks tasty bits like you."

I literally feel my face losing color and the man just cackles. I have no idea if he's joking or not, but decide against going inside.

I pull up Google, searching for local taxi numbers, shivering, but not from the cold. The adrenaline's leaving me and fear is taking its place.

"Nice phone," Crackpipe says. He makes moves to stand, but stumbles more than he can get his feet under him. "Latest model. Can I have it?"

"Uh—" I swallow. "No."

"You got money, then? Pretty treat like you has cash."

I back away, nearly toppling off the curb. "N-no, I don't carry any cash on me."

9-1-1 is looking better than any call to a cab company.

"Too bad. Girl like you could make a ton of dough 'round here. Want me to hook you up? I'm a great pimp, I'm told. Got one chick with one eyeball that gives the best head around. Maybe she can teach you somethin'—"

Gripping my phone and my bag, I spin around and just start running.

My cheeks feel wet, and I swipe them with the back of my hand holding my phone as I sprint, unsure of where I'm going or why. I'm not going to be a stupid crybaby right now. This is New York City. Surely I'll run into a subway entrance at some point.

At first, the car laying on its horn nearby doesn't draw my attention. I'm too busy dodging cracks in the sidewalk, floating trash, and loitering people to slow down. But as it comes closer and the lengthened *beeeeeeep* turns into a *beep-beep-beep*, then "HEY! McKenna!" I finally halt my steps.

Sniffing and swiping under my nose, I turn to the road. A beat-up sedan approaches at a crawl, the visor too reflected by the outside streetlights for me to see who's inside.

Words tumble out of me. "I-I don't need a ride."

"Sure as fuck you do."

The passenger window rolls down, and a face I'm all too familiar with greets my watery vision. Mason's windblown hair skews across his forehead like a sexy question mark, and despite the darkened interior, his eyes shine daylight blue.

"Get in," he says.

He doesn't get the full two words out before I'm shaking my head.

"Get *in*, Big Mack. You can't be out here. You'll be eaten alive. And I mean that in the literal sense."

My grip tightens around my phone. "I'm doing just fine. About to head into the subway."

I don't need streetlights to witness Mason's dramatic eye-roll. "You're crying. You're cold. You're scared. If you slide on in, I'll drive you home. Okay?"

My feet totter backward. There's no way I'll do what he says. If I thought ripped ketchup packets on my naked body were enough to jump out of a moving car for, I'd rather play the odds on this street corner than see what Mason has in store for me.

"Big M—" Mason presses his lips together, then amends, "McKenna, seriously. Even my asshole status can't let you be out here on your own. At least let me take you to a safe bus stop, which is five whole minutes away. That's it."

Shivering, I sniffle. "Why do you want to help me?"

Mason glances ahead, the cut of his jawline amplified by the backlit glow of his interior lights. "Because April was supposed to drop you off at my place where I could keep an eye on you. Instead, she dumps you at one of the biggest crime streets in the neighborhood. I don't let that kind of shit slide."

"Why not? I'd think you'd love it if I were harassed in your section of town. Wouldn't it prove I'm the gutless, fat, mousey girl you're convinced I am?"

Mason's stare cuts right through me. "Do not be stupid enough to confuse school pranks with deadly assault."

My mouth falls open. "*Pranks*? *That's* what you and your minions think you do to me?"

Mason's expression turns defiant. "Out here in the real world, princess, I deal with friends dying on the streets or OD'ing in their homes, gunshots as my alarm clock, and a dad with a gambling problem with gang members as his loan sharks. Apologies for considering those to be more problematic than who rubs their dick on my romance book."

I attempt to find an argument. "That doesn't give you the go-ahead to make other people suffer. I dread going to school every morning because of you—"

"Get the *fuck* in, Mack. Or I really will leave you here."

Gritting my teeth, I pull open the passenger door and fall inside, mostly because I'm cold, depleted, and ready for the comfort of home. Even if my parents won't be there and the brownstone will stand empty as usual.

Mason pulls into traffic. "You smell like cheeseburger."

"That is *it*. I've had it!" I throw my backpack from my lap into the footwell. The random act is enough to startle Mason. "You knew what April and her crew had in store for me. What they were going to do. They were going to strip me, weren't they? And leave me on your doorstep covered in ketchup and mayonnaise and milkshake, in front of all your friends, so you could all have a good laugh." I shriek, "*And you masterminded it!*"

Mason instinctually leans away from me as he drives. "Whoa, Big Mack, calm do—"

I don't. I hit him in the arm. It feels so good, I whack him again, laughing hysterically. "Such a great joke! You think I'm fat so I must devour burgers every day. And I'm such a waste of space, I'm not even worth an original thought, so you and your crew dump trash on me *Carrie*-style to make your point. Never mind I lost my mother to cancer two years ago. Who cares that I lost my best and only friend in the world and only want to survive the rest of the year so I can get out of the Hell that's now my home—"

"Hang on, Debbie isn't your mom?"

Mason's flippant question about my so-called stepmom sends me into skyrocketing rage. I push him and the car swerves. "Jesus, McKenna!"

"I jumped out of a moving car to get away from your *pranks!*" I scream, then sob. "You don't know me! My life is already miserable, okay? You don't have to—don't have—" I hiccup through my cries, and Mason glances at me fervently enough that he pulls over to a side-street and parks.

Once the engine is off, his hands move toward me.

"Put your fingers near me and I will bite them off knuckle by knuckle," I say.

"Got it." He holds them up in surrender, then retreats to his side of the car.

We sit in silence as I take the opportunity to collect myself. He dares to reach into the middle console, but pulls out a tissue, which I take without a thank you.

"For the record," he says quietly, "I had no idea April was planning on doing that to you."

"Oh no?" I swipe under my eyes, then wipe my nose. I've never been a pretty crier and usually I'm too emotional to care. "Do you think that makes you a hero? You've done plenty of other things. Spilling coffee on me, spreading rumors that I'm selling my virginity, ruining the one thing I have that makes me happy— my books—and lets not forget the nickname that everyone at school now knows me as and won't refer to me as anything else. That stuff sticks, Mason. And not just through high school. It's going to be like hardened glue on my bones for the rest of my life."

Mason palms the steering wheel. Squeezes. "I never said I'm a good guy."

"Doesn't mean you have to be an asshole instead."

"Look, I don't know why I do half the things I do."

"So now I'm talking to a four-year-old. Great." I stare out my window and say on a sigh, "Just take me to that bus stop. Please."

"I mean it. I ... I *love* being a jerk. It makes me feel good. I like the control it gives, the laughter it causes. People think I'm King at our school. You have any idea how addictive that is?"

I risk meeting his stare. "Is it because you're treated like a loser at home?"

Mason's forehead smooths. His lips stiffen before they part. "Say that again, Big Mack. See what happens."

I nod, then stare straight ahead. "I'm guessing a truce isn't in our future."

He must feel my judgment fade, because he says, "I'm sorry about tonight. I won't apologize for anything else, but leaving you in this 'hood was unacceptable. I approve a lot of things, but not this. All right?"

Mason starts the car, spins it around, and gets back on the road.

"Why did you want me to come to your house?" I ask. "And *why* enlist April to do it?"

"Because she scares the shit out of you," he says on a shrug. "And I get my rocks off upsetting you."

I exhale through clenched teeth. "I'm ready to get out of this car now."

"And…" he says, with a more hesitant tone. "I'm pretty sure I need the tutoring. My guys are all heading somewhere after year's end. East is going to college. Wyn's following suit. Rex, while not a scholar like me, has scored some full-time job in the city. And I'm—if I don't get my ass in gear, I'll be stuck here. In the same house. Same 'hood. Same fucking drama with my family."

I'm instantly suspicious. "So, it has nothing to do with Miss Lucas and her rules?"

"Fuck that. She's not gonna breathe a word and neither am I. You're the only liability, and she believes you can be belittled enough to keep your mouth shut."

I bristle at his words.

"And I guess you can," Mason continues, "but the added incentive of stellar college references can't hurt."

"Are you always so glib and hurtful?" I ask.

Mason gives me the side-eye. "Have you *met* me?"

"Actually, no. I don't feel like I know you at all. Not the true you, anyway."

My honesty shuts him up. I'm surprised I said it, but I don't have regrets. He might, though, with the way he's gripping the steering wheel, so tightly I can make out the fine bones in his hands.

As we weave through traffic in the dark, we say nothing more, both content on opposite sides of the vehicle. I don't feel safe, per se. There's no white flag from either of us waving in the wind. But it's a quiet relief to be in Mason's presence and not stress over what he's planning. I believe him when he says he doesn't want me wandering his neighborhood alone.

We pull up to my house and Mason leaves the car idling.

I startle, shocked we made it all the way back to the Upper East Side. "How do you know where I live?"

"I had plans for this house," Mason muses. "Eggs. TP. Paint-balls." He nails me with an arrogant smirk. "But we've graduated beyond that, haven't we?"

Though Mason's face is hard and angular, his words cutting and foreboding, I sense he's not telling the truth. The honesty I'm looking for shimmers behind his eyes, a cracked surface with multiple, delicate fractures.

I'm also smart enough not to poke the bear any more than I have.

"Goodbye, Mason," I say as I open the door and step out.

"Tell no one about this," he says.

"Thank you for the ride." I enunciate the words before slamming the door shut behind me.

Mason roars off, and I'm left in front of a shuttered house.

No porch light has been left on.

Lamps and candles don't shine in the windows.

My stepmom isn't waiting up for me, reading on the couch, refusing to go to bed until I'm safe inside with her.

Dad hasn't texted, wondering where I am.

My shoes scuff against the pavement as I take the stairs and pull out the keys to my empty family home.

CHAPTER 4

Mckenna

LONG FINGERS STREAK into my vision and steal my french fry.

I slide my gaze up to meet the culprit, and I sigh. He's late, but there he is. Mason.

He stands at the side of my table, his ripped denim jacket, messy hair and multi-colored bruised eye a far cry from the kids screaming their mirth as they play in the indoor jungle gym.

"When you said to meet you at McDonald's," he says, "I thought you were joking."

Grabbing another fry, I say before popping it into my mouth, "I found the irony in it."

Mason cocks his head. "Do you have some funny in you, Beckley?"

I answer, with a flat expression, "I hate Big Macs."

"I see."

Mason doesn't move. He's trying to figure me out. Good. At least I've gained his quiet attention for an additional two seconds before he remembers to switch to asshole mode.

I ask, "Why didn't you call me by my horrible nickname just then?"

At last, he moves, his proximity no longer causing little tingles along my arm closest to him. He takes a seat across from me, scanning the place. "Honestly? It seems wrong to call you that in this establishment, with all these innocent kids running around. Wouldn't want to teach them bad manners."

I close the book I was studying and set down my highlighter. "How benevolent of you."

"Guess you're still pissed." Mason reaches over for another fry, but I slap his hand away.

"You're here to study with me, not steal my food along with my dignity. Where are your books?"

Mason shrugs. "Don't have any."

"You don't *have* any—" I cut myself off on a low sound of frustration. Of course he doesn't. I spin, then push, my English book over to his side of the table. "Can you at least read?"

"Oh, my. Direct hit." Mason palms his chest in a mock gasp. "Did Ronald McDonald lend you his balls for the evening?"

I bite back a sigh. "Consider this neutral territory. You spend an hour resisting becoming a taunting dick, and I'll use the same amount of time to help you pass our English exam. Then we can part ways and act like this never happened, until the same time next week."

Mason ponders this. "Fine. But as soon as you step out onto that sidewalk, I'm pouring a soda over your head."

"Wouldn't be the first time. At least it's not a hot beverage."

One of Mason's lower eyelid twitches at my last statement, and if I didn't know any better, I'd say it was guilt over tossing my coffee all over my shirt the first time we spoke.

But, I know better. And the way to deal with Mason is to pretend he's someone else and turn him into someone lot less intimidating.

Like a toddler who's failing kindergarten and needs help figuring out his shapes.

Staring at his features, all harsh angles and hard life knocks that somehow make him beautiful isn't doing me any favors, so I start. "So. *Catcher in the Rye.* Can you summarize—"

"Is that honey beside your ketchup?"

I blink. "What?"

"That." He points to a golden, sticky puddle I made on my cheeseburger wrapper, next to a dollop of ketchup.

"Yes. Why?"

"What do you use it for?"

"Mason, really. Don't waste my time."

"I'll shut up as soon as you tell me why you have honey sharing real estate with a cheeseburger."

I sigh. "It's for my fries. I like dipping them in honey sometimes. Not always ketchup."

One side of Mason's face screws up. "The fuck?"

One corner of my mouth nestles wryly in my cheek. "Don't knock it 'till you try it." I take a breath. "Or, tell the entire school I douse my fries in sugar before eating them to pad my fat ass, I don't care anymore."

"Hey, now." Mason sits back in the uncomfortable metal chair. "I thought you said this was neutral territory."

"It is." I shove the cheeseburger wrapper farther to the side. "Can we get to what's important?"

"Let me try it."

"Huh?" I can't tell if he's being a jackass. "Mason, I'm not here because I want to be and I really don't want to play any of your sick games—"

"I'm serious. Let's see what all your fuss is about."

Before I can object, Mason reaches for a fry and swipes it into the honey, popping it into his mouth and chewing it the way guys do. Meaning, barely one crunch down before it's swallowed whole.

"Hm." Mason licks his lips. "Pretty good."

The tip of his tongue darting across his full lower lip makes me blink. I pretend to flip through my notebook to distract myself. "I'm happy for you."

"Can I have another?"

I look up from my notes. "You didn't feel like you needed to ask permission before."

He gives a one-shouldered shrug. "I'm asking now."

I throw a hand over my remaining fries and drag them closer. "Get your own, Payne."

Mason's eyes shutter. His jawline turns hard and thick. Then he motions to my papers. "Nah. You're right. I'm good. Let's get down to it."

My fingers pause in the flipping of pages. I search Mason's flat expression.

He must feel it, because he shoves back in his chair, crossing his arms, and I'm suddenly witness to the emotional storm cloud forming at his hairline and smoking forward until it darkens his eyes.

"You gonna get started, Big Mack, or are you about to go mute and useless on me like you usually do?"

Mason can't afford to buy his own food.

The thought hits my mind the same time I instinctually work to school my features into a blank slate, but I'm too late.

"What's your problem?" he asks. There's a dangerous twist to his question.

"Nothing." I straighten, finding renewed interest in scribbling down a bunch of nothing. "Take my fries. Whatever. I don't care."

His low voice is like a cold mist billowing over my head and shoulders, goose-pimpling my flesh. "I don't want your fucking fries."

"Well, I'm done with them. They're cold and gross, so if you want them—"

I gasp and jump back in my seat when his hand swipes my food off our table and it all scatters to the ground. "I said I don't *want* your fucking fries, Big Mack!"

"Mason!" I say.

He stands. "And I don't want your fucking pity, either."

"O-Okay. I'm sorry."

"Don't be sorry. Don't apologize for anything." He palms the table and leans forward so he's in my face, and I try not to flinch. "Stop being such a goddamned doormat."

My hand clenches around my pen. "I'll stop being scared of you when you stop snarling in my *face*, Mason."

Our eyes duel for a few seconds. I don't feel my breath. Saliva has disappeared from my mouth and throat. Hot, dry fire replaces it, and I'm confused whether staring into the depths of his cerulean blues is causing tingles of fear, or if I'm actually turned on by this jerk.

At last, Mason backs off. "Session's over."

I bite out, "Clearly," before cleaning up what remains on the table. My breath comes back.

Mason stalks away, his heavy steps crushing my now inedible food into the stained, worn down tiles.

I remain seated, planning on ensuring Mason's complete departure before I move another muscle the same way he probably wants to be rid of my company, but we're both sidelined when the entrance door is pulled open, and a young, scraggly guy with a bunch of other guys stumbles in.

"Mase!" the scraggly leader says. He's lean—too thin for his height, his cheeks concaved and pockmarked. When he turns to Mason, I catch the color of his eyes, and freeze when I notice they're the exact same shade as Mason's. "Glad I caught you, bro."

Mason comes to a full stop between the tables, peppered throughout with patrons. The air around him shifts, almost becoming a tangible ice cube bordering his body. His voice is frost when he asks, "What are you doing here, Brax?"

This boy—Brax—digs through his filthy jeans' pocket, losing his balance a few times as his fingers fumble. "Texted Amy. Said you were here. Meeting..."

Blearily, Brax scans the crowd, but the action is too much and he stumbles into a woman trying to eat nearby. "S-sorry ma'am. There. Meeting that chick. The hot and thick one."

My cheeks turn to fire. Brax cackles.

Mason's lips have formed into such sharp lines, they've become barbed wire. He tries to hook Brax's elbow. "Let's go."

"No, bro." Brax weaves out of Mason's grip, then gestures to the guys behind him. "I'm here with my friends. We're gonna … what we gonna do, boys? We're gonna … oh, I know!"

Brax reaches behind his jacket to the waistband of his jeans and pulls out a—

"Gun!" someone screams.

The entire restaurant freaks out, some ducking under tables, others sprinting for the door. I slide from my seat to the floor, hiding under my table, since I'm too far away from the doors. My heart skitters to keep up with my movements, but I'm having trouble breathing. I'm clutching the table's stand like I can unbolt it and launch the thing at this Brax.

Mason dives for Brax, toppling him to the ground. "Jesus— it's not a gun! It's not a gun!"

But it's too late. Outright panic blankets the restaurant, phones are pulled out and people are stepped on and shoved out of the way to escape. Children cry.

I curl up my legs, tears running down my cheeks even as I register Mason's yells.

"It's his wallet! For fuck's sake, he's pulled out a black wallet!"

He's on top of Brax, scanning the crowd frantically, most likely in the hopes that nobody—undercover or otherwise—pulls out a retaliatory weapon. In his right hand he clutches something dark, and I lean forward to see closer and realize that, yes, it's a wallet. Not a gun.

I crawl out from under the table. "He's right, it's not a gun! Everyone, please, stay calm!"

"Mack, *get the fuck back under that table right now!*" Mason bellows.

I jolt, but stand my ground. Especially when staff members sprint toward Mason and his captive. I scream, over and over, that it's not a weapon, it's a misunderstanding, but nobody hears me. When the cops crash in, manhandling Mason and throwing him over a table to lay cuffs on him, I dart forward, trying to reason with the officers.

Mason is red fury under their hands. "Get out of here, Mack! Just go! Before this gets worse!"

"It's already worse!" I scream. "I can help! My dad knows some powerful lawyers—"

Half Mason's face is mashed into the table as he's read his rights, but he manages to spit fireballs of fury at me. "*Get away from me, Mack!*"

I trip back a step, glancing over to where Brax is being contained. He's shoved against a window and searched.

"Lookee here," one officer says. He holds up a white baggie that he's pulled out of one of Brax's back pockets. "We've caught ourselves a junkie."

"Or a dealer," another officer, closest to Mason, responds. "See how much that is? Jesus. You are in some deep shit, boys. Deep fucking shit."

"It's mine," Mason says, his mouth crammed against the laminate table. "He was holding it for me. Arrest me, not him."

What?

"Mason has nothing to do with it," I blurt. "He was with me. We were over there, studying, and this guy came in and accosted him—"

The officer holding down Mason takes the time to glance up at me. "You mean, Mason Payne, miss? The boy who spends more time in my holding cell than at home with his momma? Or are you talking about his brother, Braxton Payne, who has more dope in his system than a washed-up rockstar? Or hey, what about his deadbeat pops, Jasper Payne? Why don't you alibi all of them while you're at it? They sure are upstanding citizens that need people like you to protect them."

My mouth opens and closes. "I...but Mason didn't do anything. I've been with him..."

The officer lifts Mason by his cuffs, yanking him to the point that Mason winces when his shoulder joints are pulled, but he goes willingly.

When Mason's facing me, I lift my hand. To touch him, to stop the officer from hurting him, I don't know. "Mason..."

Dead eyes meet mine. All emotion is wiped clean. "Listen to me, McKenna. I'm rotten. I'll poison you from the inside out. Run away, because I'll destroy you if you don't."

I gulp down the ball of saliva lodged in my throat and respond, "Don't say anything else. Nothing at all. Not until you get a lawyer."

As Mason is carted away, he looks over his shoulder, keeping his attention on me.

His tone is flat when he says, "Leave. Now. You don't belong in my world."

CHAPTER 5

Mckenna

I DON'T SEE Mason at school for a month.

Most of me is glad for it. Without their Bully King, his minions show less interest in me and move on to other things, like prepping for prom.

I'm able to focus on my studies without worrying about what's being planned behind my back—or what's about to *hit* my back if I don't turn around. As such, I'm lowering my defenses.

Miss Lucas seems relieved at Mason's absence, too. She hasn't said anything to me about tutoring sessions. In fact, maybe my month of kept silence without Mason's ominous shadow has proven to her that I'm good for my word, because while passing by me in class one day, she laid a manila envelope on my desk. While she was up front explaining the next assignment, I opened it and saw the reference letters she promised.

With only two months left of senior year, things are looking up.

If only I could shake the last image of Mason, cuffed, then dragged out of McDonald's in an attempt to take the rap for his brother.

I wonder how he's doing, if he's been sent to juvie, under house arrest, or worse, beaten by his dad or sent to actual jail.

The look on his face when he was carted away seemed to expect all of those things to happen.

Then I wonder why I care. Mason is horrible. Every time I show kindness, he wants me to choke on it. So why do I keep feeling the need to fill the emptiness behind his eyes? *Why* do I sense more pain in him than malice? It's only going to hurt me by drawing more attention to myself—*his* attention.

Except, Mason may never be coming back.

A thick sense of disappointment settles on my shoulders as I take my seat in English class, later than intended this morning because I'd been quizzing my dad over breakfast and trying to glean information on Mason's whereabouts. Dad, of course, gave me nothing.

The classroom fills up slowly, most students taking their time finding their seats and clustering in groups instead. Bits of conversation hit my ears, but I try to be invisible by opening up my paperback and quietly reading until the teacher comes in.

I'm so focused on the pages, I don't register the hush of the room at first. Or the quiet scattering of bodies as space is made for someone to come in.

A person sits behind me and brings with them the scent of wildness—sweat, cold river water and earth-worn grass. A smell my nose reminds me I've been missing.

I turn, and find chipped iceberg eyes staring back at me.

Mason sits, his stare raking me from my waist up to my face, studying my body as if he owns it. He settles for a moment on my breasts, watching them rise and fall with anticipatory breaths. As if sparks are connected to his stare, tiny electric *pings* on my skin follow his attention up to my collarbone, scattering at my neck, before finally dispersing once he meets my gaze again.

"You're back," I say.

Mason taps his fingers against his desk, bringing nothing with him except a military jacket, ripped jeans, heavy black boots, and a vicious stare.

Dread creeps up my neck. Remembrance at what he's capable of. All it'll take is a nod to his girls, a murmur to his boys, and I'll be back within their scope.

I spin around before he gets any ideas, hoping that his time away has been so harsh, he's become tired of making my life miserable.

Hot breath hits my ear and I grip my desk.

Mason's low voice follows, summoning the *pings* and turning the right side of my face and neck into electrical wires. "Janitor's closet in the South Hall. You know where it is?"

I nod, afraid to speak.

"Meet me there."

Is he out of his *mind*? I'd rather be lead to slaughter. At least then, I'd know what I'd be turning into.

His breathing doesn't go away. "Say no, and I'll tell Amy to get creative. You've had a lot of time off, Big Mack. There's a lot to make up for, and I'm more than willing to orchestrate it. Unless, of course, you do as I say."

I hold my book close to my chest, hating that I'm also closing my eyes in submission. The thought of more torment, the idea of inviting his torture again...

"Fine," I whisper. "I'll be there after class."

"Good."

Cold air seeps against my cheek when he draws back, and I resist the urge to hold my fingers to it and reclaim the warmth.

I didn't pay attention for the rest of class, instead reeling over what Mason wants to say to me, or do, or threaten. Time doesn't do me any favors and the clock ticks achingly slowly, as well as Miss Lucas's lecture.

If she's as affected as me by Mason's reappearance, she sure is better at disguising it. She pays attention to me only once, a lingering, silent warning behind her expression, before getting back to her analysis.

I'm not frightened or threatened by you, I want to say to her. *But I'm truly afraid of your beast.*

The bell sounds and everyone is instantly on the move, banging books shut, re-starting conversations, finding their initial cluster of friends. Miss Lucas calls over the crowd to have our assignments in by Friday, but I'm scuttling to the door before she finishes her speech and sprinting through the hallway before the tidal wave of students begins.

I make it to the South Hall and the janitor's closet, open the door and duck in before anyone notices. Because it's such a small space, I leave the door ajar, and as people pass and see me idling in a broom closet, clutching my books to my chest, it doesn't take a genius to know their echoing laughter is about me.

Nothing I'm not used to.

I chew on my lower lip, inwardly cursing Mason and his ability to make people wait even when it's not necessary.

I should go. Just leave. Stay strong and not let him think he has any power—

A tall form fills the janitor's doorframe before the door is pulled shut and I'm left in the dark.

The lock clicks and I'm left with my own breaths for company.

Instead of panicking—which I *really* want to do—I yell into the small space, "Really? Locking me in a closet so I miss my next class? *That's* your next move?"

"No, Big Mack."

Yelping, I stumble back, hitting metal shelving and sending toilet paper rolls bouncing off my head.

I can't see a thing, yet I can sense him within inches of me, his body producing waves of hormones, charisma, power, *dominance*—I can name every poison.

Fumbling for balance, I press my palms against the metal shelving, creating divots in my back as I create as much space between us as I can in this black hole of ours.

"Are you afraid?" he asks quietly.

"M-Mason." *Damn* my voice for trembling. "Turn on the light."

"You want it so bad, you go and turn it on."

We both knew the switch is behind him and I'd have to go through him first. I picture him catching me by the waist, my breasts hitting his torso, my face molding into his neck. The way my thighs respond to that image—by clenching shut—isn't something I'm comfortable with, because I don't know if they're closing in fear or to keep Mason from sensing the immediate, sexual response to his words.

"What do you want?" I ask instead.

I gasp when calloused fingers trace my jaw, but I don't flinch away. Mostly because I can't—not without banging my head against more metal.

His hand moves down, tracing my elbow then grasping my arm. "Lose the books."

Swallowing, I let him take my barricade from me, my protection. I'm in complete conflict over the softness of his touch and his commands.

His fingers start playing with the buttons of my shirt. Ones he's trained to play the right notes, to elicit the right response, and my clavicle tingles against his touch. My nipples stand in rapt attention.

"Did you miss me?" he asks.

"N-no." My quick breaths make it hard to talk. "What are you doing? Why am I here? What do you—"

"Want?" I sense his head tilt at the question. "For you to answer some questions, Big Mack. Isn't it obvious?"

His hand cups my throat, still light, still soft, and I swallow against his palm.

"Right where I want you," he murmurs, then strokes down and undoes my top button. "Did you wonder where I was?"

I feel the need to be honest with him. "Yes."

"Did you worry?"

"I—yes. After what I saw…"

"Mm. Traumatic for a girl of your stature, I know. All chicks love bad boys until those bad boys get arrested in the local McDonalds. Kinda ruins the dangerous streak."

Another button pops open.

"That's not what I mean," I say. "I wasn't sure if you were being sent to jail or if your dad was gonna hear about it or— God, Mason, those cops *hated* you. It's like they wanted to hurt you."

"Believe me, I give them reason to. Hmm." The deep tone of his realization when he hits the lace of my bra sends rivers of fire into my veins. He cups one breast through the fabric, and my back arches into his hand in response. His thumb glides over my hard nipple, and I swear to God, I mewl.

"What do we have here?" he asks in a seductive whisper. "Do you want my mouth on you? Ever done seven minutes in heaven? No, probably not. Not Saint McKenna."

"I—" I don't *know* what he's doing to me. "I'm not … this isn't me. We should go. If this is all you want me in here for then —oh, *God.*"

His mouth and tongue are liquid fire through the thin cotton of my bra. A strong arm laces around my waist and draws me closer. My head tilts back, and when things clatter, when metal scrapes, I don't care anymore.

"You're always so nice, Big Mack," Mason says into my sensitive skin. "But it makes me think, you like the opposite of nice. It turns you on."

"Not true," I say through a gasp. He's doing things with his teeth I don't think should be legal. "I deserve respect from you. I've done nothing but try to help you and you're constantly throwing it back in my face."

His free hand dives into the front of my jeans. "Then why are you so wet for me?"

I moan, biting down on his thumb when he takes it out of my pants and scrapes it across my lip.

My thighs are traitors for unclenching.

My nipple leaves his mouth with a *pop*. He straightens and I feel his breath on my cheeks when he says, "I can make you come. I'll get down on my knees and tongue-fuck you right now, if you'll only answer one thing."

I'm so absorbed in how my body's responding to him, how I can feel his hardness pressing against my stomach through our clothes, that all I can do is wait for him to continue.

"Why the *fuck* did you involve your dad?"

Mason's voice is harsh and loud, completely at odds to the beckoning whispers and seductive curves of his tongue.

I turn into a fish out of water. "I—what?"

"Your father, Big Mack," Mason spits out. "I'm in the holding cell and next thing I know, I've been given a private lawyer who gets me the deal of my dreams and I'm let out."

"That wasn't my father," I say carefully. I may be treading into the waters of stupidity, but in the cloak of darkness, I do it anyway. "It's someone he knows. All I did was ask him if he could help out a friend of mine by making a few calls—"

"So I'm your fucking charity case now?"

"No!" My knees are unstable when he steps back. "But witnessing what happened to you and how unfair it was, I had to do something! I couldn't just walk away knowing you were taking the fall for something you didn't do."

Mason's nose nearly hits mine as he dives forward, but he doesn't relent. "What happens with my brother and Me, with my *family*, is none of your goddamned business."

"So you'd rather rot in jail, then? Is that it?"

"I can handle myself. Always have. Always will. Last thing I need is some pathetic chick with a save-the-bad-boy complex running to my rescue. What is it you're not grasping, Big Mack? I. Don't. Like. You. I feel *sorry* for you. So stop thinking you see something in me. 'Cause now I'm about to either fuck Amy or Miss Lucas, I can't decide. Either way, I'm washing you off my hands and forgetting your sad ass."

I speak as though his words don't hurt. "I only wanted to help. And it looks like I did. A simple thank you would've been nice."

Mason chuckles, and its absurdly evil in the pitch black. "Oh, my mouth on your tits and my fingers against your pussy were my thanks. But now? Now, here's my fuck you."

Light blasts into my eyes and I instinctively cover them, forgetting that my shirt is open and my breasts completely bare.

I dare a peek through my fingers, fully aware of what I'll see but doing it anyway.

You're better than him. You're stronger. Your life will be so much fuller. Mason's nothing but a shit-stain on the carpeted steps to your future...

I lose all positive thinking when so many people, so many pairs of eyes, land on my exposed body.

Tears smearing my vision, I fumble to shut the door against all the pointing and laughter, but I hear Mason's voice ricochet through the hall. "Anyone else want a go? Big Mack's ready for you!"

CHAPTER 6

Mckenna

I PULL BACK the deadbolt and stare at a freshly bruised face.

It's the same eye and more of his cheek this time. What was slowly becoming the puce-yellow color of healing is back to an angry, swollen purple, and the white of his eye half-bloodshot.

"What are you doing here?" I ask Mason, but it's with a resigned tone, a *what more could you possibly think to do to me* kind of question.

Mason shoves his hands into his pockets. He wears no jacket, using an open, denim button-down shirt to cover his stained white tee instead. It's cold today—May supposedly harboring spring somewhere, but New York's decided to delay any kind of blooming flower bouquet in favor of icy pricks of snow blasting into people's bodies instead.

Kind of how like I feel upon seeing Mason on the doorstep to my home.

"I, uh, was wondering if tutoring was still on the table," he said.

I glance down at his feet. Dirty, battered, used-to-be-white sneakers stand on my stoop, one with a grayed-over lace untied.

"What are *you* doing?" he asks.

I keep my focus on his shoes when I say, "Waiting for you to shuffle your feet. Or shift in some way with a bashful apology. Maybe have your cheeks redden not from a bruise for once, but from embarrassment over how you've treated me." I shrug. "Anything, really, to show me why you think you deserve any kind of help from the girl you've repeatedly bullied."

He exhales with an impatient puff. "Look, Big M—"

"*Not* the start of getting back in my good graces, you jerk."

"Okay. Fine. Mack. Just Mack, then." Mason levels his shoulders. "I'm tired of being here. In this town. Last night with my pops was the last straw, I mean—if I don't pass my classes, I'm stuck repeating senior year, while the rest of my guys, they move on. Rex is moving into the city, Wyn's going with him. Easton got accepted into a college out of state. He swears he'll come back to practice, but ... I know they're moving on. And our band is the one thing I have. The *one* thing. They can go off and build their lives, but where will I be at?"

The question's rhetorical, but I say anyway, "Still in the craphole you've created for yourself, most likely."

A muscle ticks in Mason's healthy cheek. He purses his lips, then winces as it tightens the bruised side of his face. "Alright. I deserve that."

"You deserve a whole lot more." I lean against the door frame and cross my arms. "And worse. Much worse."

In truth, these are the most words I've ever heard Mason speak. The most I've heard him confess. But I can't let his tough life and the angry shell he's formed around himself get to me.

"Where's the trap?" I ask.

"The what?"

I peer around the doorframe, searching the sidewalk below and the road beyond that. Waiting for a red Volvo SUV to come screeching around the corner with a carton of eggs to toss at my face. Or pig's blood.

In doing so, I glaze over Mason, who I'm trying not to linger on too long, but my stupid conscience notes his shivers, the concave hollows in his cheeks. The messed up, tangled chestnut hair. And the bruises on his neck. I wonder when he last ate.

"This is a set-up, right?" I say, making sure there's no indication in my voice that this battered boy is getting to me. "Amy'll be here any second with her cohorts, and I'll be kidnapped again, and this time they'll strip me in the streets of my neighborhood. Mrs. Dawes next door is ninety. It'd probably kill her if she saw my boobs in public."

The mention of my breasts on public view sharpens Mason's eyes, but not with shame. They go dark with passion as they rake down my neck and land on my pink cashmere sweater, my nipples safely housed behind the material, but *dammit*, not impervious to his attention.

"No." Mason shakes his head, hands still in his pockets. "There's no trick, B—Mack. It's just me. Asking you for help, even though I don't deserve shit from you. I've bottomed-out, but I still want to get out of here. I *need* to leave my home. I can't turn into my brother. Or my pops. I can't..." He hisses through his teeth, a hand coming up to dig into his hairline and push it back. He stares up at my house, his jaw working, then comes back to me. "This is my last, desperate move. I get it if you slam the door in my face. I'm surprised you haven't done it yet. But I got nothing left in me. I got no one else who'd be willing to ... and I'm—I'm s..."

Good lord. He can't even get out an apology without choking on his own spit.

At last, he gets it out, and it leaves the flush on his cheeks I'm looking for. "I apologize for everything. I'll leave you alone from now on, okay?"

"Why, thank you, Mason, for promising to leave me alone for the next month, despite years of making my life hell."

"You don't know what Hell is—" he bites his tongue, yet he can't temper the angry flash over his features. "What do you want? For me to get down on my knees? Publicly beg for your services? Fine, Mack. Anything. I really want this. I swear."

Every strong bone in my body tells me to advise him to go find Miss Lucas for help, then slam the door in his face like he predicted. But the one organ I have that's fighting back, the red-blooded beats of compassion, *thump-thump, thump-thump,* urges me to open the door wider for Mason to step in.

It's what my mom would've done. Despite a person's past or their history, she was always willing to help if they needed it.

"Tell no one about this," I say, then step aside.

Mason raises his head at the gesture.

He doesn't say thank you. I don't expect him to, since in the four years of knowing who he is, I've never witnessed Mason Payne grovel before anyone.

"There's a staircase to the basement at the end of the hall-way," I say. "Go down there and wait. I'll grab some of my books."

He nods, his expression blank, but his attention darting everywhere. Mason takes in the expansive foyer, the dust-free mahogany finishes, the marbled floors. He cocks his head at the dangling, Swarovski chandelier, an addition of my stepmom's, but keeps his mouth shut as he follows my instruction and strides down the first hallway.

I'm right behind Mason when I hear my dad say, "Hey, sweetie," as he's coming down the main staircase.

I shove Mason through the door to the basement before my dad notices him. Mason grunts at the move, but stays quiet when I shut the heavy wood and spin to face my dad.

"Who was at the door?" Dad asks as he fixes his watch around his wrist.

"Oh. Delivery guy. Wrong house."

"Ah. Mrs. Dawes ordering accidental Chinese food on her phone again?"

"Probably," I say, while tucking a strand of hair behind my ear. "Where are you off to?"

"Some function or another. Debbie's joining me," he says as I follow him into the kitchen, referring to my stepmom. "We'll be out rather late. You'll be okay? Order pizza for dinner?"

It's the third "function" they've been to this week.

"I was hoping I could cook you dinner tonight, actually," I say, disappointment swirling. "Since I haven't seen you for more than ten minutes this week. You know, like we used to? When it was just you and me for a time?"

"Ah, sweets." He kisses the top of my head, then moves to a hanging, silver pot and straightens his tie through the reflection. "This is a big meeting I can't miss. A negotiation of a whole lotta funds. I have to be there. Especially if my girl's going to Yale." He looks over and winks.

My dad is handsome, as most single, middle-aged women and the few friends I have will tell me. He's the silver fox everyone speaks of—tall, full head of salted hair, chiseled features and a flat stomach despite all his company events featuring open bars.

But to this day, I still see a saddened, down-trodden man who'd come into the den in the evenings and open up Scrabble so we could both get our minds off our newly widowed, mother-less status.

Or I used to, anyway.

Scrunching my lips to one side, I nod. "Then I guess I'll see you in the morning before school."

"No can do, sweetie." Dad comes over and squeezes my shoulders. "I'm taking Debbie on a quick trip for a long weekend to St. Lucia. To thank her for all her efforts in helping me land this deal. It's a big one, honey. It'll keep us in this house and make sure you can go to the Ivy League. Really, she's working the room for us as a family."

My upper lip goes stiff, but I say nothing as he pats my shoulders, kisses my head, then departs in a wave of cologne as familiar to me as childhood memories. Debbie, for all her giggles and manicures and perfect visage, is no carbon copy of my mother, and never will be.

She knows I know it, therefore, we don't get along well.

On a sigh, I thump up the stairs to my room, choose a few assigned novels for English class and my notes and laptop, and move downstairs, where there's someone in this expansive, hollow home that actually waits for me.

Whether he's lying in wait or waiting for my help, that's yet to be determined.

Mason's turned on the lights in the finished basement and he sits on the couch in front of an entire wall of shelving containing books I've had since I could read. Everything from *Peter Rabbit*, to Nora Roberts, to a neglected Scrabble board decorates the shelves. Being in its presence brings me immediate calm.

This is my safe space. My hobbit hole, my secret library, my quiet solitude.

If Mason screws it up I really *will* match his good eye to his bad one.

"Here," I say as I come up beside him, dumping a stack of books on his lap. He jolts, but covers it up with a frown. "Start at the top."

"Wait, I gotta read all these?"

"I don't have Cliff Notes for you, if that's what you're asking. But I can help as you take it chapter by chapter."

"Chap..." he trails off, staring at the five books on his lap in awe. "I'm gonna be here forever."

"It's not a bad place to be," I say quietly, taking a seat on the other side of the couch. At the sudden vulnerability in my voice, I cover it by smiling and saying, "This is where the genius happens."

Mason doesn't like my smile. His stare narrows on my mouth

and his brows pinch together. "Something happen up there with your pops?"

"Nothing out of the norm." I scratch a fake itch on my neck. "Can we start? We have a long night ahead of us. I should probably order the pizza now…"

At the mention of food, Mason's stomach lets out an audible grumble. He covers it by shifting and focusing major attention on cracking open *Catcher in the Rye.*

I'm no second-time fool. I don't say a word about his hunger and instead tap out an order on my phone. "I'm getting the toppings I want. Like pineapple. And olives."

Mason flicks a page. "Fine. I don't care."

"*Only* pineapple and olives," I say, tap-tapping away. "It's how I like it."

"Good for you. Enjoy."

"Great." I add an order of garlic-cheese sticks and another pizza, then place my phone on the coffee table. "Go back to the first page of the first chapter. You're not even skimming the words, Mason."

"But I—"

"Do it."

We work long into the night, Mason staying over and sleeping in the basement, next to my books, beside my precious artifacts. He ends up staying the next four days.

When the pizzas come, I tell Mason there was a mistake, that the second pepperoni one was accidentally included in an automatic order I usually place when Dad's around.

Mason doesn't question it. He eats the whole pie, then belches out his thank you.

CHAPTER 7

Mckenna

IT'S like I inherited a stray cat.

...If that cat were naturally angry, preferred the darkness of dumpsters to people, and with raised fur that's tangled and mangy.

After Mason's four-night stay, where my dad and Debbie were none the wiser, Mason took it easier on me at school. He never acknowledged our time together—because that, of course, is the kind of announcement better kept *out* of cool circles, but he also didn't ... stop coming over.

"Hey, Mr. Beckley," Mason says on my doorstep one random Wednesday.

Mid-snack chew, I peer around Dad's form while sitting on the kitchen stool, instantly stiffening at the voice.

"Mason, pleasure to see you," Dad says, opening the front door wider and eyeing Mason warily as he steps around him. "Again."

"Your daughter's an excellent teacher." Mason chooses that moment to send me a wink.

I cringe, fully aware Mason often confuses "teacher" and "janitor's closet" as related words.

"Whatchu got there?" Mason asks as he saunters into the

kitchen. He nicks an apple slice smeared with peanut butter off my plate, not bothering to hear an answer.

This close, he smells like fresh rain, the sharp burst of a droplet hitting soil and newly ripped spears of grass. I glance over and see the shoulders of his denim jacket are wet and his hair sparkles with the beginnings of a storm.

He also brings with him the outside chill.

I shiver, pretending it's because the door was open and not Mason's proximity.

"I guess you're here to learn more," I say after swallowing, then grab my diet coke as I slide off the stool.

"There was a pop quiz on Monday. Remember?" Mason asks while chewing.

Automatically, I nod.

"I got six out of ten right," he says. "That's because of you. Damn right we're gonna learn more."

Dad squints at me behind Mason's back. I send him a comforting nod, the kind that says, *everything's fine, this strange boy is familiar to me, don't worry.*

"Leave the basement door open while you're down there," Dad says before retreating upstairs to his office.

As soon as Dad's out of earshot, Mason gives me an up-close wink. "Is he afraid I'll take advantage of his sweet girl's ass?"

"You had your opportunities," I say while leading him down the hallway. "You didn't take them."

I won't admit it, but it's kind of nice to see Mason in a semi-good mood, even if it always has to be accompanied with dirty intentions.

The four nights Mason stayed over, he didn't sneak up to my room, or say nasty things, or try to break me. In fact, every morning when I crept down the basement stairs to wake him up, the blanket was neatly folded with a pillow perched on top, and there was no Mason in sight.

He left early, but arrived late, willing to undergo an hour or two of tutoring before wanting to sleep. It's hard to pretend nothing's wrong when the dark purple bruises under his eyes tells me different, but I tried to be as ambivalent as possible, focusing my criticism and study on his schoolwork and nothing else.

When I saw him in the hallways at school, he'd barely acknowledge my presence. One time, he was with Amy and her crew, standing around the lockers. Amy turned and locked in on me. Mason, chewing idly on a toothpick, nudged her shoulder and brought her attention back to him. He threw an arm around her and brought her near, and she laughed and nipped at his jaw, my proximity neatly forgotten.

I tried to forget the pit lodging in my stomach at the sight of them, too.

I can't possibly be *jealous* of Amy's relationship with Mason. That's ... that's practically blasphemy, after the way he's treated me. His four night couch-stay can't possibly erase the years of torment.

Yet here he is, the heat of his body too close as we take the basement stairs into our haphazard study hall, and there's my heart, pattering away excitedly at the thought of spending another evening with this temperamental street cat.

Mason, familiar with the layout, goes into the mini-fridge and grabs a beer.

"Do you think that's wise?" I ask as I swipe my pile of books from the side table and drop them in the middle of the couch.

"Best decision I've made today," he responds as he cracks open the can. After a few glugs and a satisfied exhale, Mason falls onto his side of the couch. "Which books we got today?"

I sit nearby and crack open our next assignment, explaining the questions while referring to my laptop now and again. I'm shocked to hear Mason ask his own, pointing at my screen and then the book, leaning closer each time.

I smell him again, wild and rugged male mixed with the malt

of beer. His breath hits my shoulder and I instinctively turn my head toward it, realizing how close his lips are to mine.

In that moment, we both freeze.

This close, Mason's eyes are winter blue, silver icicles spearing jaggedly from his pupils into his irises. His lashes are coal black, despite the milk chocolate of his hair.

My breaths are short. Hesitant.

Mason's gaze skims over my face. "I can count all your freckles from here," he says.

And I notice he has none. No freckles or moles mar the flawless skin. No recent bruises, either. His stubble has grown a bit, but that only makes him appear older. Too mature for his years.

He's not moving away. Neither am I. Our breath mixes, the room is silent, and I think if I tip my chin up just a bit...

We could be kissing.

My world shatters at the thought. *I have to remember.*

Specifically, Mason's Hall of Fame moments, the ones that I carry with me the most.

Freshman year, Mason introduced himself to me by tripping me in the cafeteria. Such a tried-and-tested move, I fell into my lunch tray, splattering spaghetti and meatballs all over my shirt and anyone within spraying distance. He then opened a can of coke and poured it on my head while I was on the ground.

Sophomore year, he snuck into the girls' locker rooms during gym glass and stole all my clothes. That part didn't affect me too much. It was when he stuck my underwear to my school locker, smeared with red sharpie marker and a sign proclaiming PERIOD PATSY above it.

Immature, illogical, and utterly hurtful.

Junior year was the worst. Mason was making out with Amy in front of an open classroom door I had to get through if I wanted to complete the mid-terms. As I tried to get by undetected, Mason cracked one eye open and tagged my movements.

He unglued his lips from Amy's long enough to reach over, undo my top button and say, "Wanna join?"

"Ugh, don't bother," Amy said, her gaze clearly ranking me a zero from head to toe. "Virgins don't do threesomes, Mase."

Mason doesn't glance over at Amy. He keeps his stare on me. "I love me some virgins. They taste the sweetest. So I ask again, wanna join, little girl?"

"N-no," I mumble into the stack of books against my chest and scurry into the classroom.

"Listen up," I heard Mason call behind me. The classroom instantly fell silent. "All hail the V-card I'm about to cash in on, because Big Mack over here just agreed to a menage et trois! Who knew she wanted it so dirty the first time? Pictures to follow!"

The room erupted with cheers, hoots, and hollers, and I knew my cheeks were going as red as the boiling blood underneath.

Then, senior year, he learned my actual name for the first time while on the city bus and toppled my coffee onto my shirt in misfired rage.

Mason is not nice. He's not kind. He's broken and mean.

"Hey, what's this? You writing a book or something?"

Mason's question snaps me out of the traumatic fugue, and I react by slamming my laptop shut, nearly trapping his fingers.

"Shit, Mack," he says, withdrawing his hands. "You nearly gave me a manicure."

"You need to leave."

Mason cocks a brow.

"Leave," I say through trembling lips. "Now."

"Whoa. What's happening right now?"

"This was such a mistake," I say, standing and smoothing down my simple cotton skirt. "I won't let you do this to me anymore."

Mason stands with me, but remains a careful distance away. "Do what? Mack, what's going on?"

"*Leave!*" I shout.

Mason glances up the stairs, likely fearful of drawing my father's attention. "Not until you tell me what's going on. What'd I do?"

"What did you *do?*" I repeat with broken syllables. "Let me count the ways, Mason. You've tormented, been my bully, been my *nightmare*, for years. Suddenly you need my help and turn into this vaguely nice guy who can turn against me as soon as he's done with me, and I'm *helping* you! Why am I helping you? Why do I do this to myself?"

"Hey—I'm not here with other motives. I actually want to do better in school."

"There's one month left!" I scream. "You're too late to do any better!"

"Thanks for that."

"Go away, Mason. For good. Don't ever come back."

He crosses his arms over his chest. "I'm not going anywhere."

"Fine," I say. "Then *I'll* leave and you can explain to my dad why you're still on the property."

I tear up the stairs and out the front door, making sure to slam it extra hard so Dad will hear and maybe try to figure out what's going on, but I don't hold out much hope. When Dad's in his office, or in any sort of work mode, I cease to exist. Sounds don't reach him, not even ones of distress. All he cares about is work. His clients. Maybe a little bit of Debbie. But as far as I'm concerned, I disappeared along with my mother two years ago.

However, Mason doesn't know that.

I streak down the side of the brownstone where we have a coveted driveway that's mostly unheard of in this neighborhood of stuck-together brownstones. Dad's car rests, inky black, cold and wet, in its usual spot.

Wet.

I'm getting soaked. The rain's coming down hard, and I'm only now noticing that the dampness on my face isn't only tears. Clouds have cracked open, water is falling from the sky, and I pause beside the car, wondering what the hell I'm doing.

Hands grab me from behind, spinning me, then throwing me against the front hood. I scream, grappling for balance, but turn mute when I meet smoke-filled blue eyes, like plumes of ashes after a nasty fire.

"You don't get to leave me like that," Mason says, so close that water droplets hitting his face are ricocheting against mine. "*Nobody* leaves me like that."

"Let go." I won't let him see me crumble. I *won't*.

"No."

He holds me tighter. The car's cold metal burns ice against the backs of my thighs, the wet slickness causing my skin to squeal against it when I try to break free.

"My dad's right up there," I say.

"Then scream."

I don't. My stomach's flipping upside-down at Mason's proximity. It keeps happening, no matter how much I hate him, my body's natural attraction. A growl bursts out of me, but Mason only smiles.

His lips are chapped, yet dewy, as he murmurs his threats.

"You've done nothing but make my life hell," I say while struggling. "Every nasty rumor has come from you. You're the reason I'm only known for that terrible nickname. The reason I have no *friends*. Why no one ever comes up to me other than to laugh in my face."

"Ah. Hence your change of heart this evening."

"These are my high school memories, Mason. They're what you've given me for the rest of my life. Nothing but pain."

He cocks his head. "Welcome to my world, Mack."

I peel my lips back and say, "You don't deserve anything nice from me. *Ever*."

"I'm well aware."

"Get off my property, then. Let me go—"

"That's what you want, huh? Me to be nicer to you? Kind? Sweet?" Mason asks, his grip on me remaining strong. "I got you covered, sweetheart. But I have to warn you, that Mason isn't much better."

I murmur, "What—"

But his mouth devours mine before I can say any more.

I grip the collar of his jacket, so tight, first out of shock, then to pull him closer as he angles his head and kisses me deeper.

He's not angry. Nor hungry. He kisses me in the rain like any romance hero I'd thought only existed in my books. I have no choice but to meet his suppleness with my own candor, our tongues twining, wet heat combining with the cold spray drenching us from above.

Both his hands slide up each of my thighs under my skirt, playing with the side straps of my underwear. The slick path he leaves on my skin might as well be fire, if it weren't for the rain dissolving his journey as soon as he makes it. He cups my butt cheeks and I let out a squeak of surprise in his mouth, which he swallows whole.

I feel his lips stretch with a grin before he lifts me by the back of my thighs and settles me on the car's hood, then nestles between the V of my legs.

His pants are soaked and they press up against my underwear ... which, I'm now realizing, are damp for entirely different reasons.

Mason's upper lip curls against mine before he grinds tight circles against me. His fingers tangle in my hair, tilting my head back, and he tongues me deeper.

A singular moan escapes, swirling up my throat and into his mouth. The sexual friction is mind-blowing, revolutionary, and I wrap my legs around his waist, a silent invitation for him to be faster, harder, *closer.*

My eyes pop open when pain lances through my lower lip. A coppery tang follows. I pull away, but Mason lingers in my vision with a closed-mouthed smile.

"Did you just bite me?" I ask, holding my fingers to my lips.

"I can only be gentle with you for so long, Mack," he says in a husky voice. Rain splatters against his face. "Restraint isn't something I can master when I'm picturing how tight you'll be."

A heavy hank of hair falls against my forehead, and I push it away. It's the only sign of normalcy during this insane fantasy I must be having, where I'm pulsing and swollen with need and splayed out on my dad's car with Mason talking about having *sex* with me.

Oh my God.

My dad's *car.*

Outside.

Where anyone could see us.

"Oh, hell no," Mason says, nestling back between my legs. "I just got a taste of you. No way are we stopping now."

To my horror, he gets down on his knees, he's literally kneeling in puddles, and starts pulling down my underwear.

"We're out in public," I hiss.

He looks up, and for the first time, I'm truly meeting the devil. "Let them watch. Give your neighbors something to talk about other than lawn encroachments for once."

"But my Dad. He could look out the window and see—oh, *fuck.*"

I don't swear. Not even in my head. But the instant my underwear's slipped off and two of Mason's fingers plunge inside me, the only words that matter contain a curse.

One corner of Mason's mouth twitches at my exclamation, but his sole focus is down below. The more I let him in, the farther my legs spread, the darker his expression becomes.

Arrows tipped with liquid aphrodisiac shoot toward my center at his look. I should be fighting him off. Rolling off this car and running back into the safety of my home, where Mason can't get to me.

Can't pleasure me.

Despite the storm, the pelting rain, the very real fact that my Dad could peek out his office window, I can't run.

Seeing Mason between my legs is the sexiest vision I've ever had. I'm hot, burning from the inside out, turning raindrops into steam.

I'm the heroines inside my paperback novels, being ravished by a rebel king.

"See, I can't be gentle with you, Mack. You like it dirty." He fits another finger inside, thrusting hard, twisting almost violently. I shudder at the gorgeous feeling. "A secret part of you wants me to dominate, to take. To *own* this pussy of yours."

He curls his fingers inside me and I fall back into a merciless arch against the hood. Rain goes up my nostrils, into my mouth, but it doesn't stop the moans.

A wave builds, pooling near his fingers, and I writhe, antici- pating the orgasm. I've only done it with my fingers before, never by someone else, but Mason has me.

He's so bad, the worst, but I have to let him do this.

Because I like it dirty.

"Fuck, Mack, I gotta taste you again."

His fingers leave my body, but my mewl of disappointment is cut short when his mouth replaces his magic hands.

Whimpering, I throw my arm across my mouth and bite down on the skin to stop the ecstatic scream.

His tongue does things his fingers couldn't. And he won't stop, I don't want him to, because I'm so close. I'm almost there.

A sudden cool mist hits where his tongue should still be.

I crack my eyes open, lashes thick with wetness, and discover Mason standing above me, a dark blur in the spray.

Oh, no.

Another prank. My gut churns, twists, destroying itself over the fact that my brain is once again an idiot.

Something brutal takes its place, a hatching egg containing a McKenna that's harder, scarier, a girl completely separate from the humiliation about to ensue.

I slide up on my elbows, searching for Amy, or anyone else with a camera phone.

Mason growls, "Let me fuck you on this Rolls, Mack."

Blinking, and not because of the rain, I turn my attention back to him. "W-what did you say?"

His slick features contain sharper angles, his cheeks bright slashes in the storm. "Let me fuck you. You're irresistible. Gorgeous. Splayed out and *mine*. I wanna claim you, Mack, right here and now, in front of everybody."

The request should cause a gasp. A horrified expression. A hellbent *no*.

Yet, it only makes me hotter. The idea of Mason pounding into me, in *public*, on a luxury vehicle...

"This is a joke," I say carefully.

Mason responds with a slow shake of his head. "Not even close. You're wet for me. Drenched. And I want to take you."

As if to prove his point, he rubs my clit with the tips of his fingers. I shudder instantly.

"Say yes, Mack."

Gasping, throwing my head back, I try to speak. "I..."

"Say yes."

"I—"

"Fucking *say* it before we both cream our pants."

"YES!" I cry without thinking.

Mason unbuckles his belt. Unzips his pants. He releases his dick and my eyes bulge at the sight.

Holy. He's big. And thick. And gorgeous.

He reaches in his back pocket and pulls out a condom.

This is the point I should be rationalizing, do I really want to lose my virginity to a bad boy from the wrong side of the tracks who carries spare condoms in his pocket? To a tutoring session?

But I can't. I won't. I'm kind of tired of good 'ol McKenna, sweet McKenna, the McKenna who should lose her virginity in her own bed, with candles and love notes and probably at the age of thirty, at the rate she's going.

This McKenna, however, Mason's Mack, is spread-eagle on her dad's car waiting for a huge cock to fill her with rain falling in all directions. The bastard wants to dirty me up, and I want him to.

His arm circles my waist and pulls me into a seated position, my skin squeaking loudly against the black metal. I grip his shoulders as he positions himself between my legs, my body so filled with anticipation, I'm shivering.

"Kiss me," he says, our wet noses touching. "Focus on my tongue and it won't hurt as much."

I dart for his mouth, sucking on his lips, searching for his tongue and he meets me halfway while maneuvering my body closer.

The tip of him spreads my lips down below at the same time his tongue parts my mouth. He starts off slow, and my thighs shake. My fingers ache from clenching his shoulders so hard. But I'm nervous. Terrified.

In a sudden thrust, he spears in, and I shout, though he muffles it with his lips.

"It's okay," he says against my mouth. "Worst is over. God, you're as tight as I imagined. As hot and wet as I needed. Mack … ah, fuck, Mack … I've been thinking about this for too long."

I grip him harder and pull back long enough to search his face, suspicious and waiting for the punchline, the Pavlovian response he's planted in me. Yet, all I see is a crack of vulnerability, a surprised fugue crossing his features as he realizes this isn't a quick fuck like all his others.

I say, with a straight face, "Then do something about it."

The openness falls away and his usual mask takes its place. The devil grins. "As you wish."

He tightens his grip on my waist. Thrusts out, then in, before he pounds faster, our squeals of skin against car becoming nothing but background noise as my moans and his breaths take front stage.

Mason buries his face in my neck as my inner walls tighten and build up to … aching greatness. I've never felt anything like this before. Pleasure, pain, power, need, and want, all bonded into one.

He lowers his hand and starts flicking my clit, and now I don't need the haze of a storm to be blinded. The dull pain stops and darts of pleasure takes its place.

"Don't stop," I whisper against his hair. "Not this time. I'm almost there. Oh, my God, I'm almost … almost … *Mason!*"

I cry out through the stars in my eyes and his thumb on my clit and his dick inside me, my mouth opening and closing against the sudden thrill jolting above my bones.

Mason's broad back shudders. He lifts from my neck, his cheeks flushed and his eyes dilated and bright.

Without another word, Mason slides out of me as quickly as he speared in. I slump against the vehicle, disoriented but supple, yet so rubbery I'm unable to slide off the car and stand on my own two feet.

Completely out of character, Mason lands a sweet peck on my forehead.

He says, before he leaves me in the rain, slumped over and satiated, "I think I'm gonna grow to like this deviant McKenna."

CHAPTER 8

Mckenna

I WOULDN'T SAY Mason's heart grew ten sizes larger than its original, shriveled state after taking my virginity, but the additional time I spent with him sure made a difference in my schooldays.

Aside from eating all the Nutella out of my house and home, Mason wasn't unwelcome at my place after school. My stepmom and dad were often away on business (Debbie always accompanied him on trips) or out late for dinner engagements. The fridge was always stocked, which Mason always sniffed out, and before I knew it, he was sitting next to me on the bus home after a day of being ignored by him *and* his cronies.

I gotta say, I prefer being invisible to being bullied any day.

We'd arrive at my house, make snacks, I'd force him to learn and summarize themes in at least one chapter of our assigned reading, and then we'd have sex.

Yep, sex.

I'm Mason's secret, and the part of me that's horrified is nowhere near as large as the desire to be dominated by him.

You like to be dirty.

Mason's teaching me things I didn't know existed. He throws

my arms up over my head, locks my wrists, and uses his free hand to sink his fingers into my folds and pump, and curl, and *pound*, until I have nowhere else to look but up.

It doesn't matter if we're standing or lying down. He takes me as soon as he sees his chance, whether on the kitchen counter, the living room, the shower, the jacuzzi…

It's no longer just my dad's car that's sullied.

What we're doing is forbidden, and my feelings for Mason are so wrongly rooted, but I can't seem to stop. I don't want to, even when he barely acknowledges me at school save for a singular, searing glance that he blinks away so fast, I'm not sure it ever occurred.

In private, he'll turn feral, but it's a ferocious heat, addictive in its intensity, and I submit, because where else would I rather be?

At the moment, we're lying naked on my stepmom's Persian carpet in the formal living room that's never used, save for the annual company Christmas party hosted by my dad.

"I gotta admit something," Mason says, idly playing with my fingers.

There's no cover-up happening. Mason lies, fully splayed out with one knee up, in complete confidence and relaxation. I've curled into him in an attempt to hide my exposed bits, an instinctive move I doubt he notices, since he keeps reaching down and tweaking my nipple, his dick jerking happily in response.

"What must you confess?" I murmur, nuzzling his neck. It's these rare moments after sex that Mason's calm and at ease—but I'd never call him vulnerable.

"The first time I had you, I thought I scared you so bad, I'd never see your tits again."

I snort into his warm skin, well used to his crassness, but never so complacent that I'm not still startled by it.

"Why would you say that?" I ask.

"Because you're *you*. Cute and innocent and pure, and I laid you out on a car for your first time. I thought that'd be it for you. That I'd gone too far. But here we are, laid out on your stepmom's fancy carpet after fucking like dogs on all fours ... I fucking love it. But I'm wondering if *you* do."

I pull away from his neck, wondering why he cares. "I'm giving you what you want. I figured that'd be enough explanation for a guy like you."

"Hell, yes. But what if I said to you that next, I want anal?"

I give a one-shouldered shrug. "Sure, we can try."

Mason twists his head. His eyes turn to slits when they meet mine. "Who *are* you?"

"Maybe I'm finally turning into who I'm supposed to be." I prop myself up on one elbow. "This may surprise you, but I didn't like to be called bookish, or a nerd, or *Big Mack*, Mason. I hated being ostracized and made a fool. And yeah, when we started having sex, it was all you. Your choice, your power, your time. But I *like* this. It makes me feel good." I reach down, and with more confidence than I've ever had in my life, I wrap my fingers around his shaft. "It's oddly freeing, letting you do what you want with my body."

Mason searches my eyes. Half his mouth turns up into a smile. "What have I unleashed?"

Hand still on his dick, I stroke, up and down. "Most of my days were spent wishing I was the girl in my romance novels, getting the guy, being introduced to great sex, and having her happy ending. You've awakened at least one of those things in me. I'm not about to stop until I'm satisfied."

Mason grunts, low in his throat, as his hips take up my rhythm. "I'm more the villain in your stories than the hero."

I whisper into the shell of his ear, "I know."

Massaging the back of my scalp, Mason tangles his fingers in my hair, then slowly applies pressure. Down.

"Wait just a minute," I tease, loving that I'm the one causing his brows to furrow with pained frustration. "I want to ask you a question, first."

"Make it fucking quick."

"Prom's next week."

Mason's grip freezes on the back of my neck. "So?"

"Be my date."

"No."

I release his dick. On a growl, he grabs my wrist and places my hand back on his thick, hard, very hot and swollen shaft. "I wouldn't make that mistake twice, Mack."

"I mean it. It's the only event I'll ever ask you to."

"That's because it's the last event at school."

"Not true. Graduation."

"Sweetheart, I'll be lucky if I'm allowed on the ceremony grounds, never mind be part of the graduating class."

I nod like he's said the exact right thing. "Fine. One dance at prom then. In public. Prove to me I'm not your shameful secret, give me my happy ending, and then we can part ways."

Mason's gaze grows suspicious again. "Just like that?"

It'd be wonderful to show up at the dance with Mason on my arm and capping off a shitty high school experience by at last conquering the bully. I could throw it in Amy's face and all her minions. I can show Mason there's more to us than sex, despite his natural inclination to shy away.

One dance, just like in my romance novels.

One perfect moment in high school, just like how I've fantasized.

Mason will kiss me in front of everyone, and no one will call me Big Mack again.

"Yes," I say, breathless now. "Just like that."

Mason mulls this over by wrapping my fingers around his cock and squeezing. "Deal."

In one startling move, he rolls so fast on top of me, he might as well be performing night ops in a military exercise. A muffled squeak leaves my throat.

"Now," he says, his lips brushing against mine. "Let's seal it with a fuck."

CHAPTER 9

Mckenna

I'M NOT sure how it's possible, but...

Mason's on my doorstep.

In a suit.

While getting ready this afternoon, I was mostly convinced Mason wouldn't show up *at the dance*, never mind at my home. All I asked him for was one dance. No other expectations were set.

It was with that in mind that I let Debbie do my hair and make-up this afternoon and approve my dress—a pale yellow, strapless silk affair that sets off the red in my hair and compliments my skin—thinking I'd attend prom for a half hour, max, figure Mason wasn't coming, then leave out the back door.

Prom wasn't anything I strived for, except in my dreams. But it was also in my dreams that I was popular, had a bunch of friends, and dated the high school quarterback, so it's no wonder my real life is like dumping a pile of concrete on expectations.

Yet...

Here he is. Mason can't be farther from a clean-cut, extra muscular QB1, but he is absolutely as handsome as the footballer of my fantasies. Just a darker, crueler, demonic version, which only makes him more seductive.

"You're here," I say, once my lips are able to move again. My arm's like a limp noodle holding the front door open.

"Uh, yeah." He tangles his hand in his hair as he stares at me, but I have the feeling he's not really seeing what's in front of him. There's a glazed sheen to his eyes and a troubled line between his brows. "Was I supposed to meet you there?"

"No, I—we didn't really make plans. It's just one dance that we agreed to," I repeat, and have been repeating on a loop this past week.

His hand moves down his face, where he cups his jaw and scratches. "Right, well. I'm here now, so ... wanna ride?"

"Are you okay?" I blurt out, assessing if he's on drugs, or drunk, despite my awareness Mason doesn't do hard drugs. His brother and father do, which is enough to "fucking immunize me against that shit for life," according to Mason.

Mason's vaguely unbalanced, like he's not sure how he ended up here.

"Fine," Mason snaps, then looks me up and down. "You look beautiful."

I raise my brows. "Nobody's ever yelled at me for being beautiful but ... thank you?"

He holds out his hand. "C'mon. Ride's waiting."

My shoes are already on. Debbie insisted my outfit wasn't complete until I capped it off with her sparkling Jimmy Choo's, and she was right. After she and my dad left for their dinner engagement, the halls became my runway as I sashayed in private.

Now my feet hurt like a mother, but it was worth it. Mason's here, I have great shoes, a gorgeous dress, and my hair's behaving like it should for once.

The prom I wasn't going to attend is looking better and better.

Then I saw our ride.

"Is that..." My fingers tighten on Mason's. "No. It can't be."

A black stretch limo waits at the curb with the back door open, where Mason must've stepped out initially.

It's not the car that makes my spine tighten, but the swath of red tulle coupled with a white, veneered smile that flashes into my vision.

"That's Amy," I whisper.

Mason tries to pull me along, but I've come to a halt.

"Yeah," he says, but then his tone goes dark. "Court and Melissa are in there, too. And Amy's date."

Tug. I keep still.

Mason steps closer, using his index finger to tip my chin up. "Relax, Mack. You're with me tonight. Nothing's gonna happen to you on my watch."

"I don't know that." I search his eyes. "I have four years of proof to not *believe* that."

"Yet you asked me to be your date."

"I didn't..." I let out a fake, too-harsh laugh. "I asked you for a single dance. You're the one who showed up at my doorstep in a suit."

Up close, the suit is definitely secondhand. A few threads are loose along the shoulders, and the color is more of a tarnished gray than its once black. Its only saving grace is that Mason's in it. The guy is wearing a suit for me, to a dance he hates, and I can't lie and say my stomach hasn't turned to mush at the sight.

But is it trusting mush?

"Seriously." Mason tries tugging my hand again. "I'll be by your side the whole time."

"That's supposed to be a good thing?" I mutter out of the side of my mouth, but my feet start moving.

Mason hears. He leans close and says, "After this, we'll come back to your place and I'll eat you out until you're dry."

My eyelids flare. That means a lot of orgasms. A *whoosh* of feeling hits my core and I stumble in my heels.

"Good girl," Mason murmurs, his hand at the small of my back.

At the limo, Mason guides me in first. I cringe, but hide it the instant these girls can see my face. I don't say hello as I find a spot as far away from them as possible, but it turns out it's not necessary when I notice who's next to Amy.

My mouth drops, but so not to be obvious, I watch Mason get into the car and settle beside me. His expression has turned to stone, his cheeks so hard, lines of muscle frame his jawline.

Amy studies me with lowered lids. She's in a scarlet gown with a mermaid cut that's tight all the way down until her lower legs, where sparkling fabric and tulle flares out. Courtney's in a purple number and Melissa has chosen a simple short, ivory dress.

I clear my throat and sit back, folding my hands on my lap.

"Holy fucknut, let's cut this tension with a champagne bottle," Brax says from his position beside Amy.

Amy giggles, then nestles closer to Mason's brother.

Rage pulses off Mason in rivulets, the heat of his anger so potent, I'm afraid to touch him or acknowledge him in any way.

Brax doesn't seem to mind. He fumbles around for champagne in the side door, finds it, then holds it up like a trophy, his mouth a clownish maw and his stare uncentered.

Oh, boy. Brax is loaded.

On what, I have no idea, but it matters little when the whites of Mason's knuckles cut through his skin like blades as he grips his thighs.

The three girls titter and clap when Brax pops open the bottle, Melissa grabbing five flutes. I'm no mathematician, but it's obvious they've missed a glass. Me.

"You've had enough, B," Mason says.

Brax cackles. "Not even close, bro. We're not even at the stupid dance, yet. And since watery fruit punch isn't gonna do it for me, I'm gonna swig now."

Amy offers him a flute, but Brax knocks it away. It hits the other glasses and a couple shatter to the floor. Courtney covers her mouth with a laugh and Amy smirks.

"Whoopsie," Brax sing-songs, then tips the bottle to his mouth. "Who's next?"

"Me," Amy says. Brax passes the bottle over with a lecherous smile, and Amy daintily grins back.

I note the slyness in her expression, and, even though I didn't need it to understand what was really going on in this vehicle, it solidifies my opinion.

"Shit, bro, I've had an epicany!" Brax hoots, slapping his thighs.

"A what?" Mason asks tightly.

"Epic … epif … you know, a bright idea."

"Epiphany," I say, before I can help it.

Brax points at me. "Yeah, Big Mack Bookworm, that." Then he frowns. "When did you get here? And *why* are you here?"

"Because she's my date," Mason bites out.

"Oooooh." Brax nods sagely. "Makes complete no fucking sense."

"Tell me about it," Amy says. "Talk about an ugly duckling making her debut … as an ugly duckling."

"Fuck off, Amy," Mason says. He throws an arm around my stiff shoulders, pulling me closer. It's like being slammed against a cold, brick wall.

"No one want to hear my epitaph?" Brax asks.

Amy trails a finger down Brax's cheek. "Tell us, babe."

Mason's torso contracts beneath my arm. He's coiled to spring.

I don't like that Amy's using Brax, especially when he's so vulnerable, but I'm not sure I'm enjoying Mason's reaction, either.

"My brother, my gosh dang, freaking big boy bro who's always cutting a path for me, has fucked every single chick in this cab." Brax slaps his thighs and jiggles up and down. "Ain't that right, Mase?"

My gut hardens, but I school my face.

Amy laughs. "Braxie, shut it. This isn't the time, nor the place, to point out Mason's conquests—hang on." Her tipsy expression hardens. She glares at Mason. "You've fucked Big Mack? No way. Are you *serious*?"

Mason's hand hasn't left my shoulder. I try to move away, but he's leaving deep red marks on it as he grips me harder.

Amy face goes white. She says to Mason, "You're not denying it."

"Oh, my God..." Melissa whispers to Courtney. "Can you believe he..."

And in an instant, I'm transported to what the dance will be like when I arrive on Mason's arm. The whispers. Stares. Cat-calls. Insults. Laughter.

What am I thinking?

That this would make me cool? That being here, becoming one of Mason's *girls*, would heal the years of terribleness these people have wrought?

The sex is good, mind-blowing even, but it's not enough to bury the memories of the torture I've gone through.

"Can't blame you for eating the most famous burger in the land," Brax says. "She got that special sauce on her cooch?"

Amy sneers. "Never knew fast, fatty food was your craving, Mason. I always thought it was fine dining you were after.'"

An overwhelming urge to escape hits me at the same time the limo stops at a light. I open my mouth to say, *this was a bad idea, I need to leave*, but I don't even get to inhale.

I miss what else is said, but Mason's leap to the other side of the car is impossible to ignore. He throws himself against Brax, his arm raised for a punch. Amy squeals, champagne spills everywhere, and Courtney and Melissa scramble to get to my side.

"Mason, stop—!" I shout, but the limo's moving again and standing in a crouch, with no handhold, in heels, is a recipe for disaster. I topple to the side, narrowly missing Mason's shoe side-swiping my cheek as he struggles with Brax and I land in a heap.

I crawl up Mason's leg, gripping his blazer and trying to pull him back. The limo lurches to the side and comes to a stop, the driver tumbling out and running to the back door.

He opens it and helps me drag Mason out of the car by his feet, but the damage is done. Brax's face is bloody, already swelling, and I'm fairly certain I spot a cracked tooth when he grins maniacally at Mason's departure.

I stumble out behind Mason as the driver barrels down on him.

"—out of my vehicle!" the driver screams. "Completely unacceptable behavior! You're walking from here, kid. Lady, it's your mistake if you stay with him."

I grip the fabric of my dress as I sidle up to Mason. "I'll stay."

"Fucking punk kids," the driver mumbles as he dismisses us. "If you were my daughter, sweetheart, I'd never let you within arm's reach of scrap like that. You need to reevaluate your decisions in life."

"Thank you for your unsolicited advice," I say to his back as he climbs into the limo.

With a mild engine roar—because it's a hulking stretch limo—the vehicle lurches back into traffic and disappears.

Mason wipes his mouth with the back of his hand and starts limp-walking away. A few droplets of blood pattern the pavement as he moves.

"Wait up!" I say, toddling behind in my heels while trying not to scrape the hem of my dress against the filthy sidewalk.

"Don't know why you got out with me," Mason says without turning around. "Shoulda stayed in the car and gone to the dance of your dreams."

"That's a joke, right?" Finally, I catch up to him. "You want me to stay in that car with *them*? I might as well be a Big Mac. They'd eat me alive."

"Only because you let them," Mason mutters.

"Excuse me?"

"Big Mack Doormat, Big Mack Bookworm, Big Mack Mouse —there are so *many* nicknames for you, because you give us so much to work with."

Hurt spears my heart, but I'm comfortable enough with Mason to retort, "Not any original material, at least."

Mason whirls. "Yet you take it. Each and every time. Hell, I've treated you like shit on my shoe, and you *still* let me fuck you! Scratch that—you let me take your v-card! Like, holy shit, dude, where is your pride?"

I stop in my tracks, heat flooding into my cheeks. "I know why you're saying these things to me right now. You're hurting. Brax isn't well and—"

Mason's finger jams near my face. "Don't you dare bring up my family problems. Not if you want to come out of this without bawling your eyes out."

I grab his finger. Clutch his hand in my own and force it down. I keep holding on when I say, "I've gotten to know you these past few weeks. Not just your body and not only the random moments of tenderness when you stroke my face or kiss my forehead when you think I'm sleeping. And I know, right now, that you're lashing out, and I'm your closest target."

"Target?" Mason sneers, and it's such an ugly, old expression of his that I recoil. "More like you're my *victim*. You've always been such easy prey. I zeroed in on you out of spite. That spoiled, rich, lonely girl who thinks she has it bad but has no idea how bad it could really get. Not until I came along. And you know what?" Mason laughs darkly. He rips out of my hold and turns, scrubs at his red-rimmed eyes, then whirls back. "You're still my victim. I'm not fucking you 'cause I want to. Or even because you're willing and *there*. I'm doing it because Amy thought it'd be fun to make you feel special before bringing you down in front of the entire class at prom."

I grit my teeth against any incoming tears. "You're lying."

Mason grins, and it's a lot like his brother minutes before. "I ain't."

"You *are*." I storm toward him, stopping when my face is inches from his. "You can't fake what we've been doing. Your late night visits to my house, the fact that you're starving—"

"Stop it."

"And that my bed is the first real place of warmth you've had in *years*—"

"I said fucking stop it."

"And the escape I've brought you. Away from your druggie brother and abusive father, out of a crumbling home in a dangerous neighborhood, and into something good. Something *real*. You're just pissed I've broken down your walls, Mason Payne. You can't stand that I've given you feelings other than numbness and cruelty. That—dare I say—I've given you *happiness*."

"*Fuck you!*" Mason screams, and despite the deserted curb we're on, I look around for any witnesses. "You don't know anything about me because I've made it that way. You don't make me happy. You *disgust* me. Amy had my blessing for tonight. She brought scissors. Was gonna cut your hair when you weren't looking, rip your dress off, and push you out onto the stage. Something about, I don't know, everyone getting a taste of McKenna's Dollar Menu. Offering you up to the whole class." Mason palms his chest. "And I *knew* about it! Why do you think we were taking a limo with them? It was to get you drunk. To make you vulnerable. I fucked you to give you a false sense of safety with me. I was gonna ditch you the minute I could. It was a set-up!"

I bare my teeth and say through blurred vision, "You don't mean any of that!"

"Hell, I was gonna be the cameraman and document the whole thing! Upload it on YouTube!"

"No." I shake my head. "This isn't the Mason I've been seeing—"

"Are you fucking dumb?" He bears down on me and whispers, "I mean every. Fucking. Word. You're nothing to me, Mack Beckley. You've been nothing. You'll forever be nothing."

Mason's upper lip curls before he spins away. "You're forgotten."

"This is because of Brax!" I cry at his back. "And what Amy did by bringing him as her date. Nobody's trying to help him but you. He's surrounded by these bobbleheads that do whatever he wants, and you're at a loss. But you entertain the same company, Mason!" I'm crying now, tears streaming down my face. "You're around nothing but *bobbleheads*! And because I'm the first one to call you out, to want to help, to have real feelings for you, you become cruel—you—you—"

But it's useless. Mason's turned a corner and is gone.

I crumble into a heap in the middle of the sidewalk, doing exactly what he swore I'd do. Bawl my eyes out.

Even worse, I'm a fool to hope he'll ever come back.

♡

After a moment of letting myself cry, I pull myself up. It's obvious that Mason isn't coming back, and I can't just sit out here, feeling sorry for myself. If I do that, I'm exactly what they expect me to be - a victim worth dumping on, taking advantage of, ridiculing.

At this moment, I have two choices: I can go home, stuff my face with ice cream and watch sad movies all night, or I can go to my senior prom. Sure, I have to fix my makeup, and I would have to keep an eye out for Brax and Amy and even Mason if he winds up at the dance. But I refuse to let a group of assholes take something I've wanted so badly away from me.

I kick off my shoes, deciding to walk to prom the rest of the way. I'm hoping I can catch a ride home from someone, though I'm not sure if I know anyone who's actually going to be willing to help me out.

I'll figure it out when I'm there.

Half a mile later, my feet killing me, I reach the auditorium of the school. I can hear the music thumping from where I am. My heart skips in excitement. I know it's stupid, but I'm still looking forward to being here, even if Mason broke my heart.

I suck in a deep breath and force myself to continue inside. I refuse to let Mason ruin tonight. It may not be perfect, but it was my night and I wasn't going to just roll over and let him dictate how I felt.

When I stepped through the auditorium, I put my shoes back on. I winced at the pain, but refused to give anyone an excuse to pick on me. Let them say whatever they wanted about me not being here with Mason, but I couldn't let them get to me.

I step into the ladies' room before I do anything else. I need to fix my mascara and wash my face. A couple of the stalls are occupied by the time I get there, and the two people talking sound oddly familiar.

"...can't believe she got out of the limo to follow him, the twat," a voice says.

"Where's Brax now?" the second voice responds. "You said he was sick when he got here."

"Throwing up in the back," the first voice says. "Can you believe it? He's such a buzzkill. I don't know if he took anything before, but I can't stand the smell of vomit, especially when it's alcohol-induced. Like, okay, he has a problem and if he doesn't do anything about it now, he's going to end up in rehab or dead. Did you know my uncle—"

I dash out of the bathroom before I can hear the rest of

Amy's sentence. I shouldn't be surprised that she ditched Brax when he was too much to handle, but I can't help but feel sorry for him. Not that he deserves it. I just know what he's going through, thanks to Mason.

I step out of the school and try to find him somewhere on the football field in the back. A couple is making out on the benches while a group of friends are passing around a metal flask behind them. Where the chaperones were was anybody's guess.

After a moment, I hear the sound of heaving and I follow it, only to find Brax just behind a goal post, throwing up in the end zone.

"Brax?" I call out to him, ignoring the sharp pain in my feet. "Is that you?"

"Who goes there?" he calls in between retches.

I roll my eyes and step to him as he starts throwing up again. When I reach him, I place a tentative hand on his shoulder, patting him awkwardly.

"Brax?" I ask. "Are you all right?"

"Mack?" a voice calls from behind me. "What are you..." The voice trails off as I slowly turn around.

I don't know why I'm surprised Mason is here, but I am. I assumed he would go home, or anywhere else that isn't prom. Then I remembered the limo, how worried Mason was about his brother. Mason probably had no intention of coming here other than the fact that he wanted to get Brax and leave.

"Are you following me?" Mason asks, coming closer. He has a bottle of water in one hand and a stick of gum in another. "God, I thought you were pathetic, but after everything I did to you, you're still here?"

I know he's lashing out. But I can see the worry in his eyes.

"I'm here because no matter what you tell me, I'm going to have fun at my dance, with or without you," I tell him. My voice shakes. I'm not prepared to go toe-to-toe with Mason, but I can't help myself. Everything I've kept inside comes tumbling out and

I can't stop it, even if I want to. "I'm here because I heard Amy talking about Brax in the bathroom like he was yesterday's trash. I wanted to make sure he's okay."

"Brax is none of your concern," Mason says.

"He's no one's concern, that's the problem." I step forward. "You feel guilty about your dad. You feel guilty about not being able to stop it. So, you let Brax drink because you know it helps him. But it's going to kill him if you don't get him help. *Real* help."

"And what do you know about that?" Mason asks. He throws his arms out, stepping closer to me. "What do you know about my life? About everything I'm going through?"

"I know you're a good person deep down," I say. "I know that you lash out because you want to protect yourself and your brother because you don't trust anyone. I know that whether you want to admit it or not, you care about me. I know you're a coward. Because ten years from now when we've forgotten all about high school, you are going to regret treating me the way you did. Picking on me, hurting me, getting me to believe you loved me only to crush me, exactly what your father does to both of you. You revel in the pain. You think I'm pathetic for having hope? For believing in the good in you? You're pathetic because you are exactly your father. Instead of hurting me with your hands, you use your words."

I glance back at Brax, who seems to have stopped throwing up for the time being, before looking back at Mason.

"You're exactly the person you don't want to be, and you have no one to blame but yourself," I say. "You're going to miss me so bad when I'm gone, Mason Payne."

I step away from him and head back into the auditorium. This time, I don't turn back. I don't want Mason to follow me. I'm done with him, this time, for good.

Part Two

PRESENT DAY

CHAPTER 10

Mckenna

"Turns out, Amy's mom is a porn star."

The woman whispers it to her friend as they sit across from me at the exclusive dinner table in the middle of the restaurant.

"More bread, sweetheart?"

I cut my attention to my date as he offers me a basket of bread rolls. I take one, chewing idly.

"Never could resist the carbs, could you, darling?" my date—Charles, is it?—asks.

He leans over to whisper into my ear. "Just make sure some of that fat hits your ass. I like my women juicy."

I smile through the dry crumbs in my mouth. He makes a doting clucking sound, then dabs the corners of my lips with his napkin that he's dipped in his water glass. I let him.

His salt and pepper hair—more salty than peppery—is slicked back from his rugged, pock-marked face. The paunches in his jaw match his rotund belly, masked by a specialty tailored suit that costs more than my bi-annual rent.

"How did you come to know she was a porn star?" the woman's friend asks as she reaches for her wine. "Don't tell me it came up during school pick-up."

The woman—I think her name is Judy, she's Charles's

neighbor—*tsk-tsks.* "It was Susan's husband that found out. He swears he 'accidentally' fell upon a website advertising this mother's ... skills, but we all know the truth. He watches porn non-stop at night because Susan's not adventurous enough in bed, or maybe he's just bored being a stay-at-home dad. Then he stumbles upon his daughter's best friend's mother's breasts, and probably decides to jack off to them before informing the parents of the entire class."

"Despicable," her friend replies.

I've forgotten her name, but both of them are bottle-blonde, heavily Botoxed, and doused in expensive perfume where each woman's scent is at war for my nose's attention.

"Who?" Judy titters. "Susan's cardboard sex life or her husband's dark net trysts?"

Her friend giggles into her wine glass.

"Ladies," Charles says, resting against his chair and slinging an arm around my shoulders. "Should we get down to it, or what?"

"Of course, Charles," Judy says, angling away from her friend and, at last, resting her gaze on mine. "But I'm not quite sure why you brought your date to a co-op meeting in a restaurant. Aren't you bored, darling?"

"Not at all," I say as I lift my gin martini, and I mean it. I only allow myself one drink while on dates, and this one has become necessary. "Tell me, does Amy's mom have her own website, or did this guy find her on one of those free streaming sites?"

Charles coughs into his bourbon while Judy startles. He says, "Jane. Honey. Let's not get into the details."

"I'm only curious," I say to Charles with my best simpering tone.

Judy's friend shifts uncomfortably in her chair. "You weren't supposed to have heard that."

I offer an apologetic smile. "These young ears of mine. They tend to get piqued when forbidden sex is mentioned."

Judy nearly chokes on her red wine.

"Jane," Charles warns.

"Oh, dear," I say to him under my breath. Meanwhile, my hand finds Charles's thigh and begins a slow rub, up … up … *up.* "Have I gone too far?"

Charles's hips move enough to spoon his shaft into my palm. It's small, thick, and rigid through the fabric of his pants. No one else at the table has noticed.

He clears his throat. "Let's move to the first topic of our agenda, shall we? I'm sure we all have places we'd rather be than discussing this year's budget for the condo."

"I don't know," Judy's friend says with a smile. "Attending New York's premiere steakhouse and offering unlimited bottles of wine to your neighbors does have its perks, Charles."

"Yes, well." Charles opens his binder of notes with a frown.

Meanwhile, I've slipped into his pants and I'm giving him the chub-rub of his life. His cheeks redden with the exertion of keeping his groans contained. "My aim is to have this done before you've hit your third bottle, Karen."

Properly chastised, Judy's friend Karen quiets down. The rest of the table, previously absorbed in their own conversations, move their attention to Charles as he makes his announcements for the new year.

As he talks through his bullet-points, his voice remains steady, his shoulders relaxed, and his fingers easy as they turn pages. But his dick is hot and pulsing, along with his cheeks, and he dabs at his forehead with his napkin as he continues with his speech.

"Furthermore, the special assessment will have—will have to —be, uh—oh, *fuck*—"

Charles's hands grip the edge of the table, causing plates and glasses to lightly clatter.

I smile serenely as I remove my hand and settle it onto my

lap, where I give it a nondescript wipe with my napkin under the table.

Judy is aghast. "Charles!"

"You all right, man?" someone asks, the only other male at the table.

"The bourbon," Charles says once he rights himself. "My mouth is much too dry to be making such long speeches. Tony, please take the lead on the next item of our agenda while I wet my palette."

"Excuse me," I say to the table as I rise. "While I go to the ladies' room."

No one gives me a second glance, certainly not the ladies across from me, but that's how I prefer it. I'm nothing but a ghost attending this function, forgettable to everyone except my client. Even my name is nothing special, Jane Landers, a deliberate ruse that's completely at odds with my occupation. Jane Landers should be an accountant, a tax auditor, or perhaps even an attorney. Certainly not an escort. It's exactly the moniker that my clientele love, because when it comes to introductions at social gatherings, who would ever suspect Miss Jane Landers of handcuffing them to shower rods and spanking them until they come all over their Calcutta marble bathroom tiles?

I straighten the hem of my modest, yet tight and curve-hugging black dress, and amble over to the restrooms with the full knowledge that the only other male at the table—Tony—is eyeing my ass the entire way, despite his wife jabbing him with her elbow to quit it.

So far, it's been a successful night, probably topped off with one last go-around at Charles's penthouse apartment before I can get home and finish my written deadline by midnight.

It's thoughts of my writing—the perfect story I'm crafting—that whittle into my mind as I trek through the crowded restaurant to the restrooms on the other side, and I really should be batting them away. I refuse to let my true self sift into my fake persona, as it can become too diluted and confusing and often results in mistakes. I've seen too many girls in my occupation fall victim to feelings that should never come into play while transforming into a client's fantasy woman.

But this story idea of mine. It could turn into a book. It could change my career, and I'm finally feeling like I can start working toward a job I'm proud of—

Oh my God.

I duck behind a broad man's back, hoping I didn't just see who I thought I saw.

It couldn't be.

Shaking my head, I peer over the man's shoulder to get a second look.

Razor blue eyes lock onto mine.

My jaw clenches of its own accord, nearly fracturing my molars, but I *cannot* let him make the connection. Not here. Not in the middle of a job that's about to pay me thousands.

"McKenna!"

Shit.

I beeline away from my safe man-barrier and sprint as best I can, taking the same route I intended and hoping my talent in heels will put enough space between me and ... oh, God ... me and *him*.

"McKenna! Wait the hell up!"

When I'm passing the crowded circular bar in the middle of the restaurant, I latch onto the first young-ish appearing woman I see.

"Holy shit, did you see who's here?" I exclaim.

Her eyes widen as I grab her arm, but she's in a Hard Rock t-shirt, jeans and running shoes. Totally a tourist, and 100% what I need right now.

"No! Who?" she asks, elbowing her friend beside her.

"Freaking Mason Payne!" I say in a stage-whisper and point. "Right over there!"

True to form, Mason cuts through the crowd like shaving wire, his face a storm of emotions as he catches my eye across the room.

"OMIGOSH!" the woman shrieks. "Mason Payne from Nocturne Court is here! You guys! Look!"

Oh, thank Jesus. The woman has a cohort of other women with her, like a tourist bus of mid-Western ladies-who-drink, and every single one of them bops up and down and waves as Mason, with his devilishly coiffed hair, sculpted arms, and a jaw that cuts through glass as easily as it does hearts, pauses mid-stride, suddenly wary.

The women move forward like a tidal wave and drown him in screams. He has no choice but to smile and take selfies and accept kisses and ass-grabs as I duck, cover and roll into a detour and head back to my table.

Charles glances up and around me as I appear beside him, a deep frown in place. "Do people have no decency in public places, anymore? Good lord, the sounds those women are making."

"Charles, darling," I say while placing my hand on his arm. "I'm feeling a little under the weather. Do you mind if we leave early?" I bend and whisper into his ear. "I can make a few sounds that will drive you wild."

I refuse to look behind me. I'm not about to lose this transaction because of an unwelcome blast from the past. Like I said: thousands of dollars.

"But Charles," Judy says. "We haven't even gotten to the appetizers yet."

"Yes, but we've broken into the wine," Charles says as he stands abruptly, placing a meaty hand around my waist. "And I've said what I needed. Send me the revised minutes as soon as you have them."

Nodding uncertainly, Judy doesn't argue further and nor does anyone else. More to the point, Charles doesn't give them time.

He's too busy skirting me around patrons to the front entrance, his anticipatory grunts heavy and wet against my bare shoulder as we maneuver out of the restaurant.

"Here we are, my darling Jane," he says as a car pulls up to the curb. The valet opens the passenger side of the Astin Martin as Charles folds into the driver's seat. "Thank you from saving me from the sheer number of vapid ladies in that room."

"It's interesting, you know," I say as I settle into the cool, buttery leather passenger seat.

"What is?"

"Their talk of porn. I wonder if they've ever experienced it themselves?"

Charles laughs as he motors into traffic. "You mean, watched a video with their spouse and tried to replicate it? I don't think so."

I slide a finger down his cheek. "One doesn't need to be a porn star to possess the required talents."

Charles growls low in his throat and playfully tries to bite my finger. "Show me, Jane."

I lean back against my seat, my focus sliding to the side mirror in time to see Mason bursting through the front doors of the steakhouse and into the street, his muscular form high-lighted by city traffic lights as he watches me speed away.

From him.

"I will, Charles," I say, and fold my hand over his on the gearshift.

I don't pay attention to the rubble that makes up my heart. The permanent destruction that Mason Payne caused. "Tonight, I'm all yours."

CHAPTER 11

Mckenna

THIS GUY IS NEW.

I've vetted him, of course. Since going independent instead of using an escort agency, I've had to be extremely cut-throat and expeditious when it comes to taking on clients, and my rules are fairly simple: They must've used girls before.

I'm usually contacted through email or my website, and as part of those contact requirements, the men provide at least three referrals from girls they've employed previously. Once I receive them, I pour myself a glass of wine and look up those women via their official website and ask them directly how the client is, their behaviors and preferences, and whether the girls were treated right. If all three get back to me with positive notes, then I put the client on my roster.

Eight years of honing smarts and skills has lead me to this place of entrepreneurship. I have my own two-bedroom apartment on the twenty-ninth floor on the Upper East Side of Manhattan, a steady, questionably taxable income, and I'm my own boss.

I finish applying scarlet lipstick in my bathroom mirror, fix the straps of my ruby red dress, slip on my black Louboutin pumps, and I'm out the door by 7 PM.

Giles Bennett has sent a black car to pick me up, and it idles near the curb once I exit the building. The driver dips his chin as he opens the back door and I gracefully slide in.

We don't drive for long. Mr. Bennett has asked that I come directly to his apartment, no social meet-and-greets required. He wants to get down to business, and I'm okay with that, so long as an envelope filled with cash is unobtrusively set aside for me as soon as I arrive.

Once in the expansive marbled lobby, I'm directed to the private elevators where the security guard keys the doors open, presses the button for the fourteenth floor, and I'm neatly sequestered inside.

The ride up is quiet. No music or muzak plays in hidden speakers. Only a light *ding* sounds out once the fourteenth floor is reached and I step out onto a carpeted hallway. Apartment 1 is directly ahead and the only unit on this floor. I knock, then smooth down my hair as I wait, in case the summer wind has coaxed out any rebellious flyaways in my mercilessly flat-ironed hair.

Sometimes I wear wigs. Other times I wear colored contacts. But my favorite costume is straightening my wayward curls and going almost natural. That way, my scalp doesn't itch and my eyes don't feel like they're being scratched out by silicone discs.

The door opens, and Giles matches his online profile exactly. Thin and distinguished with a slight beak of a nose, his hair is ebony shot through with gray. His eyes are the same overcast, stormy color. He wears a white collared shirt that he's unbuttoned at the neck, no tie, and holds in one hand a short glass of whiskey.

"Miss Landers," he says, his laugh lines deepening in his tanned, angular face. "You're right on time."

"Punctuality is always my aim." I try on a lingering smile.

He steps away from the door. "Do come in."

I think I detect a light British accent, and I focus on that delightful feature as I enter his home and prepare my personality for what can only be described as stranger sex. It's what I do with these men of mine. I find something appealing about them and latch onto it tight, throughout the entire date, so when I pretend to come, or exert deep interest in what they have to say, they're convinced I mean it.

"Can I offer you something to drink?" he asks as he wanders ahead. "White wine? Whiskey?"

"Pinot Grigio if you have it," I say, and as I pass an antique side table in the hallway, I surreptitiously slide the envelope made out to *Jane Landers* with impeccable penmanship into my clutch. It's thicker than what I'm expecting—much thicker—but I'm not one to count bills in front of my clients. I only serve high-salaried men, and many would take finger-combing through their money as an insult. That, and my vetting process is thorough. I personally met with four of Giles's previous girls—women I knew as reputable, high-class escorts—over brunch, and I was comfortable with everything they had to indulge about him.

"Sauvignon Blanc all right?"

"Sure," I say.

"Make yourself at home, darling. Take a seat in the library and I'll be right there."

Giles heads into his chef's kitchen and I hear bottles and glasses clinking as I find a side room filled with wall-to-wall bookshelves and two velvet couches. I take a seat in one, cross my legs and set aside my clutch. I don't read the spines of the books closest to me even though I desperately want to. That's something McKenna would do. Instead, I raise the hem of my dress enough that the defined muscles of my thighs show, and maybe a slight peek of what's to come.

Giles walks in with a full glass of wine and a top-off of his own. He's not shy and sits directly beside me, his suit pants brushing against my bare legs, and trails a finger down the side of my face.

"My, you are a beautiful one, aren't you?" he murmurs, close enough that I smell his aftershave mixing with the whiskey on his breath.

I lean into his touch, the tip of my tongue licking my top lip. "I have to admit, you are incredibly handsome."

"I bet you say that to all your clients," he says with a tight-lipped smile, then hands me my drink.

I take the wine, recrossing my legs and angling toward him. I don't normally bring up other clients—ever—since I'm meant to be his and his alone, so I brush off Giles's statement by reaching over and laying a hand on his thigh.

"No," I say. "You are *especially* handsome."

"Mm." He leans back and spreads his legs, giving me full access.

I take the lead and my fingers trail delicate, sensitive circles as I move to the center, but he surprises me by catching my wrist.

"Tell me, how did you get into your own business?" he asks.

I jolt, but keep it inward, the way one would tense at a loud, familiar noise heard in a comfortable household. "Are you asking why I'm not with an agency?"

"That's exactly what I'm asking. Isn't there better safety precautions when you're with a company?"

I remove my hand and settle back into the couch. If Mr. Bennett wants to make idle conversation for a while, I'm more than happy to oblige. Though, he doesn't strike me as a man who is nervously delaying sex with an escort, and I've had many of those.

"It's more about their take," I respond. "I started out with an agency, but thirty percent or more of what I made went directly to them. After doing some research, I decided I was better off creating my own company." I smile over the rim of my glass. "That way, I keep one-hundred percent of the profits."

"Makes sense," he says. "But, how do you clean the money?"

My brows tic up before I can school them into submission. Bending forward, my manicured fingers dance across his inner thigh. "Dear Mr. Bennett, are you asking me if I launder money?"

"Well, it would make sense, wouldn't it? The cash you receive from men is black market. So, how do you whiten it? You can't possibly be claiming an escort service on your tax returns, now can you?"

I lick my lips, my hand retreating again. But my mind works overtime. I decide to punt his original question over to him. "I bet you ask this of all your girls."

Giles laughs, but it doesn't reach his eyes. "I'll admit, I do try. But most are with agencies, or paired with some boss or pimp or another. You're the first one I've found who is truly entrepreneurial. Yet, I couldn't find your company name in any records."

Find? He searched for my private data?

Mildly uneasy, I respond, "I don't normally provide that information. It's business-like and boring, when you should be in it for the pleasure."

I make sure my tone lilts at the end, tantalizing and seductive.

"Sure, of course." He laughs again. "Forgive me, it must be my mind for business, but I just find your occupation so interesting. *How* do you get the IRS on your side, for example? How do you stay under the radar? What's your secret, besides a smart brain? I truly admire your skill, you know."

I smile, but don't show my teeth. The conversation is getting tiring, and if he really is innocently curious, I'll nip this in the bud pretty quickly. Besides, I often receive great financial advice from clients. "Real estate."

Giles cocks a brow. "No kidding?"

I nod. "I have a real estate business, a license, and even do a few showings on weekends. Sometimes renovation projects." I shrug. "That's how I 'clean' my money, as you say."

"Fascinating. And inspiring. Of course that's how you do it. So much cash exchanges hands in real estate transactions. A good amount of all-cash down payments, too. And with renovations, you can spend fifty grand, then up-sell the unit for seven-hundred grand, and no bank or government would be the wiser. Wonderful, Jane. That is truly independent."

Uh-huh. "Enough idle conversation, Mr. Bennett. I'm feeling ... parched. And hungry."

Giles's brows furrow. "You still have a full glass of wine, darling."

I rake my gaze over his body. "That's not what I'm craving."

"Mm. I see. Perhaps once you're finished cleaning the seventy grand I gave you, then you may suck my dick."

My startle reflex isn't as contained this time. "I—excuse me?"

"The envelope I gave you." Giles makes a benign motion towards my clutch as he uses his other hand to sip his drink. He swallows, then continues, "It contains that exact amount. Clean it within the week and I won't report you to the authorities or have someone kill you and drop you in a vast, off-shore ocean. Then, if you're a good girl, we'll up the next payment to one hundred. Then two. Do you see where I'm going here, Jane?"

My face feels ashen. I stiffen. "No. I do not."

"Then I need to make myself more clear."

In a whiplash motion, Giles is off the couch and hovering, his hand clamped around my neck as he grinds the back of my head against the couch cushions. The wine glass falls to the floor and shatters. My fingers scrabble for leverage on his forearm, scraping and pulling for oxygen.

He still holds his whiskey in one hand and sips idly as I struggle against his hold.

"Here is what you need to learn, darling. Simply because I was kind to a few other girls, gracious and courteous as they sucked me off before I rammed myself into their assholes, does not mean I am kind in business. I have some dirty money I need access to. My accounts have been flagged, and I've been diligently searching for a way to claim what I am owed. I happened upon you, after asking many whores for an independent one who works only for herself. A smart one—and believe me, whores with brains are difficult to come across. Yet, your name kept coming up. Or, your pseudonym." His focus slides all the way down my body and back up. "You possess way too much delectable sin to really be named Jane."

"*Agh—ugh—*" I'm trying so hard to speak. To breathe.

"Perhaps you need more incentive."

He applies more pressure. My legs kick out uselessly.

"I've found your father," Giles says.

Despite my struggles, my body goes stiff.

"That's right, darling. I know where he is, and more importantly, I can get to him. He may not die by my hand, but he could very well perish through another's. Favors go so far these days, especially to those on the inside."

"N-No—" I can barely breathe, never mind speak.

"I'm thinking I *should* claim your body tonight." Giles sets his drink aside while still choking me. He uses his free hand to cup my privates. "Bare as the day you were born. I love it."

I squirm away, but I'm trapped under his grip.

This may sound shocking, but I've never been raped. Not by any clients or when I lived as my past self as a friendless, quiet schoolgirl who did her homework like clockwork. The idea that this man could do to me what everyone in the world thinks happens to escorts who must be *asking for it* is so gut-wrenchingly terrifying, I don't need his chokehold to stop breathing.

Giles cocks his head, thinks about it, then lifts his hand.

"Never mind. Torture and BDSM were never my style. I am a kind man in bed, you know."

He releases his grip on my neck.

Gasping, sputtering, I spear off the couch and sprint for the door, well aware that at any moment Giles—if that is indeed his name—could pounce and drag me under again.

"I'll go after your father first, darling!" he calls down the hallway. "And I will stalk you, harass you, scare the bejesus out of you, until you do what I want."

I reach the front door. Scrambling, I try to unbolt the chain locks with shaking fingers, my breaths hitching.

His voice sounds behind my ear. "You forgot something."

"No. *No!*" I pound on the door. "*Help*! Somebody!"

Giles *tsks-tsks*. His arm reaches around to unlock the last deadbolt. He swings the door open with such violence, I'm forced to step back and knock into his hard chest. "I'm merely giving you back your purse, darling. There. That's a good girl."

I take the sparkling clutch, an impulse buy I remember purchasing months ago. The woman working in the exclusive store magically came through the wall and offered me a mimosa. Patience surrounded the minimalist space with shining, imported flooring. I chose this bag high on power, money, and *belonging*.

"Remember what's in there, hmm?" Giles says, tapping the hand-sewn crystal case. "I'll be in touch. Off you go, now."

My hair falls haphazardly across my forehead. My throat is flayed like torn, raw meat.

"Go on," Giles says kindly.

I won't be told a third time. I rush to the elevators, my ankles bending dangerously in my heels, and when I can't find a stairwell to access and sprint down, I bang the DOWN elevator button multiple times.

Get me out of here.

Giles doesn't shut his door. He waits, right up until the lift slides open and I fall inside, pressing myself against the far wall.

"Bye, now!" I hear him call as the brass elevator doors slither shut.

I feel my cheeks. They're wet and hot. I swipe under my eyes with full knowledge that I resemble a terrified animal. Sifting through my clutch, and groaning at the thick envelope nestled inside, I find folded tissues and use them to dab at my face and pull myself together.

By the time the elevator brings me to the lobby, I'm as composed as I'll ever be, and I step off with a much steadier gait.

It's only money. I can figure this out. I can keep my dad safe.

I'm passing by the security desk, avoiding eye contact in case I still appear rattled, when I halt, the soles of my heels screeching with a hard brake against the varnished marble.

Tousled chestnut hair, coming to a V at the nape of his neck —a spot as familiar to my lips as breathing—bows close to the guard, deep in conversation. Muscled, tanned forearms rest against the counter. A broad back turns at the fingernail-chalkboard sound my shoes make, and arctic blue eyes freeze against mine.

"Oh, hey, Mack," Mason says.

I slow-blink.

"Nope," I say, then continue to the exit.

CHAPTER 12

Mason

McKenna Beckley was not supposed to fall into my lap like this.

"Mack, wait!" I say to her retreating back, then push off the security desk. "Hold up!"

Is she limping?

I admit, I'm not here by chance. It took a lot of negotiation and bribery to get to this location, but I did not expect Mack to literally step off an elevator and into my sights the instant I entered the lobby.

"Hey," I say, running to catch up with her. She's fast in heels, even if she looks a little ... disheveled.

Darkness settles across my brows upon assessing the state of her, because I know why she's here.

"Stop ignoring me, Mack—"

I'm forced to dodge back as she swings through the revolving doors, unless I want my nose and a bunch of blood to decorate this fine establishment.

Once space opens up, I duck through the doors and jog up to the curb, where McKenna's forced to stop and pull out her phone, probably to call an Uber.

"Have you gone deaf since I last saw you?" I say once I'm standing in front of her.

Her gaze flicks up. "What do you *want*, Mason?"

Fire can't be green. There's only molten blue, hot red, or burning orange. Yet, according to McKenna's stare, green should have a heat level. A mutant, nuclear, apocalypse-inducing melting point.

I grin. "God, I missed you."

Her eyes narrow. Her lips thin. But she says nothing, instead going back to her phone.

That's not like her.

"What are you doing here?" I ask, playing dumb. "You live in that building or something?"

I want her to admit it, what she is, what she does. The minute I figured out what McKenna Beckley turned into in the ten years we've been apart, I've been dying to confront her. Demand she stop. Figure out why the fuck prostituting herself became an option for the girl destined for Yale.

McKenna snorts. "No, this isn't my place. Go away, Mason."

Did I say I deserved an explanation from her? Not even close.

I say in a low voice, "Tell me what the fuck is going on, Mack."

She purses her lips. "Hmm. Let me think on that. No."

To this day, I dislike being dismissed. Even by chicks I haven't seen in close to a decade. A guttural growl lingers in my throat. "Fine, then I'll tell you."

Curiosity forces her gaze back to mine.

"Your dress is wrinkled. Your hair's a mess," I say.

McKenna adopts a fake, breathy voice when she responds, "Gee, Mase, after all this time away from you, I've been *dying* to hear you say those very things to me once again. Want to comment on my weight, too?"

My lips flatline. "My guess is, you're all up in disarray

because you just finished fucking whoever was upstairs for money."

Even she, McKenna "I know and predict all" Beckley, didn't see that particular missile hitting her between the eyes. She gasps and steps back, her expression morphing into something like surprised disgust.

"That's okay, darlin', I'm used to getting that kind of look from you."

She slaps me. Actually, up-in-arms, slaps my face.

"Who the *fuck* do you think you are?" she hisses, "coming at me in the dead of night and judging me after years of silence? You don't give a shit about me! You haven't given a damn since you ditched me at prom, like the predictable, clichéd broken bad boy you worked so hard to master!"

McKenna steps forward, shoving me at the shoulders. I'm so stunned, an exhale of laughter escapes my chest.

McKenna's face turns white with rage. "Now that you're famous, you think you can say these things to me and get away with it? You think I'll stand here tolerating such shit? Think again, you miserable, low-life, bag of dicks." She punctuates her next sentences with another shove, each time. I let her. "I don't care that you're a rockstar. I'm not a fan. I hate you. You don't deserve one ounce of explanation from me. Ever. Again. You got that?"

See what I mean? Green fire. Needs to be a thing.

"Loud and clear," I drawl, once her arms have safely retreated. "But that ain't gonna stop me from judging you, anyway."

She sneers, but a lot of her anger has deflated. I see it in the set of her shoulders. "Oh, fuck off, Mase."

"Seriously, Mack," I say, losing some—not all—of the cockiness. "What's going on with you? Why are you doing this shit?"

McKenna rolls her eyes. "Why do you even care?"

"Because as soon as I heard what you were doing, I wanted to rip door hinges off." I close back in, stepping into her space. "Then, when I was done stripping wood, I wanted to go after the flaccid cocks that think they have any claim over you and rip them off at the balls."

"How heroic of you," McKenna says, her attention drifting to the traffic on the street. "But I can take care of myself."

"Can you?" I hadn't wanted to focus on it, but now that I'm close enough to catch her scent—she still spritzes that sexy gardenia perfume—my focus settles where it shouldn't.

Right on her clavicle, in the delicate curves of her neck, are ripening bruises.

Outrage blasts to the surface. "Why does your throat look like you were caught in a bear trap, Mack? Did this guy hurt you? Did he fucking put his hands on you? I know where that fucker lives. I'll go right up there and lock him by the—"

"Mason, don't!"

McKenna grabs me by the arm as I stalk toward the entrance. Her hold can't contain me. Mack's grip is nothing but butterfly wings hovering against my skin and I can shake her off easily, *especially* if some douchebag thinks he can get away with manhandling a woman—

"Wait, how do you know what apartment he's in?" McKenna asks behind me, her touch lingering on my forearm.

I pause.

"Mason, answer me." Her voice takes on a warning tone. "How do you know where I was? Did you come here *looking* for me?"

I blow out a breath. It's needed, since the hot cloud of rage needs to be dispelled somehow. "I might've."

"What—why?"

Patience has never been my strong suit. "I told you. Because Rex saw you at one of our parties and it became pretty clear you were one of the hired girls."

She frowns. "Rex Sloane?"

"Fuck, Mack, don't be so dense. *Yes*, Rex Sloane. The guys you went to high school with *recognized* you. How could you not think it would get back to me?"

McKenna exhales. "I was there doing a favor for one of my friends who couldn't make her ... shift. I wasn't aware of who the band was until I got there. Didn't make the connection in time."

"So you didn't follow our rise to fame? Failed to keep tabs on me? Refused to follow me on social media and witness my climb to the A-list?"

"Get over yourself."

"Never."

McKenna wanders back to the curb, waving at a vehicle that begins slowing down. "As titillating as this conversation is, my car's here. Nice to see you again, Mason. And no, I don't mean that."

"Mack, wait."

She sighs. "What?"

"You got me. Yes, I'm here at this building because I tracked you down. I wanted to see you again. I don't want you doing this."

"Your concern is noted." McKenna moves to step around me. "Now, let me get into my car and go home."

I hook her arm, but she reacts by yanking it away.

"Get a clue, Mason! I don't want you around. Leave me the hell alone."

"I can't."

"You *have*. For ten goddamn years. Keep at it, you were doing such a good job."

The flicker of hurt in her eyes doesn't escape my notice. I shake my head and at last, come to admit why I came here in the first place. "I came to make you an offer, Mack."

Her brows scrunch together. "Offer? What kind of—" Her expression clears. "No. No way. Fuck off, Mason, I mean it. For *good*."

I try for her elbow again. "Two hundred and fifty thousand dollars."

Her arm goes slack in my hold. It gives me the opportunity to feel every tendon, each muscle type, flex and harden with contained, dangerous anger.

"How ... *dare* ... you." Mack seethes through her teeth. "Let go of me right this second, or I swear I will bite your dick off and spit it right back in your—"

"It's not to fuck you," I say. When her eyes finally meet mine again, I continue, "I'm making an offer for you to go on tour with me. Eight weeks. I'd like you to ... be my companion for that time, so I don't have to deal with all the press and the fangirls and—"

"You're making this about you," Mack says in awe. "You are *actually* making the offer of a quarter million, to a prostitute, about *you*."

My lips flatline. "No. I'm not."

"You haven't changed a bit, Mason Payne. Not one goddamned bit."

"Mack. This is for your own good. Step away from your clients for a while."

"Goodbye, Mase."

I let her remove her arm from my grip, and as she opens the car door and gets into the vehicle, I say, "You have, though."

Her head tips up above the door.

"You've changed so much, Mack. It scares me."

"Now you know how it feels," she says before she disappears behind the black tint. "To think you know someone, when you don't have a handle on them at all."

CHAPTER 13

Mckenna

MY KEYS jangle against the marble kitchen counter as I toss them across the room, and my clutch follows suit.

I strip my clothes off as I walk down my hallway and into the master bathroom, desperate to get the filth off me.

Naked, I step up to the sink, throwing my hands under cold tap water and washing, washing, *washing*.

When I look up, I lock eyes with myself in the mirror, and my lips part.

Jane Landers is no longer. The girl staring back at me is McKenna Beckley, with messy auburn-brown hair, red-rimmed green eyes, and a freckled, pert nose with cheeks that are swollen from held-in emotional turmoil.

I hate this girl.

Ridding myself of McKenna, the prissy, wimpy, mouse of a human who barely squeaked enough to speak up for herself was the best thing I ever did.

To see her come back tonight is the worst feeling in the world.

All because of two men.

Granted, Giles is worth being frightened of. He's the reason I'm turning my shower to scalding and scraping away at the top layer of my skin like there's healing to be found underneath. His money sits in my purse, collecting dread like interest the longer I don't do anything with it.

But Mason? Mason shouldn't bring this out in me. He's nothing but a high school bully I fell in love with who ended up breaking my heart so badly, many small pieces are still scattered across our hometown.

And now, ten years later, he wants to pay for my company.

The guy who guilelessly made fun of my lack of sex appeal, my virginity, my *curves* for god's sake, wants me to remain in his presence for at least eight weeks for an exorbitant amount of money, for reasons or motives yet to be revealed.

Ugh. The fact I'm considering it makes me almost as stupid as I was when I had sex with him for the first time.

Yet ... it might be an offer I can't refuse. There could be a way out of this Giles mess that doesn't include me being forever subservient to that asshole. Maybe I could use Mason's cash to pay off Giles and make him go away for good. Maybe I don't have to turn into Giles's money laundering lackey.

Maybe I can escape, use Mason as my jumping point, and never come back to Giles or New York City.

I'm a professional at making a new name for myself.

The idea of bunking with Mason brings forth a strange wash of feeling, similar to the beginnings of our relationship where he was so mean, yet my body responded to his magnetism and utter confidence. If he wanted me naked and willing underneath him, he'd get me there.

Even now, when I saw him tonight, *zaps* and *zings* hit my skin with sensitive, erotic accuracy.

Disgusted with myself, I towel off with rough swipes. I dismiss the flutter in my heart as one of the holes Mason left behind leaking air.

There are more important issues to consider.

For one, how in the hell Mason Payne found Jane Landers's current location.

Throwing on a thin robe, my damp hair falling thick and heavy down my back, I pad into the kitchen and pull my phone out of my clutch, tapping the screen until I find my Safe Number.

She picks up on the second ring. "Dude, you're fifteen minutes late in calling me. I was two seconds away from alerting the police."

"I know," I say as I slide onto a stool, my elbows resting on the counter. "It was a rough one, Dee."

Deonne Sparrow's voice rises. "Seriously? You okay?"

"He wasn't a good egg." I rub my eyes with my free hand. "I feel like I barely got out..."

"But the references! The girls before! They're not liars. We know them, we're familiar with their client list."

"Yeah," I say, "Turns out, Johns can be great actors when they're working toward a particular goal."

I hear Dee smacking gum between her teeth as she thinks. "You're saying that goal was you?"

"He wants something from me. And he's willing to blackmail and threaten to get it."

"Jesus. Usually we just blacklist the guy so no girls worth their salt in this city go near him ever again. But I guess that can't work in this scenario."

"No." I sigh. "It can't. But I'm figuring it out. Hey, did you get a phone call today? About where I was?"

Pause. More gum chewing. "I might've."

"Dee." I smack my forehead. "What is the *one* rule we have for each other?"

"Never give out our locations unless in an emergency. I know, I *know*, but you realize who FaceTimed me, right? Who was right in my fucking phone talking to me?"

I gesture wildly with my free hand. "What if he wanted to know where I was so he could kill me?"

Smack, smack, smack. "You're saying Mason 'Fuck Me Eyes' Payne, three time Grammy winner and part of the most famous rockband in the world, an A-list celeb, wants to kill you?"

"No! But that doesn't mean I want him to know where I am!"

"Why the fuck not? I get the secrecy. I mean, if he were my client I'd sew my pussy shut and open it only for him—"

"Good God, he is *not* one of my clients."

"That's not what he said."

I'm close to a migraine. I can feel it. "He told you he's a client of mine?"

"Yeah, and that you were owed money from last time. He was only here for one night, he said, so timing was an issue. If he didn't give it to you now, you wouldn't get your payment for another eight weeks. And girl, we need our money. That's all I was thinking when I gave him your address. Not to mention he's famous and I recorded the entire thing just in case he *did* show up there to kill you."

It's difficult, with a raging headache and the night I've had, to parse through Dee's words, yet I've figured out the following: Mason knows my current occupation, my call girl name Jane Landers, and how to get in touch with my emergency contact when I'm out on a job.

How did he figure all this out after running into me at a bar one night?

My forehead smooths as I answer my own question. *Because he's known longer than a chance encounter. Mason had the time to look me up, research me, and find me.*

But ... why?

"Dee, I'm pissed at you."

"Fine, but at least fuck that gorgeous piece senseless and *then* be pissed at me."

Unable to stay still anymore, I rise and pace the kitchen.

"Mason Payne offered me two hundred and fifty grand to go on tour with him for eight weeks."

"He *what*?"

Choking and sputtering follows Dee's words.

"Dee, you okay?"

"Sorry." More coughing. "Swallowed my gum. You have to go, Mack."

"It's an irresistible offer, I agree. But with our history, and the threats from tonight's client, I..."

"You need to get out. Now. We only have ourselves. There's no agency backing us, no pimp. If this John is truly scaring the life out of you, what better way to hide than in plain sight with a giant rock band and their entire public posse for two months? This guy can't touch you there."

"He can touch me when I get back," I say softly. *He can get to my dad.*

"By then, you'll have figured this out. If it's money he wants, you'll have tons of it. If it's you he's after—well, you know how to disappear. We have a failsafe for this. You're gonna be okay, Mack."

I've been alone for a long time. I'm a pro at taking care of myself. And unlike what Mason was so sure of when we were in high school, I'm a survivor.

My clutch lays open on the counter, the wad of bills spilling out of the envelope they were stuffed in.

I was Mason's ticket out when we were seniors.

Now, he might need to be mine.

CHAPTER 14

Mason

THE WORLD SUCKS.

According to the flat screen TV in our hotel suite, war would get us before climate change, but that doesn't mean I should disregard the utter shit that is reality TV from turning every human brain into mush before nuclear bombs ever get the chance.

Muttering, I toss the remote control to the side. A resultant grunt tells me I've hit my mark.

"Dude, you know I'm here, you know I'm a solid mass, do *not* throw heavy objects at my ass when I'm half-asleep," my bandmate, Wyn, says.

He rolls over on the velvet couch, one leg hanging off the sofa as he lands on his back with a sigh.

"There's a one-hundred percent chance I'll be following that up with the stereo system," I say.

Wyn frowns, his eyes remaining closed. "Relax, man. This is meant to be our time to rest before our tour starts. Need more weed? I think there's some over there."

Wyn gestures vaguely to the circular table in the corner of our expansive room, where two women in tight, braless tops and mini-skirts snort and drink.

It's a hard one to gauge, but whether I'm less impressed with the girls Wyn brought home or the crowd of managers, agents, executives and other corporate types that will soon be invading our hotel room, is something I have to think about.

Wyn cracks an eye open. "One of those chicks is for you. Or both for me. You decide."

I check the time on my watch. "You can barely get your ass off that couch. What makes you think you have the energy for a threesome?"

Wyn grabs his crotch and grins as he calls, "Ladies! My man has given me a dare and methinks I'd like to accept it. Care to escort me to my room?"

The two girls laugh softly at each other, then toddle over to our section of the suite. One grazes her hand across my shoulder as she passes. "You sure you don't want to join, sugar? I don't mind two swords in a fight."

I wait for my dick to twitch. My balls to stiffen. Hell, I'll settle for increased saliva to coat my mouth.

Nothing happens.

"I'm good," I say before tossing back a cool swig of beer.

The girl moves to Wyn. He throws an arm around each, sends me a wink, then heads to his private bedroom.

"Rex should be back soon, after he's done sucking face with Harper," Wyn says. Once he's at the entrance to his bedroom, he adds over his shoulder, "Don't tell him I said that. Last thing I need is him punching me in my money-maker before we make our tour rounds."

"Wouldn't want to mar that gorgeous jawline of yours," I say while staring out the floor-to-ceiling windows.

"Damn straight."

The door clicks shut, and the sound of feminine laughter quickly fades to moans.

I lay the empty beer bottle on its side, idly spinning it on the table as I slouch in the sofa chair and wonder what the fuck happened.

Our dreams have been reached. Nocturne Court's band of merry vagabonds, Rex, Wyn, Easton, and me, made it out of high school—some without graduating—and scrimped, scraped, begged and stole to get to the position we're in now. We dealt with seedy bars and seedier managers ripping us off in the beginning, chicks throwing up on us when we played on $1 shot nights, fists and brawls from guys who thought they were better than us, because somehow, our ability to play instruments pissed them off, broken bones, stomped-on pride, and a whole lot of facial fractures. All with empty pockets.

Despite all that and taking those years of effort straight to the bank, I feel I haven't moved an inch.

Rex is busy saying goodbye to his girl and spending time with his daughter before we leave. Easton is occupied with his wife and stepson, opting to forego our hotel suite entirely, and Wyn ... Wyn is a perpetual reminder that I'm the same dude I was in high school, just with a lot more money and bigger bedrooms.

Mostly surrounded by drugs, hot chicks, threesomes, foursomes, orgasms, money, and music.

How I always wanted it, right?

Eighteen-year-old me would've bitten off heads to get where I am now. He may not have imbibed in the copious amount of coke and opiates on the table, but he *definitely* would've taken the the free pussy going around.

I should be thankful I'm alone in this room before all the fuckery starts and the endless demands begin. Instead, I'm disappointed that my guys aren't here for our traditional hotel room drinkfest before the tour kicks off.

We're distancing from each other as we grow and fame gets old, which is terrifying. We've been aiming for fame our whole lives, and now we're getting tired of it? Pretty soon I'll be left with Wyn, who seems more than content to remain fucking the status quo. I don't think he's noticed Easton isn't coming tonight and will meet us at the airport tomorrow.

All because he's found happiness outside of this band, and *that* is the true nightmare I refuse to let happen to me, or hell, even Wyn.

The closest I've come to contentment unrelated to status and music is ... McKenna.

Or Jane.

Or whatever the hell she calls herself.

I'm pretty sure I nipped that in the bud by ruining her in high school, but even I can't claim credit for what she's turned into.

An escort.

A call girl.

A prostitute.

A hooker.

My Mack. The girl who turned into a bright red blooming rose any time the word *dick* was mentioned in her presence. The one who aimed for the Ivy Leagues and would achieve it, both through her lifestyle choices, her loner-isms and bookworm hidey-holes, and her family inheritance.

So, what happened between graduation and now?

And more importantly, why the fuck do I care?

I have the annoying suspicion that I'm so melancholy right now, so unwilling to fuck a hot chick, because Mack is on my mind.

The loner girl turned call girl whom I offered a quarter million to get out of her current life and stick to mine for eight weeks, where I can keep an eye on her.

I reach down and grab another beer from the six-pack hanging out by my feet, chuckling. *Because my lifestyle is oh so much better than hers.*

Mack's fully aware she wouldn't be trading up by accepting. She fucks the big boys now.

And here I am, alone, in this fancy-ass suite, enduring an emptiness that cannot and will not get out of my fucking chest.

A knock sounds at the door. Grumbling, I get up and stalk over, certain that Wyn ordered some kind of edible delight to join him in his boudoir. That, or another faceless snatch.

"Yeah." I grunt at the closed door.

"Mason? It's me."

My brows jump. I'm unbolting the deadlock and twisting the knob before my brain registers what I'm doing. "How'd you get through security?"

McKenna—Mack, *my* Mack—stands at the threshold, her hair tossed up into a messy bun with scant make-up on her face and wearing tight leggings and a tee.

Those green eyes, always containing the same impact whether lined in black or natural and bare, slam against mine.

"Hello to you, too," she says. "May I come in?"

"Sure. Yeah." I step back to give her access.

The moment she steps into the suite is the perfect time for the moans to sound, followed by thumps, panting, and "oh *yes*, Wyn, right there, baby!"

Mack's attention strays to Wyn's closed door.

"Nothing you haven't heard before," I quip.

Mack's jaw goes rigid. She parts her lips enough to ask, "Am I interrupting something?"

I tilt my head. "Are you wanting to join?"

She doesn't flush red like I expect her to—like the young McKenna Beckley did when shrinking into her seat at school. Or get angry, displaying that newly discovered green fire that kinda turns me on.

Mack mirrors my head-tilt and answers, "From what I gather, there are at least two women in there with Wyn. I don't do side chicks. I like it to be just me and the man, so he can appreciate every fine detail."

My jaw locks. She's made her point. I grit out, "Would you like a drink?"

She smiles and it reaches her eyes. Mack enjoys outplaying me. "Sure."

I reach down and throw her a beer, which she catches smoothly. Mack settles herself on the couch Wyn recently vacated, using the time to take in what I can only assume is the room, the price tag, the mess, and the lack of company.

"I thought you guys partied hard before tour kick-offs," she says while twisting off the metal cap.

"Times have changed." I fall back into the sofa chair, legs spread as I help myself to another beer. "That, and TMZ has moved on from hotel-trashing parties to the finer details of celebrity shade on social media."

Mack makes a noncommittal sound and drinks from the bottle, her full lips cupping the amber spout with the perfect amount of suction.

My dick stiffens to a half-chub.

Frowning, I set my drink down harder than necessary. "Mack, why are you here? You made it pretty clear on the street you weren't interested in seeing me again."

"Yeah, call me trigger happy." Mack settles her beer between her thighs and leans back. "I'm sure you can't blame me for needing to think about it."

"I dunno, most chicks wouldn't hesitate to pocket a quarter mill. Especially girls like—"

"Me?" Mack's cheekbones glow in the lamplight as she tips her chin up in defiance. "That's what you we're going to say. Girls like me, right, Mason?"

My teeth grind down.

"That's exactly what I'm unsure of," Mack continues. "You have a complete lack of respect for me and what I do. And that's okay—plenty of people feel the same. What I can't wrap my head around is why you want my company for eight weeks. Or why you tracked me down. Jesus, Mase, I'm even wondering why I'm of any interest to you. Look at this place. Look at *you*. You've achieved everything you've ever wanted." She splays out her hands. "What am I doing here?"

I scratch at my jaw. "You want the honest truth?"

"Considering it's the reason I trekked over here in the dead of night to see a man whom I vowed never to cross paths with again, yes, the truth would be nice."

"Because I can't stand the thought of you fucking other dudes."

Silence. Then, "I refuse to become your *Pretty Woman* fetish, Mason."

I shake my head while scratching harder at my scruff. "You don't get it. Rex told me he saw you at one of our after parties and it was clear you weren't there as a ticket holder. I saw red, Mack. The instant I figured out what you are and what—*who*— you do, I fucking saw blood spots in my vision. And I had to find you. Talk to you. I dunno, stop you."

Mack's lips flatline. "Scratch that. I refuse to become the Julia Roberts you save in the end. This was a mistake." Mack sets aside her drink and rises from the couch. "I'm happy. I don't need to be rescued."

I squint, peering closer at the flash of emotion that crossed her face as she said that. Unnamable, but raw. I latch onto it. "You sure you're happy? Safe? What about the guys who aren't so nice?"

Her delicate hands clench. "Guys like you, you mean?"

Ouch. "You've got no idea how I've grown these past ten years."

Mack glances around the suite. Wyn's sexcapades are still going strong in the other room. "I can take a guess."

I stand, and as she's walking away, grab her wrist. "Mack, stay. The money's good, I swear it."

Another emotion flutters through her expression, and this

one I can read. Disappointment. "You don't need me, Mason. And I ... I don't want the money."

"Bullshit."

"There are plenty of women who'd be more than happy to appear on your arm. Ones without our past and my unsavory occupation." She rips her arm from my hold. "Ones who actually *like* you."

"I don't want those chicks. I want you." I step closer. Invade her space. Breathe her in. God, she smells good. "Eight weeks, Mack. That's all. No sex. Just company."

She rolls her eyes. "I can't be so important to you that you'd give up sex."

I raise a brow. My dick spears in my pants. "You offering?"

"Hell, no."

"Then I promise no sex with *you*. I'll get my jollies elsewhere. You'd be doing me a favor. Be my companion at parties and junkets and whatever else my agent has up her sleeve so she can stop getting up my ass about showing up to these places single."

Mack moves her head side to side. "It must be so hard to be constantly set up with gorgeous, single girls by your posse of 'people' that you hire to take care of you."

I growl. "You don't know what it's like to have a girl on your arm and have no idea if she wants you for you or for your fame, money, or baby-daddy status."

"Last I checked, Sorsha Dillon wasn't any of those."

One side of my mouth folds up into a grin. "You been checking up on me, Mack?"

Caught, Mack's cheeks color, but her gaze remains defiant. "Hard not to, when that particular relationship blew up the internet for a good few months."

I shrug. "She was cool. We were cool. But then she won an Oscar and it fizzled."

Mack's intelligent eyes narrow. "You mean, you became too much of a liability to be paired with an A-list actress, what with your..." She gestures to the drug paraphernalia on the table. "Proclivities."

I say, with a flat expression, "Those ain't mine."

"So," Mack says on a sigh, unperturbed by my answer, "Now you're scraping the bottom of the barrel by hiring a hooker to be on your arm."

"Don't degrade yourself like that."

Mack ignores me. "You can't be this desperate, Mason."

"That means you're considering it, then."

"This could blow up in your face. You're also going into this with the full knowledge that I can't stand you." She levels her gaze with mine. "Why risk it?"

"You think I'm doing this to clean up my image? Fuck my reputation. I like who I am. I don't care who I date. All I know is, you're staying with me."

"I'm not going to change who I am after the two months are over. Or what I do."

My molars grind together. "We'll see about that."

She tips her nose up so it nearly brushes against my lips. She hisses. "You're not staging some sort of intervention. You proved I'm the shit on the bottom of your shoe a long time ago. You don't get to scrape it off now."

I bare my teeth. "I do what I want, when I want, and that includes you. And *you,* Mack, can't ignore an easy quarter mill. You need it. I see it in your face every time I mention the amount. So, if you can't stand my company, at least picture the bathtub full of bills I'll give you for tolerating my presence."

"And isolating me from my clients."

"Fuck, yes."

Mack hisses out a breath, but steps back. "I'm a fool to agree to this."

I settle my hands against my hips. "So you'll do it?"

Mack's shoulders slope. She mutters, "My suitcase is in the hallway."

A slow, shit-eating grin forms on my face and I move past her to grab her things from the outside hall. "Welcome to Nocturne Court's Greatest Hits Tour, McKenna Beckley."

I think I hear her whisper, "Be careful what you wish for," but I'm too busy tossing her stuff inside the suite before she tries to change her mind.

Not that I'd give her the option.

I never lose.

CHAPTER 15

Mason

"My bedroom's over here," I say to Mack once I've stacked her two suitcases against the wall next to the TV. I'm pointing across the room to the beveled double doors leading to the master suite.

Wyn and I flipped for it, and as usual, I cheated and won.

Mack follows where I'm pointing, and her forehead does a weird creasing thing. I'm sure it should wrinkle, but the girl probably Botoxes now.

I wonder if her men demand and pay for that kind of thing, or if it's her preference. I prefer to believe it's the latter. The idea she does what other men instruct opens up boiling rage in my chest I've worked to keep quiet since discovering McKenna 2.0.

"Uh, we're not sharing a bed," she says.

Being confronted by McKenna—the *real* one, not the made-up escort chick with perfect, straight hair, long lashes and staged smile—has me all sorts of conflicted.

She stands in the center of the room, hands on her hips, her baggy shirt doing nothing to hide her drool-worthy hourglass waist.

The lack of cosmetics on her face shows me the McKenna of our younger years, the shy one, the girl whose face I loved to

131

bring color to by sending her into gasping outrage, sometimes with actual tears.

Then, later, getting that same flush on her by biting down on her lips and inhaling her orgasms.

"Mason? Hello? Did you hear me?"

"Yeah." I gesture to the sofa. "I'll take the couch. You take the room."

"Is this how it's going to be for eight weeks?" Mack gnaws on her lower lip, thinking. All the blood immediately rushes to my groin. "We're gonna need a contract drawn up. I have a few demands."

"I'm not surprised."

"Like my own hotel room for the duration of my stay," Mack continues. When I don't answer, she says, "I'm not moving from this spot until I get a verbal agreement from you."

"Okay. Sure. Fine."

She peers at me closer. "This was all your idea. If you're uncomfortable now that I've actually said yes, then—"

"No. I want this. You. I mean, the convenience of having you around. I'll have my assistant draw something up in the morning before we board the jet."

"Great," she says, but doesn't sound convinced. "For tonight, I'll take the bedroom, like you said."

She walks past, grabbing the smaller of her suitcases along the way. I inhale the cloud of her scent in the air as a small wind of movement accompanies her, but I stay where I am.

"Good night, Mason," she says, her pale face peeking through the doorway before she clicks it shut.

"'Night," I say, then add, "Be ready to go by seven."

Her voice is muffled through the door. "No problem."

I fantasize about sneaking into her room, leaning down onto the bed and stroking my hand up her bare, milky thigh, but instead, I'm left with the dwindling sounds of Wyn's double love-making.

I rub my eyes with my thumb and forefinger.

I'm not sure how I'm going to explain this to the guys, but then again, I'm not sure they require an explanation.

This is my choice, my reasons, my urge to have Mack around again.

And this time, I haven't given myself an escape hatch.

CHAPTER 16

Mckenna

MY HEART *THUMPED* the entire time I faced Mason in the hotel suite's main room.

I thought I could handle standing in front of him again, especially with ten years between us. The needles of the past shouldn't have pricked my skin, memories of Mason's teenaged face interposing itself on his hardened, rugged adult man one.

My mind played tricks on me as I kept sneaking glimpses of different parts of his features, as if reality were trying to reclaim him from the Mason I've been imagining all these years.

I still remembered the first time I met his eyes, despite my efforts to bury that image along with all the others. It stuck the way some images do at the moment you least expect them—a flash of a smile by your crush, an image of your mom searching for shark tooth fossils on the beach, sharing fish and chips with your dad on the pier. Simple snapshots of daily life and quick glimpses that you know, deep in your bones, will be a picture forever interposed in your brain.

When I sat beside Mason on the city bus to school, every eighteen-year-old inch of him stiffened to such a degree it was clear he was urging his body to shatter, then scatter to the wind. But his eyes, when they met mine, told a different story. So blue they were oceanic, but so pale they were almost silver, metallic shrapnel shooting out from his pupils. One eye was puffy, swollen, and recently punched.

We connected, and I swear I saw both sides of him.

Mason's body may not yet have shattered, but his eyes were already broken.

The vulnerable kid who thought he had to be mean to gain any status in this world versus the arrogant prick with the confidence he'll succeed at anything he aims for.

Leave it to me to think she could be nice to the lost boy and have it be taken as innocent kindness. In the end, it was Mason's fractured rage that took control, a beautiful demon with a sword from the Underworld, one he'd aim straight for my heart and macerate.

I resented the power he held over me then, and I refuse to let him find it a second time.

My phone dings where I threw it on the bed, and I pick it up and read the incoming text.

Dee: You in? Can you stay with him?

With a closed-mouth smile, I text back, **Yep.**

Dee: Oh, man. So much goddamned money. The guy must be head over heels for you. Or you must've had the most addictive snake charmer in the world back in high school. You feel bad about gaming him?

I frown, then let out a soft laugh when I realize Dee's referring to my vagina as a snake charmer.

Me: No way. We both know where we stand. He's fully aware I'm in this for the cash. With the way he treated me, he's not delusional enough to think this will go anywhere.

Dee: Ah, so you're in this for revenge then.

My frown deepens. **No. I'm over it. I'm over him.**

Dee: Uh-huh.

I'm about to toss my phone on the side table and crawl into

bed, ignoring any more of Dee's insinuations, but her next text catches my eye.

Dee: Be careful, okay? We can celebrate the money and everything, but we both know why you're forcing yourself into this. Watch your back. You don't know who's behind you.

Chewing the inside of my cheek, I black out my screen, set the phone on the nightstand and busy myself pouring a glass of water in the attached bathroom sink.

I left my apartment in a rush but had the fortitude—or dumb-tude—to leave Giles's cash in plain sight on the kitchen counter inside my clutch in case he or his lackeys break in and come looking for me while I'm gone.

Dee's also been given strict instructions if, after eight weeks, my condo is no longer safe, to never step foot there ever again. I packaged and mailed a few important things to a secure P.O. Box, pocketed some paper, then walked out of my apartment, possibly for good.

I didn't linger among my things or say goodbye. Situations like this have to be considered in my line of work, and it was inevitable, with the high-risk, high-salaried clients I attend to, that a dangerous phase would come up. So, I instituted my fail-safe, which can basically be summed up as: *cut your losses and run.*

I couldn't do what Giles demanded. I wasn't about to clean his money and think he'd leave me alone afterward. He's the type of man who would demand more, expect extra, and steal bonuses, like using my body whenever he felt the need—and not paying for it.

I've met guys like him before. Avoided worse. It's because of that I know my limits, and facing him down while defying him isn't the way to go. It's best to hide out for a while, especially in a crowd, most preferably out of the country, gather my relevant documents (which were settled nicely in the small suitcase I brought in here with me), then make the call to Giles. Give him an offer he can't refuse, and provide him with two-hundred-and-fifty thousand reasons not to hurt my dad.

Mason provided the perfect opportunity to do all of that.

I have no one. I've been alone for a long time and starting over is almost a refreshing goal to look forward to, if I didn't have dangerous criminals breathing down my neck.

I ignore the skitter of unease crawling across my skin.

It can't be this easy.

Oh, but it is. Mason has no idea, but this time it'll be me that gives him the slip. I'll have his money, a clean slate, and a new country to settle down in.

And maybe the additional side benefit of hurting him as much as he's hurt me.

I pad into the bedroom, finishing my water and wiping my mouth with the back of my sleeve. The bed, luxurious and comfy, uses its siren call of fluffy down feathers and high thread counts to lure me into a catching a few hours sleep, before I assume the role Mason wants me to play.

Before I turn out the light, I twist the lock on the bedroom doorknob, my fingers brushing lightly against the wood before withdrawing.

Just in case Mason Payne gets any ideas.

Then, I pick up my phone and make the call.

CHAPTER 17

Mason

"Oh, good. You're awake," a female voice says.

Right after a pillow hits me in the face.

"What the—*ow*, Jess." I sit up, running a finger around my eye socket, wondering if a tassel thread got caught in there.

Jess, in a fitted blazer and tighter jeans, taps away at her tablet. "In two minutes, this room will be infiltrated with agents, managers, and busboys. Want to tell me why half your body's on the couch and the other half is on the floor?"

I crick my neck and pop my back. "Because this fucking thing is too small."

Jess's brown eyes narrow behind her thick, black-framed glasses. "Did you idiots party too hard last night? Is that why you couldn't find your bed? I *told* you, Mason, you need to get some rest. You guys are hitting the arena the minute you land in Tokyo."

"Yeah, I'm aware." I'm still rubbing my neck. My cheek feels stiff, and not solely from a day's growth of beard. I might've drooled in my sleep while using a hard, unforgiving couch arm as my pillow. "Is this furniture meant to be for show only?"

Jess's attention skims over the faded maroon velvet. "It's probably not meant for six-foot-five men, no. Even lean ones.

Where's Wyn? It's six-thirty and I don't even see a shirt lying around near you—oh. Hi, there."

Jess's finger pauses on her screen as she notices the person coming out of my bedroom.

The woman.

Mack steps outside the doorway in an oversized Mickey Mouse tee and ... that's about it. Her red-brown hair is mussed, kinked, and tossed to one side, and her legs glide for miles all the way down to the plush carpeting.

It's there my attention strays, right at the apex of her thighs where Mickey's yellow feet deny me any preview.

I push off the couch, scraping a hand through my own messed up, half-flat hair. "Mack, meet Jess, my assistant. Jess, this is—"

"McKenna." Mack heads over and holds out a hand, undeterred by Jess's put-togetherness versus her own. "Mason hired me to—"

"Mack's an old childhood friend," I cut in smoothly. But I make sure my directed smile at McKenna is more cutting than smooth. "She'll be joining me on tour."

Now all Jess's fingers pause on her screen. "Come again?"

"Yep. Mack'll be joining us for the entire tour. You're set to get her hotel rooms and such sorted, right?"

Jess lowers her tone. "Mason, you can't be serious."

"Oh, but I am." I hit her with my winning smile—the one that makes fans hyperventilate. "If anyone can do it, you can, Jessie."

Jess's face doesn't crack an inch. Always the professional, she answers, "Fine," then spins away, scrolling furiously on her tablet.

Mack raises a brow. "I take it you've let no one in on your grand idea to sweep me away?"

"It's no one's damned business." I scratch at my bare chest.

"Now, are you wanting to shower first, or should I? Or should we conserve the water supply and—"

"I'll shower first," Mack says, but I grin.

"In case you're wondering, no, I still don't have any tattoos," I say.

"What makes you think I care?" she retorts.

"Because I see you eyeing my pecs, that's why."

Mack's jaw hardens before she says, "They're the same pecs you wore when you were eighteen. I see no difference."

"Oh, *ouch*, Mack." I feign a harsh wince.

She and I both know there's a huge difference. My pecs and abs are chiseled like glass these days.

My attention strays to Mickey's ears, and I mean it when I say, "You've filled out nicely. Not that you didn't perfectly fill my hands senior year."

Mack flips me the finger the instant the hotel door opens and a bunch of guys stroll in.

Rex is the first to whistle, then say, "Couldn't get it up enough, eh, Mase?" before all the other guys start chirping.

Mack, to her credit, doesn't blush or flinch. She keeps that bird high in the air.

"You can tell us the truth, darling. He can't even last with just the tip, can he—holy shit, McKenna?"

Mack's eyes widen as she stares at the owner of the voice, my younger brother. "Braxton? Oh my *God*."

The awe in Mack's voice is real and true as she envelops my brother in a big hug. When she withdraws, she exclaims, "Look at you! I barely recognized you!"

Brax nods, glancing at me briefly before being drawn in by her. "I'm clean. Sober and going strong. Took a few stints at rehab—"

More like eight.

"—but Mase got me there," Brax finishes.

Mack cups Brax's cheeks. He's at least a head and a half taller than her and she has to look up to take him all in. "I'm so glad."

Brax squeezes her wrists, then withdraws. "Yep. Now I'm Mase's assistant's assistant. Bullshit work, but he pays me triple what I should make."

Mack squints over at me. "Yeah, he tends to do that."

I make an indecipherable sound in my throat, unhappy with the way my gut's reacting to my brother's hands on Mack. "Brax, you have my assistant to track down. She's about to have a heart attack over recent schedule updates. And Mack, take a shower before I cut your time in half and get in there myself. Whether or not you're still in it."

"And he's still a bossy asshole," Brax adds.

"Already knew that," Mack says, but she does as I ask and strolls back to the bedroom, every virile, non-taken male eye following her ass as she goes.

How many would she let pay to fuck her?

The thought comes unbidden but sharp. I wonder if I'll ever shake the hot-button anger that blooms every time I think about where she's ended up.

"Dude," Brax says as soon as Mack shuts the door behind her. "McKenna Beckley?"

I wave him off. "I don't wanna talk about it."

"How'd you find her?"

"You deaf? Just accept that she's here, Brax. And she'll be joining us on tour."

Brax's brows jump, but he does the smart thing and doesn't push. But, being my brother and the only guy who has more access to my history than anyone else on the planet, I can read behind his expression. And I don't like what I see.

He's confused, sure, but his eyes, the same color as mine, translate pity.

"Don't think I can't let go of my past or some shit," I spit out before swiping my shirt from the floor and pulling it on.

Brax holds his hands up. "Didn't say a word. Time to go find Jess."

"You do that."

Once Brax leaves, I don't find any additional privacy. I spin around to find Rex, East, and our manager, Spinner, watching me.

Rex immediately goes to tuning his guitar on the couch and East, sitting beside our manager, bursts into a conversation about logistics.

Wyn steps out of his room, his boxer briefs at half mast. Scratching his scalp, he says to me, "Hey man, I'm just glad there's a chick in your life other than Sorsha. That lady's the devil's work."

I glower at all of them.

CHAPTER 18

Mckenna

THE TRIP to Nocturne Court's personal jet wasn't exactly how I imagined it would be.

VIP entrances and exits are meant to be private, incognito affairs—or that's what I thought. As soon as we exit the building via the back entrance, the boys are engulfed with waiting fans and flashing phones. I spot a few press badges and a *ton* of paparazzi.

Mason and the others take it in stride, flashing smiles, scrawling autographs and accepting hugs and gropes like it's all part of the job. I guess it is.

I disappear with their other "people," flanked by Mason's executive assistant, Jess, and some kind of manager, Spinner, a tall, thin, greased up guy who smiles like he should be signing some tits, too.

Four black Escalades idle at the curb, and as security pushes through the small crowd with their black clothing and broad shoulders, we're all ushered into our respective vehicles.

I blow out a breath, my heart hammering like I'd just had to cross a deep chasm by taking a rickety bridge.

Mason, sitting beside me in the backseat, pats my thigh. "All good?"

I nod. "That's a lot of people. And cameras."

The door opens again and Brax flies in, forcing me into the middle seat. "Two chicks out there knew me as your bro, Mase. They couldn't get you so they asked *me* to sign their boobs."

"Always getting my sloppy seconds," Mason responds. "But what amuses me the most is that you're *happy* about it."

"Dude, the chicks that want you are hot. Getting the side-benefit of hot ass is never a bad thing."

"Hot ass does *not* sound like a good thing," Mason says. "Try again with some different words, buddy."

Brax leans back in his seat with a grin. I take the moment to study his profile, noticing his cheekbones still jut out and his neck is more tendons than fat. Drugs had always made him rail-thin, otherwise he and Mason could pass as twins. They were only a year-and-a-half apart, but with Brax's addiction holding him back and Mason's success propelling him forward, the differences between them grew.

I remember when Brax was at his worst, head-shaven, pock-marked, malnourished and out cold most of the time.

I'm still soft on Brax, especially back then. He didn't have the hard edges of his brother. Brax's cravings went the way of phar-maceutical bodily highs and isolated lows, books and quiet places, and preferring the comforting weight of a purring cat on his lap versus the crushing weight of social anxiety. Mason preferred live victims to direct his anger at, in public arenas.

I had more in common with Braxton than I ever did with Mason, but that's visceral attraction for you. There's no control or handle on it. It just is.

And in high school, Mason just was.

Jess breaks me from my thoughts when she turns in the front passenger seat and asks, "So, McKenna, do cameras bother you?"

"I'm sorry?"

"You were just saying to Mason that there were a lot of people back there. And cameras," Jess clarifies.

"Oh. Yeah. I'm not used to it, I guess," I say, fully aware how lame I sound.

"Lay off, Jess," Mason says. He's chosen a triple-washed vintage tee, faded jeans and black-on-black classic Ray-Bans as his travel outfit, and it irks me, for no reason, how good he looks.

"I don't need you to step in," I say to him.

"I know you don't," Mason responds. "I also don't care. You're here for a long haul. I don't need cattiness from either of you broads."

Brax chuckles into his fist, the kind of laughter that forewarns Mason from saying anything else, lest he get a claw to the eye.

Mason, of course, ignores it. "You don't like the cameras? Get used to it. They follow me everywhere I go, and since you'll be going *with* me to all the places I go, there's no avoiding them." He lowers his shades enough for his eyes to ice the top rim. "Nervous you'll be recognized?"

I give him a face. "Not at all."

"Recognized as what?" Brax asks. "Last I checked, you're the famous one, Mase. We're just your lackeys who get your spare cash."

As Brax and Mason launch into inappropriate banter, I stare ahead as the car bumps over potholes and dodges traffic, and notice Jess, still twisted in her seat.

I say wryly, "I suppose along with our apparent cattiness, we'll also have to deal with a bunch of testosterone fueled broness."

Jess doesn't respond. She eyes me through her glasses in a flat, studied way. One I'm not sure I appreciate.

"You and me?" she says. "We're the only women on this tour. Doesn't mean we're going to be friends."

She flips back around.

"Message received," I mumble.

Brax and Mason go quiet.

"Enjoying the show?" I snap. At either of them. Both of them. Whatever.

Think of the money.

I'm saved from any further cloistering small talk when we pull into the private airport and park next to the jet.

A red carpet runs from the plane's steps and down the tarmac to the waiting vehicles. The driver hops out to open our doors, but Mason opens his own and steps out.

He turns to me. "If I offer you my hand, will you bite it off?"

"Depends," I say as I shimmy into the spot he just vacated. "Are you going to yank me out of this car so I trip and fall on my face in front of everybody?"

Mason smiles. "That was the old me. The new me would instill a sense of safety in you, first. Perhaps I'll pants you in front of the whole crew when we're on the plane."

"I'll pass on the assistance," I say, and slide out and around Mason, making sure not to touch any part of him.

"You're right," he says to my back as I follow the entourage to the plane. "That gorgeous ass of yours should be for my eyes only."

I immediately regret my choice of leggings as part of my travel wardrobe.

Brax jogs up to my side as I'm about to take the stairs.

"You may not believe it," he says, "but despite the mouth on him, Mason's changed."

"He's no different from the guy who didn't bother saying goodbye at prom," I say as I grab onto the railing and hit the first step.

"Then why are you here?" Brax asks behind me. "How did he find you? Or did you find him?"

I don't answer.

"Not that I'm complaining," Brax adds as we board. "I'm happy to see you. You're looking well."

We step into the plane's interior, all buttery caramels and

supple leather, with two-seaters on one side and single seats facing each other on the opposite side. Brax squeezes my arm once I choose a single seat and sit.

I glance up at him. "You too, Brax. Sobriety looks good on you."

And it does. The baby face that lost all its filling when he was on drugs has gained back the smooth grooves of a healthy man. His piercing blue eyes shine with alertness, and while his head is shaved, there's a healthy tan underneath the dark stubble.

Brax replies with a thin smile. "Does working for my brother qualify as doing well?"

I'm not sure what to make of his last comment but I'm saved from replying when Mason clomps onto the plane with the rest of his band.

Mason's voice cuts through the air. "Brax—lay off my girl and go sit with Jess."

I twist and pin him with a stare. "I'm not your—"

His eyes bore into mine and I clamp my mouth shut. I guess we're honestly doing this, even within his inner circle. I'm expected play-act throughout the tour, starting now.

"S'up, Mack," the lead singer, Rex, says as he passes me.

He's grown more god-like than he was in high school, tall with long blond hair and Nordic features. Rex is also, according to what Mason's said, the only other person who knows my true occupation.

I look for it in his face. That inner confusion ... or disgust ... at what I choose to do that so many people don't manage to hide once they figure me out.

There's nothing.

Kindness stares back, with real interest in how I'm doing passing through his eyes.

I realize I should probably say something instead of studying him intently for a hidden insult. "I'm good. Nice to see you, Rex."

"You, too. We'll have time to catch up," he says.

"Yeah, I hear you have a daughter now," I say with a genuine smile. Rex, despite his Viking exterior, always had a soft spot for kids.

"I do. A girl at that. I'll tell you all about how to brush her hair into a perfect ponytail."

I laugh. Then, guitar strapped to his back, Rex heads to the last seats on the plane. Wyn and East pass by, nodding their hellos, and join Rex.

After chatting in the cockpit for a while, Mason plops into the seat facing me.

I swallow a sigh. Why did I expect Mason would join the rest of his band in the back of the plane?

"That's right, Mack. You have me for fourteen straight hours." He makes a show of leaning back and resting his ankle on one leg. "Want me to start a timer?"

I give a tight smile and reply quietly, "Not until the ink's dry on my contract."

Mason's head falls back against the seat. "Ah, yes. The official agreement. Jess is drawing it up right now."

"So tell me." I lean forward, resting my elbows on my knees. A small, bolted-down table is between us, stacked with magazines and two Perrier bottles. I swipe one and twist it open. "How many people on this plane know I'm a fake?"

Mason shrugs. "These are my most trusted colleagues. What I do—or don't do—in front of them is need to know only. They won't care if we have heavy PDA or barely touch in public. Wanna know why?"

I tip my chin.

"Because they're *paid* to do what I want."

I sit back, crossing my legs and taking a sip from the small, green bottle. "Just like me."

His gaze sharpens. "With one minor exception. When you suck my cock, it won't be because of the money."

I don't choke on my next swig, but I do nearly spill bubbly

water all over my mouth and chin when he blurts that out. I lower the drink, dabbing at the corners of my mouth with my finger. "Hit a nerve, did I?"

Mason's features smooth back to playful. "Not at all. I'm good, Mack. I'm always good."

"Are you? Because it seems to me you're the same guy from high school who surrounds himself with people who want or expect something from you. There's no one on this plane who's here just for your company, is there?"

A flight attendant shuts the plane's main door, then goes about taking drink orders. Since we're at the front, she'll be here any second.

Mason doesn't respond, but his cheeks turn rock solid as he clenches his jaw.

I forgot how addictive it is to push his buttons. "Want to tell me why you're not sitting with your band?"

"No. I don't. Because it's none of your fucking business."

He bites the words out, but his stare spits fire.

"And now you're thinking of the worst thing you could say to me to cut me down and shut me up," I say. "Because that's how you roll. Someone hits a nerve, and, instead of dealing with it like an adult, you lash out like a chained dog and make the other person feel terrible about themselves." I stand, gathering my things. "Do me a favor and put that on hold. We don't merely have fourteen hours together. We've got eight weeks. And I'd like to get through them without slapping you across the face within the first ten minutes."

I move to the seat behind him, and with each step, I'm anticipating a disgusted lip curl, a masochistic comment, or a venomous insult. Nothing comes.

Mason remains stiff-backed in his seat. He doesn't even show me his profile as I take the last available seat behind him.

"Mr. Payne," the pretty flight attendant says as she

approaches Mason. "Can I get you anything to drink before we take off?"

"Bourbon. Triple. Rocks."

The girl maintains professional calm despite the lethal injection Mason's put into his words. "Coming right up, sir."

I don't feel bad about picking a fight with Mason. I have to, since the alternative is to stay close and bear the prickling *zing* his presence gives off, familiar sparks igniting against my skin. Those old feelings are coming back to lay claim on my heart when I've worked so hard to turn them into dust.

I can't let Mason, with his arrogant grin and predatory strides, find the one smoking ember that remains.

The plane's wheels start moving and we pull out of its parking spot. Peering out the window, I notice all the cars that transported us here are gone. The red carpet's been rolled up and put away. It's as if the quiet solitude of a private airstrip had never been swarmed by a rock band and all the people, vehicles, and cameras they bring with them.

The efficiency with which multiple VIPs are transported, tucked away, and cleaned up after boggles my mind.

The flight attendant brings Mason his drink, then wanders over to me. "And you, Miss? What can I—"

"Aw, trouble in paradise already, kiddos?" Brax calls from his seat.

In answer, Mason stands and hurls his drink at his brother.

CHAPTER 19

Mason

WE STOP TO REFUEL, nobody choosing to leave the aircraft during the brief break while on the ground.

Mack keeps ominously quiet during the entire trip, pulling out her laptop and *tap-tap-tapping* on her keyboard incessantly. I crane my neck over the seat to glare daggers at her, which I think is the more polite approach rather than snarling my annoyance, but Mack just lifts a brow blandly in response, then goes back to her screen, pecking away again.

Sneering, I spin around and slouch in my seat and drink from my replacement scotch, since my first one is running rivulets down my brother's window seat.

I can't let Mack get to me like this. She's making me regret luring her onto this damned plane in the first place. It takes me back to our times on the city bus, Mack in her bucket seat reading quietly, and me, somewhere nearby (usually through deliberate means), ready to lob spitballs that'll get tangled in that wild hair of hers.

Hmm. I eye the cocktail napkin on the varnished wood of my armrest. Too bad I don't drink high-end scotch through a straw.

I can't resist turning back around, calculating some smartass remark in my mind as I move, but Mack catches me off-guard.

The computer that's been glued to her face is set to the side, on a low shelf under the window. She's curled up in her seat, using one of the Hermés throw blankets as a cover-up, her profile peeking through the cashmere as she sleeps.

It's Mack's most vulnerable moment, and I stand, wanting to take it all in. Her expression is softened by dreams, her lashes stark against the pale crests of her cheeks. The plane's interior lights are dimmed for night, but I know where her freckles are. Tiny constellations on the tip of her nose, a few rogue patterns on her cheeks. She covers them up, but not here. When she boarded the plane, her hair was straightened, but not now. It's crimped, curled and splayed around her shoulders, blanket, and headrest, and in that instant—in five seconds flat—she's the girl I fell in love with.

This is why you lured her onto the damned plane.

Frowning, I toss back the rest of my drink and let the empty glass hang by my side.

"Hey, creepster, wanna sit down so the plane can hit the skies again?"

I guess my brother didn't get the glass shard memo from last time. I spin the crystal in my hand, debating.

Brax rolls his eyes. "Only joking, buddy. But seriously, sit down."

I do, but I take my time, ensuring Brax understands that it's *my* choice, not his.

Sadly, Brax also doesn't understand the dimmed plane lights and the resulting hint to *shut up*. Everyone else seems to have the right idea, either sleeping or silently scrolling through whatever device is in their hands.

But, seeing as Brax is across the aisle from me, I can't avoid him.

"You gonna tell me why she's here?" he asks.

I clench both armrests and peer over at him. "Because I missed her."

Brax snorts. "So you ran into her at some bar, chatted, realized how you two were meant to be together, and you invite her on tour. Is that the long and short of it?"

"Sure."

"Yeah, I can really sense the love between you two. It's palpable."

"That's a big word, bro. Good job."

Brax frowns, but says, "If you're not going to tell me, I'll find out some other way. I know Jess is back there working on something or another relating to McKenna."

"If you're talking about a non-disclosure agreement, then yeah, of course she is. I don't invite any chick on a trip without covering my ass."

Too late, I realize my mistake.

"See, that's the thing, Mase. You've *never* brought a chick on a trip."

I keep silent.

"I get that it's McKenna," Brax continues. "She's special. She's a saint for putting up with you as long as she did and *despite* what you did. But with the way you two left things ... I'm confused, bro. And I guarantee everyone else in this crew is, too. It's only a matter of time before you have to give it to us straight."

My patience is at an all-time low. I turn to him and say, "Fine. I found out she's a high-class call girl and since she refuses to save herself, I've stepped in and bought her time with a lot of fucking dough, mostly to set my mind at ease that she's not out screwing strangers while I try to figure out how to stop her from being such an idiot."

Silence.

Then, Brax lets out a loud guffaw. Mack stirs in her seat.

"That is fucking *funny*!" Brax says through his chest laugh. "I swear, you're one of those guys that chews glass but with a witty remark before he swallows." Brax chuckles. "That was a good one, man."

"Yeah. I'm a regular jokester."

I spot the flight attendant bending into the cabinets near the cockpit. I wish I could appreciate her ass, but my gonads are numbed to anyone but the woman behind me, snoring quietly through cascading mermaid hair I'm fantasizing tangling my fingers in when I take her from behind.

Instead, I catch the flight attendant's eye and signal for another.

"You sure about that, bro?" Brax asks. "You're going straight to your concert once we land."

"Thanks for the head's up," I say wryly, then snap my fingers to make the attendant move faster.

♡

The plane touches down after cresting through clouds grayed by night, the multi-color lights of the city of Tokyo replacing the black calm of the skies above.

The cabin has stirred awake, lights put on bright, and once we taxi to a stop, all of us depart.

I wait for Mack to collect her things, then let her exit the plane first. She's bleary-eyed, feeling the time change already, but there's no time to go to the hotel.

"Mack, you're taking a car with Jess," I say once our feet hit the ground. "I gotta go with the boys."

"I assumed as much," she says with a yawn. "Am I going to the hotel, or...?"

"Fuck, no. You're coming to the concert and watching us play. Or you can fall asleep in the dressing room for all I care. I'm not letting you out of my sight this entire trip, so get used to it."

Mack idly scrapes her hair back from her forehead as we stand and wait for the cars to coast to a stop in front of us. "Why? Afraid I'll find the Asian market too tempting and decide to move here?"

"You're not exactly talking about stocks and bonds, kid," I say, pleased at the coolness icing my tone. It's at complete odds with the fire in my gut that ignites every time she mentions her fucking job.

And she knows it.

She turns and beams at me, "That's true—" Mack stumbles back a step. "My God, Mason."

"What?" My plane smell can't be *that* bad.

Mack wrinkles her nose. "Your breath. Did you empty the plane of all brown-colored liquor?"

"Maybe. After I banged the stewardess in the bathroom a few times."

I don't know why I say it. Scratch that—I do. I want a reaction from McKenna, the more fiery the better, and I anticipate that scandalized flush to her cheeks that always happens when I lob something inappropriate her way.

C'mon, Mack. I know you're still in there.

She meets my gaze with a mild expression. "Congrats on the Mile High Club. I've been there many times."

I refuse, *refuse*, to have any flush of any damn kind hit my face, so I turn away from her and stalk over to my boys who are watching their instruments be carried out and inspecting them.

East catches my eye as I sidle up to him. "Hey."

I nod in return, ignoring the stiffness that's befallen this band since last year. I know what it is, even if they don't. Once Rex and East found their women and made their families, their attention tore in half. One-hundred percent could no longer be given to our band. Wyn and me, though, being single AF, still devote an insane amount of time and energy to keeping Nocturne Court afloat, successful, and all the background suits in charge of our money happy, and this has made each band member's effort uneven and severely imbalanced.

It builds resentment.

A black feeling I dislike associating with my boys, guys

who've been with me since the preteen years, has formed in my chest, but I refuse to accept that once multi-platinum success is achieved, we'll all go our separate ways.

I wish Rex and East felt the same.

"All good?" I ask Rex as he bends to lift his second guitar case. He passes me mine.

"Yep. Let's roll," he says, barely sparing me a glance as he strides by.

My eyes narrow. The bourbon thins my blood. "You got something to say, man?"

Rex throws a look over his shoulder, not slowing his pace. "Nope."

"Mase." East lays a hand on my shoulder. "Ease up."

"Ease *up*?" I throw his hand off. "I'm not doing anything."

"Yet," Wyn mumbles. "Mase, come with me. Get in the car."

I cast around the area, noticing assistants, agents and managers busying themselves with their own things and expending extra effort in not looking in my direction. Everyone except for Mack, who stands in the thick of it and watches me with interest.

Brax is the only one who dares to touch me again by grabbing my arm. I stumble back against his yank and I'm ready to rip him a new one—

"Don't do this again, Mase," Brax says, but only so I can hear. "Not in front of your girl. Hear me?"

"Lay your hands on me again and I'll—"

"Punch my lights out, kick my dick into my throat, eat my kneecaps, yeah. I've heard it all before. Get in the car, drink some water."

The exasperation with which Brax meets my threat does nothing to temper my rage. In answer, I kick my guitar case across the tarmac. Some poor, young, assistant soul jumps back with a yelp. Mack covers her mouth with her fingers at the action, but displays no further emotion.

I'm close to snarling when Brax shoves me into the backseat of a waiting black SUV, and I can't keep on my feet. I fall into the leather, nearly face-plowing into the luxury stitching.

"You've got a concert to play at. Fans to greet. Fucking act like it," Brax says, then pushes me farther in to make room for East.

"I'm fine," I say, but accept the cold bottle of water passed through the front by Wyn.

"We know," Rex says as he hops in the other side. He pushes me into a seated position in the middle. I let him, because the space is too small and crowded to throw a decent punch.

"You're the most put together of all of us," Rex says sarcastically, then glances behind us. "I sure hope bringing Mack along was a good idea."

I follow Rex's stare and see Mack standing on the tarmac, highlighted by our car's rear lights. Once I register her expression, my upper lip curls in distaste.

Pity is something we *both* left behind in our teenage years. She has no right to pull it out now.

"She's the greatest mistake I ever made," I mumble.

Nobody knows how to respond that. Fuck, neither do I.

Maybe, it was never in question.

CHAPTER 20

Mason

THE CONCERT IS A BLOW-OUT.

I mean that in a good way. Huge arena, screaming fans, massive pyrotechnics and exploding music—Tokyo knows how to get it done.

I lose myself on stage and become someone other than Mason Payne. Or, maybe I'm still that guy, just a juiced-up version with no past or future, only present tense, with the sole motivation of living through music, jamming with lyrics, and sweating through a detox.

With the amount of liquor I ingested on the plane, I should be comatose in a horse stable somewhere, but my body knows better than to betray me on a concert night. We got it together, especially after one last whiskey shot before hitting the stage, my fingers loose and able on my bass as I assist East on his drums in our opening song.

The booze also makes it easier to handle when the guys stop talking to me and each other and they go off into their own worlds, texting their wives or some shit, talking with their own hub of "people" like their personal agents and managers, which is exactly what happened as soon as we stepped out of the SUV and into the venue.

After greeting the raging waves of hyperventilating fans waiting at the so-called "secret entrance."

The booze helps with that, too. Makes it nicer when girls claw at your shirt and skin, nails digging and tearing, tears streaming down their faces as you try to take a decent selfie with them.

I mean, I look good. Maybe a little rouge-y in the cheeks, but it's a helluva lot better than the open, crying maw of the chick beside me.

But hey, they're my people, and I do love them. It's why I'm the last to remain within the clawing crowd, signing all kinds of shit on skin and other random materials. Security hates me for it since I breach all sorts of rules, like climbing over the barricade to get closer photos with the fans, or try to reach the ones in the back.

But like I said, the booze makes it easy. Helps me coast along through complete, manic, fandemonium that seems never-ending, always buzzing, forever taking.

I don't see Mack through any of it. I assume she's somewhere within our secure area, ushered into the venue as I linger outside.

I still don't find her when we finish our concert and tumble backstage, my shirt long gone and replaced by a shiny veneer of sweat. Droplets from my hair drip into my vision and thicken my eyelashes as I search for her.

"Anyone seen Mack?" I ask the room.

The rest of the band entered before me and the giant room is quickly amassing with other people, like corporate types, our tour staff, some fans with backstage passes, some without. A few girls have also been made available for our pleasure, though someone needs to give them the memo that Wyn's likely the only dick they should be searching for nowadays.

Meh. He'll sacrifice himself willingly.

"Nah, man. I think she left early," East says as he passes me, chowing down on a sub sandwich.

My stomach rumbles at the sight, hunger replacing adrenaline with the speed of a tiger's swipe, but I ignore it.

"Early? Did she see the concert? Why'd she go?"

My questions aren't in order, but East doesn't need them to be as he reads my lips.

"It was pretty crazy out there. Might've been too much for her. She's not used to it, you know? I remember her being such a bookworm. This is probably way out of her element. Why'd you bring her along, anyway? You orchestrating some kind of high school reunion?"

If you only fuckin' knew.

"So where's she at, then? Who took her somewhere?" I ask.

East laughs and claps me on the back. He says out of the corner of his mouth while he chews, "She's your girl, not mine. Figure it out. I'm sure she's safe."

Mouth twisting down, I scan the rest of the figures in the room but don't see familiar auburn curls or feline eyes.

I pull out my phone from my pants, texting her. Thirty seconds later, I still get no response.

"Hey—Spin." I catch my manager as he walks by. "You seen Mack? McKenna, I mean?"

"The girl you brought?" Spinner mulls this over. "Not for a while. I think she may have left with Jess. Gone to the hotel."

I nod, the tightness in my chest receding. "Cool."

"And your brother."

My chest bounces back to tight with elastic efficiency. "Say what?"

Spinner side-eyes me, but I make no attempt to hide my darkening mood. He asks, "Doesn't Brax work with Jess? What's the problem?"

"None," I snap, then peel off my guitar, hand it to some assistant or another, and storm out of the room.

The security detail assigned to my ass follows me, one even handing me a spare shirt. I grab it then throw it onto the hallway floor.

"Where's my car?" I demand.

Someone employed by the venue scuttles up beside me and says, "Right this way, sir. We have a few vehicles waiting for when your party decides to depart."

"Great. Just me," I say, and follow him, bare-chested, into the cold.

The chilled weather feels *good* against my chest. It freshens my breath and clears the heat similar to a cold shower, and I slide into the waiting SUV with tinted windows, thankful I've left early enough that fans have yet to assemble near our cars.

I nod my thanks to the employee who directed me here before the door shuts, a small part of me understanding that my pissiness should only be tolerated by my friends and enemies. Hard workers and employees are exempt from Hurricane Mason, a pledge I made to myself back when I decided to work on controlling my temper.

Young Mack had a lot to do with that.

Maybe I've succeeded? I can't be sure, since the thought of Brax sitting near Mack right now for who knows how long boils my blood.

She's mine.

I sit in silence until we pull up to the hotel, a huge, white, half-circle building with glittering lights and carved domes. I'm swiped in through the back entrance and ushered into a private elevator with my security until we reach my floor. Jess has taken care of the details. All I need to do is show up, and a keycard is shoved into my hand and I'm told what suite is mine.

The perks of fame and money. It's like being a baby needing diapers all over again.

"Which room's Mack's?" I say to no one in particular while riding the elevator.

One of the two security guys clears his throat. "Um. I think I heard Jess mention she's the room beside yours."

I nod. When the doors slide open, I say, "Have a good night, gentlemen," and beeline for the door next to mine.

Except, there's one on each side.

Whatever. I'll bang on the whole hallway until I see Mack's face.

I choose the one on the left, since why not, and knock. When no one immediately responds, I pound louder.

Grumbles sound on the other side. Female ones.

I smile.

There are a few light taps and brushes of fabric on the other side of the door, probably checking the peep-hole, before it's whipped open and Mack's half-asleep expression with mostly mussed hair greets me with a *fuck you.*

"What the hell, Mase? I was sleeping!"

"You missed our concert."

"No." She rubs her eyes. Clad in an oversized t-shirt, her nipples are hard and rounded and her legs bare. "I missed *some* of your concert. Ever heard of jet lag?"

"Ever heard of being a proper guest and staying for the whole show you've been invited to?"

"I don't know, Mason, is it in the contract? Do I have to stay for each show's entirety while on tour?" She cocks a hip. "Because we both know I'm operating only on the instructions listed therein. I'm not here as your friend."

My molars grind down. "Then I guess we have to amend our agreement."

"If that's what you want," Mack says. "You're enjoying this, aren't you? Instructing me. Telling me what I can and can't do."

I tilt my head and say darkly, "We both know what you do. If I had it my way, I'd be instructing you to get on your knees and remember the taste of my dick. I'd tell you to spread your legs while I revisit my favorite meal. And I'd fuck you so hard and senseless, no client or boyfriend of yours will ever compare. Remember how big I was? Do you recall how much you begged for it?"

With each word leaving my mouth, I watch the flush creep up, from her collarbone, to her neck, to her cheeks. Her eyes glitter with insult, and I grow hard just looking at her.

I crave her.

"You have some fucking nerve," she hisses, then moves to slam the door.

I catch it easily, splaying my hand against the wood. "That's the truth, Mack. But I wasn't about to scandalize Jess with my wants and needs while she wrote up the contract."

She sneers. "You're still drunk."

"Brax in there with you?"

Mack startles. "Why the hell would Brax be in here with me?"

I shrug. "Just a question."

"So you're drunk *and* unreasonably jealous. Go to bed, Mase. It's late."

"Can't. I have too much adrenaline pumping through my veins. It's what shows do to me. I need an outlet."

Realization brightens her eyes. "You won't find it with me."

I step forward. "Won't I?"

"Mason, don't." She holds up a hand, as if she can stop me from stepping into her hotel room.

"You're on my dime. I can do what I want with you."

Those bright sparks in her eyes pop off. She palms my chest, shoving me back. "Just because I do what I do, just because I'm here because you're paying me does *not* mean I'm here for your pleasure. Got it, you jerk?" Another shove. Laughter bubbles out of me as my shoulder jerks back from her force, which only makes her fiercer. She makes a sound of disgust. "That's how it's gonna be, huh? You're going to lord my choices over my head and talk about prostitution every chance you get, use me as an *object*—"

She cuts herself off. I smirk, but I'm noticing the calculation rippling across her features.

Mack straightens her shoulders. She lifts her head. Then she takes one step into the hallway.

I hedge back to make room for her, but not so much that I'm trying to make her comfortable.

"That's what you want, isn't it?" she asks, without the fire. "You know what? Fine. Have it your way. Use me, Mason."

The laughter dies in my throat when she reaches for the hem of her shirt and peels it off.

She's not wearing anything underneath.

Mack stands naked in the hallway. And she's toned—god*dammit*, she's gorgeous. Her stomach is flat and pale, with the dot of her belly button and two bordering lines of muscle running down the sides. Sides that flare into hourglass hips, her hairless apex, and thick, flawless thighs.

My gaze runs up to her tits—full and rounded, with large rose nipples peaked by the rush of cool air. Her chest heaves, raising them.

Her body's so different from what I remember. The softness has hardened into crafted muscle, a carving made to appeal to various clientele. The eighteen-year-old girl is long gone, replaced by luscious curvature and flawless real estate.

But ... I bet her ass is still ripe as a peach. I bet I can spread her cheeks and lift her until she settles on my cock.

I bare my teeth, unable to decide whether to bite every inch of her or growl at her to get back inside her fucking room.

"You're out in public," I say, and it pains me to do the opposite of what I want. "You should probably put that shirt back on or go back inside and shut the door."

"It's a closed floor," she retorts. "Reserved for Nocturne Court and their staff."

I arch a brow. "You think I want my fucking staff and band-mates to see you like this any more than TMZ?"

"They're all at the after-party. It's only you here, coming back early. And me, you're newest employee, ready and willing to ride you all night long."

Passion doesn't accompany her words.

"I'm here for your pleasure, aren't I?" she continues. "You want to put your quarter million to use. I understand that. So what's your vice these days, Mr. Payne? Do you want me on my knees? On all fours on the bed? How about anal? Lately, clients love when I choke on their dick while deep-throating them. Is that what you want to try, too?"

I've lifted my attention from her body to her face. Throughout her speech, she's defiant. Stands her ground. Prepares herself for whatever I demand. Except for one thing.

I see it when her lashes flutter. The way she blinks. How she swallows after she's done talking.

The girl's in pain. It hurts her to say these things to me. To offer herself up as a meal.

I move until I'm cupping one side of her face and tilt her chin until she has no choice but to keep staring into my eyes. My thumb brushes against her bottom lip, smooth as silk against my callouses. She wears no make-up, instead donning a stubborn mask.

Her cheeks and forehead are smooth and emotionless as porcelain, and I know what she's doing.

I say, close to the tip of her nose. "So you'll be my play doll, huh? Do anything I want?"

"Anything."

"Mm. A quarter mill is a lot of money." I tilt my head until our lips are almost touching. "I think I'll start collecting my dues right here."

Then, I claim her mouth.

We're in full view of the hallway and probably a few hidden

cameras, but I cease to care when her taste hits my tongue and I'm transported back to honeysuckle and sage—scents and tastes so foreign to my world but familiar in hers. Skin scented with flowers, hair smoothed by expensive oils, and lips, exfoliated and buttered and meant to shape against my own.

At first, she's stiff. But as my tongue coaxes, her lips part, a supple invitation to explore further. Mack's fingers wrap around my wrist. I'm still holding her face, directing her angles so I can taste all of her, *remember* the feel of her, and on instinct, she bows forward, her naked body melting against my half-clothed one.

My other arm wraps around her waist, pulls her closer. She moans when she feels me, hard, against her stomach. And yes, her ass remains as squeezable as it was when we were younger. Probably the only reminder I have that she's still her.

Mack's mouth opens further, her tongue joining with mine, and I groan, deep in my throat, my hand moving to tangle in her hair.

I wait until Mack hitches a breath, for when she gasps my name and pulls at my arms to drag me inside her room. I can do anything I want with her. Push my fingers in. Splay her against the wall. Spin her around, spread her legs, and ram into her from behind until she cries out in ecstatic mercy.

I do none of that.

I pull back, dropping both my hands from her body. Cool air comes between us.

Mack slow-blinks, her cheeks flushed and burned raw from my day's stubble. "What…"

"Those clients of yours?" I say. "They'll never know what it's like to touch you like that. To have you melt in their hands and go wet simply from their tongue playing across your lips. When I have you, and make no mistake, I *will*, it will be because you want me, Mack. Desperate for my touch, my strokes, my tongue.

Not because I've paid you or the fucked up notion that you owe me."

Mack collects herself, but doesn't cover her body in an attempt to regain dignity. No, her dignity's reclaimed when she props her hands on her hips and retorts, "When money's involved, there's always a debt owed. A favor to ask. A crime to commit. No cash is free, Mason, and I won't be the moron who buys into your 'I'm doing this for your own good' speech."

I get in her face, my expression playing no games. She doesn't wince when I dart forward. I growl, low in my throat, "Don't you ever proposition me like a client again. *Ever.*"

Mack's brows go rigid. "It's what you expected. It's what every guy wants."

"Not me, Mack. You are not my whore." I lean back, but make sure I keep her attention when I say, "You're simply ... mine."

She's silent when I storm away. It's clear our tables have turned. There was a time when Mack offered me her french fries and I was sent into a tailspin of rage at the notion she felt sorry for me. I can fully comprehend her sense of pride in this moment and the refusal to back down and have someone swoop in as a savior.

Problem is, unlike her, I have no shame, or decorum, when it comes to doing what I think is right.

Mack is anchored to her spot outside her room, watching me leave.

Before keying into my room, I toss over my shoulder, "You're in my world, now. So get the hell inside your room before word gets out to Brax there's a hot naked chick haunting Nocturne Court's hallway."

CHAPTER 21

Mckenna

IT'S three days after Mason and my's stint in the hallway, and he's been avoiding me ever since.

Well, I can't say he's ignoring me. Mason demands, as per my contract, that I accompany him everywhere, including cars, soundchecks, and when he decides to retreat to his next hotel suite. It's never to invite me into his room with him, as what's *also* part of my contract is the requirement that my room always neighbor his—preferably with an adjoining door that remains befuddling, since he's never tried to use it.

Mason demands my presence, yet doesn't talk to me.

We're on tour stop #3, Berlin, hotel number #4, and Mason's demeanor hasn't changed.

Not since he played music on my tongue. Strummed guitar notes in my mouth.

It's a far cry from the Mason I'm currently dealing with, who seems to want me around only to prove, all these years later, he can still dismiss me.

Mason and the rest of Nocturne Court have hit the stage, and I'm hanging back in their dressing room, enjoying the detritus they left behind. I'm required to be at the concert, but Mason has left it up to me whether I want to watch the show or wait back-stage, an allowance I'm sure he wants me to be grateful for.

"What'd that meatball sub ever do to you?"

Brax's question breaks me out of my stare-down with the sandwich tray.

"It went soggy on me," I say before opting for the ham and swiss option.

Brax makes himself comfortable on one of the reclining leather chairs, tipping a bag of Skittles into his palm and throwing them all in his mouth. "Yeah, not sure why Wyn requests marinara-soaked subs when he doesn't get to them until hours later, but that's a rock star for you."

I'm oddly fascinated by Brax's ability to form complete words while chewing with a wad of candy in his mouth.

He notices and points to his lips. "My new fixation. One thing you learn from being an addict is, you'll always be an addict. Doesn't have to be drugs. Now I've moved onto sugar."

"How are you dealing with that? I mean, is it going well?" I place my sandwich on a paper plate and take a seat next to him.

"Sure. If you factor in having your big bro as a bodyguard who never lets you out of his sight, even if I wanted to sneak something as innocent as a blunt. Which I don't."

I roll my eyes. "He has a certain way of keeping an eye on people he considers problems, doesn't he?"

Brax murmurs in agreement. "Ever since he was a kid. It's like, since he's cleaned up his life, he needs to absorb other people's fuck-ups as his own and fix them his way. Like he sees himself as some sort of mentor or idol, but won't admit it."

"You think he's changed his life for the better?"

"Well." Brax pours more candy into his hand, shaking them in thought before tossing them back. "He started to. When he hooked up with that actress chick, he was at the top of his game. The band hit the Billboard charts, raked in cash, he reduced his drinking and recreational weed use, really got into the music and the art. And hey, he hired me, the newly sober little brother as a ride-along, to show me how climbing out of the sewer can be done. Right? The Payne sewer rats scrabble their way up to become millionaires. One of them, anyway."

Brax's last sentence rubs me the wrong way. I never knew Brax and Mason to be in competition with one another, but I also haven't been around them in a decade. As proven by Mason smoking weed, which he wouldn't touch as a kid. I keep quiet.

"Lately, though, I'm sensing big bro going downhill. He's upped his drinking, even around me. Used to be, if I were in the room, he'd take steps to ensure he wasn't rubbing his alcohol use in my face. Now, it seems he doesn't give a shit."

I remember back to when the tour started and we left the jet, Mason tripping over his own feet down the stairs. Trying to start fights. Kicking his own guitar case across the tarmac.

"I don't know what has him so lit," Brax continues. "When I try to talk to him, he shuts down. Pretends nothing's wrong. Acts like I'm the idiot who's reading too much into things."

"I know what that's like," I murmur, then bite into my sandwich.

My comment centers Brax's attention on me. "You being here came as a surprise, McKenna. A big one. Like, I remember how you guys were those last months in high school. It's foggy and laced with a lot of coke, but my memories are there. But I also remember how you ended. If I may be so bold, why are you back with him?"

I guffaw, almost spitting out breadcrumbs. Swallowing and dabbing at my mouth, I say, "We're not together. It's complicated."

"Ah. The good ol' complication bit. I get it." Brax nods. "I know when I'm being dismissed."

I lay a hand on his forearm. "I'm not brushing you off, Brax."

He stares down at my fingers.

I say, "I agree with you when you say Mason tries to fix

things he thinks are broken. Especially when he doesn't see any fractures within himself."

"*Yes.*" Brax meets my eyes. "You say it so much better than I do. You've always been so smart. And super intimidating, especially when you stepped into our neighborhood. You still doing good? Last I heard, you were off to some college that wouldn't look at me sideways even if I had the cash and Mason's rockstar name to give them."

"Oh. That." I lift my hand away from his arm. "I only did a year there. Life doesn't always go as planned."

"Cryptic." Brax offers me Skittles, but I shake my head, lifting my sandwich instead. Yet, I keep feeling his stare. "You seem different, though. Still a brainiac, but ... did something happen to you? Is that why Mason's swooped in?"

"I, um..."

I've never been ashamed of what I do. But in this instance, the contract's fine-print blares into my mind's eye and the money I'll miss out on if I screw anything up. I also can't ignore the lingering sense that I want Brax to stay proud of me. And that, if I tell him the truth, his eyes will shutter the same way everyone else's does when they figure out my calling.

I set my sandwich aside. "I have to go to the bathroom."

"Was it something I said? I'm sorry, McKenna. I don't mean to offend."

"You haven't," I assure. "I'll be back. Okay?"

"Yeah. Fine." Brax tips the rest of the bag into his mouth, and I get the feeling it's to cover his hurt at being left alone.

"I—" I stop myself before I say *I promise*. Promises are all too easy to back out of, and I don't think Brax deserves that.

"See you soon," I amend, then leave the dressing room.

Bathrooms are down the hall, the women's even farther, taking me so long to find that I actually do have to use it once I push open the door and rush to a stall and lock it.

When I'm finishing up, the door creaks open again, and I recognize Jess's voice.

"I know, Derek, I know," she says as her heels sound against the tiles.

Through the crack in the stall, I see her set her purse on the sink and pull out her cosmetics bag as she nestles her phone between her ear and shoulder.

"No, I'm keeping Braxton out of the loop for now," she says. Once she finds what she's looking for, she looks up to the mirror and touches up her lipstick. "He's unstable, unreliable, and here because of nepotism. It's the trifecta of a bad idea. I can't very well inform Braxton that Rex and Easton are leaving the band and expect him to keep his mouth shut to Mason."

My fingers freeze on the lock to the stall.

"If Mason finds out," she continues, "Der—Derek—listen to me. He'll lose it. I've worked for Mason long enough to know he'll walk off the tour, and we can't afford that. Not if this is the last leg of our cash cow. It's what's good for him. Yes. What's best. I'll talk to Spinner as soon as I see—"

Through the mirror, I see Jess's gaze lower and land on my shoes under the stall. I inwardly curse, thinking maybe I should've crouched on the toilet so I could've heard more.

"I have to go," she says. "I'll call you back at the hotel."

Cringing, half of me is afraid to open the stall door. I stay put, warring with how to better phrase the question, "What the *fuck* is going on?" so I can actually elicit a truthful answer.

Jess sighs and says to the mirror, "It sucks, being the only woman on staff for so long. I got comfortable thinking the women's bathroom was my own private conference room." She clips her makeup bag shut. "But you're not staff, are you, McKenna?"

Put on the spot, I have no choice but to shimmy out of the safety of the stall.

Jess turns so her hip is leaning against the sink. "But Mason's paying you, so I guess you're something. An important something, I'd say. A quarter million's worth."

Jess clucks her tongue as I step up beside her to wash my hands, pretending like I'm unaffected by what I overheard.

"Care to tell me why Mason's paying you so much?" she asks.

I shake my head while running my hands under the sink. "It's confidential."

"That it is. I'm the one who wrote up the contract. Mason was incredibly tight-lipped about the whole thing, only gave me the bare bones."

I want to squirm under Jess's shrewd study, but I remind myself it was not my choice to be in the bathroom at this exact time and listen to information I shouldn't be privy to.

"It made me want to do my own research on you," Jess says.

I lift my gaze until it meets hers in the mirror.

"And what I found out..." Jess tucks her cosmetics bag in her purse before pulling the strap over her shoulder. "You really need this money."

I keep my face blank and don't break our stare-down. There's no way she could know about Giles and the deal I struck with him. It's like a mantra in my head: *she can't know she can't know she can't know* that prevents even a flicker of emotion from showing.

"If you're trying to intimidate me," I say. "You need to do better than that. Who doesn't want that kind of money?"

"You're a difficult one to figure out. There isn't much about you online, except for one small thing. I know about your father, McKenna."

My hands freeze halfway to the paper towel dispenser. My brain jumps between relief that Giles isn't mentioned and dread that my father is.

Jess says, "Mason's too self-absorbed to ever consider looking into your past because he thinks he knows it already—but he doesn't know shit, does he? As I was saying, you *need* the money.

For your dad, your broken family, whatever you want to call it. So if I were you, I wouldn't do anything to jeopardize that."

I pull down a few paper towels, scrunch them between my hands, then toss them into the trash can on the side. It forces me to lean around Jess, who isn't moving a muscle. Her brown eyes are trained on mine.

"Mason deserves to know what's going on with his friends," I say to her.

"You haven't been around long, but it's been long enough to notice Mason isn't exactly at the top of his game," Jess says. "He's on a downward spiral, McKenna, and this news? Not only will it derail him, it'll kill him. In his mind, this band is all he has. It's the thing that pulled him out of Hell and made him famous. To be told it's breaking up ... well, I'll leave it up to you whether or not you want to be the one to break him."

"Guilting me won't work, either," I say. "How about just telling me the truth? Why are they leaving?"

"I don't trust you enough to give you the truth, same way you don't trust Mason enough to tell him what really happened to your family. And to you."

I swallow a retort, the tang of Jess's words bitter at the back of my throat. "What, so now I'm expected to walk around with this news and be Mason's sidekick without telling him Rex and East want to dissolve the band? How can I be expected to do that? If he finds out I've kept it from him, he'll—"

"You're the one who signed the contract, not me." Jess moves to the door, her expensive perfume splicing through the air. "And to finish your sentence, yeah, he'll fire you, kick you off this tour, and leave you penniless. He's vindictive like that."

I have no doubts Jess is right. What I have trouble dealing with is the different faces of Mason. The mean one in high school who could go fuck himself for all I cared, or the benevolent rock star seen on glossy pages? What about the brother who would do anything for his sibling? And I can't forget the man from three days ago, who kissed like he had to make up for ten years of leaving me behind.

Some were easier than others to dismiss. The problem is, which one would I be deceiving? Which one would I hurt *by keeping this information to myself?*

Lately, Mason is nothing but a jumble of contradictions. I've never hate-liked him more, but I can't go back to the girl I was with him. That yellow-bellied, stupidly innocent, idiot child who never spoke up for herself.

Jess opens the Ladies' door. "While guilt and blackmail may not work for you, you better do all you can to make sure he *doesn't* find out until that cash hits your bank account, McKenna."

I scrape my hair back from my forehead. "This may surprise you, but it's not that black and white for me."

Jess isn't swayed. "You don't give a shit about Mason. I've come across plenty of girls like you. You're after the money. Remember that and it'll be easier to lie to his face."

The door smacks shut behind her.

CHAPTER 22

Mason

I'M BACK at the hotel shining like a star.

Whether it's residue from sweating my heart out on stage or the sparkly sheen of playing a flawless set, what's it matter? Both ways, I'm downright satisfied.

My shirt was lost somewhere between hitting the stage and stepping into my suite, but it's one of many white tees tossed into scrabbling hands—or ripped from my body.

Chest heaving, I yank a hand towel from the attached bathroom and scrub my face, slick back my hair. I scratch at my scruff with the white cotton, and my attention diverts to the adjoining door.

Mack.

I've been treating her like a sourpuss lately, but I don't have a conscience over it. She baits me with her body, then undercuts that passion by turning it into a business transaction. The fact she turned the tables on me pisses me off. We're not teenagers anymore. We've moved past humiliation and pettiness.

Or ... I thought *she* had, anyway.

Before I think it over, my knuckles rap against the wood. When there's no response, I knock harder. When there's still nothing, I pound with the side of my fist incessantly until the door flings open and Mack barks, "*What?*"

I lean against the frame with my elbow, hand on my head and fingers digging into my damp hair. "Hi."

Mack squints. At me, at the light in my room. Behind her, the room is dark and cool. She's back in an over-sized t-shirt, her hair all over the place and her face bare of expertise—exactly the way I like her.

"Oh, so now you're choosing three in the morning to talk to me?" she says.

"I'm on a high," I admit. "Can't help it. The concert was insane—we played like we were back in high school, totally in sync. Honestly, Mack, it hasn't been that way in so long … it was fucking epic. And all four of us stayed afterword to sign autographs and meet fans. That never happens. We even posed for pictures. *That's* a rarity. Usually Rex frowns and stalks off to a corner, East is too shy and reserved, and Wyn threatens to pull out his wiener if the paparazzi so much as captures his profile. But no, man, there we were, totally rising above all our petty shit."

Something flits behind Mack's expression, and I take it as her being miffed that I've ignored her for days.

"Have a drink with me," I say.

Mack rubs her eyes. "Go find your brother and celebrate. Or the rest of your band. I'm sleeping."

I shake my head. "It's not them I want to kick back with right now."

"I wouldn't think it'd be me, either," she says. "I thought I pissed you off so much you were ignoring me until I crawled up to your feet and kissed your toes for forgiveness."

I smile. "Nah, I've grown out of that."

Mack sighs. "The answer's still no, Mase. I'm tired, and—"

"You have to abide by the contract."

Her eyes meet mine again. "You're serious. Are you aware what time it is?"

"Perfectly." I grow serious. "And I also know that you're mine to do with as I please so long as we're on tour."

"I'm not a toy, asshole."

"Didn't say you were. But you *are* subject to my spoiled rockstar whims. I'm only reiterating what you signed. You're to be at my side, as requested, no matter what time of day."

"Does it please you? To force people to hang out with you when they really don't want to? Is that how you're still making friends?"

I don't let the barb hit. The night's been too much of a rush, and Mack's annoyance with my presence only makes the adrenaline taste sweeter. "What's your poison? Scotch or vodka?"

"My poison is you," she mumbles. She combs her hair back, then drops her hand at her side. "Let me find some pants."

"Scotch it is."

"Beer," Mack corrects.

"Fine. Beer. See you in five."

The adjoining door clicks shut.

I pour myself a scotch on the rocks and grab Mack a bottle of beer from the fridge, then kick back on the couch near the bay windows overlooking Munich. As I stare into the outside, the foreign landscape lit with the same neon lights as my hometown, I'm hit with the random urge to explore the city with Mack.

We never actually tour the places we're in, mostly because there's no time to appreciate architecture when your stay at the epicenter encompasses about twenty-four to forty-eight hours of cars, hotels, venues, and crowds. I've been around the world a few times, and I can vividly remember blurs of color and open mouths screaming my name. Not much else.

With Mack, I'm thinking of a stroll through some of the gardens, maybe some old villages, and the quiet solitude of having a woman by my side as we figure out where to stop for lunch.

The thought strikes sideways and I grimace before lifting the glass to my mouth. I'm not supposed to yearn for that kind of shit. Especially from *Mack*. We had it okay back in high school, when she broke through my defenses, but that was temporary. I was back to screwing it up before graduation hit, and I'm probably fucking it up now.

I'm forcing her under contract to be here.

Preventing her from doing her so-called job.

Now, convincing her long-term that she doesn't need to sell her body, that's a work in progress.

I know that body. Traced it with my tongue. And damned if I'm going to let strange men have at it again.

There it is, that thought of fixing her situation by having her by my side. Grumbling, I stand and refill my drink.

"All right. I'm here."

McKenna appears and steps through the adjoining door, clad in athletic shorts and the same tee. I note the lack of a bra and the peaks of her nipples budding through her shirt.

She stands in the middle of the room. "Where do you want me?" she asks.

"Don't be like that," I say when I hand her a beer. "You can move about freely and you know it."

"Just making sure I didn't miss any fine print," she says before settling into a sofa chair adjacent to the couch.

Her gaze travels to the windows much like mine did, but I doubt she's thinking of goddamned gardens and villages and lunch.

I resume my position on the couch, tipping back my drink. We sit in silence for a moment, Mack proving her point that she doesn't want to be here, and me enjoying Mack's presence without her ruining it with her quick mouth.

"Are you happy?"

The question catches me off-guard. I search her face for the trap.

"I mean it," she says, staring at me levelly. "Are you happy, doing what you do, being part of Nocturne Court?"

"Absolutely," I say without thinking. With the way she searches my eyes, I guess she's looking for more. "It's what we always dreamed of, back in my moldy garage. I got the hell out of there and made a ton of money doing it. I got to escape my pops. I could pay for Brax's multiple rehabs and he finally got clean. Also moved myself into new neighborhood in a fly zip code, and I've never looked back."

"I'm glad you got out of there." Mack sips her beer. "But I always thought you were destined for escape, not just through your band. You would've carved your own path, too."

I frown. "I did carve my own path. With my buddies."

Mack nods. "Yeah, but you were so damned determined to raze our school and climb out on top. You hated everything, especially hand-outs. It was like, if you weren't going to get the hell out of there, you were going to burn it to the ground, anyway."

"I was an angry kid. I didn't think life had been fair to me, so I thought spitting in its face was the way to answer back."

"Don't I know it." Mack takes another swig.

I stare at her harder. "Are you looking for an apology? For everything I did in high school? Fuck, Mack, most of my memories are with a coating of red rage."

She laughs hollowly. "I'll never expect an apology from you, Mason."

Part of my chest flickers to life. "I was unfair to you. Borderline cruel. But do I regret it? No."

Mack glances at me, eyes wide with insult.

"I don't want to change it because it ultimately led to *us*. You and me, in your basement, pretending to study but really just making the excuse to fuck. You, listening to my rants when my brother got into more trouble. Tending to my bruises when Pops blamed me for the cops showing up to our door again. You, letting me stay nights in your fancy townhouse, hiding in your basement away from your parents."

Mack's hand slips from the bottle, and it's not from the condensation. It's her only show of emotion.

"I didn't care that I was basically an injured raccoon you were trying to nurse back to health and hide from your folks down in your crawl space," I continue. "You helped me, Mack. I didn't escape by myself."

"Wow." Mack licks her lips in thought. "Gotta say, that might be better than an apology."

I lean back against the cushions. "Let's not forget you were also a tasty piece of ass. What made it even better was that you were my dirty little secret at school."

"And there you go, ruining it again." Mack shakes her head in honest disappointment. "I guess I should be thankful you stopped sleeping with Miss Lucas when you started hooking up with me."

I eye Mack over the rim of my glass. "That made you jealous, huh?"

"You were an addiction I couldn't shake. God, you introduced me to things that I … I didn't know my body could do. Of course I wanted you all to myself."

"And now here we are," I say, stretching my arms over my head. "While I still lay claim to being the best lay you ever had, you've probably well surpassed me in the skills department."

Mack stares down at her bottle. "You can't resist bringing that up, can you?"

"I'm not sure you can blame me, considering the sweet, studious Mack in high school has turned into … you."

Mack bows into the cushions behind her, not restful, her upper body curved over her drink like she has to protect it. "I haven't gone bad, Mason. I wish people would understand that."

"You've taken on more risk. Put your life in the hands of strangers. Involved sex with money, which is one of those things that could get you killed."

Mack smiles sadly. "Don't tell me you're concerned."

"If you don't give a shit what I think, what about your pops? Your family? How are they with all this, or have you adopted my dirty little secret for your own?"

"Dad's not really around anymore."

Mack's mom died from cancer when we were kids. It'd be a shame if she lost her dad, too. I say, "He was a decent guy. I'm sorry for your loss."

"He's not dead," Mack says. "We've just … grown apart."

"So he doesn't know?"

"No. He's pretty isolated where he is."

"Where's he at?" I ask. "Did he buy some tropical island with his wads of cash and take his wife to drink Mai Tais the rest of their lives? Why'd they ditch you?"

"He's in jail." Mack finishes her beer in two large gulps.

My drink freezes midway to my mouth. "Say what?"

"Yup. Good old Dad, CFO of a major corporation, embezzled funds to maintain our lifestyle and even participated in a ponzi scheme. He was caught. End of story."

"Uh, I feel like there's more to it than that. Mr. Beckley is a *criminal*? When the fuck did that happen?"

"About halfway through my first semester at Yale."

I scrub a hand down my face as realization sets in. "Ah jeez, Mack."

"Everything was taken, auctioned off, used to convert to funds for restitution to his victims. Everything."

"Including the funds used to pay for your tuition."

"I never got that scholarship," Mack admits. "But it wasn't too concerning, since I figured Dad would be more than happy to pay for my tuition, especially if I also got a job and showed some independence. And I did all of that. What I didn't account for was his inability to hold up his end of the bargain."

I lean forward on my elbows. "Was there any way you could keep going to school?"

She shakes her head in the negative. "I had to drop out. I was left with nothing, barely even the clothes on my back. I had to figure something out, fast, or else I'd be on the streets."

Picturing McKenna Beckley navigating the street world was almost laughable, if it weren't so incredibly sad and almost true. And Jesus—frightening as shit. She wouldn't have lasted. Not for a minute.

Correction: save for the fact she found a lucrative black market career that propelled her back into wealth.

Fuck, I barely know her at all anymore.

"I wish I knew that happened to you," I say. It was around the time Nocturne Court experienced cash flow. "I would've..."

She scoffs, "You would've helped me?"

"Why not? You were there for me during one of the shittier stays of my life."

Mack eyes me warily. "Generosity isn't in your bones, Mason."

"When it comes to you, it would be." I rise from the couch, muscles stiffening with anger. "I wouldn't have left you in the dust, Mack."

She follows my rise and doesn't blink when she says, "You already did. When you left me in the street, you never even turned your head to look back."

My lips thin, and I'm pissed at myself for being the first to break our stare. "I was an idiot back then. I didn't desert you to hurt or punish you. I—"

"You did all of that." Mack pushes to a stand. While on her feet, she barely hits my shoulders, but her presence is heavy and forceful. "And you're doing it now, by proving how much control you still have over me."

I bare my teeth. "Need I remind you, you're here of your own free will. And, might I add, a nice cut of dough. I'm not forcing you to be here."

"I'm not talking about the money. That's my choice to accept. I'm talking about your determination to stop me from doing my job. Or, dare I say it, this ridiculous idea you have to *save* me."

"Because it's not you. That Jane chick you play? She's no one. This isn't who you are, McKenna."

"You have no idea who I am anymore."

"Maybe not, but I know you're better than this. You're not a—"

"A whore? A prostitute?" Mack steps closer. "But I *am*, Mason. Learn to accept that bitter taste in your mouth. That bare-breasted chick you left in a janitor's closet at school became a hooker and she *likes* it."

I rasp, "You're fucking lying."

And my gut sinks at the thought of being the one who damaged her.

"Don't, Mack," I say. "I know where you're going. Don't go down the same hole I had a helluva time digging myself out of."

"That hole, as you describe it, couldn't be farther removed from yours. We've always been different from each other, Mason. Complete opposites. So wrong for one another we should never have met in the first place."

"You really believe that?"

She sets her shoulders, but she's fidgeting with her hands. "I do."

Anger builds up in my chest, so tight it begs for release, but it's what she wants. Mack is goading me with the daring expectation I'll do exactly what she predicts.

Explode.

Say things I can't take back.

Humiliate her.

I step forward and lay my palms on her shoulders. They're

thin and boney under my large grip, fragile as a bird's, but housed in a body forged to withstand eager male hands.

"I'm sorry about your dad," I say. "I really am. And I hate that you lost your placement in college and had to figure out other ways to survive. Without your family. I know what that's like. But I'm not backing down. That money? It's for you to start a new life. Without your alter ego, Jane. Start over, Mack. Be happy."

Stunned into silence, Mack lifts her head and searches my eyes. "Who *are* you right now? You don't rescue women or do things out of the goodness of your heart. You shouldn't care what choices I make or who I make them with. You—"

I cup her jaw. "Don't get it twisted. I'm still a dick." Unable to resist, I stroke the exquisite softness of her cheek. "But you? You've always been better than me and deserved a helluva lot more."

Her breath heats the bottom of my palm, where her lips touch my skin. She doesn't move and neither do I. Not until I lower my head and our noses almost touch. Her chin tilts up, and I take that as an invitation to coax her lower lip into my mouth.

Until Mack pushes me away.

"Unless you're willing to pay extra," she says with a blank, emotionless smile, "you're not getting near my bare skin again. Face it, Mason, the innocent girl you had under you is long gone." Mack backs up until she's at the adjoining door. "And she's not coming back."

I don't move to stop her from leaving. Refuse to say any additional stupid words. I've already said too much.

I just stand there, out of scotch, watching the girl I thought I knew slam a door in my face.

CHAPTER 23

Mckenna

AFTER I SHUT the door to Mason with a satisfying *smack*, I lean against it, covering my face with my hands.

I don't cry. Tears haven't been a part in my life for a long while.

But I heave, my chest filling then concaving, as I try to wrangle my emotions back into line.

Mason shouldn't be able to *pull* at me like this. I can't believe I was that honest with him and told him about my father.

And that I almost told him about Giles.

Giles accepted my offer—a quarter of a million dollars in exchange for my dad's freedom—and I'm still reeling from the reality that I'm making deals with criminals.

It was on the tip of my tongue, where that money was going. It wasn't to start a new life, though it boggles the mind to think Mason could have such a rainbow unicorn view of changing my situation. Almost like he has blinders on—stubborn, brick ones, the same make and model as his brain, where he can't see all the cracks and fractures in his plan. Or refuses to.

Typical Mason. Only makes decisions based on *his* facts, without ever bothering to consider that maybe, offering me a wad of cash and binding me to him for eight weeks isn't enough for me to want to end my career, and then—what? Beg to stay in his arms? Ask to be his roadie for life? What the hell does Mason Payne *want* with me?

But isn't that what you're doing? Throwing hard cash at Giles, then turning your back, hoping it doesn't catch up to you again?

Maybe, except for the very different stakes: one for my life, and the other for my heart.

I push off the door in a huff and step into the bathroom to splash some water on my face. Glancing up at the mirror, I'm deliberately bare. No lip gloss, no mascara, nothing. I haven't dressed nicely since setting foot on Mason's tour, hoping that plain vanilla, regular McKenna Beckley would just bore him to death and he'd lose interest. The girls he wants are glamorous, gorgeous, lithe and confident—a lot like my Jane Landers. His ex, Sorsha Dillon, is a testament to that. Even her *name* brings about a certain awe.

I can't understand why he continues to pursue me.

It's like we're back in my basement and he's touching me for the first time, showing me that despite all the blinking, red, flashing signs saying otherwise, he's the right choice. He's safe.

"There's so much you don't know," I say to my reflection. To him.

I'm keeping so many secrets. Ones he'll hate me for.

History shows just how dangerous he can be.

Yet, I'm still picturing us standing in the middle of Mason's suite, so close, his energy vibrating against my skin. His words testing my barricades. When he stroked my face, he was feeling for faults. Exploring until he found the give in my foundation and cracked it open until it crumbled.

I shut it down before he could.

But I'm aching for that stolen kiss.

♡

The next two weeks is a blur of jet lag, city night-scapes, and foreign sounds. I barely have time between stepping off an airplane, sitting in a car, and making the next hotel my home before we're carted off again.

I don't know how the boys do it, but all four members of Nocturne Court maintain endless stamina and velvet voices, trucking through their tour like true professionals. If they complain about the ache in their arms, they don't say it in public. If their voice boxes hurt, they don't hoarsely call for tea or bourbon. Everything private, all things personal, are done in their quarters, away from the public eye, with the added touch of their closest employees scurrying quietly to gather whatever the rock stars are after.

I once ran into Rex in a hotel hallway—was it in Denmark? Maybe—as he murmured into his phone, his voice taking on a croon reserved only for the love of his life. Rex had a way with his audience, he sets off a spark with the crowd, but nothing compared to the glow blooming across his features when he spoke to his daughter and girlfriend.

I was struck frozen for a moment, one foot in front of the other, while I witnessed the exchange, and my immediate thought was, *is that why he's leaving?* Family?

And Easton, too?

Mason doesn't have that kind of epicenter to walk home to once everyone finishes the tour. He's a loner, always has been, but I always seem to be the only person to notice how *lonely* it makes him.

Nocturne Court is his family.

And they're leaving him.

Rex lifted his head and caught my eye. When his brows furrowed in confusion, I realized my sweet, internal *aww* at the way he melted for his women had turned into impatient anger.

"Just tell him already," I blurted, then scampered off to my room like a person trying *not* to get involved.

But was already so, so deep.

Today will be different, I think as I lift the covers from my body and greet the morning in … I take a quick peek out my window and yep, there's Big Ben, so yes, London is where I'm at, and tie up my hair to grab a quick shower.

The daily schedule's already different. Usually, I accompany the band to rehearsals, press conferences, meet and greets, and the like, becoming a shadow like most of the staff on tour while the boys bask in the spotlight. Mason doesn't make any further moves on me. In fact, he acts cold, distant, and professional to the point that I'm wondering if he really is tiring of my presence and is readying to let me go.

There's been no more attempts to get me to leave my job, not a single brush of a finger against my skin, and barely an attentive wave when I step into his radar. Mason's manipulation is unparalleled, and I'm thinking he's trying some reverse psychology on me. It'll never work, but it's surprising how much I wish for the passionate Mason, even if he was mean and inappropriate. At least then, I know what I'm getting. And how to handle him.

Mason Payne, what are you up to?

This morning, I'm meant to join the band and entire staff for brunch in a reserved ballroom, a treat for everyone's hard work thus far.

At home, I have a very rigid morning routine of preparation, primping and priming. Either pilates, barre method or spin class at 6 AM, a blow-out at my neighborhood salon, waxing of wayward areas not tended to by laser hair removal, before finally, an hour sit-down in front of my vanity, applying the careful guise of Jane Landers before heading out and meeting clients for late afternoon lunches, dinners, and after-parties.

Here, I sleep in, wear my hair in natural long waves (always turning into a tangled, thick mess within forty-five minutes), don't shave, though electrolysis has taken care of most of that, barely tend to my face, and wear leggings and tees more than couture.

It's oddly freeing, and the satisfaction is endless. I'm doing all this, being myself, to the tune of a quarter million dollars, and there's no sex involved. Either Mason is becoming the best client I've ever had, or he's turning into the greatest mistake.

Because I'm getting comfortable.

And that is usually when the danger lurks and Mason's passive circling turns into a bloody bite.

Once out of the shower, I brush on a coat of mascara, pinch my cheeks, and give my hair a quick scrunch with some curl spray, calling myself done in the hair and make-up department. Since it's a nice brunch in the heart of London at a very grand, historical hotel, I opt for a white sundress with lace trim and cream espadrilles for my feet, thankful my last pedicure in NYC is holding up.

When I step out of my suite, I follow the trail of staff to the elevators, passing Mason's room. My ear's perked, but I hear nothing on the other side, not until I'm almost past the door and I catch a quick, high-pitched moan. It's out of tune, almost child-ish, and definitely female.

My stomach lurches. It shouldn't, but it does. My heart throbs unexpectedly, and I tell myself it's because of the money. If he's entertaining himself in other ways, despite putting a hooker on his payroll, then I truly am in trouble.

Mason is fickle, at best. Vindictive, at worse. And pure evil when he's bored.

My dress's pocket vibrates right as I tell my feet to move faster, and I pull it out to read the text.

Private Number: I've changed my mind, darling. I need the money sooner than expected.

. . .

My gut loses another few levels. My fingers tighten on the phone as I debate how to respond, but Giles gets there first.

So sorry, but this isn't a request. 8 weeks is far too long, love. I'm already missing you at 3.

Trembling, I thumb out a response. **I don't have the money yet. But I can get it to you soon.**

Private Number: Did I mention your father is about to have the most terrible accident? So much blood, darling. No one's going to help him, not even the guards. I don't think he'll make it through the night. So, in lieu of your gorgeous body convincing me from doing something I'll regret, please wire the funds immediately.

My breath whistles through my teeth. I hold the phone closer to my face, like proximity will change Giles's threat.

Think McKenna, THINK.

I've dealt with plenty of assholes. Mason gave me the fast-pass in handling volatile men. All I have to do here is calm Giles down and have him rest easy for a few days while I figure out how to get the cash early.

"McKenna? You coming?"

I glance up long enough to see Jess holding the elevators for me with a crowd of about ten behind her in the lift. Her expression makes it clear she'd rather the doors shut in my face, but her loyalty to Mason trumps the petty gesture.

"I-I'm fine. Go without me. I'll meet you down there," I say.

I didn't school my voice enough, because Jess frowns. "You okay? Did you get some bad news?"

"No, yeah. I'm fine. I'll be there shortly."

Jess shrugs one shoulder, her duty of mild concern fulfilled, and releases her grip on the doors. She disappears behind the silver metal sheen.

Standing in the deserted hallway, the luxury carpeting under my feet provides a cloaking effect of sound. Shut doors are muffled. Voices are turned to whispers. Any further moans go unheard.

It's then an idea strikes.

I text Giles, **I can get you half by this weekend.**

Three ellipses pop up as he types a response, and the wait is death-defying. Will Giles accept the offer? It's over a hundred grand, but not the full amount. But it has to be enough. It *has* to keep him off my back and my dad safe. For now.

At last, Giles's response pops up.

Alright, darling. You win. You're lucky you have such a flawless face. That guile of yours reaches me even when you're across the pond. Send me half by Saturday and we have a temporary deal.

I close my eyes and hold the phone against my chest, breathing deeply. *I did it.* My dad is safe for the near future.

A creaking door, a muffled bang, and a resulting giggle draws my attention behind me, down the hallway.

Mason's door opens, and my breath stops halfway as my body instinctually anticipates meeting him. Tightened nipples. Drawn-in stomach. Bobbing throat.

Old habits are hard to break. Even while under threat, I crave a glimpse of him.

Yet, the legs that step out first aren't his. They're bare, golden and long. The body that follows oozes grace and self-assurance, capped off with a shining wave of honey-gold hair. A pert chin lifts up and grass-green eyes meet mine, framed by glass-carved cheekbones.

"Hello," she says to me in a musical voice. She reaches her hand back and draws Mason out of the suite.

He's busy looking at his phone and doesn't see me at first, but when he eventually glances up, when I'm still frozen like Bambi on the ice pond, his brows do an infinitesimal jump.

I shouldn't feel relief that he's fully clothed. Nor should I be focused on the rouge imprint near the corner of his mouth, a perfect facsimile of female lips meeting his skin.

"Oh, hey, Mack," he says. "I thought you'd be downstairs with everyone already."

"You have something on your face," I say, then turn and opt for the stairs.

Horrified, I leave as fast as I can. I've become the reluctant first witness to Mason Payne and Sorsha Dillon, newly reunited, and I don't want to show him that I care.

CHAPTER 24

Mason

BRUNCH ISN'T EXACTLY my thing.

I don't crave it, don't meet friends for it, and frankly, I eat my breakfast before dawn and my lunch after one in the afternoon, and I'm happy with that. I don't need some trendy mash-up that's just an excuse to drink tomatoey or orangey acid with alcohol and talk shit about people you know behind their backs.

I'm explaining all this to Sorsha during our descent to brunch, and she's nodding along, but I'm noticing her lackluster stare as she opens a compact and checks herself out in the mini-mirror.

"I'm boring you," I say, leaning against one elevator wall and crossing my arms.

Sorsha dabs at the corners of her lips, perfecting that dastardly raspberry pink she has on that won't wipe off my cheek unless I use some form of chemical.

"Not at all, babe," she says, moving her profile to and fro in the mirror. She smooths down some baby hairs.

I feel the need to point out the giant mirror behind her, actually a whole wall of it, but I'd rather skip our versions of pleasantries.

"Wanna tell me why you showed up at my door at four in the morning then?" I ask. "Drunk as a skunk?"

Sorsha casts an annoyed look my way. Even with a frown, she's gorgeous. Wide, anime-like green eyes, flawless, spa-maintained skin, gel-plumped lips, and golden hair for days. She's tall and works out about as much as I do, except she uses a trainer that makes her run up staircases and hills before he appreciatively smacks her in the ass and they fuck.

Yeah, they fuck.

It's why I dumped her appreciative ass and haven't seen her in months, yet last night she made it a priority to shove herself back in. She tripped into my suite the moment I opened the door, giggling and smelling like sour champagne, what was once a chic up-do hanging lopsided on one side of her head and smudged mascara trailing down her eyes like a sad noir clown. I righted her with a hand on her arm, and she fell into my chest in tears.

"I-I miss you, Mase," she said, sniffing and garbling. "Oh my God, I miss you. I was at this awards show and I thought, where's my guy? Where's my prince? He's here in the UK and he's not visiting me. Why doesn't he care about me anymore?"

"Because you fuck your staff when you think I'm not looking," I deadpanned as she sobbed into my shirt.

She smacked my pec with a weak hand. "That's a lie. The tabloids told you that."

"No, my own eyes showed me that when I walked in on you in your guest bedroom doing it doggy-style with a guy who's poindexter head doesn't reach your chin."

"You're so crass," she mumbled into my skin, then pushed away, sneering. "Why do I even *like* you?"

The question forced me to think about Mack and the things I did to her. The stuff I'm still doing. "Chicks dig a guy who treats them like shit, I guess."

Though I'm not as triumphant as I once was. It's a pussy

move, to bring a woman to tears. I wished someone had told me that as an eighteen-year-old punk. Would've saved me a lot of shoes being flung at my head, and submitting to hurled insults while their faces crumbled with hurt and heartache.

Ah, Mack. You're the first girl I broke. I'm still thinking of the way you cracked in half and how I was responsible.

I tried shooing Sorsha out the door, but she was too wobbly-eyed and unsteady to go anywhere far. I called down for a separate room, but with Nocturne Court's presence in the hotel, all other rooms were sold out by those clamoring to get a peek at us —press and fans alike. Reluctantly, I opted for the couch and Sorsha took my bed. There were a few drunken sneak-ups once we both went down, when Sorsha crept into the main room, naked, hair tousled, face clean, and while I appreciated the view, all I could think of was Mack next door, asleep in a ratty, over-sized tee, her hair all over the place and sober as a nun.

It didn't matter my dick twitched, anyway, because Sorsha fell dead asleep while climbing on top of me. I carried her back to bed, and that was that.

Except it couldn't end there, now could it? Mack had to be the first witness to Sorsha gliding out of the room, looking to all the world like she spent a satisfying night with her ex. She does that—appears exceptional after a night of heavy drinking and drug-use. It's been embedded in her since she was discovered at sixteen and her agent introduced her to nightclubs, underage drinking, and unlimited lines of coke to keep her entertained off-set.

She's hungry, she says, which is why I thought to order her room service. She ate a few pieces of fruit and declared herself done. I told her of my brunch plans and she looked up at me with a blank stare.

"Babe, I came for a fuck, not a date," she said.

I cock a brow. "Yeah? Well, good. Okay. Then we can part ways."

"Except I didn't get my orgasm."

"It's not coming from me, Sorsh. I gotta go. I'm already late."

Her eyes narrow. "You never pass up an emotionless screw. What's going on?"

"Nothing. I just don't think the timing's right."

"Don't tell me you're hurt over what I did." She laughs. "You're the coldest man I've ever been with. I was trying to get a rise out of you! Boil up some emotion in that brain of yours! My mistake, thinking sleeping with my personal trainer would affect you."

"You and I, we liked trying to piss each other off. We were even angrier in bed. It wasn't good for either of us."

"For you, maybe," Sorsha mumbled, then stood. "I liked how we played together."

This was going nowhere, fast. "Let's go."

She sighed with disappointment, but followed me to the suite's door, then stepped out first, as that's what she does.

Right into the eyeballs of McKenna Beckley.

Something curled in my gut at the sight of her and her expression as it computed who was coming out of my room with me. A snake, rather pleased with itself, coiled and slithered within, waiting for the emotional response to what she'd thought I'd done.

There was nothing. Not even an eyelid twitch. Mack made some comment about the lipstick on my face. Strange disappointment coated my frown when she said that, a foreign feeling at missing the mark when making someone jealous, and it made me uncomfortable.

Then Mack spun around and took the elevator on her own. She didn't hold it for us, and I smiled.

So she *was* affected by Sorsha's presence.

I *tsk-tsk'd* under my breath. "Rude, Mack."

Sorsha glanced over. "Who was that?"

"No one." *Someone.* "C'mon, now we gotta wait for another elevator."

"You're doing that stone-faced thing," Sorsha said as I ushered her forward. Then her expression cleared. "Do you *like* her? That small woman who has the same amount of hair as a toy troll?"

"Don't be mean," I chastised. "That only looks good on me."

So now here I am, in an elevator with my ex, waiting to depart on a lower floor so I don't have to take her to the lobby and face cameras.

Once the floor to the ballroom hits, I peel away from the wall and head out, but Sorsha stops me when she unexpectedly presses up against my chest, and lays her lips on my own.

"I ain't lying," she says as she leans back with a smirk. She's inadvertently fallen into her cockney accent, back when she used to be known as Maggie Dildendorf.

I tend to bring out the traits women hate about themselves the most. I'm still not sure if it's a weapon of mine or a flaw.

"I miss you," she says. "I miss your fucked up ways even more."

I stroke a finger down her cheek. "That's what worries me, darling. Safe travels."

Turning, I leave her in the elevator. She doesn't chase after me and has pulled out her phone and pressed it to her ear as the elevator doors slide shut. Typical Sorsha.

The carpeted hallway's deserted as I make my way to the ballroom, but up ahead I see a flash of leg disappear through a door. A milky, toned calf with a cream ribbon thing lacing up her skin and attached to her sandals.

Mack? Did Mack just witness Sorsha's kiss?

Part of me's delighted with this turn of events.

I'm no idiot—I'm sensing the parallels. Sorsha's need to get a rise out of me to prove I still have feelings for her versus my instinct to push Mack into furious emotion to showcase that yes, I'm still present within her shattered heart.

Hey, nobody said I wasn't as fucked up as my ex.

The banquet brunch is a cacophony of noise when I step in, plates being passed, laughter exchanged, surrounded by the comfort and ease of people who've been around each other twenty-four-seven. The buffet-style food is laid out in the back, and my stomach rumbles as soon as I spot pancakes.

Nodding, waving, but not stopping, I make my way through the tables, grabbing a plate once I'm near the food.

My plate's piled with brunch food by the time I turn to find Nocturne Court's table, where I know Mack will be waiting because I've demanded it. I scan the tables, find my guys and gal, and move to—

Wait a damned minute.

My brother's in my seat beside Mack, his arm thrown around the back of her chair, their heads close together in conversation.

Mack glances up, acknowledges me with some kind of bland slow-blink, then goes back to Brax.

My smile drops.

My strides become a lot more pissed.

My food crashes down next to Brax, and he jumps.

"Jesus, man," he says.

"You're in my seat," I say.

"*Your* seat?"

Wyn gestures to Brax with a fork. "Let him have the table, man. We gotta talk logistics on the next show, anyway."

East leans back, crossing his arms and enjoying the current show. Rex eyes my plate, the pile of food toppled by my firm drop.

"I thought you hated brunch, Mase," he says.

"I dislike the *act* of brunch, not the food of brunch," I snap, then turn back to Brax. "Out. Before I drag you up by your shirt-collar."

"Dang, bro." Brax throws his hands up. "I was only entertaining your girl until you got here."

"I'm not his girl," Mack pipes in, and *there* it is, what I want. The death glare. Not whatever that blank look was when she saw me at the buffet.

"His tour companion, then. Friend buddy." Brax rolls his eyes. "I'm out of whatever you two got cooking."

Brax stands, leaving me, the band, and Mack at the table. I fall into my seat and dig into a stack of pancakes, finding I'm ravenous.

"Active night?" Mack asks wryly.

"Why?" I say through the side of my mouth. "You curious how I spend my nights with a woman?"

"Not in the least." Mack pushes a sad, bruised strawberry around her plate.

I smile while open-mouth chewing. "Uh-huh."

"Ugh," she says. "Learn some manners."

I swallow, then lean into her ear. "Decorum isn't part of the package when I'm focused on playing the notes of a body. Stroking, strumming, until I use that rhythm to make us both come. Preferably at the same time." I steal her strawberry. "Remember how that was?"

The color on her cheeks tells me she does.

I smile and lean back.

"We should have more studio time after the tour," Wyn's saying. "I think Mase is inspired to actually write these days."

I slide my gaze over to Mack who steadfastly ignores me. "My muse is rather stunning, I'll admit."

Mack's jaw locks, but she says nothing as she picks up her OJ. In fact, she seems to be glaring at Rex.

"Yeah, Rex," she says. "Shouldn't you guys be booking studio time for your next album?"

Rex pauses in his chewing, and suddenly I'm witness to a

random stare-down between my tour-campanion-friend-buddy and my lead singer.

"We still need to sort that out," Rex says.

"Oh, really? Now seems to be a good time," Mack says, then motions around the table. "Everyone's here."

"Spinner's not," Rex says, referring to our manager. "He's the one who has our calendar. And I'll thank you to butt out of our business, Mack."

"Hey." My tone whiplashes across the table. "Don't talk to her like that."

Rex shoots me a look. "Ah, don't don the shining armor, Mase. It's not a good look on you."

"Don't patronize me," I say. "Mack has a point. Why haven't we booked studio time? We always do in the middle of a tour. To get our schedules straight once we hit home."

"We're delayed this time, okay?" Rex says. "It's not a big deal. East, back me up, man."

I'm looking between Rex and East, trying to figure out what their silent exchange means. Or their random team-up.

"Boys," I say carefully. "What's going on?"

"Dude, nothing," Easton says. "Quit it with all the sensitivity training."

Mack makes an annoyed sound in her throat. Her fork clangs against her empty plate. "Can I talk to you privately, Mason?"

Rex's head jerks back up. Easton goes still. And Wyn ... Wyn reaches over and steals one of my pancakes.

"I guess," I say, and stand, whipping my cloth napkin locker room style at Wyn's face before throwing it across my plate.

"Great," she says and pushes out of her chair.

"Mack..." I hear Rex say.

She tosses him a closed-mouth smile. Whatever's going on with them, it's weirding me out. Makes me think I'm missing something. It's not sexual, whatever it is. Rex would never jeopardize his relationship with Harper, but...

"What's going on?" I ask Mack.

She responds my grasping my forearm and dragging me out of the ballroom. Once we're in the hallway, she finds an emergency exit, and we go through, walking up one floor until we're at the base of the next staircase and settled in quiet privacy.

"What do you have going on with Rex?" I ask again.

Mack makes a sound of disgust. "If you think for one second that I'm banging Rex on the side—"

"Actually, no. Didn't think it for a nanosecond."

She bites her tongue. "Oh. Well. Good. But enough about Rex, or your band, though you should do some sorting out there."

"Why?"

"Mason, I don't have time for—" Mack's expression flickers like she's warring with what to say. Then she takes a breath. "Look. You said yourself there's distance growing with some of the members of Nocturne Court. Most especially Rex. Explore that, okay?"

I screw up my face. "*Explore* that? What are you, Therapist Mack, now?"

"Just—just figure your shit out, if this band means so much to you."

I respond without hesitation. "This band is everything to me."

Her lashes flutter. She says softly, "Then talk to your bandmates more. And not with crude jokes or sideswipes or whatever you guys do. Take it seriously."

"Here we go. Don't tell me you pulled me aside to talk about my perceived immaturity levels and how I've never grown out of the little boy that could. You still got that tag on me, huh? I'm still the guy you think you can improve—"

"I don't want any of that." She waves me away, and I'm oddly insulted at her dismissal despite hating her tendency to never believe I'm good enough. "I'm only judging by what I see, and you guys aren't as close as you were starting out. That's all I'm saying."

"Uh-huh. Well. Thanks for your observation." I cross my arms. "Anything else?"

Mack squares her shoulders. "You and Sorsha."

Both corners of my mouth tilt up slowly. "So you *do* feel something about that."

"It didn't sit well with me, but not in the way you're thinking." She scrapes her hair back, a habit I'm finding I'd like to do to her myself. Before licking down her neck and scraping my teeth against her breasts.

"Then what?" I add, because I'm an asshole, "You're looking pretty close with Brax, anyway."

"I—what? God, Mason." She throws her hands against her hips. "Can you stop being so infuriating?"

"No."

"Just because I do what I do, doesn't mean I throw myself at any male specimen for cash. Not Brax, not Rex, and *not you*—"

I cock my head. "Why not? Isn't that your business model?"

"*Aargh*." She points a finger into my chest. "You are such a son of a bitch."

"It's not like I try to hide it."

"I don't want Brax. I don't want Rex. And I don't want you, okay? I'm only trying to keep to our agreement so I can walk away with the money you promised."

A tiny bubble of bitter acid pops near my ribcage at her matter-of-factness. She can't possibly mean that. There's something between us.

I'm boring holes into her forehead with my stare, but she spars with verbal swords. "You're just mad I didn't react to you and Sorsha getting back together."

"Correction. We're not together."

"Fine, screwing, then. Whatever. My point's still made—I

don't care who you decide to be with. I'm only here because of an offer I can't refuse, and that's a whole lotta *cash*."

I clench my jaw. Work it back and forth. Try not to rage against what is fast becoming an infuriating argument.

But she's not done. "See, Mase, you keep thinking I'll realize this changed man and suddenly decide that he's the one to save me. But when I look at you, I still see a broken boy." She steps up, and I don't back down. "One who destroys his toys because he likes being surrounded by ruin. These days, you collect broken things, like me, thinking you can rebuild them the way you want, but let me tell you, I am not looking to be put back together again, especially by you. In fact, I want some of that money you promised me, in my hands, right now."

To hide the staggering shock, I offer a quick, venomous smile. "I don't buy it, Mack. This whole cold hard cash chick standing in front of me."

"I want half. Especially after seeing you with your ex this morning."

"Ah. It all makes sense now. You're jeal—"

"Don't insult me. I'm afraid of history repeating itself. You're vindictive Mason, and cruel when you want to be, and because I'm not doing what you want, I'm afraid you're going to punish me for it."

"Even if I wanted to, I wouldn't. There's a contract."

"Paper has never stopped you. You'd happily set fire to our agreement in a hot second if it meant you could get the satisfaction of seeing me crumble. So give me half of what I'm owed. Right now. I promise I'll stay on for the next five weeks, but I demand some kind of assurance. Tangible *proof* that you're not going to Mason me the way you did in high school."

"*Mason* you?"

"Yes. Leave me high and dry. Kick me off the tour because you're bored. Because you're an asshole." Her voice takes on a beggar's edge that I don't think she notices. "Please, Mase. Give me this failsafe. Then you can find any girl you want and sleep with them all day long for all I care."

Balls of coal smolder in my belly, awaiting their fire. Mack flings these words, sneering, her entire body language indicating she can't stand the sight of me. I'm ready to prove her wrong.

"Fine. You can have the money."

Her brows pinch together. "Thank you."

"On one condition."

Her forehead smooths, like she was expecting a catch all along.

I invade her personal space, and this time, she doesn't back away. Her gaze glitters with challenge.

"I hate this," I say, so close to her lips, my voice becomes a rasp. "It pisses me off you have such a concrete view of me. But you know what? Every *bit* of me wants to prove you fucking right."

She snorts. "Typical. If someone thinks you're a dick, you might as well spray your dickness all over them, right? Why bother trying to change their minds?"

This is the moment. The time I've been craving, when I unleash my most lethal smile.

"You can have the money," I say, "If you give me Jane."

Mack falters. Her legs lose their stiffness and she presses against the stair's railing as if she meant to all along. She says carefully, "I don't follow."

"Don't play dumb, Mack. It's not in your DNA. You come to my room tonight, and you come as Jane Landers. And I get to do with you as I please."

Her mouth works. Mack's eyes flit back and forth, everywhere but at me. "I don't think that's a good idea."

"It's the best damn idea I've had since signing you on to this tour. I'll be the asshole you've never shaken off, and you be the hooker you keep telling me you love embodying. Let our alter egos rule." I smile. "And let us fuck. You're gonna work for your advance."

Green fire explodes in her eyes. "How *dare* you."

I laugh, but with a warning. "You want half the cash upfront? You do your job, and you do it well." I tip her chin up with my finger. "After all, you keep telling me how much you covet this job, how you'll never leave it. And you've absolutely fucked clients a lot less appealing than me. So show me, Mack. Show me what it's like to fuck without feeling, since it's only ever been one-sided for me. Give me the best fucking client experience you've ever come up with."

"If you do this…" she whispers fiercely. "If you do this, I'll hate you. During the gap in time where I didn't see you for ten years, I've been nothing but coolly indifferent toward you. I'd see you on TV or online and think *nothing*, because that's how I decided to view you after high school. But now?" Mack angles so our faces come closer, like two tigers in a cage. "I'll do it, but I'll despise you for it. And I won't ever forget the way you used me and my body to prove a fucking point."

I bow so our foreheads almost touch, then say, quietly and simply, "Good."

I drink up her silence, then storm off, my boots clanging against the metal as I take the stairs and throw open the emergency exit.

Mack's been goading me since the night I found her in a luxury hotel lobby. I'm tired of fighting it. So I'll give her what she wants.

What she constantly dares.

She wants to see the old Mason so bad? Well, he's more than happy to greet her.

CHAPTER 25

Mason

Night falls with little fanfare.

We didn't have a concert this evening, instead taking an extra twenty-four hours to rest up in London and give our staff the day off after treating them to brunch. I spent the afternoon tuning my bass guitar, raiding the mini bar, avoiding the more elaborate ruses by fans to sneak up to our floor, and thinking of McKenna.

No. Jane.

Tonight, I ordered her to be the sex kitten she profits from, because I'm a curious man. Calling her the opposite of who she was in high school doesn't come close to what she's become. Where is the girl who kept caring, no matter how many spiked chains I threw her way? What happened to replace the sweet, married, 2.5 children, corporate woman I thought she'd become?

And why the fuck do I care?

There was a time I couldn't prevent droplets of compassion from sinking into my blood upon being around her. No matter how hard I tried, and insulted, and fought, she stood her ground, and I respected that. But the dilution wasn't enough to drown the hate of my childhood, my circumstances, my life. My black-ink hatred was fueled by other people's distaste and judgment, the automatic brush-off of such a screwed up kid.

Mack's hatred of me satisfied my hunger most of all.

These days, most of my working parts want her to keep hating me.

I'm sipping on scotch in a complementary crystal glass, gazing out the window at the foreign skyline, when I hear a knock on the door.

Turning, I check the clock. She's fifteen minutes late, but I assume that's deliberate. A show of power, what little she has of it.

"Come in," I say, and head to a sofa chair. I sit, crossing my leg at the ankle, and sip from my scotch in the gloom.

The door creaks open, golden light spilling into my suite from the hallway and outlining a shadowed, curvaceous form. I've deliberately left the lights off in the room, relying on the backlit city and keen vision as my strongest senses.

"Stop," I say.

Mack, or this Jane, halts in the small foyer, the door slowly shutting behind her and taking all the gold shimmer with it.

But it's enough light to glimpse her smooth angles and flawless beauty.

She'd smoothed her hair to the point that it falls iron straight, down past her breasts. Her eyes are lined in black kohl, a prominent framing of the jade in her eyes. Her brows are perfect arches, her shoulders bare, save for a smattering of light freckles I know belong to Mack, and she wears a tight, simple black dress that probably costs more than a night in my suite.

Porcelain shaped legs stand at an angle, her black pumps lifting and muscling her calves. Her bare arms hang by her side.

The last piece of her I note is the scarlet of her lips. Slightly parted, not upturned or downturned, but lined with grim acceptance.

"Take it off," I say in the dark.

The crack below the door allows me to see her shift, lift the straps of her dress, and slide her arms through. She shimmies out of it without a word, and I wonder, with the way her chin juts out at my request, how long she'll give me the silent treatment.

She won't win.

"Come to me," I say, lying in wait.

Her heels remain on, the soft clips of her shoes the only sound as she walks, hips swaying, in black lingerie.

I salivate at the sight of her. My tongue is desperate to dip into her and lick, taste, and suck until she becomes a part of my blood again, but I refrain from any movement, other than sipping my drink.

"Turn."

She does, the full view of her rump a mere arm's length away. Her g-string is as thin as the laces on my dress shoes, her cheeks rounded, plumped, and raised.

I bare my teeth, wanting a bite.

"Your hair," I say. "Put it over one shoulder."

She shows me her profile as she uses a slim hand to brush the silk of her hair to one side, showcasing the line down the middle of her back, the clasp of her bra.

Even cast in shadow, she's sexier than any woman, more alluring than any top-shelf scotch, and probably angrier than a bag of feral cats as she does exactly what I instruct.

"Bend over," I order.

Her shoulders stiffen into sharp angles of pride. Mack wants to rip my head off, but Jane knows the rules.

She bends over, her hands resting on the glass coffee table.

Her ass just became a lot more delectable.

"Spread your legs."

She does, but her head remains rebelliously high.

I dip my index finger in my whiskey, then bring it up to her exposed folds. As soon as I touch her, I hiss in a breath.

She's soaking wet. Swollen. Fucking delightful.

I trace her with my finger, sinking in only by a digit, then retreating.

Mack tries to hide it, but I note the trembling in her knees. It's not from the strain of holding her position.

"Let me ask you something," I say, my voice tight. My cock strains against my pants, demanding its due.

She doesn't respond.

"When you fuck a client, do you ever come?"

Still, she says nothing.

"Do they ever pleasure you so hard and fast your head spins? Do you let them take your control, fill all your holes, and scream from multiple orgasms? Or..." I dip my finger again, then idly trace the outside of her folds before moving her thong aside and circling her clit. She shudders. "Do they disappoint you so deeply that you go home afterwords and fill yourself with your fingers, fuck yourself into oblivion?" I smile. "After tonight, I'll make sure it's the image of my face, my cock, that you finger-fuck to."

Despite the goading, she doesn't answer. I don't expect her to. No, she's a pro.

I lower my head, using the darkness like a curtain as I lean forward and say, "It's nice to finally meet you, Jane."

And I indulge in a whiskey tasting.

♡

McKenna

I hear him behind me, shifting. A brush of clothing, a lifting from the seat.

I stay where I am, hip jutted out uncomfortably, preferring to face the wall than stand in front of Mason in full, *come fuck me* attire, the dark silhouettes of our environment creeping across his face as he sits, still as stone, and directs me to pose in front of him.

Tries to get me to break character.

Heckles and pushes, then, when that doesn't work, traces my delicate area with the penmanship of a cursive writer.

It's why I gasp when his finger disappears and his hot mouth hits my core. Mason's tongue spears the most sensitive part of me, and I buckle, my head falling low, my teeth biting down on any moan that wants to escape.

I push against his lips, asking for more even as my brain demands I straighten and saunter away. My fingers twitch like they want to reach behind and tangle in his hair. My hips join the dance of his tongue and the suck of his lips around my clit as he coaxes, beckons, *summons* me to come—

A dry, calloused hand grips my shoulder, brings me to a stand, and spins me around. A hungry mouth hits mine and parts my lips, exploring as though he has a right to, tasting of alcohol and me.

He cups my face with both hands, his thumbs caressing my cheeks so softly compared to the duel of his tongue in my pussy, stroking and sucking. He's taking me like I'm property, like I'm *his*, and my damn head falls back to let him plunder.

Holding back a moan, I grip his biceps, but I'm not pushing him away or snarling at the audacity of his stolen kiss. Because I'm not Mack. I can't be.

I'm Jane, and he's nothing but my next client.

Stay cold.

Remain calculated.

Don't betray me, heart.

His tongue strokes against mine, then, when I gasp for air, claims my breath.

Mason lifts me by the thighs, directing my legs to circle his torso as he continues to own my mouth, and walks us to the bed.

I fall against the mattress first, with him on top of me. His erection presses against my slit, so thick behind his jeans, hard and grinding. He moves in circles, but I refuse to moan again. I won't. My body can experience the pleasure. I'll even let it reminisce about the old days, like the first time Mason Payne's fingers stroked me to ecstasy.

My mind, however, will stay my own. He won't take it, or claim it, or make me weak with second-guesses and *what ifs.*

This is nothing but a transaction with a fool. A man who thinks he can take what he wants, especially if he's told he can't have it.

It's not until he elicits a moan that I realize, despite the cloak of protection I've put around my mind, my body is betraying me. My clit is so swollen, it's begging for the lace to be ripped so there's no longer anything between Mason and me.

Breaking our kiss, Mason rises on his hands so he's hovering above. "Take off your bra."

I open my eyes, and despite having them closed for so long, he's set in stark relief. The slashes of cheek bone. Eyes remaining the color of daylight despite the surrounding night. Strands of hair falling down his forehead. And the bunched muscles of his shoulders and arms, coiled and ready to spring. His arms are stronger than I remember, bumps and ridges undulating beneath his skin, his strength seeping out in testosterone-fueled waves.

He'd lost his shirt. When did he take off his shirt?

"Look at me," he says.

I am. My eyes score every inch of him, except for his stare.

"I said, *look at me.*"

I don't.

"Mack—"

I clench my abs, lift up, and wrap my legs around his waist, using my strongest muscles to flip us around so he's on the bottom and I rise to the top.

My hair goes everywhere and I swoop it to one side, sitting on him, taking control, and initiating my own rhythm.

Mason groans beneath me. I grind harder. I'm building to orgasm despite our remaining clothing, and I bite my lower lip as I rub against his denim and take myself there.

"It's Jane," I say to him. "You don't get to call me anything else."

His hands grip my hips, fingers digging into my skin as he tries to direct the flow to better stroke his dick.

I peel the straps of my bra off, not all the way, but so they dangle against my arms and showcase more breast. Then I remove his hands.

"This is her time," I say through my sharp breaths. "Not yours."

"Oh, yeah?" Mason says, the muscles in his stomach contracting. "'Cause you still look like the girl who begged me to fuck her in high school. There ain't no Jane here. Just my Mack."

I lift up to my knees so I can undo his jeans and release him. His dick springs out, hot, hard and swollen. I feel like if I even graze it with my fingers, I'll send him over the brink.

Mason's breathing between his teeth as he looks on.

I grip his cock and hold it against my sex. Its tip nearly hits my belly-button, and I stroke, up and down, letting the lace of my underwear cause more friction on one side, more delayed pleasure.

Mason throws back his head, the muscles in his neck bulging as he groans.

"This is what you want," I say, then shimmy down until it's my mouth against his tip instead. "So ... this is what I'll give."

Eyes closed, I embody the Jane I've refined over the years when my lips first circle his shaft. I think back to the first time I held a stranger's dick and sucked it for money. Convince myself it's no different to what I'm doing right now. I shouldn't remember this particular cock and how it was my first ... everything. It gave me my first orgasm, quickly becoming the organ that I wanted to replace my fingers for the rest of time. It tastes the same, too—amazing how I remember that. Salty, sweet, scented with raw male—

I scrunch my eyes shut. Picture someone else. A regular. A new client. Anyone but Mason as I twist and squeeze and bring about throaty groans from my subject.

I'll stick to my talents. The ones I've crafted to perfection. The sucking and cupping and swirling. The grazing of teeth against his most sensitive areas. The wicked smile I toss his way before flicking my tongue rapidly across his tip, causing his hips to grind, his hands to tangle in my hair and direct my head lower, my mouth adapting to the sudden deep throat.

Tears prick in the corners of my eyes, but with them closed, I can hide the pain.

None of it is real, and heart, if you're still listening, this is what makes me break.

"Fuck..." Mason growls, his hands now bunching the sheets as he splays out, receiving my artwork with utter abandonment.

His dick pops out of my mouth and I crawl back on top of him, sliding my underwear off, and he watches every movement as I re-position and hold him against my slit and rub, back and forth, until he's slick with me.

"Jesus—" Mason starts to say, but when my folds take him in and I slide all the way down excruciatingly slow, he has no words left.

God, he feels good. It feels *so* good. No one fills me the way Mason does, and the tiny moan that escapes my lips is mine alone. I start the pace, giving my clit what it wanted so badly. My heart may be in pain, but my body's aiming for pleasure, and I can't resist the gorgeous male specimen beneath me from helping me get there.

In the brief moment I've relinquished control, Mason uses it. He flips us again and he's on top, pushing in hard, harder, but not so painfully that it hurts. I want him deeper. I lift my hips to tell him so and Mason doesn't disappoint.

Our skin smacks together, our friction building the kind of heat I haven't experienced in *years*. My nails scrape across his back and the part of me still functioning rationally is glad I get to mark him.

We build to orgasm together, our faces close, but still so distant. I vaguely hear him continue to coax, "Look at me. Goddammit, *look* at me," but I don't listen.

I bury my face in his neck when I come, when I clench around him and soak him in orgasm. When I shiver with electric shock and my nails dig deeper into his skin.

My hair provides the extra coverage I need when we both shudder with release and the rhythm stops.

Mason's heavy on top of me, but it's not suffocating. It's warm, and firm, a body that covers and protects me fully.

It's why I have to get out from under. Now.

"Wait—" Mason says as I twist out of his hold and our connection is broken.

"It's over," I say, pleased with how cold I sound. I didn't think I had it in me after experiencing him inside me again.

I scoot to the side of the bed, digging around the floor for my underwear, then stand and find my dress.

"You serious?" Mason sits up in bed, unabashed, his dick on full display.

"Are you satisfied?" I counter.

"Well, yeah. That was ... fuck, Mack. Where'd you learn half that stuff?"

The lights from the city outside highlight his expression enough that I notice the wrinkles in his forehead as he answers that question for himself. He then tries a different tactic. "You can hang out here, you know. We can order up some food. I know I could use a fucking stiff drink."

I finish pulling the dress's straps over my shoulders. "I don't linger after sex with clients. And that's what this was. Sex. Fuck-ing. You paid for my skills and you got them. So it's time for me to go back to my own room, eat my own food, then go to sleep in my own bed."

A moment passes where nothing is said between us. Nothing containing words, at least, since Mason's stare takes all of me in, tries to process, then concludes he doesn't know shit right now.

"After everything that just happened…" Mason pauses, shaking his head. "Now. Now is when you choose look at me."

"Now is when all is said and done," I retort, then head to the door.

"Mack, please. Wait."

I freeze with my hand on the door handle. "No. You don't get to do this. You *used* me tonight, Mason. You took our history and you threw it in my face when you demanded I come to you as Jane. Maybe you were curious, maybe you finally wanted the chance to see what it's like to fuck an escort, but either way, you didn't see me as Mack. You didn't *treat* me as me. And you did it purposefully."

Mason pulls the sheet around his waist. "Wait a damn minute—"

"You never think of the consequences," I say on a hollow laugh. "Like what it would do to force me into my alter ego so I could screw and pleasure you senseless. All you saw was control. Power. *Manipulation.* Your trifecta of habits that never ceases, no matter how much older you become. It never occurred to you how much that would hurt me, did it?"

His furrowed expression smooths, becomes blank, then abject realization hits. "Mack, that's not what I meant to do. I wanted you to face this. To understand that you don't *have* to be this Jane Landers you've crafted. I wanted you to become so immersed in us that you'd lose the mask and become Mack. It's why I wanted you to look at me while I was inside you. I wanted to bring you back, McKenna."

I scoff. "Bullshit. This was a power move, to prove to me who's the boss—"

Mason's mouth twists fiercely. "Yeah, fine, it started out that way. I'm not gonna lie—you pissed me off, and—"

"And what's the first thing you do when a toy isn't doing what you want? You break it. Destroy it so no one else can have it."

"That's not—fuck." Mason scrubs a hand over his face. "Fine. My temper fucks me over a lot. But with this ... when we ... Mack, when we were together just now, I couldn't stay angry. Only you've been able to do that and I didn't think you still had that power, but here we are. You stripped me bare. That couldn't have been Jane. That was you. It was *you* in that bed with me just now."

My cheeks ache with held-in tension, but I can't let his words convince me. He's too good at it, too talented at twisting the situation so he comes out clean. "You forced me under contract to appear tonight. This wasn't emotion, and it certainly wasn't love. It was like I really was a prostitute to you. It's what you saw me as. What you *bought*. Well, you got what you paid for." I throw the door open. "Not everything goes your way just because you changed your mind."

"Mack, wait. Listen to me. I didn't want to hurt you, I wanted to bring you *back*," he repeats, and the rough honesty in his voice can't be ignored.

But it can be shut out.

I slam the door behind me.

CHAPTER 26

Mason

I DON'T SLEEP.

I spend the rest of the night back in that sofa chair, stewing over a few glasses of scotch. I'm not a smoking man, otherwise I would've gone through a pack and a half of cigs. I *am* the occasional joint man, but searching through my luggage brings me no luck (damn international travel) and I'm not in the mood to interrupt Wyn and whoever his conquest is to see if he has any weed.

Alcohol swiftly becomes the only mind-altering soother I can find, and make no mistake, I relish the taste as I watch the coming morning bloom through the windows, the burned orange sun phasing to bright yellow as it rises and sends its peachy, reflective rays into my once comfortably numb and gloomy room.

Plans with Mack backfired. Harking back to the asshole she once fell in love with didn't work out so well. Shifting gears mid-screw and treating her like a sex goddess didn't go so hot, either.

The bed's still unmade since we were in it, the sheets tangled and pillows twisted. *Fuck*, that wasn't the Mack I remembered, with her mind-blowing skill and confidence, the way she circled her hips and how she clenched my cock … but perhaps that's the point.

She thinks I used her, when in fact I was only trying to find her again.

Standing against the window, I tip the bottle to my mouth and glug. *Too bad I lost her years ago.*

After last night, hell, even before, there's no way she'll listen to me. Mack's made her choices, and I guess my work is done. I've failed her.

Glug.

Pounding at my door shocks me to the point that a dribble of scotch runs down the corner of my mouth as I drink from the bottle.

Frowning, I turn to the door. The pounding stops, but after the *beep* of an unauthorized keycard, the door shoots open and Jess storms inside.

"Do you want to explain *this*?" she says, holding her tablet up with the screen facing me, her brown eyes wide with anger behind her glasses.

"Dude." I gesture at her with the half-empty bottle. "What the fuck time in the morning is it? How are you in my room? And what's with the key I didn't know you had?"

"You don't get to ask the questions. *I do.* Read this article, Mason." Her gaze lands on the bottle dangling in my hand, then rakes me up and down. "That is, if you're not too morning-sauced to see words. How much have you had?"

"None of your fucking…" I'm striding toward her as I say it, but trail off as the bold print on her tablet becomes visible.

MASON PAYNE FEELS THE PAIN WITH NEW MADAM.

· · ·

"And this." Jess pounds at the screen without even having to look at it, and scrolls down, her fingers sliding along the edge of the glossy screen so I can see more.

MASON PLAYING HOOKER WHILE ON TOUR.

PAYING FOR SEX IS THE NEW NAUGHTY NOCTURNE

NOCTURNE COURTS A LADY OF THE NIGHT

I inhale deeply as Jess keeps scrolling ... and scrolling ... and scrolling. "Well."

"Well? *Well?* That's all you have to say for yourself?"

"Well," I repeat. "The press isn't very original, are they? Or creative. Except for maybe the last one."

"*Mason!*" Jess screeches. "Take this seriously. McKenna Beckley is a *prostitute*?"

I flick one more millisecond of attention onto Jess's screen, then shrug. "So?"

Jess's mouth drops. "You are certifiable, you know that? How could you bring a hooker on tour?"

I toss the bottle of scotch on the bed, no longer acquiring a taste for it. "Maybe because I don't give a shit."

"You may not care about your reputation," Jess says, her finger springing forward and landing against my chest. "But give some modicum of respect to your band's rep. Or your staff. Or this entire tour that's cost us millions of dollars. Your label's already breathing down my neck at this news. So are your managers, and agents, and anyone else with a Google alert on your ass."

My eye tics, the only sign of stress I'm willing to show. "Has anyone spoken to Mack? Is she all right?"

Jess ignores me. "We are in the *middle* of a worldwide tour! If tickets suffer because of this, you are in loads of trouble, you understand? You'll have to find the lost funds somewhere. And we can't, let me stress again, we *cannot*, fumble this tour. It's the most important—" Jess claps her mouth shut, then shakes her head at me on a growl. "You've sunk to low depths before, Mason, but this is a new level of sludge."

I say, after taking a minute to control my snap of temper, "I've been willing to entertain your rampage thus far, Jess, but you're toeing the line. You are my employee. Insult me all you want, but don't you dare go near McKenna. You do *not* have the freedom to insult my guest."

Jess laughs, but there's no mirth behind it. "You had me draw up a contract for this." Jess throws her hands against her head. "You've made me culpable in this. Goddamnit, Mason! What if the cops get involved? Hiring a hooker is illegal. What if you go to jail? Then this tour really is done and your band—"

"*Enough*," I snap. "Calm down. You're acting like I've murdered someone for chrissakes. Mack is a childhood friend—"

"Who is a call girl. I made you a *contract* for sex!"

I hold up a hand. "No, you did not. She was never accompanying me as an escort, so everybody take an Oxy already. As I said, she's a friend, she's here as a friend, and what she does in her spare time is none of anybody's damn business."

"When you hired her on as your 'friend,' you took her right to privacy away," Jess says. "The whole world now knows who she is and the press will be relentless if she stays on with us. You have to cut her loose, Mason."

I respond without hesitation. "Absolutely not."

"You don't get a choice in the matter. The higher ups demand it, and hell, Mason, grab some awareness that doesn't involve yourself and do it for your band. This could really damage Nocturne Court, and it worries me how little you care."

My fists clench along with my jaw and I pace the room, feeling caged. "I care. Mack's on this tour because I *care*. And if the guys want an explanation so bad, where are they now? Why is it only you coming in here like a bull in heat screaming Nocturne Court's ruin?"

Jess sighs. "Because I'm the only one you'll listen to. The rest of the guys ... they gave up reasoning with you a long time ago."

My brows scrunch together. "What kind of bullshit talk is that? You all had a meeting already? Without me?"

Jess doesn't deny it. "It's been agreed that McKenna has to go. Immediately. We'll give her the funds as promised—so long as you swear on that long-swinging dick of yours that it's not in exchange for sex—we'll get her on a plane home."

"I said no."

"You've been out-voted, Mason."

"Are you serious? A fucking quorum has decided who I can bring on tour with me? What's next? No emotional support animals allowed?"

"No one's trying to screw you over. We're trying to save you."

"Save me?" I laugh, loud and open-mouthed, my chin tipped to the ceiling. "That's fucking rich. What about the girls Spin makes sure are in our dressing rooms after shows and all the NDAs they have to sign? What about the escort service I know he has on speed dial that Wyn hits up regularly? What about all those, huh? How is Mack the bad one, here?"

"Well," Jess says softly, holding the tablet against her stomach. "If that's all true—"

"You *know* it fuckin' is."

"Then all I can say is, decorum. Under the radar. On the down-low. All the words that mean it's kept from the public eye. You've been outed, Mason. That's the problem. Not Mack."

If it weren't for the disgusted look on Jess's face, I might believe her. "The only people that knew about Mack was me and—"

I stop talking the instant another person's name hits me smack in the forehead.

"Goddammit," I mutter. "God-fucking-damnit."

"Mason, where are you going?" Jess spins around as I storm past her and toss open the hotel door. "Mason!"

I don't listen. I don't feel her pulling at my arm, or pressing her palms against my chest to stop me.

I'm too hellbent on punching my best friend in the face.

♡

The side of my fist cracks against the door to Rex's suite. When there isn't an answer as soon as I would like, I turn to Jess.

"You got a spare stolen key on you? Or was that goodie just for my room?"

"I'm *your* assistant," Jess retorts. "Therefore, I only get access to you. Can we go back to your room now? We need to talk about this."

"Nope."

Crack-crack-crack. I'm willing to keep doing this until either someone answers or I beat the door down.

"Jesus Christ!" The door opens with my arm mid-swing and Rex stands on the other side, clothed and showered. He wrinkles his nose at the sight of me. "Mase, you smell like a sour keg—"

I elbow past him and swoop the door shut before Jess can wriggle her way in.

This guy's my friend. We've been through some thick shit together. I try to remember that as I seethe, my knuckles aching to punch, in his small foyer.

"You leaked it to the press?" I ask.

"Huh?"

"Mack. What she does. You sold the story to the press?"

Rex's brows shoot up to his hairline. His neck flushes red in the V of his open-collared white shirt, but experience tells me it's not from embarrassment.

It's from rage.

I step up to him.

"Bro, you better fall back," Rex says, "before one of us does something we regret."

"Pretty sure that's already happened. I was just railroaded by Jess about the media getting a hold of Mack's occupation, and the only people who knew about it were me, her, and *you*." I jam my finger into his chest to enunciate my point, and he flicks it away on a growl.

"You know what I'm gonna do?" Rex says as he falls back and strides further into his room. "I'm going to pretend you're not accusing me of betraying you, the friend I've had close to twenty years despite all your shit and your shitty temperament and your generally shitty nature."

I spread my hands wide. "Why are you friends with me then, bro?"

Rex spins on his heel and points. "Because I *love* you, you fuckin' prick! How do you think it feels to have you barge in here accusing me of outing Mack's secret? Why would I do that to her? To you? It's fucked up, man, but it's not because of me."

I ask quietly, "Was the voting because of you?"

Rex exhales heavily. "The what?"

"I'm told a consensus was reached to vote Mack off the island for reasons of cleaning the tarnished reputation of Nocturne Court. And that you were part of it." I scratch the side of my head in mock confusion. "Or is that another baseless accusation?"

Rex's throat bobs. "Now that it's out, Mack has to leave. A part of you must know that. She can't stay on. She'll be harassed, and so will we. You know she's already getting death threats?"

I raise my head. "Mack knows this is going on? It's six in the morning! Who got to her before me—"

Rex shakes his head. "She doesn't know yet. The letters and emails were intercepted by both the hotel staff and our people. But it's only a matter of time, Mase. For her safety, she needs to go."

"Don't pretend this is all being done in her best interest," I remark. "This is for the good of our brand."

"Is that a bad thing?"

"Ah, fuck all of you." I flick my hand, dismissing him and heading to the door. "If it were your girl who was going through this, or Easton's wife, none of this would be happening. Security would circle, sharks would be laid in our waters, and no one would fucking get near them. But because it's Mack, and she's not as pure and clean as your women—"

"Watch your words, man."

"She gets left behind. Because she's not good enough, amirite?"

Rex searches my face, despite being ten feet away. "As far as I know, Mack's not your girl. She's someone you brought along with you, either for her protection or your entertainment or who the fuck knows what—that's your business. But the point is, it's no longer private. It's the public's. And we have to take the steps needed."

"Without my input."

"Mase, let me ask you something." Rex moves closer. "Are you angry because you think we believe Mack isn't good enough for us, or are you pissed because you think *you're* not good enough for us?"

I sneer in response. "I don't need this shit."

Rex digs his hands into his hair, but he won't break our stare. His jaw moves like he's working up nerve.

"If you're gonna go all Dr. Phil on me," I say, "might as well go all the way. Spit it out, man."

Rex sweeps his arm out. "Can we sit?"

"No."

"Fine. We'll stand like tools in front of the door where Jess can hear everything."

I make a sound of annoyance. "Alright. Jesus."

We make our way into the small sitting room, and I fall into the nearest chair. "What?"

"I'm not supposed to tell you this," Rex says as he takes a seat across from me. "Not until the tour's done. But I'm not standing for it anymore. Especially given current events."

"Aren't you boy scout of the year."

"You're fucking impossible." Rex rubs at his eyes. "Easton and I are leaving the band."

I dart my chin forward. "Say what?"

"We're done, man." Rex drops his hand from his face. "At least for the foreseeable future."

Rex must mistake my dead silence as an invitation to keep going and not murderous intent, because he continues, "I shouldn't be telling you this, it's majorly on the DL, but ... Harper's pregnant. And I want to be there. No, I fucking *demand* to be there for it all. I don't want it to be like it was with my Stella. I missed so much of her toddlerhood—fuck, I still am. I gotta be with my family, man. It was a tough decision, really fucking rough, but it's the only—"

"How long?" I bite out.

Rex lifts his head.

"How long have you known you wanted to do this? Before the tour?"

Rex screws up his face like I've nailed the truth.

My first instinct is to rage. I'd like to start with the glass coffee table between us and toss it against the window, shattering glass and fracturing whatever lies down below. Then I'd like to punch through the walls and kick at the row of liquor bottles standing sentry on the side table, ready for Rex's libations.

But, more importantly … "Why didn't you talk to me?"

"Because I didn't know what to say. Or how to approach it. This band is everything to you, Mase. It brought you out of your black hole, it sustains you, and I was gonna ruin it for selfish reasons. But they're reasons I can't ignore."

"So this is actually happening. Nocturne Court is ending after this leg of the tour."

Rex doesn't say anything. He folds his hands between his spread legs, leaning forward, always fucking *searching* my face for emotion.

"What's East's excuse? He knock Taryn up, too?"

"Mase, c'mon…"

"No, man." I stand, the chords of muscle in my body tensing and tangling. "Let's get it all out in the open. You're both breaking up the band for your girls. Good for *you*. Such upstanding men. I guess it didn't occur to you that leaving me and Wyn in the dust, your best friends, would destroy us. Jesus, does Wyn know, too?"

"He does. We wanted to wait to tell you as a group. As a brotherhood."

"Becoming a family man has really gummed up the plumbing up there." I point to his head. "You guys just don't want me fall apart during your last great memory. Rage against you on stage. Let the cat out of the bag and break our fans' hearts by publicly outing your plans to ditch. Yeah, I guess I'm fucking unpredictable like that."

Rex stands. "You are, Mase."

I stand so we're nose-to-nose. "Then here's some predictability for you."

I punch him in the side of the face. "Fuck you, *bro*."

CHAPTER 27

Mckenna

THE SHOWER DOESN'T CLEAN me.

The water droplets only make me dirtier.

Mason's marks linger on my skin, his nips and sucks turned into reddened, sexual reminders of what we did last night and scattered across my neck, breasts, and inner thighs.

At each juncture, I picture him, leaning down, his mouth claiming that part of my body, and I shudder.

Not with disgust, but with desire.

The escalating conflict in my head makes me scrub harder in an attempt to erase him. Coming to his room as Jane was meant to prove to Mason how fucked up the situation was, *he* was, for asking it of me.

I'm not supposed to remember the orgasms fondly, or crave the taste of him again. I'm *definitely* not supposed to stroke my clit, pretending it's his fingers at my core and not my own.

It's all too much, and I step out of the shower, toweling off like I do every time I finish with a client despite my failure at thinking Mason could be categorized as the same.

I catch my reflection in the mirror, my cheeks pink, my eyes bright, my hair soaked tendrils sticking to my face. In no way should sex with Mason have revitalized me, but here's the proof.

I look enlivened, even after a night of no sleep.

He used you. Just like he used you before. You're nothing but a novelty to him.

It's all true. There's little point in reminiscing over something that will never become my reality.

I comb my hair back and dress in tight jeans and a loose-fitting blouse, unsure of what the day will bring. Mason has sound check in a few hours, then one last concert in London before flying to Iceland. With everything that went on last night, we didn't talk of any plans for me today.

Staring at my luggage that I never fully unpack, my duffel bag sagging sadly on the ottoman in the corner, I know what I should do. Pack up and leave. Take a stance. Last night went over the line.

But I can't.

I need the money too badly. I have to save my father. Maybe even myself, though I'll never admit it to Mason.

My cell rings the moment I'm perusing the room service menu, thinking Jess wouldn't scream too much if I ordered up some scrambled eggs and fruit. I put the menu down and glance at my phone's screen, but don't recognize the number.

"Hello?" I say once the phone's against my ear.

"You are receiving a collect call from the Otisville Correctional Facility—"

"Dad," I whisper. I lose the will to stand and fall back against the bed.

A knock sounds at my door right as I'm about to accept the charges.

"I don't need cleaning right now, thank you!" I call, not getting up.

"It's not the maid service." Mason's voice, muffled but maintaining its potency, comes through the door. "Open the door, Mack."

"McKenna? Honey?"

Dad's voice sounds tinned through the speakers, but I hear him clearly.

"Dad?" I answer, my voice choked with tears. I ignore the continuous bangs against my door and Mason's increasing threats.

"Oh, honey." There are multiple puffs of air after he says it. At first I think it's laughter, but then I realize he's crying, too. "I can't tell you how good it is to hear your voice."

"How ... how'd you get this number?" I ask.

"Mack! Open up! We need to talk, damnit!"

I burrow my chin closer to my chest and angle away from the door while cradling the phone, like that's enough to block Mason out.

"A guard gave it to me," my dad says. "Said you called the prison and wanted to pass along your new number to me. I gotta say, Kenny, you almost shocked my heart into stopping when I got that message. It's been years."

Hearing my dad's voice brings forward a childhood comfort I thought was long ago destroyed. It brings back memories of story-time before bed, hot milk toddys brought to me while sick, stern lectures when disobeying house rules—all those parent moments that are just a routine part of life, until that life is altered against your will and those simple memories become precious artifacts.

It's enough to distract me from his words, until my survival instinct kicks in. *I never contacted the prison.*

"I know, Dad." I say, wiping under my eyes. "I never figured out what to say to you after you were arrested and we lost everything. Honestly, I still don't know what to say. But you should know, it wasn't me that gave you this num—"

A *beep* comes from outside the hotel door, and I watch with annoyance as the lever's pulled down and Mason strolls in, the door shutting ominously behind him.

"Mason," I snap. "I'm on the phone. Could you give me a minute?"

"Did you just say Mason?" my Dad asks from the other end of the line. "As in, Mason Payne? Are you with him, Kenny? I don't think that's a good idea—"

The phone's pulled from my grip.

"Hey—!"

Mason hangs up on my father, then tosses the phone across the room. "What I have to say is more important."

"You son of a bitch!" I rear up from the bed. Palms splayed, I push against his chest. His hammering heartbeat under my palm startles me, but I cover it with outrage. "That was my *father*, you jackass! And I have no way of calling him back!"

For a brief second, awareness brightens his stare, chased with a stab of guilt, but he blinks it away. "Listen to me, Mack."

"No!" To my horror, tears blur my vision. But I dare not let them fall. "I'm sick of listening, of doing what you instruct, of being your good little companion while you waltz around doing whatever the fuck you want. Get *out* of my room. Last night doesn't give you permission to stomp around where I deserve privacy and piss your testosterone everywhere."

"Everyone knows."

"You have such gall to bust in here right now," I continue, ignoring what he has to say. There's *nothing* he can voice to fix this emptiness growing inside me. A hollow tomb he's constructing with his bare hands. "After what you did. I'm not some object you get to keep in your attic and pull out and play with whenever you remember I'm there. I'm a person, Mase, and unless you're here for some kind of repentance—"

"You're not hearing me." Mason steps into my personal space, a not-so-subtle urging to sit back down on the bed, but I put my hands on my hips instead and practically chest-bump him.

He repeats, "Everyone. Knows."

This. Man. He gets me so angry, so volatile, that I don't feel like myself. I'm unhinged and hurting, and when set against the stone cold look on his face, it's like I'm the only one who cares that it's happening.

"Knows *what*?" I yell.

"Who you are. What you do."

The sharp insults I planned to fling lodge in my throat. I back away, but my thighs hit the side of the bed, and I have nowhere further to retreat. "They...?"

Mason nods, and while he never appears happy, at this moment, his features are especially foreboding. "Someone—I don't know who, but mark my words I *will* find out and skin them alive—leaked who you are to the press, and it's not about being a long-lost childhood friend. I'm not going to try and pretty this up for you, Mack. It's all over, the fact that you're a call girl. The tabloids here have the story, and so do the ones in the States. Your face is plastered everywhere."

"My..." I hold a hand to my forehead and crumple into a slow sit on the bed. "Oh my God."

Mason looms above, unmoving, his hands hanging at his sides. I don't expect comfort from him. It doesn't matter, anyway, because my stomach's in turmoil. My throat's swelling, and all I can think of is my father.

I risk meeting Mason's eyes, though he's hard to see through the blur. It's like my heart's pounding in my head and pulses into my vision, throbbing sound waves creating an aurora of light and darkness around his form. I may pass out. "Did you...was this you? Because of what went down last night? What I said to you? Are you punishing me?"

"It didn't come from me," Mason assures.

But it *is* something he'd do, as punishment, retribution, petty revenge. It's definitely a tactic he would've employed years ago.

"You and I had an agreement," he says, "and I honor

promises. I—fuck, Mack—I wouldn't ruin your life like that. I'm fully aware how nasty the press is."

"My life..." I say as realization hits. I massage my neck as I stare off to the side. "Yes, it's definitely ruined. I've been publicly outed and shamed. No client will ever want to associate with me again."

"I'm sorry, Mack."

The sincerity is there in his tone. I can hear it. Yet, I've experienced enough of Mason Payne to wait for the inevitable truth. He never means what he says. There's always a deeper menace lying dormant in the wings, until the perfect moment when he decides to unleash it.

"You don't mean that," I say, both shocked and impressed at how dull my tone is. "You got what you wanted, Mase. I can no longer be an escort, have sex with strange men, make all the cash I need to—to—" I choke.

Giles will punish me.

My father will die.

The contract between Mason and me is null and void.

The money promised is gone.

Mason touches my shoulder. "Mack..."

"Don't touch me," I hiss, then shoot off the bed. I dart across the room, as far away as I can get from him.

I peel my lips back and glare. "You *wanted* this! To destroy everything I've worked for! All because of your fucked up sense of decency. *You* can be the asshole, the beast, the dick who does whatever he pleases, but God forbid I exercise my free will and decide to be an escort. How dare I sully my innocence, right? How *could* I ruin the sweet, innocent, *stupid* little McKenna Beckley who you hold so dear in your memories? Do I have that right, Mason? You wanted that girl back, the one who cracked your heart open so wide you had no choice but to hurt her to protect yourself."

Mason responds with a low growl. "You are so, so wrong. You

had the perfect set-up. A jumping off point where you could've done whatever you wanted—be a doctor, lawyer, bio-fucking-scientist, it was all written in the stars for you. But then your dad got caught doing wrong. Your world went upside down. So what?"

My eyes widen at his blasé tone, but I should've seen the signs. The building blocks to anger.

He continues, "My dad did illegal shit all the time, did more time in jail than he did sitting on the couch at home, drinking and smoking and wailing on his kids. Hell, my brother did time, too. Life can be *shit*, McKenna, no one knows that better than me. And all signs pointed to me staying in my shit-hole and never coming out. No one thought I'd make it. I sure didn't think I'd be a millionaire before I'm thirty. Or have a platinum-selling album with my best friends. If anyone should've made it, it was you. *You* should be the one on top, *you* had the primer needed to pull yourself out of the gutter your father put you in, and instead, you squandered your chances by thinking you deserved to stay down."

"You're disappointed in me? Is that it?" I'm so angry, I'm shaking. "I had a good life, Mason! I may not be a millionaire, but I was living high, and now it's been taken away from me. All because I agreed to have you back in my life. My fucking mistake."

"Are you happy?"

The question makes me pause, but he doesn't deserve to see the hesitation. "Yes."

"No you're not."

"Doesn't matter now, does it?" I yell, spreading my arms. "My career's done."

"That was no career. A 'career' means you're making some-thing of yourself, striving towards success."

"Stop it! Stop talking like you're better than me!"

Mason's eyes go wide and white with rage. "You think that's

what this is? I'm trying to preach to you? God fucking *dammit*, Mack, that's the opposite of what I'm doing! I'm trying to show you who the good one is, here. Who deserves the better life, and it's not me! I sold my soul a long time ago—I'm on the brink of losing everything, and you know what? All I can think of is you. How this media leak is going to affect your everyday like you won't believe. And I don't want to be the one to do that. You hear me? I don't want to be the one that ruins you again!"

During our exchange, we moved closer to each other, bit by bit. I'm trembling, shaking, my face hot with heightened emotions, and his features mirror mine.

"Then maybe," I say in a low whisper, "you should've thought of that before you bought me last night."

Mason jerks back like I've slapped him. "That became more than just a transaction and you know it."

"You asked for Jane. You got her. And now you've destroyed her." Heaving, I spin on my heel and head toward my duffel. "I need to leave. I can't be here anymore."

"That's probably a good idea."

Nodding, I start throwing things haphazardly in my bag. My cheeks are wet and I swipe away the dampness as fast as I can, but the tears keep coming down.

Mason doesn't come up from behind to comfort, but nor does he move. He just stands there, watching my movements with an inscrutable look on his face.

When I beeline past him to the bathroom and toss my toiletries in a clear baggie with one fell swoop, he says quietly, "I'll give you the money."

I'm halfway back to my luggage when I halt, the bag of toiletries dangling in my hand.

"The cash we agreed upon," Mason clarifies. "I'll still give it to you."

Don't do me any favors flies to the tip of my tongue, but I bite it back.

To deny Mason would mean I still harbor a decent amount of pride, of which I have none left. I'm adrift and exposed. Without that currency, I don't know what Giles is capable of or what he's already reconsidering.

I don't have a choice.

"Thank you," I say in as calm a voice I can muster.

Mason responds with a single nod. "I'll call my bank now. Give me your details, and I'll have it transferred into your account within the next forty-eight hours."

With shaking hands, I pull up my bank information on my phone, write the numbers down on the hotel memo pad, and hand it over. We don't speak during any of it. In fact, I can't look up and meet his eyes when I pass the paper to him.

He folds it and shoves it into his pants' pocket. "There will be a car waiting for you downstairs to take you to the airport. I'll have Jess book you a plane ticket home."

I nod, horrified that I'm sniffling, so I turn my back on him instead and busy myself with packing.

"Mack..."

I don't turn, but I hear his exhale.

"It's going to be tough. Getting home. I won't be able to fly you private."

"I'll be fine," I say, not bothering with folding my clothes. "You can stop worrying about my welfare. I'm a big girl who's dealt with worse."

Like when my father was outed and the news articles circulated. He was the nation's pariah after what he did with innocent people's money. Debbie got past it by ignoring it all and pretending she was never married to my father in the first place. But I was forced, every time I stepped outside to camera flashes, to understand that good people can be rotten at their core, even daddies who remember to put smiley-face sticker notes in lunchboxes.

"Yeah, but..."

"Mason, go. Please."

There's shuffling behind me, and I like to think it's Mason turning to leave and not the muffled sound of my heart shaving down its size, peel by peel, until there's nothing left but a small, black coal.

Once the door clicks shut, I buckle to the floor. I fold my arms around my head and cry into the fabric of my luggage, confident no one will hear me.

CHAPTER 28

Mckenna

I'VE NEVER DONE a Walk of Shame before.

The epitome of shame in my life would've been during my first time with Mason, when I was left on the hood of my dad's car in our driveway, in the rain, soaked and shaking. Other people in that position might've scurried inside their home, shot upstairs and jumped straight into the shower to warm up what was fast becoming a cold, cold soul.

I did none of that.

Mason left through the gates, and I watched the V of his back and I smiled.

He was just as soaked as I was, and just as shaken. I knew it.

Though there was a dull pulsing between my legs, any blood had long since been washed away. I scraped my hair back with both hands, likely resembling a wet seal as I slid off the car, and on jellied legs I went back inside.

No longer a virgin, and dirtied up in the very best way.

I had sex in public where we could've been caught at any moment, with one of the hottest, most unattainable guys in school. Mason was brutal, nasty, and amazing with his hands. A controversy of traits my brain had trouble untangling but my body sure didn't.

It was my first experience with the forbidden, and as it turned out, sweet, bookish McKenna *liked* it, regardless of the consequences.

This time, when Mason left my hotel room and I slumped into a shower of tears, I still refused to feel shame. It's a useless, weighed-down emotion that does nothing to help my head remain high or my heart to stay strong.

I grab my luggage, throwing my duffel over my shoulder and dragging my roller case behind me, right when a knock sounds at the door.

I open it with my free hand, and there's Jess, her tablet out.

"Good. You're ready to leave," she says as greeting.

Nodding, I drag everything, including myself, into the hallway.

Jess starts moving and talking at the same time, keeping a comfortable space in front of me with long strides.

"I'm to escort you to a car downstairs. It'll take you to the airport, where you'll board the nine a.m. flight to LaGuardia." Jess glances back. "Economy seat."

"Sure. Fine," I say.

We stop at the elevators where Jess uses a long, manicured-black fingernail to press the down button. I'm content waiting in silence, sure that Jess, given the opportunity, would lecture hard and long about my choice of occupation.

"I hope you know the contract's null and void," Jess says while staring at the closed elevator doors.

I adjust the strap of my duffel, also staring forward. Chin high. "Yes."

"Because it's illegal," Jess clarifies.

I sniff. "Yes."

Jess turns her head and I feel her consideration of me sliding up and down my profile like tiny spider legs. "You're taking this rather well."

"I don't stay where I'm not wanted. I'm happy to go home and figure this mess out on my own."

"I wouldn't go straight home if I were you."

I flick a glance her way.

Jess wrinkles her nose like it pains her, but she says, "The press will be there. They'll be everywhere you regularly haunt. You should go some place they don't know. A friend's. A hotel. Get your bearings before you face them. Maybe even hire a lawyer."

Slowly, I nod, suspiciously grateful for the unsolicited advice. "Okay. Thank you."

"Unfortunately, you won't be getting the money agreed upon, so you'll have to figure out another way to finance this mess."

I snap my head around. "Excuse me?"

Jess shrugs, which *definitely* doesn't pain her. "Like I said. Illegal. Null. Void. We don't have to give you any of the funds agreed upon. You're lucky we're paying for your ticket home."

So you can get rid of me faster and attempt to untarnish Mason's questionable rep.

Except, that's not my top concern. "I just spoke to Mason, and he said—"

The elevator doors ding open and Jess sweeps an arm out for me to go in first. "You're not getting the cash. End of story. So don't make a scene."

Jess enjoys this brief spurt of power. It's written all over her expression. Usually, her mean-girl satisfaction would bounce against my smooth-as-marble exterior, but her words dig a hole in my gut.

"That's not what Mason—" I start to say, but I'm sidelined by the person leaving the elevator who nearly runs me down.

"Shit—sorry! Jeez, you're so large, too. With bags, I mean. Large with bags. Should've missed you by a mile. Sorry, Mack."

After rebalancing my luggage, I glance up and notice Wyn. A

woman dangles on his arm, dressed from the night before. She offers me a smeared-lipstick smile.

"No problem," I say to Wyn. "I'll just … sneak past …"

Wyn shuffles out of the way, clad in low-riding jeans and a muscle shirt. His longish, sandy hair is un-styled and swept to the side. "I'll get out of your way. Let me help, though."

He untangles his arm from the woman, lifting my roller case and setting it inside the elevator. He looks to Jess as he does it. "How come no one's helping her? We have like eight security men a piece. Someone could be assisting in getting Mack comfortable."

"She has me," Jess clips out.

"You gettin' some muscles by doing some bicep-curls with that iPad? Why don't you put them to use?"

Jess doesn't smile. "If you'll excuse us."

"Yeah, yeah." Wyn steps out of the elevator, but presses a reassuring hand against my shoulder. "It sucks how this all went down. We didn't really associate in high school, you and I, but I know what you did for Mason back then, and I see what you've done now." He spares a glance at Jess. "Don't be ashamed about any of it. Mase needs a girl like you to kick him sideways. Otherwise, he never sees the light. We're going through a rough patch now, but I really do think your presence made a difference. I don't want you to go home. I think Mase needs you more than ever."

My brows pinch together. "Thanks for those words, Wyn, but I just saw him, and he seemed fine with my exit strategy."

"You and I both know he puts on an act when he's faced with something he doesn't like. It was a double-whammy for him. First he finds out about the leak—which I don't judge, by the way." Wyn sends a wink over to his girl. "Then, Rex tells him we're disbanding after the tour."

I stiffen. "Rex told him?"

Wyn nods. "Rex got a black eye to show for it. And a swollen cheek after Mase blamed him for leaking your information to the press."

My mouth drops. "Are you kidding me?"

"Wyn, move along." Jess says. "McKenna has a plane to catch."

"Jeez, woman," Wyn says, but does as Jess asks after he squeezes my shoulder first. "You were good for him, Mack. I'm sorry we're repaying you by sending you packing. If it means anything, it wasn't my vote."

I offer him a half-smile. "I appreciate it. I'll, uh, see you around."

"Yeah." Wyn walks backwards down the hallway for a few steps, hands in his jeans, his "date" toddling beside him. He studies me the entire time it takes for the doors to slide shut between us.

I'm gifted with a few floors of silence before Jess speaks again.

"Even if the section containing your payment is void," Jess says beside me. "The NDA is not. You're not to whisper any of what you've learned to the press, especially about Nocturne Court's planned separation. Not in retaliation or revenge or pettiness. Got it?"

"If you bothered to know me at all this past month," I say to her, "You'd understand that's the last thing I'd do to those men." I turn to her. "I am the epitome of discretion. I fuck powerful men for money. My job demands it."

Jess's cheek twitches.

I'm distracted by further barbs when an incoming alert sounds out on my phone. Pulling it from my purse, I notice it's from my bank.

An amount of $250,000 will be deposited in my account, pending authorization.

With a subtle smile, I black out my screen, my phone dangling at my side.

I got what I wanted.

Therefore, all signs point to being done with Mason Payne.

I wish I felt any sort of satisfaction.

CHAPTER 29

Mckenna

I'M glad I stuffed my hoodie in my purse.

Jess, ice queen that she is, allowed me the decency of leaving the hotel via the private entrance so I could avoid the media. The driver of the black car didn't recognize me—or didn't care, making the trip a comfortable, silent ride.

It's when I'm dropped off at airport departures when things go haywire.

I'm recognized immediately, both by passengers and waiting press. The stares and pointing, I can deal with, which is what most plane-goers and their companions decide to do. But the vulture descent of cameras and microphones take me back to when Dad was arrested and the incomprehensible, explosive newsworthiness of my family.

Of course, they've made the connection.

"Miss Beckley! McKenna! How do you feel, following in your father's criminal footsteps?"

"Are you two gonna be penpals in prison?"

"Were you so damaged by your father's conviction you had to turn into a sex worker?"

"Who are your other famous clients, other than Mason Payne?"

"Did any other men from Nocturne Court use your services? Was there ever a threesome? An orgy?"

"Will you sell photos of your clients? Sell your client list?"

Relentless questions *ping* against my arms and shoulders, worse than bee stings, more terrible than a backstabbing knife.

Who did this to me?

I scramble for my hoodie, shoving my arms in and throwing the hood over my head, burying myself in the familiar-scented fabric as much as I can.

Once I'm through the inner doors, the swarm disperses, but not the voices. They're shouted through the glass, enough to bring the attention of more onlookers, and I scurry through check-in and security, pretending its someone else who's dirty laundry has been exposed.

A cloying silence descends after walking through to the gates. I have less people, an off-season ticket, and no access to unauthorized individuals to thank for the brief solitude I'm given.

Jess booked me a middle seat, but after speaking to an attendant at the gate, I'm able to move to a window. I pretend the stuttering in my voice is from fatigue as I explain that I'd really like to curl up against the plane's hull and sleep for the majority of the trip.

At some point, I expected this. Living such a high-risk lifestyle brings about high stakes.

I only wish karma didn't come for me so soon.

When boarding commences, I disappear into the line of passengers, no longer an obvious sore spot among regular commuters. Blending in is something I became quite good at about a decade ago, and I use it to my advantage now.

I take my seat, burrow deep into my hood, and quietly slumber until the plane's wheels hit New York City.

After collecting my luggage, I call a car through my phone's app and tear through the arrivals section, noticing a cluster of press and beelining past before they realize it's me.

I find my waiting car, dart in, and breathlessly confirm my address with the driver. Tilting my head back, I take a deep, exhausted sigh as we pull out, passing another media crowd.

The car drops me off in Chelsea, in front of a brick building with cast iron windows and doors. I buzz up, wait for the acknowledging *beep* of the door unlocking, then haul my bags and myself up two floors.

I knock once at door B2. It flies open.

"Dee," I say through a quiet burble of tears.

Her dark brown eyes soften. "Baby girl," she says, and sweeps me into her arms.

◦◦

"How could this have happened?" Dee asks as she hands me a glass of chilled white wine before settling beside me on the couch. "You're always so careful with your identity."

"I'm honestly at a loss."

I'm cupping the wine close to my face like it's soothing and warm with mint tea fumes hitting my nose.

I tip it to my lips for a long, much-needed swallow.

Well, at least I have the soothing part down.

"Mason wouldn't do that to you, would he?"

"I don't think it was any of the guys. Because of this, Mason's getting a lot of unwanted attention, and so is Nocturne Court. They wouldn't do this to themselves on their last—I mean, on their tour."

"So, none of them knew. No one but Mason."

I nod, then amend, "Well. Rex did. But I don't think it was him. He's got enough going on in his own life."

Dee leans back against the cushions, nursing her wine glass. "Someone gained access to the information, a person wanting to look deeper into who you are. Were you a threat to anyone there?"

I lower my brows. "I'd bet money it was Mason's stupid assistant, Jess. She didn't like me from the beginning."

"Could be. Wait a minute, you don't think..." Dee's eyes go wide as she mulls something over. "Giles?"

The mention of his name causes wine to burn my throat when I forget to swallow. In an automatic motion, I search for my phone beside me and check the screen for any notifications from him. I've yet to tell Giles I've landed *or* that the money's on its way. The media frenzy had me all sorts of frazzled and only now is my brain tipping back on its axis.

"Shit," I say. "I have to call him. Let him know I'm here—"

Dee lays a hand on mine. "It can wait. Get some sleep, first. You look like you've had none of it."

I squeeze my phone tighter. "I shouldn't make my black-mailer *wait*, Dee."

"Giles doesn't know you're here, right? Sure, he's probably aware of the news, but you're not at home, and he has no idea where I live or who I am. You're safe here. Use this time wisely." Dee pats my knee before standing. "*Sleep*, for God's sake. You've been through the wringer."

Dee's motherly tendencies are nothing new. She's always looked out for me, especially at the start when I was just getting into the business. We're the same age, but she's the one who introduced me to the escort world. She was my roommate in college, and when shit hit the fan with my father (Dee's first real exposure to media madness), and Dee witnessed not only my family's, but *my*, downfall, she tentatively confessed what she'd been doing to afford her tuition, food, board, and line-up of designer bags she displayed on her single shelf in the dorm.

She'd done it as I was boxing up my side of the room to leave campus in disgrace, and muttered the truth so softly, I had to stop folding my sweaters to catch it. True fear lit her eyes when I asked her to repeat it, then say it again so I could absorb what Dee was actually proposing I do.

It wasn't even her confession that was most shocking ... it was my reaction. I slowly sat on my stripped mattress, clutching the edges at the seams, and considered her avenue of funds.

I like sex. There's a part of me that becomes extra horny when illicit toys, words, or places are introduced. I wouldn't say I love it rough, but I gravitate toward different from the regular missionary. The way I lost my virginity proves that.

I never looked at my dad's car the same way again.

It was difficult, at first, to accept strange men into my figurative bed, but after a while and with Dee's training, I was able to turn it into giving and receiving orgasms, a skill-set, a pleasure center, a way to get off without the strings of a relationship tangling me at the center.

Eight-ish years later, Dee no longer works as an escort. Even though we worked the same job, the major difference between her and me was that she stayed and graduated college with a finance degree she now uses in a sky-rise in lower Manhattan.

There's no further need for her to languish in a devilish place with illicit cash.

Dee's straight-laced life is also why she's sitting here, telling me to catch some zzz's before transferring a quarter million dollars to a dangerous man threatening to kill my father and who will make my life hell unless I give him what he wants.

She's gone soft on me, my Dee.

I nod and smile at her anyway as she leaves for her room. She's already set out bedding for me to use on the couch, but I doubt I'll need it. I'm too wired, too uneasy, to even think about dreaming, and I send another furtive glance to my phone.

Get this over with.

The glass of wine has settled like a calm blanket against my shoulders, but it hasn't affected my trembling fingers. I text fast, before I can second-guess my intentions.

· · ·

I'm back in NYC. I can have the money for you by tomorrow. Send me the details and I'll wire it to you.

My phone shocks the bejesus out of me when it vibrates with an incoming call instead of a text.

It's from a private number, but I'm well aware who could be calling right after I send a text confirming my presence and a large amount of cash.

I swipe to open the call and hold the phone to my ear. "Yes?"

"No. I want to meet."

Giles's smooth voice filters through, but the sound sends shudders down my neck. In a pure defensive move, I summon Jane. My alter knows how to handle men like this and keep them calm, because it's men like this that become the most brutal if they feel they're being mismanaged.

"There's no need," I respond. "In this day and age we can wire the funds and be done with each other."

Giles chuckles, and he might as well have sent ice cubes tumbling into my ear canal. "That's where you're wrong, darling. I've seen the news. I know how compromised you are."

"That shouldn't affect our transaction."

"It affects my ability to trust you."

A rock drops into my gut with a *plink*, but I mentally kick it away. "It shouldn't. I was able to secure the funds despite the media leak. And I can prove it by sending you the full amount tomorrow."

"And if you do not, you maintain the ability to disappear. Even now, I don't know where you are, Jane—I mean, McKenna."

His use of my true name, and the way he says it, so delectable and slow, sends bile into my throat.

"I simply can't have that," Giles continues. "And so, we will meet, and you will wait until I've confirmed the funds are in my account. Only then may you depart my company."

"I'd never do that—disappear. Regardless of where I go, my father's a sitting duck to you. I won't compromise him."

"Again, darling, there's no way I can know that for certain. Words are pithy things, aren't they? Come to my apartment tomorrow afternoon. You remember where that is? And wear the same dress as last time. You were absolutely *divine* in that outfit."

The outfit you strangled me in? "I'd rather meet somewhere public, if all we're going to do is stare at our phones while the cash is transferred."

Giles tuts through the speaker. "Sweet McKenna. I'm amazed you're the same woman as the mature, sleek vixen that entered through my door mere weeks ago. I cannot be seen with you in public. You understand."

It's not safe. I'm not safe.

The warning blares behind my forehead with blinding fortitude, *but I don't know what else to do.*

"You know," Giles says, "despite the current time, special visiting hours are still in place at the penitentiary. If you shake hands with the right people, of course. Shall I give them a call?"

"No," I say quickly, breaking my thick silence. "That won't be necessary. I'll be there."

"Excellent. And might I say, I am *absolutely* looking forward to meeting this secret McKenna Beckley. Is she any less skillful than Jane Landers, I wonder?"

Click.

The phone remains at my ear. I use my free hand to massage my throat, since my heart seems to have lodged there and won't move down. My neck feels hot, my pulse erratic, and I'm confident I'll be walking into a viper's nest tomorrow afternoon with no guarantees to *anything.*

There's nothing to stop Giles from continuing to come after me, even if I give him the money he demands. This time.

My dad will always be in danger, and I don't think I'm his hero in this story, if he even deserves one.

My life is in pieces. I knew the risks, but didn't understand the force with which I could be taken down. My face is everywhere, plastered with Mason's, but in an ironic twist of fate, Mason is coming out of this the good guy.

And, according to my latest Google alert, I'm one of the most hated women in America right now. Death threats will commence shortly, save for the one I'm currently courting with a white collar criminal.

I fall back against the pillows, staring blindly at the ceiling.

Maybe I should've listened to Dee and caught a few hours of ignorant sleep.

Because now, I'm pretty sure I'll only sleep when I'm dead.

CHAPTER 30

Mason

THE SHOW MUST GO ON.

I hate that fucking saying, yet I've heard it come out the mouths of everyone I'm surrounded by, Jess and my brother included.

It sucks about Mack, but the show must go on. Put more money on the table, man!

McKenna's flight left on time. She's gone. Can we get back to professionalism now, Mason? The show must go on.

"Yeah, but for how long?" I mutter as some kid dabs anti-glare powder on my forehead before our photoshoot. He freezes mid-tap, and the death glare I send him doesn't help.

"They should really clarify when they try to pep talk this shit to me," I say to him like he knows what I'm talking about. "The show must go on ... but only for four more weeks. Then we'll all do what we fuckin' want. Doesn't matter your dick will be tied to a chair for the remainder, Mason, 'cause you're our puppet, and you'll do what we want *including* fucking who we want you to fuck. Amirite?"

The kid's anime-sized eyes ping-pong furtively between me and his boss, who's currently tending to Rex three chairs over. She's adding extra pancake dust under Rex's left eye.

"Relax, Mase," Wyn says beside me. His head is tipped back and his eyes closed as he's worked on, submitting to the foul-smelling theater makeup like he's at the goddamned spa. "We prep, we pose, we leave. That's all we gotta do this morning."

"You, maybe," I mumble, then flinch as the kid's brush gets too close to my eye. "I still have some heads that need rolling."

"Still don't know who leaked the info, huh?" Wyn asks.

"Yeah, and I guess I'm not getting an apology," Rex calls from his chair.

"Both of you, shut it," I say, then turn to Wyn, waving the kid away. "Unless you've found some quality info regarding the narc, I don't want to hear any more about Mack. And *you*," I say over Wyn to Rex, "you deserved a punch to the face for keeping quality info from me."

Easton chooses this time to speak. "I'm so glad I can only half-hear most of this."

I glare at him. "You're next."

Loud munching draws my attention away from my band members. Brax rattles a half-empty bag of chips on the nearby couch as he digs his hand in for more. He's not looking my way, instead studying the floor.

"Enjoying your break, Brax?" I ask him.

His chin snaps up. "I'm on break?"

"Exactly."

Brax wipes his mouth with his sleeve and rolls up the chip bag. "What do you need, *boss*?"

"A new band to play bass with."

Brax wipes his hands together and stands. "Other than that?"

I slouch in my seat, submitting to more of the kid. "Water'd be good."

"Coming right up."

Brax wanders to the craft services table set up behind us. When he comes back, the photographer also enters the room and makes noises about rounding us up.

I'm praying this doesn't take long. If it does, I'm walking off, contract or no contract. The sense of betrayal hasn't lessened, and it's such fake-ass crap to have to stand with Rex and East pretending.

I'm still not sure what the point of pretense is.

Brax comes up on my left and hands me a bottle of water.

"Did you know, too?" I ask him.

"Know what?" Instead of meeting my stare, Brax's attention goes back to the floor.

"You're well aware of what I'm talking about." I crack open the lid of the bottle.

"Look, I…" Brax shuffles around. Still not looking at me. "It's complicated."

"Yeah, complicated like Jess warned you to keep your mouth shut and for some reason you find her intimidating."

"She's a fucking dragon lady in a tiny suit!" Brax defends.

I say, in all seriousness, "You should've given me the heads up. As my brother."

"Ah, don't do that. Don't give me all the guilt."

"I was side-swiped, B. Did not see this coming, while everybody else did. Do you know what it's like to be the town idiot?"

"Actually, yeah, I do."

I dial it back, swigging on my water. "Right. I didn't mean—"

"I know, man." Brax throws a hand on my shoulder and squeezes. "Truth, it's been eating me alive, what I've done, and it's a relief that you now know and you're not trying to kill me for keeping the info from you."

I sigh. "I'm tired of trying to kill people."

"Yeah? Would've thought Sorsha'd be next on your hitlist."

I gain tunnel vision when I look back at Brax. "Why her?"

He shrugs. "Since she's the reason this all went down."

Cold plastic crunches beneath my grip. "The reason for what, Brax?"

"You know, Mack leaving, the press knowing what she does, that stuff."

I might as well've doused Brax with the rest of my ice water, because his face loses all color as I stare at him silently and realization sets in.

After working my jaw, I say, "Brax. Explain."

"I—ah, fuck. You didn't know. You didn't..." Brax backs up a few steps. "What were we just talking about?"

"The band breaking up, you fool," I snap.

Brax's head bobs forward. "Nocturne Court's *breaking up?*"

East and Rex snap to attention.

"Fucking shut up, Brax!" one of them says, but I don't know who, since all my focus is on my brother, and will remain there until I laser holes in his head.

I leap to my feet, water bottle spraying and cracking against the floor and the make-up kid dancing back like I've set fire to myself.

"Brax, tell me what the fuck you know about Sorsha!" I roar.

Wyn jumps so high out of his meditative state, he sheds skin.

Brax holds up trembling hands. "Okay, okay ... I ... she ... she tricked me, Mase. I was in the lobby arranging your car service, since Jess is always sending me on these stupid dog errands, and I ran into her. Sorsha talked about Mack like she already knew something was up, she was all suspicious about Mack, you know? So I repeated the joke you said to me. About Mack being a call girl. I was just kidding! But Sorsha for this look on her face like it could be true, and ah fuck, I knew I screwed up—"

"You said that stuff about Mack? To my ex?"

"It's not like I confided in her, man!" Brax's voice rises a few octaves. "Jesus, stop surrounding yourself with such dragon ladies! They're intimidating! I just wanted her to back off!"

"I'm sure she ran off the instant she was fed that kind of candy. Fuck, Brax. *Fuck!*"

Wyn comes up behind me, attempting to soothe. "Mase, take a—"

"Touch me and die," I spit out. "Mack's life is ruined because of this shit. *My* shit. And you." I point to Brax. "I don't know how you could've been so stupid as to—"

"To what? Repeat what I thought was a joke? Confide in a beautiful lady who was paying attention to me? Being nice to me? I'm nothing but an invisible dick in this group. The only other person who noticed me around here was Mack."

"And you betrayed her," I say. "The girl who always paid attention to you, even when we were kids, you threw under the bus. Because a Hollywood chick was *nice* to you." I ball my hands into fists. "I am so close to—"

Rex and East sidle up beside Wyn. Rex says, "Mase, perhaps you should take this somewhere else…"

I take the sobering moment to glance around the room, where all staff has stopped moving, lights are dangling from inattention, and make-up brushes are frozen in mid-air.

I swallow. "You're right, Rex, like you usually are. I'll take this somewhere else."

Blasting past Brax and the rest of the crew, I throw open the door.

Brax calls behind me, "Mase, where are you—"

But I don't hear him after I slam it shut behind me.

I wasn't kidding. A certain head needs to roll, and if I have anything to do with it, I'll be throwing it off a plane.

CHAPTER 31

Mckenna

DEE LEFT for work at 5 am, but made sure to have a full pot of coffee ready when I crack my eyes open a few hours later.

I've never considered myself old, but when I sit up on the couch, I wince when my back pops.

My best friend's furniture sure isn't the same as the five star hotels Mason and his band were staying at.

Mason.

The name forms a cloud in my already dark morning mood. It seems I can't leave his company without some form of disgrace.

I also miss my bed. And my old life. Today, I'm hoping to conquer some of the terribleness that's seeped in, starting with my afternoon meeting with Giles.

Giles leaves a bad taste in my mouth, so I pad over to Dee's open kitchen and pour coffee into the biggest mug I can find. I prop a hip against the counter and sip as much as the hot liquid will allow, not bothering with cream or sugar. The bitter beans are a welcome balm against the bile and acid that Giles brings out.

Knuckles crack against Dee's front door. Coffee spills against my nightshirt, scalding my chest.

"Jesu—"

I don't even get the curse out before the pounding starts again.

Not Giles. It can't be Giles. Too Soon. Too…

He can't know I'm here.

I set the mug down with both hands, yanking a paper towel from the roll on the counter and tip-toeing to the door.

As quietly as I can manage, I peer into the peephole.

And gasp.

Mason's hard eyes flick up and icepick into mine through the small hole.

"Open up, Mack," he says.

I don't. I splay my hands against the cold metal of the door, mouthing *how in the hell? Why is he here?* to myself.

"I can see the shadow of your feet."

There's no way he knows they're my shadows. Could be Dee's.

Crack-crack-crack.

I shriek and jump back at the unexpected shaking of the door as Mason pounds.

"I know that cry, have *tasted* that sound, and it ain't your friend's."

Fine. If this is how he wants it.

I throw the door open, my expression stern and unmoving. I pretend there isn't a giant coffee stain on my shirt as I stare him down.

He arches a brow at my silence, arms crossed against his chest. "Can I come in?"

"No." Unable to resist, I add, "How did you find me?"

"Same way I found you the first time, sweetheart. You have one friend. Dee. And you're not about to head home, what with the stable of press camped out on your street."

"You shouldn't be here."

"Here I am, anyway."

"You're halfway through your last tour. And you just left? You could've texted. Or called. Or, I don't know … emailed."

Another brow arch. "Would you have read what I wrote? Or answered my call?"

"Probably not."

"Exactly." Mason presses a hand against the doorframe. "Let me in, Mack."

I don't move back. "I'm really busy today. I don't have time for this, or you."

He lowers his head. "I wouldn't have come if it weren't important."

This close, the lightning streaks of gray in his eyes flash to full effect. They're more storm than blue today, hidden frustrations creeping through like dark clouds.

After a brief war inside my head, I say, "I'm not offering you coffee, because you're not staying long."

He nods, and when I step sideways, his bare arm brushes against my breasts. If it was intentional, his profile as he passes by gives me no clues. But the electric surge happens in my chest anyway, and I angrily rub at a spot between my breasts to erase the tingles.

"So?" I say, trailing behind him in the kitchen. "Why are you here?"

Mason stops at the large windows overlooking the Chrysler and Empire Buildings. "To apologize."

I lean my elbows on the kitchen counter, cupping my half-filled, lukewarm coffee. "Let me get this straight. You flew all the way back to New York to … apologize?"

Mason Payne doesn't say sorry. He never has.

He turns to face me. "I know who leaked the information about you, and it was in my control. I could've stopped it."

I slide my index finger around the rim of my mug, pretending interest while my stomach somersaults with Mason's confession. "Who was it?"

"Sorsha."

I nod, pursing my lips like it's no surprise. "I guess I had it coming."

"Why would you say that?"

"The way she was on your arm. How she looked at me. Her use of power. People like that, man or woman, do everything they can to stay on top. And she wanted you."

Mason doesn't bother to deny it. "I cussed her out on the phone on the way here. Told her there's no way we're getting back together. Brax apparently let it slip to her what you do, but it was an idiot mistake I'll make sure he pays for. And I'll do what I can. Use my publicity people to spin this enough that the public'll get bored and move on. You'll get your life back. It's not enough, I know, but ..."

"It's more than you've ever done," I say quietly.

"Huh?"

I shake myself out of the distracted perusal of my mug. "Look, I appreciate you telling her to fuck off. But the damage is real, and I'm dealing with it. Thank you for coming by and telling me the truth."

"You're dismissing me."

I straighten. "I told you, my day's tight. I have to..." *pay off my criminal blackmailer with your money* "...meet someone."

A heavy silence falls into the room. Old me might've shifted uncomfortably under Mason's thick scrutiny, but this me puts my hands on my hips and waits for his inevitable temper to snap forth.

"You're right back at it, huh?" he says.

I blow out a breath. "Leave it to you to jump to that conclusion. What I do is my business."

"Even with everything going on, like your *public demise*, you can't resist the dick?"

"That's crass. And disgusting of you to say to me."

"I just—I can't—" Mason digs his fingers into his hair on a

growl. "You frustrate the fuck out of me. Confuse the shit out of me. Drive me *nuts*. What's going on with you?"

I throw my hands up. "Why do you keep searching for the McKenna you used to know? She doesn't exist anymore, Mason! There's just me, a survivor, a loner, a woman who made a damn good life for herself before you pushed back in, and now I need to clean up the shattered pieces *you've* left behind."

Mason rubs at his chin. "Who're you meeting?"

"None of your damn—"

Mason rushes forward, grabbing my arm and bending low to my face. It doesn't hurt, nor does it scare me. My heart *zings* at the contact. "I'll pay double for your time this afternoon."

I shake my head, despite him being so close, his masculine scent an ambrosia flare against my nostrils. "This isn't a meeting I can miss."

"Miss it."

The tip of my nose touches his. "No."

"Damn it, Mack." His hand tightens on my arm. "Don't make me tie you to a chair."

"And do naughty things to me to make me stay?"

His eyes narrow, and the lust that fills them snakes through me and coils at my core. I like baiting him. I keep daring myself to go further, to see how much I can push him, regardless of the danger.

"Is that Jane talking, or Mack?" he asks.

"You're frustrated," I say. "Maybe even a little sad. Your band's breaking up, it's getting to you, and you're taking it out on me."

He grinds out, "Stop trying to read me. I'm not one of your storybooks."

"People keep leaving you, Mason. Aren't you tired of it?"

Mason's voice takes on a warning tone. "Don't shrink me, either."

"You're angry over how well I know you. But this time, I

don't want to help you or fix you. I learned my lesson the first time. So let me be."

His other hand sneaks up and cups the side of my jaw. He tips my face up, searching for something.

Mason's upper lip curls once he finds what he's looking for. "Nah. There's no Jane here."

I keep insisting to myself I don't want Mason Payne. I don't think about him, don't need him, *cannot* get addicted to him again. All these years later, there's still something about him that causes my mind to go at war with my body. My body enjoys him. My body *wants* him.

Mason must read my thoughts, because his eyes go black.

"Stop looking at me like that," he warns.

I made the mistake of trying to redeem him in high school. I couldn't accept him for what he was. Now, we're both irredeemable. Why can't he accept what *I've* become?

"Sweet Mack," he murmurs, stroking my cheek with his thumb, "It's amazing, all the naughty things I want to do to you."

The promise makes my thighs clench. Dampness coats my underwear and all it will take is a biting of my lip or a devilish half-smile to have Mason gripping my ass-cheeks, propping me on the kitchen counter, and committing each sin listed in his stare.

I want to give him a sign. Trigger his sexual desires.

If it weren't for a soft voice in the back of my head.

Listening to it, I lift my head enough so my lips brush his, a bare whisper, a light promise.

The butterfly touch shocks him, because he jerks back.

"What was that?" he asks.

"A kiss."

"No." Mason takes a step back. "Our kisses are explosive. Mouths collide and tongues claim and I do everything in my power to get you to moan. That wasn't our kiss. That was ... that was ..."

I angle my head. "Gentle?"

His lips part for a moment. Mason stares at me blankly. "Yeah."

I close the gap he's made between us by stepping forward and tilting my chin up. "What if that's what I want?"

Halfway through my question, my voice becomes a surprised whisper. It's difficult to ask for sweetness from a beast, especially when his face loses all color at the request.

"I ... Mack, I ... don't know how to be gentle."

I hold a hand to the side of his face, his scruff tickling my palm with electric pin pricks, his full lower lip caught underneath my thumb. "Then let me show you."

"Jane?" he asks, so quietly I have a hard time catching it.

I shake my head. "Me. Mack."

I lead him to the couch and have him sit down. I'm only in a t-shirt, so it's easy to part my legs and straddle him, underwear and jeans as our only barriers.

With both hands, I cup his face, lift his mouth to mine, and seal my promise with a blossoming kiss.

My hands slide down to his neck, his muscular, wide shoulders, and wrap around him as I deepen the kiss.

When Mason's tongue tries to plunge—to *take*—I reel him back with soft strokes. He grunts, shifting underneath me, but reluctantly allows the kindness.

I break our connection to place sweet kisses along his jawline, to that tender spot between his neck and his ear, then tongue the delicate shell of his ear, blowing light air, and I'm smiling.

Mason groans, his hands tightening on my hips. He tries to grind, his hardness spearing against the tough denim of his jeans and feeling like the *best* vibrator in the world against the thin fabric of my underwear. I want to grind down, too. Rip the barricade away and have him fill me.

But, closing my eyes, I also want *this*.

Mason and I have never made love. Been kind to each other during sex. We've never been vulnerable.

I want to see if it's possible to tame Mason Payne.

"Wait," I whisper close to his ear as I reach down and squeeze the front of his pants.

Mason's head falls back. "Fuck, Mack, you're killing me with this."

"Patience," I say as I move my kisses back to the corner of his lips.

Hooking my fingers at the hem of his shirt, I get him to lift his arms so I can peel it off. Then I work on the zipper and button of his jeans.

Mason wants to help. He frantically tries to unzip faster than I'm doing it.

Laughing, I push his hands away. "I got this."

"I want to bend you over the coffee table, expose those peachy cheeks of yours, and ram you so hard—"

I laugh again, then find his hot, swollen, thick shaft and pull it free.

Laughter dies in my throat.

Not from his girth or size or anything I haven't seen before. No, it's from the way he's looking at me.

He says, even as I squeeze and stroke him, "I never realized how beautiful you are when you laugh."

I scoff uncomfortably, breaking our gaze, then slide down and take him in my mouth.

I'm supposed to be the gentle one, not him.

To prove that, I lick delicate swirls and twirls, never sucking too hard and keeping my teeth at bay. Massaging, kissing, laying the balanced groundwork for an aching build-up, I enjoy every moment Mason groans, or shifts, or tries to push my head to take all of him.

I don't.

I tease, and prompt, and play.

"Mack…"

Right when I know I have him, I stand, peel off my underwear, and straddle him again, positioning his dick so it enters me achingly slow, joining Mason in the excruciating wait.

I'm so hot, slick and swollen I almost come as soon as he buries his tip, but I bite down and endure, ever so slowly, until I come to a soft, rocking rhythm, my hands on his shoulders, my eyes on his.

His dick filling me whole.

"Don't look away," I say, my breaths becoming uneven.

Mason takes hold of my hips. He doesn't break our stare. "I couldn't, even if I tried."

"I want you to see me come."

Hair falls into my face. Mason pushes it back and keeps his hand molded against the side of my neck, meeting my rhythm, holding my stare.

"Come with me, sweetheart," he grits out as my hips circle and sway, trying to take him deeper.

The clenching need comes first, the tightening of my walls that signal an incoming tidal wave of pleasure.

I tilt my head back, my hair cascading down my shoulders, but Mason directs my focus back to him.

"Always on me," he says, when I'm finally able to make him out through the building haze. "Just like you promised."

"Mason, I…"

"I know, sweetheart. Keep going."

"I…"

"Yes. Fuck. Keep doing what you're doing. Don't stop. Don't change. Don't—"

Mason parts his lips on a roar and I cry out, bearing down on his shoulders and riding him until that sparkling joy at my center meets every other part of my body.

When it's over, there's dampness on my cheeks, and it's not sweat. I bury my face in Mason's neck to hide it, breathing hard.

His arms come around me, holding on tight.

I never pondered the consequences of approaching such wildness with a gentle, offering hand.

My heart answers with the consequence, and it's too late to stop a shard of red from breaking off and landing against the erratic beats of Mason's chest.

CHAPTER 32

Mason

I'M NOT sweet or kind.

No one calls me nice.

But I'm holding Mack like she's precious as she breathes against my neck, her body warm and supple, my dick still captured by her slick folds.

No, you fucking moron. It's not only your cock that's captured by her.

I frown as I nestle the top of her head under my chin. I have no clue what to do with that realization, except hold onto her a little longer.

She lifts from my neck, her features composed. "I have to get ready."

My grip tightens at her waist. "Sweetheart, we're not having sex like that and then you leave."

She tucks a lock of hair behind her ear and regards me blankly. "Why not? It was nice, right? Got us both off—"

"Don't do that."

She attempts to push off my legs. I keep her there.

"Do what?" she huffs.

"Cheapen it."

"I'm not. I have to go, Mason."

"To another client," I surmise with deceiving calm. "Despite your exposure, you're meeting a guy who's going to touch all the places *I've* marked first, and you honestly think I'm about to let you."

"Not that I'm obligated to explain, but you have it wrong." Mack pauses. Calculation drifts behind her expression. She adds, too sweetly, "Besides, who are you to talk to me about what not to do? You're the one who left your band hanging mid-tour and costing millions of dollars in lost ticket sales."

"Don't jump to conclusions," I say coolly, keeping her steady on my lap despite her small struggles. "There's some B-list bass player more than happy to take my place while my piss-poor excuse of a band takes the stage. How am I supposed to go up there, anyway? What face am I saving? Rex and East are checking out. This tour's now a joke and I refuse to become the idiot punchline."

"I see. So you left them before they could leave you."

A storm cloud might as well have settled over us. "Watch what you say to me."

"Let me go, and you won't have to hear anything else out of my mouth about you running away from your problems. Again."

I sneer. Tilt my head and give her a sidelong glare. "Be very careful, Mack."

She lays her palms against my chest. Pushing. Digging her nails in. "We both have issues to resolve. I really need to solve mine and I'm only being given one chance. I'm not going to let you ruin it the way you ruin everyth—"

"Don't finish that sentence."

"Think about it, Mason! Think about what you're doing! Any time things get tough for you, you make it worse. You'd rather someone hate you than try to help you fix whatever's broken inside, so you do the worst to them. Like leave Rex and East in the dust during their last tour before what was probably an extremely difficult decision to focus on their family. And *Wyn*, who's done nothing but be loyal to you."

"You don't get to psycho-analyze me when your illegal career just exploded in your face."

Mack smacks my chest. "My *lucrative* career that you fucking ruined! Because you're an asshole!"

I clench my jaw at the tears forming in the corners of her eyes.

"I've always thought about quitting," she says. "You think I want this to be my life? I'm almost thirty. Too old for a lot of rich men and God, too damned *tired* of dealing with the risk. But I wanted it to be on my terms. My way. And you took that choice away from me, because you could. All I've done since we've known each other is try to help you, and each and every time you've thrown it back in my face tenfold. Hurt me. Enjoyed inflicting pain. You'd rather destroy every single one of your relationships than have anyone get close to you."

Mack rises, and this time I let her.

"You really don't get it," I say, but Mack doesn't hear.

"If you're here to witness my final downfall, you won't," she continues while standing over me. Her voice rises. "Fuck with me all you want—make me another offer I can't refuse, ferry me across the ocean, have your ex expose more secrets, give it your goddamned all. I won't let you take my pride. You hear me, jackass? I'll *never* let you take away my dignity."

"Sit down," I say, reaching for calm like I would a stiff drink.

"This isn't your home or your hotel. I'm not under your *contract* anymore." Mack's chest heaves with righteous indignation. "You don't control what I do here."

Leaning forward, I picture the whole damned top-shelf bottle hitting my mouth. "You still don't get it, Mack."

"Don't bother enlightening me," she snarls. "Get out. I have work to do. Plans to make. A life to rebuild." Mack points at me and says through stiff lips, "Without. You."

"Goddammit." I shoot up from the couch. The sudden movement has Mack dancing back. "I didn't fly to NYC to enjoy your humiliation in real-time. I didn't ditch my band so I can deepen the plunge of the knife shoved into your back. I came to fix things, starting with my idiot brother and involving Sorsha's publicist who *will* understand what it's like to have dragon fire breathing down his neck until an apology and retraction is made. And ending with you. You didn't deserve this, Mack. Even my cold, black heart understands you didn't deserve to be outed. And you didn't deserve what I did to you the night of prom, either."

Mack asks, with quiet menace, "I see. You're feeling some sort of ... well, not shame. Mason Payne can never be ashamed. Why would you ever want to do something like that for a girl you thought was as good as a fast-food hamburger?"

"*Because I want to help you!*" I roar.

Mack's eyes go wide. Her mouth snaps shut.

"I'm here because—because—*fuck*." I quell the deep need to punch something. "I want to do good by you, okay? You have more self-worth than I do in the tip of my dick. Somehow, you kept it when I chipped away at you in high school and maintain it now. I'm not proud of what I've done when it comes to you, McKenna. But what I will not tolerate, what I will fly across the ocean and put my tour in jeopardy for, is to tell you you're good enough. You were good enough back then, and you're fucking gold standard now."

Mack hesitates, emotion skirting across her features, then says, "I don't need a pep talk from you of all people—"

"You still love to write?"

"I—what? Yes." Mack slaps her thighs in frustration. "I still love writing stories."

"I noticed when I wasn't annoying the shit out of you, instead of having your nose buried in a book this time, it was your computer. You're writing something."

"A book," Mack admits, but her resulting glare tells me this is the last thing she wants to be talking about. "But it's stupid, and going nowhere, and you don't have to pander to me because you feel pity."

"That's the last emotion I feel." I close the space between us and put my hands on her shoulders. For some reason, she lets me. "I told you I'm here to help you, and I am. It's not easy or smart, but I've never been either of those things. All I know is, you are what drives me. Whether it be driving me nuts, or horny, or for someone to talk to … it's all you. And I can't leave that behind. Not this time."

"You don't know what you're talking about." Mack sighs. "Your impulse control has always been lacking—"

I slam my lips over hers, deepening the kiss and communicating what my lack of words can't. *I want you. I need you. We can both feel worthless together.*

I wrench away when Mack gasps for breath and say through a ragged exhale, "You wanted to show me how to fuck gently. But you're no glass sculpture. You're not gonna break, but I'll still stand by you. Face the fucking press and media questions. You have worth, Mack. You have a helluva lot of worth to me, and I'm not going anywhere until you figure that out."

Mack's shining stare searches mine. In a surprise move, she holds both hands to my cheeks, bringing me in for a closer study. She whispers, "Take your own advice, Mason," then lets go.

Mack walks away, leaving me hanging in the middle of her best friend's apartment. She glances over her shoulder before heading into the bathroom. "You know where the exit is."

And locks the bathroom door behind her.

CHAPTER 33

Mckenna

WORTH.

A word I never believed Mason knew the definition of, since he exuded so little of it. And if anyone deserves it the most, it's him. He has talent, drive, strength, stubbornness, pride.

They've never gone away, despite the odds stacked against him since he was born. All traits I should've reminded him of in Dee's living room, but couldn't.

If I did, he would've stayed.

Maybe we'd become something.

And that, more than anything, makes me question *my* worth.

I finish setting my make-up in the bathroom mirror. I've yet to unlock the door and step out, but I doubt Mason's still there. He's never taken well to outright dismissal and has probably stormed off to either get black-out drunk somewhere or punch something.

Doesn't matter. That can be Mason's afternoon.

I click my compact shut and shove it in my travel cosmetics bag, then pad out of the bathroom in search of my heels. Donning the designer suede pumps gives me a sense of power, even if it's false.

I call a car on my way down the elevators, having been texted the address by Giles a few hours earlier. As if I've forgotten where I was last strangled.

The nerves haven't hit me yet. My head's still in the clouds with Mason, and perhaps safer there.

Clutching my phone tight in my fist, I slip into the waiting car. I've chosen simple beige slacks and a billowing cream tank to match the sleek Jane-face I've put on. I'm not about to be Giles's puppet and wear the dress he wants. It's a tiny form of rebellion, but I'll jump at the chance to maintain my independence in front of that man.

Thankfully, when I step outside and into the car, there's no other cameras around to match McKenna to Jane.

Too soon, the driver pulls over to the curb of the luxury building I was hoping to never set eyes on again. Clutching the phone in my lap, I peer out the window, assessing the mirrored gray exterior all the way up.

"You okay back there?" the driver asks.

His question snaps the elastic drawn taut around my gut. I pull my gaze away. "Yes, fine. Thank you."

Once out of the car, I smooth my slacks and brush errant strands of hair out of my face—clear distraction tactics, but I need something to do with my hands other than have them tremble in front of me.

Doing this alone seems stupider the closer I come to meeting Giles again, but doing this with someone—like Dee or even Mason—is even more frightening. Why drag them into this complicated mess and put them at risk? My reputation's already in tatters. There's no need to drag their lives down with me.

A security guard eyes me as I push through the revolving door. He murmurs something into the landline phone pressed against his ear, then places it down once I'm in the lobby.

"He's expecting you. Go right on up, Miss Beckley," he says.

I nod, and though my heels make confident clacks against the marbled flooring, my attention skirts everywhere, looking for cameras or anything else that could've tipped Giles off that I'm here.

I smooth my hair again when I enter the elevator and turn to the doors, using my blurred reflection in the brass as a mirror into my future. A whole canvas of obscured uncertainty.

The elevator slows and I take a deep breath as the doors soundlessly slide open. My shoes don't make any power sounds at all as I stride down the carpeted hallway and stop at Giles's door.

Knocking softly, I suck in another inhale. I can do this. Make this quick. Give Giles the money, ensure my dad's safety, then start a new life somewhere, anywhere, else.

Thinking of my rainy day fund stashed in an untraceable bank deposit safe gives me a sense of calm. I have a way out of this.

The door swings open to a pine-filled, woodsy scent that I still smell in my nightmares.

"McK—oh. I see we have Jane today," Giles says as he appraises me head-to-toe. "Come in, darling."

Never will I give you the real me.

The thought takes me back to the sex I just had with Mason, and how that's the most real I've been with anyone in a long time.

Giles appears as misleadingly dashing as ever, with tousled, thick brown hair streaked with just the right amount of gray, a blue button-down open at the neck, and smokey gray suit pants capped off with designer, lacquered black shoes.

"Drink?" he asks. His back is to me as he reaches for two crystal tumblers at his mahogany cocktail bar in the main room.

"No." I don't bother with platitudes or manners. "Can we get this over with?"

Giles ignores both my answer and my question, pouring me a glass of bourbon. He spins around, handing me the glass.

"I said no." I hold my purse and phone in front of my stomach like a shield. "I don't want to be here, Giles. I'd like to get this over with."

Giles smiles. In some circles it could be considered serene, but I recognize the reptilian curve of a snake when it's in front of me. "In due time, darling. Sit."

He directs me to the lounge area where he places my unwanted drink on a coaster where I suppose he wants me to sit.

"I'd also like assurances that my father will remain untouched after the transaction is completed," I say, remaining where I am. Perhaps if I sound professional and detached, it'll become real.

Giles straightens from placing my drink on the coffee table. "You have my word."

"I don't believe your word to be enough—"

A thousand tiny, crystal shards burst against the wall above my head, the sound so shocking I lose the voice to scream and inhale a strangled gasp instead as I flinch and duck.

Giles latches onto my forearm and pulls me against him so I have no choice but to stare into his face as he bends close, his breaths hot and shallow as he seethes.

"Some men might enjoy your spirited behavior, but not me," Giles spits. His eyelids are so stretched, the whites of his eyes are more obvious than his irises. He shakes me by my arm that he's pressed up between us, his fingers spindly vises that'll surely leave a bruise. "*I* get to ask the questions. *I* hold the power."

I breathe through my nose, afraid to keep looking at him. Afraid to look away.

"Now is the time to apologize, *McKenna*," Giles says against my harsh breaths. His grip on my arm tightens. "Be a good little girl, now."

My lips part, but nothing comes out.

Giles lifts my arm and inspects it. "Do you like this appendage? Wait. Silly me. I should be aware of your most important asset by now."

With the movement of a viper's strike, Giles cups my vagina, his fingers spearing through the thin fabric of my pants like it's non-existent. The resulting pain burns through my struggles, but he still has me by the arm.

"*Stop!*" I yell.

He digs in harder. "Say you're sorry for acting so very immaturely and I will, my darling."

"I..."

He dips his head like he can't hear me as he continues his assault. "You what?"

"I'm sorry!" I cry, hitching with a sob. "I'm sorry for insulting you. For being immature. I'm sor—"

I stumble back after an abrupt release. I hold a hand to my mouth to quell the sobs, but nothing will work to slow down the erratic, panicked beats of my heart begging to be let out of this cage. *What have I done by coming here?*

"You are nothing but a pawn whore who's caught herself up in a very dangerous web," Giles says. "I suggest you start acting like it."

I swallow, attempting to control my gulps of air.

"Now sit."

This time, I do, the places where he assaulted me rubbing raw against the cushions.

Giles snaps his fingers, and a man in a black suit comes out of the hallway as if he were standing there waiting for Giles's call the entire time. My eyes follow his movements in a silent plea for help, but I might as well be positioned in his blind spot. He hands Giles an electronic tablet.

Giles taps his fingers against the screen as he speaks. "I have my details right here, my darling. If you would be so kind as to hand me yours."

The last thing I want to do is give Giles access to my bank account information, but my logic, still operating smoothly despite the jarring situation, insists I can close the account the instant I'm out of this room.

Besides, there's no knowing how much Giles has gleaned already.

I pull up my information and hand him my phone without argument, which he takes, pulling a face of surprise as he sees how much is in my checking.

"I stand corrected," he muses. "The whore business treats you well."

"It's all yours," I say in a cracked voice, despite Giles going nowhere near my neck. "Take it, and let me and my father go."

"How daring, continuing with your demands."

"It's not a demand if we've made a deal," I whisper.

"Come again?'

I peer up at him, saying with stronger emphasis, "We made a deal. The money in exchange for my father and I's safety."

Giles waits a few beats. "Mmm, your father, yes. But I don't recall making any kind of deal about *you*."

In that moment, I realize just how very, very sharp the precipice I'm balancing on has become. My heart drops out of its protective barricade and into the deep unknown.

Giles snaps his fingers and the man in the suit reappears in the doorway.

"Take her to the table," Giles says.

I rear back. "The table? What do you—?"

The man strikes halfway into my garbled question, holding me in a bear trap as I scream and fight against his hold.

"Let me go!" I scream in between gnashing teeth. I'll mar any part of him I can find. Kick him in the balls. Stomp on the sensitive tops of his feet. Bite his fingers off, but he brushes my defenses off like he's swatting at a butterfly.

"You're getting what you want!" I say to Giles as the man drags me out of the room. "Please! Let me go!"

"In due time, my darling," Giles says with ineffable cheer. "I have some branding to attend to, first."

As I'm dragged through the vast hallways, my screams echo to the ceiling.

CHAPTER 34

Mason

I AIN'T NO STALKER.

There's no harm in noticing the bar across the street from Mack's friend's place, or that it looks good enough to catch a few beers in, and there's no problem in happening upon a barstool that gives me a perfect view of the front entrance of said building.

If Mack happens to leave and I just *happen* to glance over and notice, what's the big deal?

Nothing. It's a free city. I can drink and brood where I like.

I step into the small building. It's surprisingly crowded. I shake the morning off, my leather jacket suddenly overwhelming in a bar filled with people. With so many bodies, I don't think Mack will notice my presence – not that it matters whatsoever, because I'm not doing anything wrong – but I try to take a seat somewhere where I'm hidden from view.

The music is some upbeat country song. A couple of drunk co-eds try and dance in the middle of the bar. I don't think it's supposed to be a dance floor, but nobody stops them. A couple of pretty girls next to me openly stare and whisper to themselves. One even has the balls to smile at me. I know that smile. I lived for that smile. Before...well, I don't want to go into it.

The bartender chick comes over, wiping down my area as I straddle the stool.

"Jeez. Wish I were the girl who's got your dick in a pinch," she says without looking at me, focusing on wiping up.

I take enough time to drag my attention from the stained windows over to her. "Whatever special you have on draft'll work fine," I say. I realize I'm being rude and add, "Thanks."

I almost growl at myself for the aforementioned politeness. That's Mack, all over me, even though she doesn't leave anything behind. I almost hate her for it, but Mack is someone I can never hate. I've tried and failed so many times before, it's exhausting.

She replies with a salute. "You got it. Big fan, by the way."

My lips peel back in a smile, but it's barely genuine. I'm too busy waiting for Mack to show herself and the plans she's made straight off my tour and her downfall.

A descent you played a big part in, asshole.

It'd be easy to plead dumb and insist I had no idea what Sorsha was up to, but I'm not a coward. I'm aware of how cunning she is and how she manipulates with sex. Brax didn't stand a chance, and I can't blame the poor schmuck who spends more time in rehab than with women in the outside world for blabbing to a gorgeous celebrity who must barely seem real in his eyes.

My job now is to fix it. Only problem is, how can you give a woman her credibility back when she never asked for it in the first place?

I think back on the recent sex between us and how real it was. How *good* it felt, almost like we were *us* again, but with careful intentions. I touched her like she was precious. Stroked her like a shining jewel. Kissed her like she was mine.

I flex my fingers and curl them into a fist, trying to forget the way she felt in my hands, the way I longed to feel her again. Everything's all fucked and I'm trying to fix it, but there's that small voice in my head that tells me I will never be able to fix it.

I try to distract myself but I can't. I keep thinking of her.

I keep thinking about Mack Beckley long enough to want to hitch a ride on a bar stool until I can see her again.

Fuck. I'm screwed.

The cold pint's slid in front of me and I down half of it in one gulp, then signal for a shot of Jack. My eyes rest on the surface of the bar. A couple of peanut skins are nearby and I resist the urge to swipe them onto the floor.

Clearly, I'm in this bar to think, not stalk. And I have a lot of goddamned pondering to do.

The noise of music and people dulls my thoughts. The music changes to some terrible pop song heavy on synthesizer, low on actual lyrics. It repeats the same phrase over and over again. One of the drunk co-eds has fallen and her friend is too drunk to properly help her up.

When my phone rings, I chance ignoring it since it can only signal bad things. My band mates. Jess. Managers. Hell, the record label. All with threats and stress, and each and every one figuring that deciding my future behind my back is much more preferable than dealing with the repercussions of me finding out.

It goes to voicemail. I order another beer.

My head buzzes with alcohol, but I'm not drunk. Nowhere near it. If I were, I don't think my thoughts would still be coherent enough to reason with them.

The phone buzzes against my ass again. On a growl, I pull it out and check the display.

Brax.

The one fucker I shouldn't ignore.

Goddammit.

I swipe to answer then snap, "What?" as I hold the phone to my ear. The noise around me is suddenly louder and I turn in my stool, my back to the music, to the makeshift dance floor, hoping it helps me hear him better.

"Dude. How long does it take you to answer? You ignoring me?"

"Yes." I'm not going to lie to him. I flick my gaze across the room on some dumb hope of spotting Mack in the crowd.

"Okay, well, you shouldn't, asshole," he says. He doesn't bother to hide his frustration in his tone. I don't care, honestly. I'm too focused on other shit to baby him. "I have some big news I've been trying to tell you all fucking day. But you won't pick up your phone because you're a pussy and are afraid to talk to all the big boys and deep pockets you've ditched."

I belch, then take another long swig of beer. The two girls from before start playing with their hair, trying to get my attention. I purposefully ignore them. They're trying too hard it's not even fun. "Get to the point, fucker. I haven't got all day."

"I don't know," he says. I can picture him, tilting his head up, arms crossed over his chest, looking at the sky. "Maybe I should make you wait for it. Beg for it."

"I'm hanging up," I snap. I can't believe I picked up this twit's call in the first place.

"Wait, dude. Fine. Goddammit, you're no fun," he says. "It wasn't Sorsha who said that stuff about Mack."

I freeze. I'm ready to take a swig of beer but stop. Wait. Say nothing. Instead, I remain silent, which Brax misconstrues.

"The prostitute stuff," Brax clarifies. "That's all over the internet. You know, the event that made Mack leave us early—"

"I'm well aware." Even to me, I'm impressed by my careful dictation as I speak, in spite of the volcano about to spew some lava all over my poor, misguided brother. My words are warning shots, clipped and firm. I can barely speak. There's too much going on in my head. I grip the beer tight, surprised glass hasn't shattered and the bar isn't covered in cheap beer. "Who dared to do it, then?"

Brax pauses. I know he's hesitating. And he calls *me* a pussy.

"Brax," I snap. No more warning.

"Okay, sorry," he says quickly. "It was Jess."

I clench my teeth. I don't know how to respond. I want to break something. Hurl this pint across the room and watch it smash to pieces. I can't believe what I'm hearing.

This time, Brax construes my silence correctly.

"I know, right?" he says. He's still uncomfortable, his voice strained, but finds more confidence the more he speaks. "Totally out of left field. But when Mack left, then you left, I got suspicious. Did some digging of my own. A lot of people think I'd only make friends with junkies while in rehab, but no one thinks to remember that we're not junkies first. We're people with careers, and families, and aspirations. Some of them illegal, sure, but—"

"Brax." I pinch the bridge of my nose with my fingers. As much as I appreciate his explanation, I don't have time for it.

"Right. Sorry. The point I'm getting at is, I know a hacker or two, and I might've called in some favors to break into some of the blogs that broke the news first." He clears his throat. "And it turns out, the emails providing the scintillating information about you and Mack came from Jess."

"She wouldn't," I say, shaking my head even though Brax can't see. The girls have given up, leaving me alone, something I'm grateful for. I take a small sip of beer. Before I can ask for another one, the bartender puts it down and gives me a little wink. I can't bring myself to smile my thanks at her, so I nod instead. "Jess isn't so stupid as to use her personal email to leak information."

"Well, right," Brax says as though that much is obvious. "The email to the blog was from a dummy account. But without getting into computer speak, which is way over my head, my boys traced the IP address, got into Jess's emails, and saw *her* exchange between someone else who wanted the information made public."

In an attempt to sort the circular chain of individuals Brax explained, I push the rest of my beer away and take hold of my new one. I'm too confused to even bring it to my lips "Come again?"

But Brax continues as if I haven't said anything. "Do you know a guy named Giles Bennett?" he asks. He keeps talking without giving me a chance to speak, which is probably a good thing because I have no idea who he's referring to. "'Cause that's who gave Jess the info—she seems to be on his payroll, by the way—and asked for it to be leaked. It didn't take much, since it's obvious Jess has had it out for Mack since the beginning."

"Giles, Giles..." I say the name repeatedly, because it's signaling *something* in my brain. I just can't place it. I pinch the bridge of my nose again. I'm sure the bar tender probably thinks I'm drunk enough to think I'm underwater or something. "Who the fuck is Giles?"

The guy sitting next to me turns to look at me over his shoulder. He shots me a look. Judging by the pressed suit, the slicked back hair, I take it he's never heard of me or my music before. He sneers but turns back to the girl he's talking up – one of the girls I ignored.

You're welcome, dick.

"That your girl?"

The bartender draws my attention as she saunters up and points out the window. Her eyes linger on the glass .

"If so, she's hot," the bartender says.

I follow her direction. For a moment, it's hard for me to make out anything because the glass is so stained. However, I manage to find a clear area and narrow my eyes. Sure enough, Mack's exiting Dee's building with long strides, head forward, sunglasses in place...

Hang on.

I frown, tilting my head to the side.

"Bro? You still there?" Brax asks. There's a note of worry in his voice.

Leaning forward, I get a closer look before Mack shoots into a waiting vehicle. I notice the sleek hair and tailored clothing. Her heavily lined, lipsticked mouth.

She's Jane.

She's fucking *Jane.*

I want to scream at her. My fingers curl back into a fist and I slam it against the bar. I don't even notice as pain shoots through my hand.

"Watch it, man!" the douche next to me says, standing up as though preparing for some sort of fight.

I don't pay attention to the pain or to the douche. My attention is focused solely on Mack. I press my lips tightly together.

Having the kind of exposure and disgrace she's experienced apparently did nothing to deter her from continuing to put herself at risk. I smack the varnished bar again, this time with an open palm, cursing under my breath.

"You alright there, bud?" The bartender asks. She looks at me as though I've grown a second head.

"Fine. Just fine," I mutter.

"Hello?" my brother calls from the other end of the phone. "Mase, you there, buddy? Answer me, man. Come on. I drop a bomb and you go dark? You okay?"

I'm far from it. I'm too enthralled in my own thoughts that I don't remember to respond to Brax. Or maybe I do. I don't know, and quite frankly, I don't care. Besides the rushing water echoing in my ears, I hear nothing. My only focus is on what a goddamn fool I've been. I don't feel the beer in my hands. I don't notice the bartender say something to me and then walk away to help other people.

Mack warned me all along she's not the girl she used to be and to stop looking for her. I could've sworn I glimpsed her a few hours ago, riding me with softness. I thought she had been true, had been completely vulnerable for me. I thought she was her real self in that moment. How could anyone have walls up during that experience? I, myself, was stripped of everything I thought I knew. I wasn't myself. I was someone more, someone open and wanting to feel things I hadn't allowed myself to feel in such a long time.

I shook my head, scoffing at myself. A strand of hair falls in my face but I don't bother to swipe it to the side. This time, I force my head to turn and remember the beer the bartender dropped off. I take a generous gulp , the amber liquid soothing the ache that developed in my throat. It's as though I want to scream but can't.

My head buzzes with the amount I drank in such a short time, but even then, it's not enough to take away what Brax told me. I also can't get the image of Mack out of my mind, her on top of me, completely undone and free. I couldn't believe I was arrogant enough to believe I received the kind of attention from her no goddamned client ever had. That I was special.

I'm an idiot.

An ass.

I don't understand how I could not have known I was just another...

It doesn't matter.

I tak another swig, letting out a hiss as my head swims. At least the thoughts are muddled. At least it helps drown out the memories of my time with her, but only slightly. I can still smell Mack's scent. I can still feel her skin in my hands.

I've been fooled. I don't do well with being made a fool.

I finish the rest of the beer and stand. I need to get out of here. Get some fresh air.

Standing, I throw a few bills against the bar and stalk outside. I bump into a couple of people on my way out. Some barely notice me, one guy swears. I don't care. I can hear familiar murmuring and I glance down at my phone and realize Brax must still be on the other line. I press the phone back to my ear as I watch the black car depart, taking the girl I thought I used to know with it. I'm surprised it's taken her this long to leave, but traffic is a bitch.

Mack wants her old life back? Then I'm more than happy to let her have it.

"Mase, seriously. Say something or I'm gonna think this is a dead call," Brax says.

I say, while glaring at the back of the vehicle, "Well B, as my brand spanking new Executive Assistant, you can tell the big boys on top there's no need to continue their freak out. I'm boarding a plane back to the tour tonight."

I know when I'm not wanted anymore.

CHAPTER 35

Mckenna

"STRIP HER."

My foot finds its mark against Suit Man's groin, but he only grunts. That's supposed to do more damage than elicit some sort of inconvenienced noise in the back of his throat. My back is pressed against his hard, yet pudgy stomach, and he uses a meaty hand against my forehead to hold me still and keep me facing Giles. I can feel his sweat smear my skin and it takes everything inside me not to empty the contents of my stomach on his fancy expensive shoe.

Or, maybe I should.

I say through my clenched jaw, "Don't you fucking touch me."

My voice comes out weaker than I want it to, but I don't look away from Giles.

Giles gives me a wry glance on the other side of the metal table. "Darling, we're past that."

I fight anyway. Despite being dragged into a small, windowless room with nothing but a metal table, a fireplace, and a sofa chair, I'm not about to cower.

The table appears freshly cleaned—streaks of cleaning solution blur what should be shining silver, as if it were recently used. I can smell the strong scent of chemicals from where I'm standing. Black straps with metal clasps hang down the sides, and I notice cuffs on the ends of them.

Oh God Oh God Oh God.

Stop looking.

I gulp. I'm trying my damndest to keep Giles from noticing my distress. I'll put up a fight, but I'm scared. I don't know what he's planning to do to me, what he wants, and that's what terrifies me the most.

I take a slow breath in, trying to steady my nerves.

"Either you take off your clothes willingly, or Mike here will do it for you," Giles says.

Suit Man—Mike—grips me so hard, his fingerprints will leave red marks on my face, but I can't seem to stop struggling. It's like it's in my DNA to push, punch and spit until something worse happens. It's the only semblance of control I have, and if I give it up now, what does that leave me with?

"McKenna. Dear. You're trying my patience." Giles pinches the bridge of his nose with annoyance, clicking his tongue against the back of his teeth. He moves to the fireplace, giving me his back as he pokes at it with something iron. "Is that better? You'd like a little privacy? I didn't realize you were so modest, what with your history."

"I'd like to leave," I say. My voice cracks and I wince,. That's not showing my confidence at all. I clear my throat and continue. "You have your money. I've done what you wanted. There's no—"

"I say when we're done, and if you'd listen to my instruction, you'd be out of here in a jiff." He continues to poke, his shoulders hunched to his ear as he does so. I can hear the metal of the fire poker grind against the inside of the fire place and I shudder. "I'll only repeat myself once. Take your clothes off yourself, or Mike will tear them off you and it won't be as pleasant."

Abruptly, Mike releases me. It takes a few seconds to gather the strength back in my legs and hold myself up. But with unsure fingers, I do as he asks, because I can still feel Giles's hands on my throat, cutting off my air.

I hate that I'm doing this. My fingers find the button to my pants and shake so much it takes me a moment before I finally pop the button through the hole. I suck in a gasp. My mind overwhelms with possibilities of what will happen. And the more scared I get, the more difficult it is for me to follow instructions. And if I can't do that, I can't fight back.

I need to get a grip.

My pants go first, then my shirt. They pool silently beside me, the thin silk fabric soundless and delicate and completely at odds in this harsh room.

I take another breath, my eyes on my clothes. A feeling of resignation goes through my body and I realize that I have no control. To think otherwise is foolish.

"Bra and panties, too," Giles says without turning around. I have no idea how he knows I've stopped unchanging, how he knows I haven't removed my underwear.

A whimper sounds out, and I realize it's me. I clamp my mouth shut, but it's too late to pretend Giles hasn't heard it. Or Mike. I shut my eyes, lecturing myself. When I open them again, I realize the corners are wet with small beads of tears.

Mike steps forward when I remain frozen, so I move to unclasp my bra, then slowly, painfully, pull down my underwear.

I swallow. I hate myself. I hate every minute of this.

I stand completely naked, my soul stripped bare, for this man's hungry, unapologetic gaze. I don't need to be anything to him. Quite frankly, I don't want to be, but I hate that this is what I'm reduced to and I hate the shame that crawls inside of the pit of my stomach and stays there like wet cement, sinking as far as I can breathe.

It's better than them doing it, I tell myself, reminding myself.

That's the only thought that keeps my limbs moving.

"Good girl," Giles murmurs, his back still turned. "Mike. Set her down for me."

I turn for the door, picturing a sprint through the hallways and a successful escape, but Mike clasps my arm and shoves me against the table before I can get farther than that, even in my mind. I try not to notice how bruising his thick fingers are on my skin. I try not to whimper as he moves with me. When he yanks me to my side, I can't help it. I can't keep doing this. I can't keep standing here and letting this happen to me.

I scream. I scream, cry, and scratch, but he lays me flat like I'm nothing to him but a skinned salmon filet. I scratch at him but his grip tightens. I'm certain I'll have bruises, but if I survive this, I welcome the marks on my body. I will wear them proudly, like battle wounds.

I manage to catch his underbelly and he grunts. His eyes slice a glare at me and he releases his grip in order to place his fingers on my throat. I know it's a threat. I know he's telling me he has no problem doing worse to me if I don't contain myself. His fingers dig into my skin and I'm gasping for air. I choke, trying to suck in anything I can.

"Enough," Giles says. "I know she can be a handful, Mike, but she's a tulip compared to you. Really, she shouldn't be giving you any trouble."

This seems to knock some sense into Mike. He releases his grip on my throat only to grab my arms yet again. He holds my arms down and straps them still, then spreads my legs and locks them down, too. I become sure: *I'm going to die here. The money was nothing but a ploy to kill me. Giles is a psychopath.*

I think of my father, and the lengths I went to in order to save him, despite his complete shut-down and inattention after my mom died. I think of Debbie, who'd prefer to let my dad rot in jail than deal with the repercussions he caused. Maybe she was right. Maybe I should have listened.

I think of Mason and the unexpected surprise of his gentle

touch. How those moments with him this morning cushioned the blow of my memories, and the sheer shock scoring through me at the realization that he's actually changed.

I can fix this, Mack. Let me fix this.

Oh, Mason, I think. *You can't fix what I've utterly broken.*

I flutter my eyelashes, slowly opening my eyes, and a lone tear falls down my cheek. I itch to reach up and wipe it away, but I can't. Mike has me fully restrained.

But, Mike's left my eyes and mouth free. I'm not blindfolded or gagged, but I'm not sure that's a good thing. I train my attention on Giles and what he's doing by the fire, his last words before locking me in this room a glaring alert in my mind.

Branding.

That can't be good.

At last, Giles turns, and he doesn't have what I thought was a fire poker in his hand. Instead, it's like a cattle prod with a circular end, the type of iron stick farmers use to brand their cows' haunches.

My lips part. Sweat collects on my temples at the growing heat in the room and the sudden, animalistic fear taking over my body even though I don't quite understand what's happening.

"Now, I realize your career's in jeopardy after unfortunate recent events," Giles says, slowly walking over to me. The end of the cattle prod glows an orange-yellow color from the fire. "So sad. How *ever* did your information get leaked?"

The gleam in his eye tells me exactly how it leaked. It was him. Giles sold me out. But … "Why?" I croak, not taking my eyes off the end of the prod. My mouth goes dry just looking at it.

Giles's lips spread wide. "I love my games, darling," he says, as though it's the most obvious thing in the world. "And preventing you from receiving that money, well, I salivated over how you were going to get yourself out of that pickle. What you might be willing to do. Unfortunately, I underestimated both your wiles and your pussy." Giles's lips pull to the side before he asks, "How was it fucking a rock star, anyway? That's the one boon I didn't gain with Jessica. As much as I encouraged her to, she never fucked Mason Payne to better get into his head." Giles shrugs. "Or maybe he never wanted to fuck her. Either way, here we are."

I keep still and silent, trembling and exposed on the table. I don't want to think about Mason being in a similar position with another girl. That's the last thing I want in my head right now.

And Giles knows it.

He likes his games.

Fuck him.

"Mason paid you well, at least," Giles muses. He tilts his head to the side, furrowing his brow. "You must be extremely talented to be worth *that much* money. I figure, I should sample the goods myself. Why not? I earned it, haven't I?"

He drags his attention down my chest, pausing to appreciate my breasts, then goes lower. It's only his gaze and yet, I feel absolutely disgusted with myself, with the situation we are in. It feels like he's touching me, exploring me in a way I definitely don't want, especially not from someone like him.

The chains rattle with my tugs, but it does me no good. At least it feels like I'm actually doing something instead of letting this happen to me.

"What are these?" Giles asks.

The dry pads of his fingers dance across one side of my hip, while his other hand holds his weapon steady. I flinch at the idea that he might accidentally brush my skin with the other end of it.

"Marks of some kind. Fingerprints," Giles deduces, "that are not my own. Hmm."

His tone turns dangerous. The knuckles on his hand holding the brand have turned practically white. "Who touched you, my darling? Who dared to leave their marks on you first, before I could claim you for myself?"

He slaps my outer thigh, hard. I choke on a whimper.

At least it's not a branding from the cattle prod, I remind myself. But I have a feeling he'll use it eventually.

"That won't do." Giles tsks-tsks. It's unnerving how soft his voice is, how I can feel his anger and frustration, but he isn't actually yelling at me. I almost wish he would. He's too controlled. I can't predict him, and that scares me more than if he were raising his voice with a threat. "For now, my handprint will cover it, but if I *ever* see another man's fingers on you from this point on ... oh dear, you do not want to picture what I'll do."

He shakes his head.

Smack.

I whip my head to the side, away from Giles, refusing to let him see my tears.

Despite his warning, I still didn't expect him to slap me. To spank me like I'm some kind of child who misbehaved.

The sick fuck.

"Better yet," Giles says with a smile, his eyes never leaving my center. "Why don't I claim ownership to the goods myself? It's not like you're a working girl for much longer."

Giles steps closer, the prod hot, red and glowing at the end.

"No. Please," I find myself whispering. I close my eyes, trying to get rid of the tears so I can speak without my voice shaking, without sounding so pathetic, so weak.

"Just think, McKenna-Jane, every time you strip for another man, any time you take your clothes off to bathe or to fuck or to change for the day, you'll be reminded of me," he continues, as though he hasn't heard me. "That you're now mine." He holds up the prod. "This, my darling, will pay off your debt, with the added bonus that I can call upon you at any moment as my own." He chuckles and glides a finger down my inner thigh. I flare my nostrils, closing my mouth to keep any bile from spitting out. I don't want to anger him, not when he's so close to me with that branding prod. "Even when I'm not there."

I want to throw up. I consider changing my mind. Maybe spitting at him will enrage Giles to the point where he does yell, where he forgets his carefully crafted plans and actually behaves in a way I can do something about. I decide I have nothing left to lose. I urge myself to do it, since that might turn him off, make Giles back away. Hell, I'll pee myself—anything to stop this madness, this nightmare, from continuing.

"These are my initials," Giles murmurs, his attention never straying from my body. "They are going to look so wonderful on this bare pussy of yours."

A cry unlike any sound I've made before leaves my throat. The fear is so thick in my throat, I can't throw up. My denial is so stiff, I can't release my bladder willingly.

But it's not just fear. It's disgust. I'm so disgusted with myself, with what is happening here, that my entire body has gone numb as a way to survive.

And even survival is unlikely. Sure, he'll keep me around so he can play with me, violate me whenever he decides he wants to, but right now, I am alone and there isn't any sort of escape.

No one knows I'm here.

"Stay still, my darling," Giles says, finally meeting my eyes. There's no life behind them. He's dead inside, same as me. "This will only singe for a few moments. The smell, however ... well, picture yourself at a picnic barbecue."

"N-*no*—" I choke out, but I can't even get it out right.

"Oh, yes." A flicker of amusement touches his face and the corners of his lips turn up.

A game. This is all a game to him.

He loves his games.

The cattle prod comes down, and I'm screaming as if it's already landed against my fragile skin.

A second of searing, *everlasting* pain rockets through my core when he starts to press it against my skin. I scrunch my eyes shut, my mouth stretching wide for a final scream—

A roar.

I catch my breath, swallow my scream. I try to see what's happening, but everything is going so quickly, it's difficult for me to keep up.

A grunt.

Since I'm still restrained, I crane my neck, looking for some sort of hint as to what's happened with Giles, what Mike's doing. These sounds are all wrong.

The pain recedes.

I look down and see the brand is no longer on my skin. I let out a cry of relief, tears blurring my vision even further, distorting my reality even more.

Am I dreaming? Or is this real?

The clatter of iron hitting the floor jars me from my muddled thoughts and I angle my neck to try and see.

"Who the f—"

A loud *thwack* cuts off what Giles was about to say, and suddenly, his crumpled form falls to the floor.

"Hey!" Mike exclaims.

He reaches into his jacket, and I'm sure it's for some kind of weapon, something to stop ... who? Who's here? What's going on?

I blink and shake my head, hoping my clouded thoughts clear up. I don't know if it's my position on this table or if it's something else, but I can't see anything. All I know is what I hear—Mike is going for his weapon and someone is actually trying to save me.

There's a struggle between Mike and the assailant. I don't know if Mike has his weapon out, or even what the weapon is.

The stranger is surprisingly silent. I don't know if it's a man or woman. I don't know if he's here to help me or if he's here to take me for himself.

Someone moves to my left.

Giles has gotten up. He's rushing towards a figure behind my head, wearing a black leather jacket. I cry out a warning. I hope I've helped him in some way. I hope I was able to warn him in time, and my eyes scrunch shu as I brace for some kind of impact. Because I have to be next.

You're afraid. Don't be afraid, be brave. Even if this doesn't work out, you're supposed to be going down with a fight, right? Don't make things easier for them by cowering. If anything happens to you, look them in the eye when they do it.

I clench my teeth together, preventing a battle cry. The voice is right. If I am going to die, I'm going to die with my eyes open.

I open my eyes to two shadowed forms struggling against the fireplace. My first thought is that it's Mike having second thoughts about torturing a woman, but then additional sounds reach my ears.

I blink once, twice, getting rid of the moisture that accumulated from trying not to cry and the panic I feel at being branded with a cattle prod.

Mike is fighting with someone. The stranger. Black Leather jacket.

I narrow my eyes, trying to get a better look.

A growl reaches me, and my entire body freezes.

I know that growl. That fueling riptide of rage unleashed from that mouth.

Mason? I mouth his name, the terror yet to leave my throat, but my eyes are wide open and follow the fight.

Mason lands a punch against Giles's jaw. Giles staggers back. Before he can catch his balance, Mason engages an uppercut to his torso. Giles lunges, but Mason pushes Giles's head down and rams it against the brick mantel of the fireplace.

I wince, the telling crack of brick against bone filling my ears and embedding itself there. I will never forget that sound for as long as I live.

I furtively search for Mike, doing as much as I can to watch Mason's back and hope neither Giles nor Mike has a gun. Whatever weapon Mike had been reaching for, I can't see it anymore. Giles definitely doesn't have it by the looks of things. It could have fallen to the floor, out of reach for anyone to grab, which would honestly be the best thing.

Where's Mike?

I had been looking for the weapon, but now I realize I don't see the man.

Lifting my head as much as I can, I glance around the room and eventually land on a slumped form in the corner.

Mike, unconscious. I let out a sigh of relief, tears blurring my vision once again. I wish I wasn't so emotional. I wish I could be strong when I really needed to. Mason must've gotten to him first, after knocking Giles to the ground.

"You think you can touch her?" Mason roars, drawing my attention back to the fight. "Without consequence? You think you can lay hands on her, *mark her*, without me coming to take off your head?"

I've never seen Mason like this. I didn't think I ever would see such a thing. So angry. I still can't see his face. Not really. But I can hear him.

Another punch.

I flinch.

I know Giles is a bad guy. I don't regret what Mason is doing to him. But I can't help but squirm.

Slam.

Toss.

I'm finally able to catch Giles as he slides against the wall, barely conscious.

"I'll kill you." Mason seethes. He walks into my line of view, leather jacket tight against his muscles. He doesn't even notice me, notice that I'm watching him. "With my bare fucking hands, and enjoy watching the light die from your eyes. I'll kill you by crushing your throat, first."

Giles writhes on the floor, gurgling from a likely broken jaw. Mason lifts a booted foot and readies to slam it down on Giles's neck.

I look away. I have to. I know Giles deserves pain, deserves some kind of retribution for all of the wrong he's committed, but this?

"Mason…" I let my voice trail off.

Blue fire shoots into my soul when he lifts his gaze and meets mine.

"Help. Please," I say. I don't think Giles is going to be a threat. Not anymore. And I don't want to stay here, naked and vulnerable, while Mason beats him to death. I want to go home. I want to put everything behind me.

Mason's jaw goes rigid. After a final study of Giles, fairly harmless on the floor, Mason steps away and strides to the table.

With one hand, he cups my jaw, using the other to unbuckle the cuffs on my wrists.

"Mack," he murmurs, his eyes flickering across my face, taking me in. "Holy fuck."

His study of the situation, of the way I'm splayed out and the position I've put myself in, shines in his eyes. For a moment, I worry he's judging me. I worry he's ashamed of my choices.

In response, soft sobs leave my lips. I don't want to cry in front of him. I don't want him to see me as weak.

"Oh, sweetheart. Baby, no."

With gentle, calloused hands, Mason lifts me into an upright seated position and folds me against his chest. His fingers dig into my hair, pulling me closer as he kisses my temple.

"I got you," he tells me, his eyes meeting mine. There's an intensity there, a promise. "You're gonna be okay."

I clutch him so hard, my grip gouges against his muscles, but Mason doesn't flinch or move. He just lets me.

I'm aware we don't have minutes, or even seconds, before either Mike or Giles recovers, but I can't seem to release him. Mason's smell, his warmth, his presence, is everything I've wanted.

"If I let you go," I whisper against his neck. "I'm afraid you'll disappear. That you're not really here."

"I ain't going nowhere, Mack." Mason holds me tighter.

After another kiss to the top of my head, he leans back to hold me by the shoulders. I'm ashamed to meet his eyes.

After a few seconds of assessment, Mason takes off his shirt and pulls it over my head, the warmth of his body lingering in the fabric.

"I'm an idiot," I say as he straightens the shirt against my torso, then moves to unbuckle my ankles. His fingers shake against my skin as he does so. I can tell from looking at him. He was afraid for me. "I can't believe I thought I had this handled."

I look away. Despite the fact that he's too busy freeing me to pay much attention to my face, I feel too guilty to even glance over. This is my fault. Maybe I'm not responsible for how evil Giles is, but I got myself into this mess.

"Hey." Mason pauses long enough to hold a hand to my cheek. "You're going to tell me everything, but not right now. Right now, I'm getting you out of here and taking you somewhere safe."

Mason glances down near my inner thighs, and I cringe at what he must see. Heat floods my cheeks and I want to press my legs together, to keep him from seeing anything, but he stops me. Gently, he places one hand on my thigh and I release a breath. I get used to his scrupulous study of my body. His lips have thinned. His free hand is down at his side, curled into a tight fist.

Giles's poker touched me, only for an instant, but it was probably enough to leave a mark.

With a deep breath, I look down, too, and see the bloody,

swollen half-circle there above my slit, almost like a crescent moon.

But no initials.

"Oh, thank God," I say with a haggard exhale. More tears fall and I let out a shaky breath. "Thank God it didn't..."

"It's going to hurt," Mason says, his fingers whispering along the edges of the brand before getting back to the straps. "But it won't be a bad scar. I don't think."

I shake my head. "It's better than..." but I can't get the rest out. I'm choking on fear, adrenaline, *relief*, confusion...

"Okay. You're all right." Mason moves faster in unbuckling my ankles. "I'm getting you out of here."

Mason lifts me in his arms at the same time Giles makes noises on the floor.

"You motherfucker," Giles says as he rolls onto his knees clutching his nose. "You're about to learn what it is to—"

Without warning, without saying anything to Mason or even thinking about what I'm doing, I slide off of the table. I clutch Mason's arm for a moment, needing to find my balance.

"Mack?" Mason questions, but I ignore him.

When I'm more sure on my feet, I walk over to Giles. He's still muttering about killing Mason. I can't stand it. This man has completely violated me in ways I could never fathom before now.

I kick him in the face, if only to shut him up.

"How dare you!" Giles says, spitting up blood. "You filthy, dirty slut."

I kick him again. This time, his head bounces off the wall. I hesitate, surprised that he's still not unconscious, but also because I am the one inflicting such horrifying pain on him

"I'll kill you. I'll *have* you killed!" Giles says through a rapidly swelling, bleeding face.

"Not before I access each and every one of your hidden bank accounts and drain you out of every penny you got," Mason says, coming up next to me. He places his hand on my lower back, offering me support. "Better yet, I'll send all the info to the cops. I'm sure they'd be mighty interested in the workings of Marvin Giles Vandersleuton."

Giles's eyelids flutter.

"That's right," Mason continues. "I know your real name. Got my guys working on accessing your shit right now. So, do me a favor. See this woman, the one who you treated like nothing more than an object, a plaything, as someone who doesn't matter? The one who just kicked your face in? Go on. Take a look at her."

When Giles's head slumps sideways, Mason forces it in my direction by bending and digging his fingers into Giles's jaw.

"Yes. Fine! I see her," Giles says, then wrenches away, spitting blood.

"These are the last few seconds you're gonna take to study her," Mason says. "After this, you're never going to see, speak, or fantasize about her again. Got me?"

When Giles says nothing, Mason prompts, "My guys are a phone call away, asshole. I'll send everything to the cops. And I do mean *everything*, including your proclivity to abuse hookers and all the pics you take to document it. Your personal information is *mine*, motherfucker."

"Okay. *Okay*," Giles repeats when Mason lifts a fist. "Leave. Go, already."

Mason straightens to his full height. "My pleasure."

As he turns, the frost in his gaze transforms into an inferno when he meets my eyes. Without a word, Mason lifts, then carries me out of that terrifying room and through the hallway without a hitch in his gait.

It's only when we're out of the apartment and enclosed in the elevator that Mason sets me on my feet. He hooks an arm around my neck, slams me against his chest, and fiercely kisses the top of my head.

"Christ, McKenna," he says as he breathes into my hair. "You're fucking trouble, aren't you?"

"Do me a favor," I murmur into his bare chest, my arms wrapping around him and fingers digging into the muscles on his back. "Don't let me go until I'm steady enough."

"Do you know when that'll be?"

I clutch him tighter. "Not for a long, *long* time."

CHAPTER 36

Mckenna

"WHAT'S THE PLAN?" I manage to ask the second we step out of the elevator. I keep my voice down, afraid someone may overhear us. "And you should at least let me walk."

"What happened to holding onto you until you're steady enough?" Mason asks, looking down at me with an arched brow. "You're fucking stubborn, you know that?"

I can tell by his voice he wants more of an explanation of what happened. I want to give it to him. I will. But we have to get out of here, first. Who knows if Giles has other men around here. Who knows if they'll be looking for us.

What I do know is that unless the lobby is empty, Mason is going to get caught carrying me in only a t-shirt, him being shirtless, and that would be just under a best-case scenario. If they noticed the blood on him, the way he's gingerly holding his hands, there's a good chance they may call the cops and the wrong people will get arrested.

"Look, Mack, we need to get out of here," he says, though it's obvious. "And the most direct route is to take the elevator down and cross the lobby."

"They'll see—"

"Two people, drunk, doing the walk of shame," he says.

"That's it. But I still have to carry you, even if your pride doesn't want me to."

The elevator pings and the golden doors slide open. We step inside and the doors quickly shut. My shoulders sag in relief. We're almost away from this mess, away from Giles and everything he planned to do to me. I shudder just thinking about it, blowing out a breath.

"Do you trust me?" Mason asked, wrapping the crook of his index finger under my chin and tilting it up so I can lock eyes with him.

I nod my head once. It's all I can muster. I can't even stand up straight, not yet. Maybe it's a good thing we're going to play it like this. I don't think I'd be able to walk as quickly as I think I can.

"I'm going to get you out of here," he says, just as the doors open.

At that moment, a couple of people walk in just as we stumble out, our faces angled away from them. I think, for a moment, that we're in the clear, that we're good to cross the lobby and leave.

"Oh my God, are you—?"

Mason's grip tightens on me. "We have to hurry."

The voice says, "Mason! Can I take a quick picture? I'm a huge fan."

Mason drops me to my feet and cuts his body in front of me to make sure no one catches sight of me and takes a picture. The last thing we need is someone selling this hot mess to a tabloid.

He urges me out of the building through the revolving doors. When we're out, his shoulders slope and he and turns, giving me a look that says *that was close*. With that, he scoops me back up in his arms before I can protest.

Mason ferries me to his waiting car with the speed of a cheetah that has the drop on its prey. It happens so quickly that anyone we pass by is unlikely to notice I'm clad in only a t-shirt and Mason's shirtless. Never mind the blood splattered against Mason's skin.

I don't know how much time has passed since Mason came to get me. I don't know how his car hasn't gotten towed on the street or how there hasn't been a long line of cars piling up behind his, honking and yelling. Part of me doesn't care.

I slip into the cool interior on the passenger side, my head falling against the headrest. I close my eyes as Mason rounds the front of the car and gets into the driver's seat. It felt like I had been in that room for hours, if not days. Every minute that ticked by was an hour. But I see it's still afternoon. The façade of time tricked me, and I'm grateful for that.

With a low purr, the engine starts and he pulls away from the curb. There's a loud honk but Mason doesn't even swerve. He forces himself into the street, not caring who he inconveniences. I want to laugh, but I'm too tired.

We sit in silence, the only sound the *whirr* of the air conditioning. Since I'm only in a shirt, my skin starts to prickle with goosebumps. As much as I revel in the peace, in the safety the car provides me, there's only so much of the silence I can take.

"How did you find me?" I ask while blearily staring ahead. It's the first thing that comes to my mind. "I'm grateful, but I didn't tell anyone, and I didn't know anyone actually knew where I was."

"Easy," Mason says. There's a hitch in his voice. He sounds nonchalant, like we're talking about something innocuous as the weather, but from my periphery, I can see the glare in his eyes. His knuckles go white against the steering wheel. "I sat across from the entrance to Dee's building at some bar and waited for you to come out. When you finally did come out—*as Jane*—I pretty much fucking lost it." He turns his head to look at me completely now, and my chest tightens.

I feel the need to say, "It's not what you—"

"Let me finish," Mason says.

The whiplash tone has my head going the same speed when I turn to look at him in anger, but it's in that moment I remind myself, as the muscles in his jaw tense and he blinks rapidly, the tendons of his arms going rigid underneath his skin, that minutes ago he broke into an apartment, bloodied himself, and beat up two men, all to get me out of there. He did all of that for me. And while it was never my intention to get caught up in that, I could understand why he's still upset. Me arguing with him, defending myself, will only give him a target to unleash his pent-up frustration on, and that won't be good for either of us.

I clamp down on any retorts I might have and look back out the window. The skyline of buildings soothes me. It reminds me that I'm no longer in that cramped room. I am free.

"I keep trying to tell myself you're gone," Mason says. His voice is low, almost like he's talking to himself rather than me. "The Mack I knew is no more. Then this morning happens, with the kind of sex that *you've* only probably read in your fairytale romances, and I find the Mack I lost. I see enough of her that I'm turned into this pathetic-ass puppy panting on the other side of the road, waiting for the pretty lady to exit the building and give me a cookie."

"Mason, I—"

"And then who comes out but the woman who tempts, who seduces, who *fakes*, and I think—she got me." He shakes his head, like he still can't believe that he let himself fall for it, for what we had. I want to reach out to him, reassure him that I'm right here, but I don't want to interrupt. "I was dumb enough to think the real Mack was somewhere under that temptress, when really, it's the other way around." Mason glances at me. "Jane's the real you."

I shake my head. This time, I try to say something but I don't get a chance to speak.

"That's okay, sweetheart." He scoffs, a smile on his chiseled face that doesn't quite reach his eyes. "I'm fine with it, considering how I treated you back then and hell, now. We do what we need to survive, and you got the money and ran. I get it. I figured that was my exit cue and I made arrangements for the first flight out as you got into the car."

I furrow my brow and turn to face him. "But … you didn't leave."

"Nope." Mason smacks the steering wheel with open fists. "I promised you no strings, and yeah, that should come with no hard feelings, but I can't fucking stop. I can't fucking stop raging at the woman who's ruining your life, this Jane you've created in the face of your dad's demise, of *my* past treatment of you, and so that's why I followed your car. Because despite being publicly outed as a paid escort, you *still* couldn't stop."

I shake my head, tears filling my eyes as I rest my head on the headrest. My vision is blurred and I gently close my eyes. A tear escapes my face and crawls down to rest on my jaw. "You have it so wrong," I tell him.

"Clearly." His hands twist on the wheel like he wants to protect himself from me. Like I'm capable of hurting him. Part of me wants to reach out, to break that wall he's put back up and tell him that I don't want him to push me away. I don't want him to lock me out. Even if I may deserve it. "I walked into a fucking butcher's shop," he continues. "What the *fuck* kind of guy was that? How did you get wrapped up as his hooker and why—s

"Stop. Just stop." I put up my hand, my head hanging down. My matted hair falls in my face, shielding my profile from his view.

"No." His voice is sharp. I can hear the fury behind it. The emotions he kept bottled up – the anger, the concern, the compassion he has for me, the emotion he doesn't want me to know about in order to protect himself from being hurt. "You don't get to cut off our conversation. I'll lock you in this car if I have to."

I flinch at his words. My entire body stiffens. I know he

doesn't mean them. I know he would never restrain me against my will, but I can't help my reaction so soon after what I've endured. Judging by the way he's stopped talking, he must have noticed as well. He sucks in a breath and waits, as though he's trying to think of the words to continue.

He lets out a sigh and looks away, out his window. I can see the tension in his neck, the way his jaw is clenched. I know part of him is sorry that he's used such a phrase, but he's not willing to apologize for it. Not yet.

So I wait. I close my eyes, trying to get hold of my body's reactions. I don't want to stop him from talking to me. Clearly, he has a lot he needs to get off his chest and I want to give him the opportunity to do just that.

Finally, he clears his throat. He tilts his head in my direction, but his gaze in on the dashboard of the car, on the traffic that's accumulated in front of him. We are at a red light now, though we wouldn't be moving, even if the light was green.

"All this time, you've insisted you're safe, you're smart, you're making more money than you've ever dreamed of and you're *happy*, and then I find some sadistic dickhead branding you with a fire poker," he says.

"It's ... he's ..." I try to explain but I can't find the words. Part of me thinks Mason won't understand. How can he?

"He's *what*, Mack?"

Mason bangs his hands against the wheel again, but much harder. I flinch again and I hate myself for my reaction. I hate that I am weak, that I am scared, that I can't do something as simple as tell Mason exactly what's going on so he knows the truth. Why is this so hard for me? Is it because I don't want him to know it? Because I'm ashamed of who I am?

"Why are you still hooking?" Mason demands to know. Now, his head turns so it's facing me completely. His eyes are wide like he's trying to understand but doesn't. "Why couldn't the cash I gave you be enough? *Fuck.*" Mason's voice turns sandpaper rough. He looks away again, gaze dropping to his lap, where his hands are digging into his thighs. "Why couldn't *I* be enough?"

I close my eyes just as his voice cracks. Pain rips across my chest. I thought I endured the most pain I would ever feel in that room with Giles tonight. If I close my eyes and imagine myself being branded again, I am sure I will still feel the hot metal searing my skin.

But I was wrong.

Because the pain I feel now, in this moment, because of Mason, knowing that I've hurt him in some way, is much worse than I anticipate. To be honest, I don't even realize I have the capabilities to hurt him at all. I feel no satisfaction in his pain the way I thought I might back in high school, after everything he had put me through. In fact, the last thing I want him to endure is misery, especially because of me.

A few heavy seconds weigh between us, the only sound coming from the car's engine and the blinker as Mason tried to change lanes. It's practically impossible. We are deadlocked.

I chew my lower lip, then say, "He was blackmailing me."

My voice is small, like the squeak of a mouse. I don't know why I say anything at all. Mason has already made up his mind about what happened. I've already hurt him more than I can remedy. What good will this do?

And yet, he needs to know the truth. Even if he still wants to be angry with me, if he wants nothing to do with me anymore, fine. But he needs to know because he deserves the truth. After rescuing me, after damaging his hands and risking his life to save me, I want him to know everything.

Mason manages to move the car an inch before the light changes red again, and turns to face me. "What did you just say?"

"Giles," I clarify. My gaze is on my hands in my lap. I turn them over so I can see my palms. It gives me something to look at, something that isn't Mason. It's easier to speak when I don't have to look at him, recognize his disappointment. "At first he wanted me to launder money for him through my business, which I did, which I wanted to do … but then you came along, offering me a quarter million, and I thought…" I let my voice trail off and shake my head once. How silly I had been to think I could get away with it.

Mason exhales heavily. "You thought you could pay him off," he finishes. "Get out of his debt so you wouldn't have to do his dirty work."

I nod. I curl my fingers into tight fists. I hope he can understand.

"You took the money to pay off your blackmailer instead of starting a new life for yourself." He seems dumbfounded by my words, as though he hadn't thought it could be anything other than what he assumed.

Part of me is sad that he would think so low of me. Then again, I try to understand it from his perspective.

"He threatened my father," I continue. I close my eyes. I try not to remember. It's too much for me. Anger burns my blood and a small feeling of helplessness curls in my stomach. Coming after me is one thing, but my family? I let out a sigh, reminding myself it was over. It's finally over. "And I had no choice but to believe it."

"Jesus, Mack." He blinks once, twice. He's finally able to move the car a bit more. I'm not sure if an accident caused the traffic or if it's the fact that it's a Saturday afternoon in the city. I'm just glad we're making progress and getting the hell away from Giles. "I wish you would've told me."

I shake my head, rubbing my hands on my thighs. Because it's my bare skin, there is no friction, and I'm not able to wipe off the perspiration. "It was my mess to clean up," I say in a low voice.

I can't believe I let myself get caught up in this. I've been such a fool. Mason risked a lot to get me out of there. Blood rushes to my face and I grind my teeth together. I even sink my nails into my thighs—not because I want to hurt myself, but to remind myself that this is my fault. I don't deserve Mason's kindness. Let him be mad at me.

"I..." He lets his voice trail off, pulling up to another red light. Traffic has cleared a bit. "I think we both need to learn to lean on each other when shit gets tough."

The statement is so out of place on Mason's lips. I pull my gaze away from the tiny crescent moons I've left in my thighs so I can look at him, not sure I heard him correctly. There's a good chance that I've imagined it.

"Mason..." I say, letting my voice trail off. I want to reach out to him. I want to touch him. I want him to know how much I appreciate what he did for me. So, I try and find the words and I hope they're enough. That he understands I mean them, and so much more. "I'm so grateful for what you did today. Honestly, I didn't think anyone would come for me. I wasn't expecting to be saved. I knew what I got myself into."

"Don't bullshit me, Mack. No way you knew he was going to fucking brand you."

I let out a breath. He's right, of course. There's no way in hell I could have predicted that.

"Regardless," I continue, "I just, I want you to know that you don't have to believe we're something." I look down again. "We're too messed up for that."

I don't mean that. At least, I don't want to mean that. I love Mason, and maybe it's not exactly a conventional love story, but I don't care. I want to offer him an out if he needs one. I don't want him to feel obligated to be with me.

Mason places his hand on my thigh. I look up, surprised by his touch, by the shock of life I feel spark through me. How does he have such power over me? He had it back in high school and he has it now.

"Are we?" He shakes his head and takes his foot off the

brake. He eases on the gas as we pass another red light. "Mack, I want to be messy with you." He presses his lips together and waits, as though he's trying to figure out what to say exactly. He runs his fingers through his hair, glancing at me from his peripheral. "I thought I lost you today, okay? And not the past McKenna or your alter ego, Jane. You. The Mack you are now. The messy, frustratingly stubborn, devastatingly gorgeous, the only woman to bring me to my knees. To make me weak. And I realized, I would do anything for this Mack. For you."

I clench my hands on my lap, worried my heart is falling for his words. I clear my throat as the silence drags on. I know he wants me to say something, but I'm not sure what he wants me to say. Hell, all I can do right now is feel. My heart bursts at his words, and even though I am so joyful at hearing them, there's still a black cloud hovering close.

Because, I realize, I want them to be true so badly. And I'm so worried that they aren't.

Not because I don't trust Mason, but because I don't deserve him. And I worry he'll realize it if I give into my hope and my own feelings for him.

The car behind us honks, and Mason drives forward, ripping his gaze from me.

"It wasn't Sorsha," he says. "It was Jess who outed you. And it came from Giles. Meaning, that douche-mouth was never gonna accept the quarter mill at face value. He wanted to ruin you. Then denigrate you. He wanted you isolated and alone so you would have no choice but to go to him. So you wouldn't feel comfortable going to anyone else. He wanted you broken and weak."

Mason's hand snatches away from my thigh like he had been burned so he can grip the wheel so tight, he may break it. I press my lips together, lifting my own hand. I hesitate. I want to touch him. I want to comfort him. But I'm not sure if I would help him or make things worse. I decide I don't care. I lay my hand on his hard forearm, tendons and muscles pulsing.

"You didn't let that happen," I say in a small voice, though I make sure it doesn't shake. I want him to know that he saved me, that he's responsible for keeping me from spiraling into that consuming isolation.

"Actually," he says, his voice flat, "it's Brax that didn't let it happen."

I pause, tilting my head to the side. Out of all the things that could have come out of Mason's mouth, that certainly isn't what I expect him to say. "Really?"

He nods, though his eyes are focused in front of him. "Brax met some people in rehab, computer geeks who like exploring the dark web or some shit." He shrugs, like he has no idea what any of that means and doesn't actually care. "He reached out to them."

"Brax knows hackers?" I ask, testing the theory out for myself. It sounds just as ridiculous as I expect it to.

"Yeah, Brax is still making friends in high places," Mason says, false humor lacing his voice. "You know how he is. I swear, that kid is always surprising me."

"Sober surprises, thanks to you."

"Say what?"

"You helped him," I say. "Stayed with him. Did everything you could. Saved him. He's lucky to have you, Mase. I don't think you realize the positive effect you had on him. He's lucky to have a good big brother looking after him."

Mason makes a sound in his throat as he makes a right turn. "I'm not a good guy, Mack," he says, his voice firm. It's like he doesn't like talking about this. He won't even look at me, not even from the corner of his eyes. "You gotta stop seeing me in that light."

"You became one for your brother," I insist. Perhaps it's not my place, but I can't help it. I've started talking and I can't stop now. "You think I don't remember the sacrifices you made for him when we were young? The jail time you did?"

Mason shrugs it off even though I know it's something that still burdens him to this day. "He's the only family I got," he says as though everything he's done is no big deal. "I couldn't let him go down our pops's road. What sort of brother would I be if I did that?"

"And you saved me today." I laugh softly, squeezing his forearm then letting go. I place my hand back in my lap. I feel lighter, talking to Mason about all of this, about the good person he tries to bury away. "I was wrong, Mase, when I said you haven't changed and meant it as a bad thing. You've always had good in you, even if you refuse to believe it." I pause. "I was wrong about a lot of things. And I'm ready to admit that maybe I don't actually know what I'm talking about half the time. I just think it's important that you know what a good person you are. If you don't believe me, fine, but I want you to hear it."

He's silent for a long moment. I don't know why, but I hold my breath. I wait. I hope my words sink in. I hope they squeeze through the cracks of the armor he's built around himself because he deserves to know he's good. He's not like the kid back in high school. He's grown. He's changed. And I see it.

His fingers caress my forearm but he doesn't hold it. His gaze is on his lap, but when he speaks, he's talking to me. "I want to keep finding the good with you."

I stiffen at his words, but not with tense foreboding. With hope.

I clear my throat. I uncross my legs only to re-cross them the opposite way. I forget I'm cold. There's a rush of blood through my body, warming me in a way I don't expect. I don't want to allow myself to hope. I don't want to take that risk. And yet, I can't help it.

"I'm going through a lot," he continues after a moment, his hands twisting the wheel, "And so are you. I don't even know if this is the right idea. But I want to…" He lets his voice trail off and lets out a small, frustrated grunt. He comes to another red light and while he doesn't slam on the breaks, the stop is jerky. "Honestly, Mack, I don't know what I want. The fact that I'm even considering…" He shakes his head. "It took me a while to come to this point, and seeing you naked on a butcher's table certainly helped."

I let out a breath. "I understand if being with me is too much for you, Mase. I would never want to force you to be with me until you're ready." I caress my thighs with my knuckles, trying to keep my eyes from spilling the tears that have accumulated in them. The truth of the matter is, I don't deserve Mason. And I realize it now, with absolute clarity.

All this time, I've been holding onto my past, using it as a reason for why I do what I do in the present, and the person as the center of it all is none other than Mason. He's my crutch, my excuse, and that's not fair to him when he hasn't actually done anything wrong, at least not now.

I don't deserve him. I'm as bad as he was then. At least he's grown. At least he recognizes that his actions weren't okay and he's changed. I've changed, certainly, but I've grown bitter and helpless, as though I blame all of my problems on other people rather than the right person. Myself.

"Mase," I say. My voice is garbled like sandpaper. I clear my throat, hoping that will help, but knowing I have to get this out, even if it doesn't. "I think I wanted to get back at you for everything you did in high school. I know I did back then but… I couldn't let it go. And I blamed you. But after being around you, and seeing the type of person you are, you make me want to be better. You make me want to forget the past, accept it for what it is, but release it. Let it go. I don't want to be broken. And I know you're not the person who can fix me. Only I can do that. But…" I let my voice trail off. I still have no idea how to tell him what I feel for him. A small part of me is still afraid of his brutal rejection, of the emptiness I would feel if I never got to see him again.

But that's his choice, and I need to be honest because I haven't been with him. And after everything he's done for me, he deserves my honesty.

"I care about you," I tell him.

He's silent for a long moment. I can feel him thinking, and I'm not sure if that's a good thing or not.

"We've been through a lot," he says as we pass residential buildings. "A lot more than most. Tough times. But I realize that if I have to go through these tough times, there's no one else I want to get through these tough times than you." He looks at me from the corner of his eyes. "I don't want to lose you again, Mack."

I say, so low he almost can't hear me, "I don't think you ever lost me, Mason."

"Mack. McKenna." Mason says my name like he's cherishing it, then pulls over, flipping on his hazard lights. The resulting horns and the blocking of traffic on this one-way street doesn't phase him.

He looks at me softly, taking me in. I shift with obvious discomfort under his gaze. It's like I don't want him to see me for who I am. I don't want him to see my flaws. I don't want him to remember the parts of myself, the darkness, I'm trying to forget.

But there's something about how he looks at me. Like the honking, he doesn't even seem to notice them. Or, if he does, he accepts it's there and moves on to look for something good inside of me.

After his cursory gaze, his eyes meet mine and he says, "Are we doing this? Are you sticking with me?"

I suck in a breath. I want to. God, I want to. But I also don't feel as though I truly deserve him. After everything he's done...

You have to stop punishing yourself for your decisions. You both made mistakes. You can both forgive and move on. Together.

I offer a tentative smile. "I can't very well leave my hero without his heroine, now can I?" I ask.

"Ah, Mack." Without warning, Mason turns and reaches for me. He pulls me into his arms, enveloping me into rugged warmth I didn't realize I needed until this very moment. I place my head over his heart, melting into him..

He says, "I can't believe I'm saying this, but I'm totally fine being your anti-hero"

I feel safe. Mason's heartbeat keeps a steady pace and reminds me I'm not chained anymore, that I'm with Mason, and I can have a life where I don't need to sell myself in order to survive.

"We have to figure this out," I say into his chest. My fingers trace his collarbone. "Your band. Getting out of this job of mine. If these last weeks have taught me anything, it's..." I let my voice trail off, trying to find the right words to say.

"That we like each other more than we hate each other?" he guesses before placing a kiss on the crown of my head.

I laugh, despite myself. "No," I say. "It's that maybe we love each other, and that's why we can't stay out of each other's business."

For a moment, I worry that I've said too much. We discussed caring about each other, but love?

"Love?" It's as though Mason can read my thoughts. "You love me?"

"I..." I swallow and let out a breath.

Part of me, the part that wants to stay hidden, considers taking it back. The last thing I want to do is push Mason away. Maybe we aren't at the point where we can love each other, but there's always a chance we can be friends. Except, I don't want to be friends with Mason. I don't think I can. We have too much history between us, and my feelings for him are both fierce and wild. I don't think I can contain them, even if I want to.

I take a deep breath.

I'm tired of being scared. I'm tired of living my life frightened and on the fringes. I want more. I don't want to live with a fake name, in fear of rejection or pain. My entire high school years were shrouded with that and I refuse to let my adult life be filled with more of the same.

Maybe I said too much. Maybe my feelings are much stronger than Mason's. But that's okay. They're the truth.

"Yeah," I say. "I do. I love you, Mason."

Mason still holds me. I hope that that's a good sign. I don't want him to think about whether he loves me or not. It's not something you have to think about. You either know it or you don't.

"Mase," I say, pulling away. "You don't have to love me back. I understand. I just, I think it's important that you know the truth. I'm done keeping things from you. And if love isn't something you're ready for, I get it. You have a lot on your plate." I reach up and curl a stray strand of hair behind his ear, letting my fingertips linger on his skin the way he did to me not so long ago. "But if there's a chance of you feeling the same way, or growing into that feeling, I'll wait for you. I'll give you your space so you can figure out what you need regarding the band, and when you're ready, I'll still be here."

He furrows his brow, thumb tracing his bottom lip, deep in thought. "You would do that?" he asks, as though he can't quite believe it. "For me?"

"I would do anything for you," I admit. "Mase, you saved my life. You could have broken your hands. You're my hero."

Mason scoffs but I can tell my words please him. He looks down at his lap, his lips curling into a smile that crinkles the skin around her eyes. For a moment, it strikes me and I'm paralyzed. Rarely do I get the chance to see Mason smile so fully and I wish I had the ability to take mental snapshots so I can remember later that I have the power to make him happy.

"You never cease to amaze me, Mack," he says. "I don't deserve you."

I roll my eyes. "Oh, please. Not this again."

He laughs, the sound so pure and unexpected, I can't help but laugh as well.

Without warning, he catches my lips with his own, one hand on my cheek, the other holding my chin. The kiss is gentle, but there's something possessive about it, as if he's saying I belong to him with his lips instead of his words.

"I love you, too, Mack," he says after he breaks away, resting his forehead on mine. He drops his hand from my cheek to take my hand in his and lace our fingers together. A shock ripples across my skin and leaves me tingling. "I always have."

I raise a brow, though I'm not sure he can see it and it's not important enough for me to pull away and show him. "Have you?" I ask instead.

"Since the very beginning." Mason kisses my temple and I sigh, content.

"I hate to be that girl," I say after a moment, "but I want to make sure we're on the same page. What does this mean? I know I want to be with you, but I understand if fuck buddy and girlfriend can't be used interchangeably right away. If you need time..."

I let my voice trail off. I'm not sure what I'm offering him – an out, maybe? Maybe I'm projecting. Maybe I'm the one who needs time. But I won't know until I hear what he has to say about it.

"Well, we love each other," Mason says.

"Our own fucked up, sweet, delicious, fiery kind of love," I reply with a grin.

Mason pushes away enough to search my face. It's almost as if he isn't sure if I'm making a joke or if I'm being wary of entering into a relationship—if that's what this is going to turn into—with this kind of feeling between us. "That's the only kind of love I want," he insists. "Look, I know it's not going to be easy. We both have our share of demons that we're still fighting, some with each other. But I know I love you. I know I refuse to lose you again. And I know I would do anything for you. I'm not saying we're going to have a fairytale. We're going to argue and fight and it probably won't be healthy. We'll scream and shout and say stupid things at the wrong times. But I know I love you. And I know that you're worth it. Whatever this is between us is worth it. I'd like to at least try. If you are, I mean."

"I know," I say. "I want to. Try with you." This much is true. I drop my eyes to look at Mason's lips. I know he just kissed me, but it feels like forever ago, and I'm suddenly desperate to feel his lips on mine again. "Now kiss me like you mean it, before we have to get back to the real world and start cleaning up both our messes."

Mason leans in, and I meet him halfway, hoping that one day soon, we'll take each other all the way.

When our lips collide, my eyes flutter shut. I've kissed Mason plenty of times before, but he still somehow has this power to make the butterflies in my stomach crash into each other. I don't think I'll ever get used to his kisses, the way his tongue draws out my bottom lip, the way he fights me for dominance, for control. I'm jelly in his arms. I'm not sure how I'm still solid mass.

I love you, Mason Payne.

Words I never thought I would say—or mean.

But I'm so glad I do.

Former Bully. Big brother. Rock star. Friend.

And ... my unintentional good guy.

Epilogue

MCKENNA

I STARE at the unread email in my inbox, my finger hovering over my laptop's touchpad, but I don't dare click it.

"Mason?" I call.

There's no response.

I know he's in the shower, the hard, hot spray probably *whooshing* out any other sounds. It's been fifteen minutes, but Mason loves his time in there, throwing his muscular arms up, his fingers tangling in his wet hair, rivulets of soapy shampoo running down the bulges of his shoulders, his pecs, his abs, the V of his torso as he stretches tall…

Damn it.

I blink myself out of the fantasy. I can't think about sex right now. Even mind-blowing sex in the shower.

"*Mason?*" I cry out.

Heavy footfalls follow my yell. Mason appears at the French doors to my home office fully naked, not bothering with a towel before he tore out of the bathroom.

"What? What is it?" he asks, his chest heaving. He glances

around the room, droplets of water splattering against the hardwood floor. "Is someone here? Did Giles truly have the balls—"

"No. No," I assure, standing from my chair. I pull the bedsheet I've wrapped around me tighter.

It's almost lunch time, but Mason and I were up *very* early, having sought out each other's bodies almost at the same time. The heat of him beside me is like a Siren's call, and I can't help but roll closer almost every night, stroking his arms, his back, reminding myself that he's mine. That, of course, causes him to groan awake, one part of him waking much faster than the rest. And like a lighthouse guiding a lost ship, my legs spread to receive him.

"Then what is it?" Mason asks. He wipes water from his face, his long lashes clumping with dampness. "You all right?"

"Fine. I guess. I mean..." I bite my lower lip and fidget with the top of the sheet. "There's an email."

"From Giles?"

I shake my head. "It's been six months, Mase. I don't think Giles is coming after me anymore. Or my dad."

Since the showdown with Giles, I've been making weekly calls to my father, checking in, tentatively getting to know him again. I can't say I feel like a newfound daughter, but the conversations have been pleasant. And the fact that he's alive and unhurt. I've yet to gather the courage to visit him in person, but right now, I'm content with the baby steps we're taking.

"I've been keeping tabs on that dickcheese," Mason says, his lips curling. "He's left the country and gone back to the UK. Brax has his computer guys looking into Giles's tech, making sure he has no plans of revenge against us. And if he ever does, I'll be on top of it. He's not going to hurt you again, Mack."

I step towards him, then all the way to him. I lift my hands to cup his cheeks, uncaring that the sheet puddles to the floor. Trying not to think of the half-moon brand on my core. Or if I do, to think of it as a new moon. I might get a tattoo to cover it one day, but right now, I just want to heal. "I know that. I do."

Mason searches my eyes, and I hope he sees what I feel for him. "I fucking love you, Mack."

I smile. Go in for a kiss. When we part, I murmur, "I know that, too."

Mason's arms glide around, pulling me closer. He's damp, but warm and hard. My body molds against him like puzzle pieces fitting together, and I lay my cheek against his chest and listen to his heartbeat. Right here, all fear goes away.

"So what's the email then?" he asks, his voice rumbling in his chest and against my ear.

I swallow and clutch him tighter. "It's *the* email."

"Wait. Back up." He must mean that literally, because he pulls away and rests his palms against my shoulders so he can better read my expression. "*The* email?"

I nod, pulling my lips into my mouth.

"What's it say?" he asks.

"I haven't opened it yet."

"Seriously?" Mason glances over my shoulder. "Why not, Mack? You gotta."

I hate to admit it, but I say, "I'm too scared."

"Okay." Mason lets out a loud exhale, then stares deep into my eyes. "You've been a sex worker for almost a decade, mingling with high risk clients, and you recently faced down a psychopath with a red-hot cattle prod, *and* you managed to snag a screwed up, broken down rockstar who clearly doesn't deserve you. You can't open an email?"

I point at my computer. "This email will dictate my future."

"Our future is already written." Now Mason cups my cheeks. "This will simply be icing on an already fucking fantastic cake."

I swallow. Nod. Gripping his wrists, I say, "Okay. I can do this."

"You can," Mason says as he releases me and I turn back to

my desk. "Because this whole time while I was getting to know the new you, I thought you were the one who needed to be changed. Fucked that up pretty good."

I pause beside my chair. "How'd you screw it up? I'm here, aren't I?"

"You're here because you're the only one who could tame me." Mason's eyes soften to a warm blue. "Make me better. I'm working on my anger issues because of you and dealing with being a former rockstar in way healthier ways, all due to you. Frankly, Mack, I don't know what I'd do—or who I'd turn into—without you. So, whatever's in that email, we'll weather through together. Make it work. And most importantly..." Mason raises his brows. "We'll keep fighting for what you deserve. And that's a fucking book d—"

I hold my hand up. "Don't jinx it!"

Mason laughs. "Then stop with the suspense and open the damn thing."

After blowing out a breath, I fall into my chair, and before second-guessing anything, I click on the email and read.

Mason, who's clearly been abducted and replaced with his alien doppelgänger, waits patiently and silently behind me. I don't even hear him step closer.

"Oh my God," I whisper.

"What?" Mason asks. Then, when I don't answer because I'm rereading, he follows up with, "Well? Gimme something, Mack, I'm standing here in a wet birthday suit."

"I..." Spinning around in my chair, I say to him. "I got it."

Mason's lips part. "Seriously? You got it? The fucking book deal?"

My smile could split my face open. "*The* fucking book deal. The one my agent's been negotiating, the one I've been drooling over getting, the publishing house of my dreams—"

Mason doesn't let me get anything else out. He sprints to

where I am, scoops me from the chair, and spins us around in circles, letting out a loud *whoop!*

"I knew you could do it, Mack." He presses his lips against mine with a hard smack. "I *knew* it. You got your dream. You did it."

I hold onto his neck, tight as can be, and meet his eyes. "I can't believe I did it."

Mason's eyes soften again, and I swear, it's my favorite sight in the world, being able to melt this dragon man with a simple smile.

"I can," he responds. "I've never met anyone like you."

I laugh under my breath. "I was thinking the same thing."

"Then I guess it's good we're together." He grins.

"So, I know you're hanging onto me naked, and I'm also naked, but I want to say..." I grow serious. "I love you, Mason Payne."

Mason responds without hesitation. The man who could barely love himself. "And I love you, McKenna Beckley."

"Yoo-hoo! Anyone hom—" Wyn halts by my French doors. "Oh, sweet Jesus, naked office kama sutra. I'm out."

I'm already yelping and scrambling out of Mason's hold, searching for my sheet. Mason, never shy around me or any of his bandmates, storms out of my office, hard dick swinging as he chases Wyn down.

"Wyn, goddammit, why don't you ever fucking *knock*?" he calls down the hallway.

Wyn's echoing voice counters, "Why don't you ever fucking lock your front door?"

"Because we were expecting you!" Mason yells, then catches himself. "Except most people *announce* themselves before walking in!"

"Excuse me for thinking the two of you would be dressed and I dunno, in your kitchen making lunch, since it's the middle of the afternoon."

"I don't have time to make lunch when my girl looks the way she does twenty-four seven—"

"Okay, that's good," I say once I reach the hallway, sheet wrapped tightly around me. I catch Mason and drag him into our bedroom. "Cute banter's over. We'll meet you in the kitchen, Wyn."

"Already there," Wyn answers, his voice muffled with ... whatever he's found to eat in our pantry.

Once Mason and I are both dressed and Mason's copped a few feels before we can get naked again and truly celebrate my big win, we head to the kitchen, where Wyn's found a stool to hang out on and made himself a sandwich.

"Make yourself at home, bro," Mason says as he opens the fridge.

"Will do." Wyn wipes his mouth with a paper towel. "Since I got nothing else to do these days."

Mason bends down, finds two diet cokes, and rises. "Hear that."

"You two," I say, sitting beside Wyn. "Acting like your careers are over and you're not even thirty."

"We hurt, right here." Wyn melodramatically pats his heart. "It'll be a while before we pull ourselves together."

"Don't I know it," I say as I accept the soda from Mason. "But you two are resilient on your worst days, so I have no doubt you'll come out of it better than you were before. And more successful."

"You'll have to excuse her," Mason says, propping himself against the counter. But he says it with a smile. "Mack's all positive and shit because she landed herself a five-figure book deal."

"No way!" Wyn's enthusiasm is genuine. He pops up and envelopes me in a warm, muscular hug. "Congrats, Mack. You've been working your ass off."

"You don't know the half of it," I say with a laugh, but I look to Mason over Wyn's shoulder, commiserating on the late nights of freak outs, the tears of frustration, the constant rejection letters, and not to mention the difficulty of landing an agent to even take my manuscript to a publishing company.

But through it all, Mason was there, my worries turning into his, and my solace becoming him.

"What's the thing about, anyway?" Wyn asks as he withdraws.

I try for flippant. "Oh, you know, just…"

Mason offers a wicked smirk. "Tell him, sweetheart."

"What?" Wyn glances between us. "What am I missing?"

It's at that moment Dee strides in, her ebony hair slick and straight down her back, and her pantsuit uncreased despite it being in the middle of the day when she spent most of her morning at her desk in her office. She holds a bottle of wine in one hand and her phone in the other.

She says as she places the bottle on the counter, "It's your classic, heart-wrenching underdog story. A plucky street kid becomes suddenly famous, and his only connection to the real world ends up being his best friend from kindergarten, a quiet girl turned cutthroat publicist." Dee arches a brow and turns to me. "Enemies to lovers, right McKenna?"

"Ah, so you based it on real life," Wyn says.

"Who you callin' plucky street kid?" Mason asks him.

I say, a little more defensively than intended, "I wrote most of it before ever I met up with Mase. And I've always loved romance novels. Been obsessed with them. It was only a matter of time before I challenged myself to write one of my own. Mason—he's not the Deacon in my book."

"But you were inspired by my boy, weren't you?" Wyn asks, grinning. He looks to Dee and stage-whispers *"Deacon rhymes with Mason,"*, but she avoids his eye.

Ever the opportunist, Wyn continues, "I'm Wyn. You must be Dee."

"I know who you are," Dee says, allegedly to him, but her

calculating brown eyes are trained on mine. "And I brought this gorgeous bottle of wine to celebrate your book deal."

I scrunch my brows. "How'd you know? We only just found out and I haven't texted anyone..."

Dee laughs. "Honey, I knew you had it in the bag the minute you told me your dream was to become an author. And"—Dee side-eyes Mason—"A little birdie might've texted me when he had a minute."

"Celebration time!" Mason claps his hands, then spins to find glasses. Dee, already familiar with the apartment Mason and I share, pulls out a drawer and finds a wine opener.

"So, you're Mack's friend, huh?" Wyn isn't giving up.

On a sigh, Dee pauses in uncorking the wine. "Now's the time you should stop picturing me naked. I don't date cave men."

"Hey—" Wyn starts, but mid-chew, he searches his scruff and sure enough, mayo and mustard have nestled in the corners of his lips. He licks it away, then says, "Well, fine. But I promise you I'm a lot more flavorful in bed."

"Oh, yeah?" she asks, getting back to uncorking. "How many women have you brought back to your lair?"

Wyn answers without hesitation. "Plenty."

"Then search your phone to find them again." There's a *pop* as Dee releases the cork. "Because I'm not gonna be one of them."

Wyn glances at me. "But I thought..."

I stare back at him with widened eyes, channeling into his head, *Don't make that mistake. Don't do it.*

Dee carefully tilts the bottle towards the closest wine glass Mason's set out. Those who don't know her would find this a completely innocuous move. Mason and I, however, brace for impact.

"Thought what, exactly?" she asks.

"Ah, you know..." Wyn clears his throat. "You used to ... with

Mack ... I mean, Mack was a—lady, and I heard you did the same—"

"If you value your penis length, you won't finish that sentence," Dee says. The bottle lands on the counter with a smack.

Wyn lifts his hands. "I'm only—"

"I am a senior-level Portfolio Manager of a major hedge fund in the heart of the Financial District, and I'm the only female to have made that position—and *not* by being on my back. My yearly salary would make you blush, if you weren't an overblown, overpaid top forties musician who's more famous for his good looks than his brains."

Wyn grins at Mason. "Hear that? She thinks I'm cute."

Mason replies with a narrowed gaze, "I think I should also be insulted."

"I know guys like you," Dee continues. "I've dated guys like you. Been paid by many like you. And, I've decided, I don't like guys like you. Not anymore."

Dee turns to me. "Cheers me quick, McKenna. My lunch has been cut short but I wanted to be here and drink our first celebratory sips of wine together. I'm proud of you. I love you."

I accept wine from one of her hands and cheers her glass with a light clink.

Dee takes a sip then winks. "We'll celebrate big time later."

"Count on it," I say, taking a big gulp of my own.

I did it. I can't believe it.

Dee heads to the kitchen archway, but tosses over her shoulder, "And Wyn, just so you're aware, even call girls like being asked to dinner first."

Wyn raises his brows. He eyes Dee during her entire trip from the kitchen counter to the exit. Her bottom half, at least.

"I think she likes me," he says once she shuts the front door, then rises. "I'm gonna go see if she likes me, too."

Mason chuckles. "I think you got the answer to that one,

bro."

"Nah. Ladies can't resist me. Eventually."

Mason rounds the counter and throws an arm across my shoulders. "Good luck to you."

Wyn salutes, then departs quickly after Dee.

I roll my eyes while laughing. "Now, there's a couple that will never become a hashtag."

"Don't speak too soon." Mason kisses the top of my head. "Some folks said the same thing about us."

I widen my eyes in mock surprise as I look up at him. "No way. Us? McMason?"

"Yeah, babe." Mason rubs his thumb across my lower lip. "Us."

"I like how you say that word," I purr.

"Oh, yeah?"

I lick my lips, then smile. "Uh-huh."

Mason cups under my legs and lifts. I let out a delighted shout as he cradles me, and I wrap my arms around his neck.

"Let's finish this bottle in bed," he says, nuzzling my ear.

Giving into the shivers, I turn so my mouth is closer to his lips.

"After," I murmur.

"Oh, yeah." Mason grins. "After."

Mason carries me over the threshold of our home, holding on tight, our low laughter mingling together.

We don't shut the bedroom door behind us.

❧

Don't stop reading! Let Wyn take you to his small town with city-girl Dee in this opposites attract, small town romance, available now! Take me to Lover.

Keep reading for a special sneak peek.

sneak peek of Lover

DEE

He looks ridiculous.

Wyn Riley is a lot of things, but a preppy country club member he's not. He's barely squeezed into a light blue polo shirt, so tight he might as well have borrowed it from Mason. It has awful success in showing off the boulders of his biceps and the rigid muscle of his torso, the fabric so stretched, I can tell his nipple piercing is a hoop and not a bar.

My core clenches again when he steps into the light of my office, his slacks untailored yet fitting against his tree-trunk thighs and nether region like a bonus peekaboo layer of skin.

When I first ran into Wyn in the hall, on the way to pour my third cup of coffee as I waited for him to show, the one thing that pinged into my mind was *pecs for days.* Now, I'm cataloguing every fine piece of him, reserving the last blank section of my brain's readout for his ass. He's yet to turn around, and I'm appalled I'm waiting for him to do just that.

"That looks good." Wyn gestures to the steaming mug in my hand.

Startled, I unfreeze and round my desk, taking a seat in my chair.

"Can I have some?"

"No." I pretend to busy myself with papers as I wait for him to sit across from me. After a minute of motionless silence, I look up. "Are you going to take a seat?"

"Uh . . ." Wyn shuffles in place, a wrinkled khaki blazer thrown over his arm. "Not sure I can, ma'am. This outfit's a little tight."

My attention flings itself against his groin before I can stop it. On an inward curse, I force my eyes back up. "Don't ma'am me. I'm not your mother."

A wince crosses his face. Curious, I angle my head but keep my expression blank.

"So, are we going to do this?" Wyn folds his arms, thinks better of it, then lets them hang at his side.

"Sure. You can stand. I doubt this will take long." I turn to my computer, bringing up the spreadsheet I'd created when I arrived at five. "The amount in your checking is pitiful, as well as your savings. I see you own a property upstate with significant debt. If we sell that for a reasonable sum and pay off your creditors, coupled with your consistent royalties from Nocturne Court, I'm pretty sure I can double, maybe triple, what you're making now with the right strategy. What's with this four-figure payment every month that digs into your royalties? You haven't logged it as anything but 'miscellaneous.' If you halted those payments, I could add it to your investment portfolio."

"I'm not selling."

I jolt at the unexpected conviction in Wyn's voice and spin on my chair. "Excuse me?"

"I'm not investing, either."

I frown. "Wyn, I'm not sure you understand what I do."

Wyn lowers his chin, his oceanic stare seemingly slipping

into my body and glaring directly on my soul. "I perfectly comprehend what you do."

I say, quieter, "I thought you were here for my help."

"I am. To a point. Give me advice, but leave it at that. You're not getting control of my money, and neither is this succubus firm."

Leaning back in my chair, I hold his gaze for a moment, although the time drifting between us sends shivers down my chest. If Wyn loosened his hair tie, I'm certain I'd be attempting to tame a lion. "We don't just take over. You, as the client, have complete decision-making control."

Wyn's brows come down. "I don't believe you."

Straightening, I flatten my palms on the desk. "Fine. If advice is what you want . . . at the rate you're spending, you're bleeding money. And if you won't tell me what you're spending it on, my best advice is to clean up your debt, triple your assets, and find a new job. Otherwise, you'll be worse off in a month than you are now."

"How worse off?"

My lips thin in thought. "That miscellaneous money you're sending out? Forget about paying it next month. Or any others."

Wyn exhales through his nose, and for a moment, I read true worry in his expression before the skin around his eyes relaxes and his hands unclench. "You're the money lady. Tell me how to do this without investing in anything. Explain to me how to keep making my payments without losing my shirt."

"A job," I say, softening despite the thorns in his voice. "Maybe sell your instruments. Stop renting studio space. And then, when it gets too tight, think of releasing your property upstate."

"I can't . . ." Wyn trails off and glances out the window behind me, the line of his jaw cutting through his skin. "This is all I am. Giving up my music would be like signing away my soul. I don't belong in a place like this, an office, wearing these—fuck, this costume." He pulls at his shirt, the telltale sound of a tear cutting between us. The stretched-out fabric falls from his fingers, and I wonder how much has ripped and if his back is exposed and how those muscles might ripple as he tenses.

A disgusted sound leaves my throat at my imagination's unwanted brashness, but Wyn reads it in an entirely different way.

His stare grows shadows as he glowers at me. "This may mean shit to you, but I need to find fame again and my song-writing can do that. It has to. That success is what shot me out of the gallows and made me *me*."

Closing my eyes, I try not to react to the hollowness in his tone. It makes me think about his home life, and if we grew up similarly. It never occurred to me I'd have something in common with Wyn or we'd share the same pain. But his voice, it sounds too much like my own when I'm alone, late at night, curled up in luxury sheets but swallowed up by the darkness coating my heart.

I sever the emotional pull toward him by opening my eyes, telling him what I told myself all those years ago. "Then you have to give up some of your assets."

"Assets." He laughs mirthlessly. "Sure, 'cause that's what they are, not a poor man's collection of trinkets."

"Wyn, I'd love to help, but save from moving your money around, I can't—"

I cut off, my attention drifting from the intensity of Wyn's bottomless gaze to the glass wall separating my office from the hallway. Dennis passes by with his usual dismissive flair, until his attention falls on Wyn and he stops in his tracks.

My coffee nearly tips over in my hands. I let loose a guttural whisper. "Jesus, no."

"What?" Wyn asks. "Do you have more tough love to dole out

because I gotta admit, lady, you suck at it. Do you make all your clients feel like losers, or—"

"Shut up."

"Pardon?"

"Shut up and listen." I shoot up from my seat, my words coming out rapid-fire. "My coworker thinks I'm engaged to you" —Wyn's brows do a slow rise—"and he's about to come in here any second. I know you don't owe me anything, but if you could —*hey*, Dennis!" Bright, fake cheer coats my voice.

Wyn staggers back, fully disarmed and appalled at the sudden veer in conversation.

"What are you doing here so early?" I ask Dennis, smile straining. "You never show up until nine thirty."

"Well, if it isn't the happy couple!" Dennis ignores my question and offers his hand to Wyn. Wyn takes it, but his hand is more stunned than firm when they shake. "Now I understand why I never see you around here. Early morning sessions are your jam, huh?" Dennis winks. "I get it. Our Dee's irresistible, especially before regular business hours."

Swallowing, the paper coffee cup crumpling audibly in my hands, I wait for Wyn's reaction.

He blinks at Dennis. "Before . . . business hours?"

"Yes, well." Dennis chuckles, taking back his hand and resting it on his stomach. "She's a rare jewel around here. She always seems to be open."

I take a breath. Long and deep, internally lecturing myself that launching over my desk and digging my nails into Dennis's eyeballs would do nothing but bring down an HR nightmare on my head.

Wyn sneers. "I never thought hard work could be used as such an insult."

Dennis jolts as if he's unexpectedly called out. "I didn't mean it like that—Dee's a favorite at this firm, especially with the big man. She works so much for our clients. I never thought she'd have the time to get a boyfriend, never mind a fiancé. Yet here you are, in all your . . ." Dennis looks him up and down. "Fashionable glory."

Wyn's pecs twitch under his shirt, loosened now by a tear in the back. "Veiled insult number three. Wow, you're good."

Dennis lets out a boisterous laugh, but retreats a step. Or two. "Just having fun with ya, buddy. And making sure this whole thing is real. Dee brought up the existence of your relationship at *such* a convenient time. And now, here you are, at yet another opportune time. Our boss is due down this hallway any minute."

"I didn't realize our personal life was such a concern to you," Wyn says. His eyes move to me, the question in his face urging me to speak, but I'm too mortified to say a word.

"Only when it comes to my upward movement in this firm." Dennis's smile curves with snakelike precision, like he knows I'm desperate and he has nothing to lose by insulting the former Nocturne Court member. "Dee has herself a secret, one I'd love to cash in on, yet I can't seem to when this *relationship* with you comes with this firm's handling of Emerald Spin Records."

Wyn's nose twitches as he absorbs the information, cogs turning in his head. As lazy and messy as he appears to be, I'm aware of his hidden smarts. Before the creditors came down, he'd been managing his upstate property quite well, making improvements and increasing the value until a sudden turn last year when everything—well, to use his words, went to shit.

As if proving my suspicions, Wyn says, "I get it. If you out her, I'll take my complaints to Emerald Spin and have them pull their account from Whitecrest Investments."

"And lose my well-deserved promotion. I see you're aware of Dee's hidden . . . talents." Dennis nods somberly, as if the turd actually cares about my particular outcome. "I was rather hoping it might come as a surprise."

"Dude, if you knew me, you'd understand my past is no convent, either. My best buddy's dating an ex–call girl, too. I assume you know who he is—Mason Payne. If my math is right . . ." Wyn looks to the ceiling, brows furrowed as he pretends to count. "That would be *two* Nocturne Court members you'd piss off. And we won't wait for corporate approval before we drown you in a sewer line." Wyn lowers his head and nails Dennis with a glare.

Dennis clears his throat, retreating from Wyn's looming shadow. "Listen, no harm, no foul. But you might as well be aware, since this is technically a client-employee interrelation, you two have a duty to report to HR."

Speaking of HR nightmares . . .

"Dennis," I warn. He's finally pissed me off enough to make my voice curdle. "Not now."

"Why not? It's the perfect time. Larry'll be here any sec." Dennis thumbs the door. "Want me to get him?"

"No," I say, at the same time Wyn says, "Sure."

Both my and Dennis's heads swivel to Wyn.

Wyn turns to me with a suspiciously wide grin. "Why not, *honey*? We're telling my family this weekend. We might as well tell your firm, too."

My mouth opens and closes before I gulp it into submission. "Shouldn't we talk about this, *dear*?"

Wyn shrugs. "Not much to chat about. The smartest supervillain in the world seems to have uncovered our tryst. We have no hope of hiding now." Wyn moves his saccharine smile to Dennis, who answers with a wry sneer.

"I'm doing you a favor, advising you on our company handbook," he says.

"Something tells me, if Dee left and the firm fell into your hands, you wouldn't be able to match her skills if you copied all her spreadsheets."

Dennis ignores Wyn's observation. "Better yet, why don't you two announce your engagement at our banquet coming up next week? All our top clients will be there. Including Emerald Spin representatives. Wouldn't that be nice?" Dennis looks between the two of us.

"That would be perfect," I respond, the words coating my teeth like unbrushed fuzz, "but we'll have to get back to you. Wyn's schedule is . . ."

"Wide open."

I stare at Wyn, who spreads his hands and widens his eyes innocently. "What? I'm good to go."

Papers might as well turn to dust in my clenched hands.

Dennis claps, the sound sharp in the thickened air. "Well, now that this is all sorted, I have work to do. Nice to meet you, Wyn. And, uh, congrats on your upcoming nuptials." Dennis gives us two thumbs-up before backing out through the doorway. "I'll keep mum until the banquet since I can't *wait* to see you two take center stage and make the announcement to our entire company and clients."

"Snake," I mutter at the same time Wyn says, "Fuck off and die, panty-muncher."

We share a look, my lips tipping with amusement before I blink and set my lips straight. "I'm so sorry about that. I can explain."

Wyn flicks his hand toward the door. "No need. It was all pretty self-explanatory."

"But you must be confused. Or insulted. Or both."

"Not really."

I squint at him. "I've been talking about you as my fiancé at work, and you're not thrown by it?"

"Don't get me wrong." Wyn laughs. "I shit a few bricks when you babbled out your confession."

"Excuse me. I didn't 'babble.' There was only so much time to inform you before—"

"You didn't let me finish." But he says it gently, his expression infuriatingly soft. "I was about to finish with, it ain't so bad."

I press my lips together. "I'm not sure if you were in the same office as me these past ten minutes. This is *very* bad."

"Why, though? So you need to fool your dinky coworker and boss for a while. I'm cool with going to a few functions or two. This banquet gives me a chance to talk to the label *mano et mano* —they've been avoiding my calls. I could even get them to take a chance on my songs. Then, when a few weeks pass, we end it." Wyn shrugs. "People break up all the time."

"This might not be enough to stop Dennis."

"Then we'll break up amicably. I'll still take my issues to Emerald Spin Records and tell them to kick Dennis to the curb."

"You just told me your label won't talk to you."

"Dennis doesn't know that. All he sees is dollar signs if he gets you kicked out of this firm. I doubt he's done his research on me yet. And when he does, it'll be too late. Our relationship'll be made public and he'd be a fool to humiliate me in front of the label with you on my arm. If he's smart, he'll bide his time and keep quiet. So will we."

I close my eyes, giving my head a little shake. This isn't going in the direction I was prepared for. "The press could get ahold of it. I wouldn't put it past Dennis to leak this early somehow and really put us under pressure. Your name could be back in the tabloids, Wyn. Wouldn't you hate that?"

Wyn shuts his mouth and moves to stare out of the skyscraper window again. When Nocturne Court was at their height, the members were stalked relentlessly and the women they dated even more so. Wyn usually had a different girl each week, sometimes multiple. They dubbed him Wingman Wyn, since he was the only single one who refused to settle down, and they often caught him with his pants down. "It wouldn't be the worst thing in the world."

I suppose he misses those days. "Are you serious? Mason and

McKenna endure *so* much crap online, and you've seemed to flow under it all, maintaining your privacy and barely breaking the surface. Why would you want to change that?"

His eye tics like he's struggling to hold back a wince, and I realize I might've hurt him with that comment. "The press passes me by because I'm not considered relevant anymore. I don't have kids with another celebrity, and I ain't dating any, either. You're looking pretty pale. Do you need water?"

I'm so thrown by his change in topic all I can do is shake my head.

"Oh. Well, I'll take one." Wyn moves to my mini fridge and helps himself, humming at the sparkling water options. He finds a bottle, his twist of the cap making a *pfft* sound in the silent office.

After taking a long swig, he wipes the back of his hand across his mouth, covering a large belch.

I exhale through my teeth, silently pleading with my wall to magically transform into an escape hatch.

"There's something you haven't considered," Wyn says. "Maybe I don't mind being your fake fiancé for a while."

My mouth falls open. I have to clasp the edges of my desk to keep from toppling into my chair. "You . . . what?"

"My family's up my ass about my single status. My job is nonexistent. My perfect brother keeps being perfect with his perfect wife and kids, and thank you for reminding me—the press considers me a worthless pile of unnoticeable shit. Fuck, maybe you *should* come with me to see my family this weekend. Maybe we *should* pretend to be a couple for a while. It could benefit the both of us."

"I can't tell if you're joking."

"You're still white as a ghost over there." Wyn snaps his fingers. "Because you hate me. Yep. That's a problem."

My chin pushes into my neck as I regard him. "I don't *hate* you."

"You've never liked me."

"I don't know you. There's a difference."

"Because you don't *care* to know me."

"Stop repeating my words back to me with different emphasis." This time, I allow myself to fall into my chair and cover my face with my hands. "This is bad. This is so, so bad. I like my job. I love who I've become. I can't lose it all because of a stupid lie to keep a bloodthirsty coworker off my back."

"Exactly. So let's do this."

I peek at him through my fingers. This barrel of a man squeezed into designer, preppy duds with his hair coming undone and his cheekbones cut from stone wants to help me.

God. *Dammit.*

"Quit being so excited about this." My voice comes out muffled against my palm.

"Why not? It's a chance at redemption for both of us. Or maybe just me. Who the fuck cares. Your secret will be safe, I'll get some free fancy food at some banquets or fundraisers or whatever, and you can do some noninvesting gobbledygook with my money without taking a cut—"

"Wait a minute."

"—*and* meet my ma and bro and get them off my back for once." Wyn stops to take a breath and I jump in.

"Wyn, I thought I made it clear there's nothing I can do with your money if you won't let me grow it."

"Move it around. Transfer shit."

I sigh. "There's more to it than that."

"Then figure it out. I'll help you if you help me."

I stare at him for a beat, licking my lower lip in thought. Wyn catches the movement, and something akin to fire licks at my core. Fire I quickly stanch. "From my vantage point, it looks like I'm doing two things for you."

"Yeah? I'm keeping your secret under wraps and saving your ass at this vulture job of yours. That's two things, too, gorgeous."

I stiffen at his easy use of such a loaded nickname. *He thinks I'm gorgeous?* I drown the thought quickly. "I'm using this statement loosely, but maybe this could work. At the very least, it'll buy me some time to figure out what to do about Dennis."

"It can, and awesome. I'll pick you up at four on Friday to head to the sticks."

I rub the back of my neck, feeling a headache creeping on at spending more than ten minutes with this man. "This is a transaction. Nothing more. I'll do you a favor, you do me a solid, and then we'll part ways."

Wyn cocks a brow. "Didn't I just say all that?"

"Well, I'm confirming it."

"Okay. Consider it written in blood." Wyn steps towards me, offering his hand.

I stare at it for a moment, then lift my own to clasp his in a shake. I haven't lifted from my seat, yet my heart ratchets up at the contact, the roughness of his palm scraping against my sensitive skin before I pull away like he's given me a static shock.

For a moment, his hand hangs in the air above my desk, his expression slack-jawed like he was as unexpectedly affected as I was, before he shakes it off with a comical smile.

Wyn heads to the door, offering me a salute before he leaves. "See ya in a few days, wifey."

"Ugh. Don't call me that."

"Your choice, gorgeous."

"Don't call me that, either," I snap.

"Looking forward to this weekend, doll!" Wyn says, stretching his lips wide with a fake grin.

The door clicks shut just as his infuriatingly perfect ass disappears from view.

What happens when you mix a giant man and a prickly woman into a small town?

scan here to start reading —>

all in kindle unlimited

If you like your grump to be a single dad (or a dad-to-be), read:

Trust

Rock

Play

If you like your men to fall in love in a small town, read:

Lover

If you like your playboys with a dash of suspense, read:

Dare

If you like your tattooed bad boys and morally gray heroes, read:

Rebel

Crave

If you like thriller with your romance, read:

To Have and to Hold

From This Day Forward

If you want enemies to lovers with a side of secret societies and gothic academies, read:

Briarcliff Academy Series

Rival

Virtue

Fiend

Reign

Thorne of Winthorpe Series

Thorne

Crush

Liar

If you like dark romance and mafia men, read

Titan Falls Standalone

Cruel Promise

Corrupt Empire Duet

Underground Prince

Jaded Princess

About the Author

Ketley Allison has always been a romantic at heart and loves writing over-the-top, plot-twisty romance and characters. Ketley was born in Canada, moved to Australia, then to California, and finally to New York City to attend law school, but most of that time was spent in coffee shops thinking about her next book.

Her other passions include her two daughters, wine, coffee, Big Macs, her cat, and her husband, possibly in that order.

Visit Ketley's Website:

facebook.com/ketleyallison

tiktok.com/ketleyallison

instagram.com/ketleyallison